I AM MARY TUDOR

This is my book; the book of Mary Tudor; Queen of England.

Herein I am to set down the happenings of my life; and, for my soul's sake, to set them down with truth. God willing, I will write the things I did and that others did to me; the things I said and that others said to me. Above all the thoughts of my heart I must search out, for none knows them but me. I need to examine not only the things that happened to me, but myself that let them happen. So, for the first time I speak of what till now I have not dared admit even to my own heart.

I tell, among other things, the truth about my father King Henry the Eighth, and how I both hated and loved him; but loved more than I hated, so that I mourned his death many a long day.

My memories would seem to stand out clear, especially the memories of early childhood. But a child may be mistaken; and a royal child, especially, believe he has of himself remembered things he has heard or read; for the doings of such children are, from their first hours bruited abroad, are set down in letters and documents. And what has been told is not always true but something only half-remembered; and sometimes the truth is, of intention, falsified. But in this I have been fortunate. For those whose honesty cannot be questioned—such as my mother, my lady-governor the countess of Salisbury and that dear nurse of my infancy lady Bryan, sweet Margaret; these that were in the heart of affairs, spoke while events were fresh in their memory.

As for myself, I am a woman to speak plain though it be to my own hurt. Here then is the truth about the woman Mary Tudor, Queen of England.

I AM
MARY TUDOR

Hilda Lewis

Arrow Books

Arrow Books Ltd
3 Fitzroy Square, London W1

An imprint of the Hutchinson Group

London Melbourne Sydney Auckland
Wellington Johannesburg Cape Town
and agencies throughout the world

First published by Hutchinson
& Co (Publishers) Ltd 1971

Arrow edition January 1974

Made and printed in Great Britain by
C. Nicholls & Company Ltd
The Philips Park Press, Manchester

ISBN 0 09 908270 5

To my husband

My most grateful thanks to Alice Clarke, librarian, of Nottingham University; to Professor W. R. Fryer, of the Department of History; and to Mary Stacey, of Nottingham City Library.

Chapter One

'Will it please the King's Majesty to look upon the child?'

My father made no answer but still presented his back to my lady countess of Salisbury and to the babe she held out upon a fine white cushion.

My mother propped upon pillows implored him out of eyes dark-ringed with the pains of childbearing. She knew the agony of his most bitter disappointment. The child was not the longed-for, prayed-for, desperately-needed son. She, herself, had known that first, cruel thrust at the heart; but God had seen fit to send her a girl and already she had accepted the child with a deep thankfulness. After the long and desolate grief of four miscarriages she had borne a living child. She was a mother.

'Sir, I pray you.' . . . From the great bed came my mother's voice; the low, gentle voice with the pretty foreign accent of Spain she never lost.

At that he did turn but his sullen face did not lighten. He liked a pretty woman—and she was pretty enough to please any man. But in this moment—pale face a-glisten with sweat, light curls dark and dank, eyes deep-sunk into her head, she had lost all claim to prettiness. Lady Salisbury was uncomfortably aware that she had done her Queen some disservice; she should have waited until the women had brought the Queen back to her usual charming looks. A tender man must have found her beautiful in this moment; but he was not tender, my father; nor was he one to bear disappointment well. Now, unsmiling, he turned from his wife to throw a careless glance upon the new-born child.

'A fair and lovely child, sir; well-made and strong,' lady Salisbury told him.

Without thinking he put out a finger. The tiny hand curled about it, held it. His face changed; he was always a lover of children.

'Why Kate,' he cried out, and now there was warmth in his voice, 'you have done well enough and shall do better! You shall give me half-a-dozen fine sons!' And she, fair hair dark yet with the sweat of her labour, smiled.

My father was King Henry the Eighth of England; my mother his first and undoubted wife, Queen Catherine of Aragon; and the babe her only living child, Mary Tudor. I tell this tale of my birth as I had it from Lady Salisbury, my mother's true friend and my own. Through her eyes I see it all—the birth-chamber at Greenwich Palace in the dark of the winter morning; four o'clock on the eighteenth day of February in the year of grace fifteen hundred and sixteen.

Of the joy throughout the country she told me also; of bonfires smoking red to the winter sky, of oxen roasted whole, and cakes and wine for all. Four times the people had been disappointed; now, at last—the heir.

Three days after my birth I was baptised in the chapel of the Friars Observant that stands hard by Greenwich Palace. Down a path all hung with arras lest I take cold and beneath a Canopy of Estate carried by four knights, I was carried by my lady Countess of Surrey into the chapel. At the door a very great congregation waited to conduct the Princess of England to her christening—princes of church and state, high officers of the realm, and my lord Mayor of London with all his aldermen; there waited, also, the ambassadors of Christendom together with illustrious foreign visitors—all, all to pay their respects to the new-born infant.

'The chapel was a miracle of beauty,' lady Salisbury told me. 'The hangings were cloth-of-gold and every cup and plate of pure gold; before the high altar stood the silver font brought from Canterbury for the christening of the long awaited child. At the font, itself, stood the great cardinal, Wolsey, archbishop of York, Papal legate and new-made lord Chancellor—the most feared, most hated man in England.'

From my earliest childhood, I too, had hated and feared him; feared that square, yellow face beneath the scarlet cap. The cardinal's hat I never saw him wear; it was carried before him upon a cushion, as though it were the crown itself.

'Even when he took you at the font to perform his most tender office his eyes were hard. There he stood, that bulky figure all in scarlet satin, and his shadow falling upon you!'

As it was to shadow my growing years—childhood and girlhood alike! A gentle godfather my father had chosen; my mother's enemy and my own!

So I was baptised with every Christian ceremony; and thereafter lady Salisbury—herself royal Plantagenet, that had been appointed

Mistress of my Household—knelt before the high altar offering me to God. Now to the sound of trumpets my titles were declared. *God give good life and long unto the right high, right noble, right excellent and puissant Princess Mary of England, daughter to our lord the King and to Queen Catherine his wife.* They say that, even then, I turned to the sound of the trumpet, for I was born with a passion for music.

My first memories, like those of any child, are of my father and mother. Everyone knows how my father looked in his middle and later years—there are portraits enough. But who remembers him in his young years? He was twenty-four when I was born; and as soon as I was old enough to think anything at all, I thought him the handsomest man in all the world; the merriest and the kindest. As for that last—I have had time and time enough to question it.

He was a tall young man of excellent proportions—his shoulders broad, his middle elegant, his legs shapely. Of those last he was vain, standing always that they might be seen to their full advantage. A blue-eyed, laughing young man. Yet those eyes could redden with anger and seem to sink into his head; and that laughing mouth could shrink to a button scarce to be seen within the golden beard.

He was altogether a golden young man; hair and beard of the self-same red-gold. Tudor gold. Gold blazed from him as from a sunburst; from doublet and cloak, from shoes and feathered bonnet all sewn with jewels. And these adornments that might have sat heavy upon another man, he carried lightly; for he had every grace, every accomplishment. He danced, he ran, he rode, he hunted and hawked; he wrestled, he jousted with incomparable grace, forever showing himself better than the best.

In music he was gifted above all men. He sang in a voice to break the heart with its sweetness; he composed to his own notes words of his own devising. Each instrument—lute or flute or virginals, he touched with a lover's hand; and each one, obedient, yielded up its secret. From him I inherited my passion for music; and such skill as I may have, is but a faint echo of his own.

And that true ear of his served him well in foreign languages. French and Italian came easy to his tongue; when he spoke to those ambassadors his simplest words sounded—when he chose—like the most gracious compliment. To all other ambassadors he spoke in Latin; and, never in my life, have I heard any man speak it easier. From my earliest years I was put to the Latin; I speak and write it perfectly. But I speak and write it as a scholar; he, as a thrush its native notes.

So much for my father. Now for my mother. To me she was—and

will be till I die—the most perfect being a kind God ever created. Never a mother so tender, so loving; never a wife so true, so gentle, so patient yet withal so honourable to her own conscience. She had a shining integrity, an enduring courage. I thought her beautiful—nor was I the only one. There is a portrait that goes by her name; the artist is unknown to me, and to her was certainly unknown for he never in his life set eyes on her. The heavy woman with the heavy chin is not my mother. If you would truly see my mother as I knew her before sorrow set its mark upon her then look at Michiele's portrait. She smiles out from the canvas serene and beautiful; she might, indeed, stand for the picture of Our Lady. The mouth is sweet, the rounded chin delicate but firm. I shut my eyes and see her very clear— a fair Spaniard; the complexion pink-and-white, the eyes as blue as my father's, the hair smooth beneath the bonnet, red-gold, matching my father's thread for thread.

As a very little girl I saw her a happy young woman, the laughter forever on her lips; but later—though for me she could always smile— the laughter died. Her cheeks were pale then with a grief I did not understand. As for her shape, let lady Salisbury speak. 'She was small and slender and elegant; her colouring, Madam, much like your own; more English than Spanish. Well, sorrow dims all beauty and constant childbearing thickens the sweetest shape.' But even then the ambassador of Venice said she was handsomer by far than Mistress Anne Bullen whom everyone acknowledged—or affected to acknowledge— the beauty of the court.

In one thing my father and my mother were alike—profession of their faith; but, beneath that profession, how different! To him religion was a pleasant enough affair. God had been good and he was always pleased to say his thanks. He heard Mass five times a day—when he was not hunting; he was punctilious in every rite—if time did not press. He was pleased to go along with God—as long as God went my father's way; but when from a divergent path some bright bauble caught his fancy, then, humming a little tune, he followed that other path.

But my mother came of a line devoted to God. Her father and forefathers had burned heretics that the purified soul might be forever saved. And though her gentle soul fainted at such deeds she would not, I think, have questioned their rightness. For the union of the soul with God was the truth by which she lived; and for that truth she would, herself, have gone to the fire.

'In that one way they were ill-matched,' lady Salisbury said. 'She put God and her conscience before all; before him, even. But in every other way the match was good—each complement to the other; he all-demanding, she all gentle obedience. And, in looks, too, they were well-matched. For all she was some six years older you would never have guessed it; not at first. He was tall and well set-up—if anything he looked older than his years; and she, small and slender, quick and bright, looked younger than he. But constant childbearing is not kind to women; nor is grief kind, neither.'

For all her constant pregnancies I was her only child. Four children she had already borne and three of them sons; and all still-born save for one, that, christened in triumph and joy, died within a few days. That she had given him no living son was the first cause of my father's unkindness to her; and later, to me. And cause for disappointment he had! He *needed* sons. He was but second in the new line of Kings. Desolation of civil war—the War of the Roses—lay behind him; but not far behind. He could not rest until he knew the Tudors secure upon the throne; and to him that meant sons. But had my mother been lively as Venus and fruitful as Niobe, I doubt she would have kept him faithful. Even at the time of my birth he had found himself another bedfellow—pretty, complaisant Mary Bullen, sister to that same Anne who was to cast her black shadow upon my mother's life and upon my own. Nor did he stop at two mistresses; constancy was not in him.

Until I was four years old I was in the charge of lady Bryan—sweet Margaret that looked so kindly to my needs. She had charge of my clothes, my food and the whole ordering of my day; it was she that taught me my English A.B.C. Though, as befitted the Princess of England, I had establishments of my own, my first two years were spent almost entirely in my mother's apartments. 'Never a child so happy, so loved, so admired!' Bryan told me. 'Such a pretty little thing with a mass of flaxen curls, a wild-rose skin and large blue-grey eyes; small-made you were and graceful. No-one ever stinted to tell you how pretty you were! It was gossip in all the capitals of Christendom!' But if they had stinted to admire me, I should have admired myself. Better than the letters of my hornbook I could read my mirror's message; I was a vain child. Well, time and sorrow have cured that fault!

From the moment I was old enough to understand, my mother led me gently from love of myself to love of God; a long, hard journey— a life-time's journey. Yet she made it not so hard. If she was devout, she was gay. If there were Masses and prayers, there was pleasant chatter of ladies at their stitching and songs other than hymns. In my mother's apartments I learned to thread my first needle, to choose my wools with an eye careful to colour, to make my first uneven stitches. And there was music and dancing aplenty. Here I first placed my small fingers upon the virginals whose keys I could scarce press down; here, not wholly steady upon my feet, I made my first dancing-steps, my mother holding me by the hand. *God likes us to be merry but always we must serve Him first—even though it be with tears,* she would say. She was the most profound influence upon my life; nor did death alter anything save to make me more careful of her teaching, more grateful for her love.

But, for all that, it was some time before I knew my mother as *my mother*; understood the relationship between us. Other women had the intimate handling of me—Catherine Pole my wet-nurse, Margaret Bryan, and above them all, ordering my household, my lady Salisbury. But with my father it was a different matter. There was no man to come between him and me. Before I knew her for my mother, I knew him for my father. Did I catch but a distant glimpse of him I would cry out and leap to come to him so that my nurse must grip me tight. He would appear suddenly in the nurseries or in my mother's apartments to lift me in his arms and throw me almost to the ceiling and catch me again. I cannot remember that I was ever frightened as I went flying into the air; I knew his arms were strong and sure. He was the golden god that walked in sunlight. When I was very small I thought he *was* God. I was learning my *Pater noster*, each word explained to my infant ear; but a little one can understand only according to his capacity. *Our Father* . . . and he *was* my father; that *is in heaven* . . . for what was heaven but a place of delights where delicious foods were served such as I was never allowed in my mother's apartments, and where all backs were bent and he alone stood upright; where all was hushed until himself broke the silence with his laughter? He was God; and I was not afraid of him; not yet.

For his part my father delighted in me. I was a credit to him—a pretty, merry child, forward of my age and already a useful pawn in his hand; the *Pearl of England* he called me. When he entertained visitors from abroad, and especially when ambassadors were present, he would have me brought in that they might see the treasure he had to bestow. Lady Salisbury told me of one such occasion and I repeat it in her words.

'You were not above two years old when your father came into the Presence Chamber carrying you in his arms. You wore, I remember, a gown of Tudor green all stitched with tiny flowers—a smiling baby; a pretty sight. The King went to his place and set you on his knees. Your godfather, the great cardinal, was there and some half-dozen ambassadors. Wolsey came forward to bend his bulk and kneel to kiss your hand. All must kneel to salute Madam Baby, even the great cardinal; after him knelt the spendid ambassadors, each in turn. You did not so much as look at them. Your eyes were fixed upon a dark-robed priest; you knew him—Master Dionysius that made music for the King. You began to call out, *Priest! Priest! Music! Music!* as well as you could say the words; nor would you be quieted until he was let to play for you.'

Music and priests. These I have loved above all earthly things, for both alike speak to the soul.

'Someone sent for a lute and your father sat holding you while the good priest played and sang . . . a little hymn it was, a child's hymn. And you sang with him in your baby voice. It was a rare sight; the priest in his dark gown, tonsured head bent upon the strings—a lute is a lover's instrument, not a priest's; and you in your flowered gown, in your father's arms, bright head upon his breast.

'When he was finished, Madam, you clapped your little hands laughing the while; and your father turning to a foreign gentleman, cried out in delight, *By God, Mr. Ambassador, here's a little girl that never cries!* He spoke in Latin that all the foreign gentlemen might understand; he had an easy way with Latin as though it were his English tongue!'

Here's a little girl that never cries! Well, the little girl has made up for it; she has cried enough since—enough and enough!

As I have said, my father was well aware of my value in the marriage-market. At a very tender age I was betrothed to the new-born Dauphin of France; I had been promised before his birth.

It was my lady Salisbury that told me of that infant betrothal.

'It was early October; you were but two years old and the groom's eyes scarce open upon the world. He lay, no doubt, in his cradle, sucking his thumb, if he had learned so much! You were all in cloth-of-gold; you mother feared lest you find it over-heavy but your father said, She must learn to carry herself—a Queen! You wore a little cap of black velvet all bright with jewels and underneath it the fair curls flowed. The betrothal took place in the chamber of Madam the Queen; you stood by the French ambassador that was proxy for the groom; it was all very pretty and very solemn.'

So it may have been! But I remember nothing; not even the great diamond they put on my finger. Nor did it signify anything at all, this first of many betrothals that came to naught. For my father, pricked thereto by Wolsey, had his eye always upon a more advantageous betrothal. He contracted me to this one and to that—the infant Dauphin, that loose-liver the King of France himself, his other son the duke of Orleans; to the Emperor my cousin, to the King of Scots and to half-a-dozen others; once I was betrothed to two grooms at once.

And always it was Wolsey that busied himself in the affair—Wolsey taking bribes from France, from Spain, from any that offered; how many bribes no-one will ever know. But the man grew fat in goods, in girth and in pride until like an over-blown bladder he burst.

All these things I did not then understand; I knew only that I was *the* Princess of England, the future Queen of France; and that men paid more honour to me than to my mother the Queen. So I played in a never-ending sunshine, and did not know how soon the butcher's son from Ipswich should cast his shadow between me and the sun.

Chapter Two

I was four years old when I passed from the care of my dear Margaret Bryan to the care of one who was to become even dearer; from my mother's apartments to my own establishments. Now I had my own officers—my Chamberlain, my Treasurer and my Master of the Wardrobe. I had my priests and my confessors; my ladies and my waiting-women. I had my Masters of the Horse, the Falcon and the Hunt, each with his underlings; I had my men-at-arms obedient to their captain. I had my cooks, my serving-men and every menial that pertains to a royal household—and all wearing my livery of green and white. Over the whole household, and over myself, lady Salisbury ruled, taking her instructions from my godfather the dreaded Cardinal. To him went her daily reports upon my health, my lessons and my conduct.

I wept, at first, missing my mother and her familiar rooms, missing my dear Bryan; and above all missing my father. But my lady Salisbury was a woman of wit and integrity; she loved children and knew how to make life happy and interesting. And, if she must make her daily report to my godfather, she was, no less, in constant communication with my mother, for they were fast friends. So quietly, discreetly, my life was ordered more in accordance with my mother's wishes than with the Cardinal's; and, indeed my lady Salisbury whom I shall now call my lady-governor had but to say *Madam your mother would wish . . .* for me to obey immediately and with a good will.

For all my great establishments I led a simple life. My amusements were few and always lessons came first. As for my meals, in spite of all my cooks, they were simple beyond belief. At dinner and supper I was allowed one dish only—meat and bread; occasionally, an especial treat, I might be allowed a pudding of my own choosing. Many a farmer's child fared better than I. It was now that I began Latin, French and Spanish, also; my lessons were well-suited to my age and I learned quickly. My chaplain came daily to instruct me in divinity and in religious practice; my confessor to hear my childish faults. My mother finding such sweetness in the practice of her faith, and my father so punctilious in his devotion, I was already devout, loving above all things church services and church music. Then I would feel God's love all about me and, within that love, blessed and secure. I knew, by now, that my father was not God; but that next to God, I must obey him—not only because he was my father but because he was the King. And this seemed to me right and proper, for still he walked godlike.

My lessons in dancing and music were now serious affairs—though none the less pleasant for that! As far back as I can remember I have loved dancing, being light upon my feet; as for music, from babyhood I have loved listening, sitting very still, never offering to interrupt. Even at two I would reach up trying to touch the keys of the virginal or the strings of the lute. Now that I must study music seriously, my father, seeing my especial delight in the virginals, had a set made for me—small enough for small fingers; its ivory keys were a delight to touch, its case of inlaid rosewood a delight to see. It went with me wherever I might go. When I was taken to court visitors were expected to ask that I might entertain them; and my father consenting, there I would sit playing with fearful care lest I disgrace him. I doubt not my listeners managed to conceal their yawns in the face of the wonder child.

I was often at court; for neither my mother nor my father could endure long to be without me. Here, as at home, there were lessons and simple meals, but there were masques and dancing and music; at dinner my father would often send for me to take me on his knee and feed me with tit-bits from his own plate. And, wherever I went, there were compliments and the bent back. I was a little child and some that bent to me old and honourable; but I was a Tudor princess. My father bade me always remember it . . . though later himself tried to make me forget it.

I lived for the most part at Ditton Park—a short journey across the river to Windsor or Richmond; a longer one down to Westminster. But long or short it was always joyful. My lady Salisbury holding me fast by the hand, I would run now to this side of the boat, now to that, anxious to miss nothing of the river all gay with craft and everyone cheering as the royal barge went by. Sometimes, when my parents were in residence, I would visit them in the Tower and my father, himself, would take me to watch the lions and the tigers; they fascinated me but they frightened me, too. The Tower was for me the best palace of them all. I would stand entranced watching the ships go by while my lady-governor would tell me from what country they had come or for what port they were bound. She would show me the places on the globe and tell me what cargoes they brought or carried away. But of all things, what I liked best was riding through London; I loved the booths and the crowds and the smells and the warmth and the greetings. London has always been my most loved city.

And there were other journeys when Ditton was being cleansed, for after a few months air within a house grows stale, you can smell it in the hangings; only the great cardinal could afford to change his hangings every week. And, besides, there are layer upon layer of rushes to be removed and the mess beneath them cleared away—old bones, decaying bits of meat—and worse. But sometimes there's a silver penny and once there was a golden ring.

So out we would set leaving the house to brooms and scrub-brushes and lye and fuller's earth; and a long procession it was! Outriders and men-at-arms; baggage trains with beds and bedding, clothes and presses, baths and cooking-pots; and, wrapped with especial care, my musical instruments and silver dishes for my own use. Then, a little later would follow priests and tutors and more men-at-arms; and, in the midst, riding with my lady governor, on horseback, or in the litter as distance and weather dictated, my own small self.

Along the rutted roads we would go where people stood to blow their kisses and to press forward, a posy or a cake in their hands. And so through the springtime country—for such house-cleaning is never done but in spring—to yet another of my houses, sparkling-clean, to be greeted in all reverence and love. And I would run here and there, remembering this and that, my lady governor at my heels, enjoying the adventure of it all.

At this time, my father and mother were lovers still and good friends. Of course I knew nothing of the shadow that already threatened my mother's happiness; and her life. But later, when untimely I lost her, lady Salisbury would speak of her answering my questions.

'They were truly happy in each other and in you. Yes, his eyes did sometimes stray but not for long. Your mother was pretty enough to call them home again. She was a merry woman then! She was shrewd too, and honest; a more truthful woman never breathed. Your father would go to her for advice—and take it, too! And that was part of the trouble. It made Wolsey jealous; he feared her influence. He was always one to favour France at the expense of Spain—it paid him better. But she, loving her own country, would press its claims against France. Wolsey was forever jeering at her as Spain's best ambassador; so he lessened the King's trust in her and with it his love. True she did love her own land, but she loved her husband better: she always put his welfare first. So Wolsey had his revenge by throwing pretty women in the King's way—he knew your father's weakness. There was Mary Bullen, old Norfolk's niece. Your mother was hurt, naturally; but she gave no sign. It was the way of men; and the girl was too simple to hold him. And she was right, your mother; he tired of her soon enough so she married and left the court.'

About that other pretty face—Eliza Blount—she did not speak. I was three years old when the Blount girl left the court to marry and bear her son; my father's son. That the child was indeed my father's son but not my mother's was a fact I must, all too soon, accept, though without understanding: but to that I will come in due time.

In those early days I never saw my father angry but once. It was Christmas and I nearing my fourth birthday. To me he had always shown himself laughing and merry so I must forever remember that first time. We were keeping the festival, as usual, at Greenwich. There were the usual gifts for me; but already I had silver pomanders enough to keep me from the plague as long as I lived, cups of gold and silver more than I could house and jewels enough to cover my small person several times over. I made my way about the company, presenting my own gifts and offering thanks for those I had received. But all the time my mind was upon a gift the like of which I had never seen in all my life; and upon one giver I could not thank.

It was a sweet, silly thing to catch at a child's heart however puissant a princess she might be. An old woman had brought it. 'Very poor,' said the man that had taken it from her. 'She left it with me and went away.' I can see it now—a small rosemary bush aglitter with tinsel spangles. A little tree straight out of heaven. I walked round it scarce taking my eyes from the charming thing, *Pretty! Pretty!* I kept saying.

Suddenly the words died in my throat. I was doing wrong. How or why I did not know. I turned to meet my father's face; his eyes had gone small with anger—an anger I did not understand. I was soon made to understand, for he burst forth in a torrent of words.

'Trash! Take that thing away! God knows from what plague-stricken hovel it comes!'

I stood speechless, tears rolling down my cheeks; the sight enraged him further. He that never hid his own feelings, required others to hide their own.

'The girl prefers trash to pure gold! Your daughter's a fool, Madam, a fool!' He kicked out at the little tree so that it fell; dirt from the gilded pot bespattered his jewelled shoes. He roared for a servant to take the thing away.

Afterwards, I think he was sorry, for he sent me a standing-cup of pure gold filled with silver pieces. It could not comfort me for the loss of my little tree; still less for the knowledge that my father was an angry man whose anger could rise without any cause a child could see. It did not make me love him less; the fault I felt to be within myself. I strove even more anxiously to please him.

I was but three-and-a-half when I was betrothed for the second time. And now my groom was no new-born babe but the Emperor himself, my mother's nephew, Charles V of Spain. He had but recently been elected Emperor of the Holy Roman Empire, to the open anger of the King of France and the hidden anger of my father; for each had coveted the honour for himself. Charles was not quite twenty and the most powerful ruler in Christendom. From his father he had inherited Austria, from his mother, Spain. She was alive still, a woman crazed with love for a dead husband and Charles ruled in her stead. From his grandmother of Burgundy he had inherited the Netherlands; as for princedoms and dukedoms in Italy and elsewhere, you could scarce count them on the fingers of both hands.

The first I heard of the betrothal was from my mother. 'You are to wed the most glorious King in all the world,' she said, 'and the kindest and the noblest; a noble Spaniard—there's nothing nobler. And he's my own nephew, my sister Joanna's son. Poor Joanna! When she lost her husband she lost her wits! But that's no tale for a child's ear—save this, perhaps. True love lasts for ever; it never changes. But that's a thing you are too little to understand!'

Of the high policies behind this match, of my father's careful balancing of one power against the other, I had no notion, I saw only that he was pleased, that my mother was pleased and that the frightening Wolsey was pleased.

It was lady Salisbury that explained it all later.

'Your mother was happy in the match because she loved you and she loved Spain; she believed the betrothal was for your best happiness. Your father welcomed it because the Emperor was a more glorious son-in-law than the baby Dauphin; and powerful to help against France if need be. And Wolsey, for all he favoured France against Spain, was delighted. His finger had been in this betrothal. He'd more than a finger in getting the new-made Emperor his title. There'd been some understanding between them that if Charles became Emperor he would help Wolsey to the thing he desired most in the world—the

13

triple crown. To be Pope; to command all Christian Kings—and especially your father, his difficult master! To be Pope Wolsey would have sold his soul.

'But meanwhile you were still betrothed to France; and the Emperor himself to a French princess. So the matter must be kept very secret. Your father was not the man to let one bird go before the other was safe in his hands. He meant to keep both fast in his grip. But you cannot keep a secret like the betrothal of princes—especially from those ears it most concerns. King Francis pricked up his ears, and to keep him sweet your father agreed to meet him in France and openly proclaim their brotherhood. He took, as was fitting, your mother with him.'

'I remember it. The first time my parents went away together; the only time, I think, I missed them; but I enjoyed it, too.'

'It was about this time that your mother began to be troubled. It lay heavy upon your father that he had no son by her; it lay heavier upon her, for Eliza Blount had given him a fine healthy boy. So far your father had kept the child hidden in the country; but a King's son, though he be a byblow, cannot be kept secret and your mother knew . . . she knew! But she had great dignity, great courage; she hid her grief, and her fear. Even then she must have known her future threatened—and yours, too, maybe.'

Of that meeting at Ardres—*the Field of the Cloth of Gold*—all Christendom knows. How, overnight, there sprang up upon waste ground a palace of crystal all hung with flutings of white satin, the bare earth carpeted in cloth-of-gold and every chair, stool and table covered with the same glittering stuff. And how the two Kings met, each striving to outdo the other in splendour and in loving greeting; and each hiding the suspicion in his heart. Such waste of gold, of words; and nothing gained, nothing at all.

Of this great meeting I knew nothing, save that my parents were across the sea. And they, being absent, I was taken, by my father's command from Ditton to Richmond to receive, in his place, such visitors as the lords in Council decreed.

'It is a hard thing for such a little child,' my lady-governor said; and indeed I had scarce passed my fourth birthday, 'but you have been well-schooled in right behaviour; and you are a child with a will to be good; the *will* to be good—that is the thing! So we shall all be proud of our princess—your father, your mother and the whole country; and not least pleased, myself that have taught you.'

At Richmond I enjoyed myself. Never such a June for blue skies and sunshine; or, perhaps, grown older, we remember with heartache the summers of our childhood. Even then I loved pretty clothes; and since I was to receive in state, I had pretty clothes aplenty. I was a happy child, friendly and never shy. How should I be shy when everything I did was right; when I was the centre of all love, my father's *Pearl of England*? But for all that I did my lessons with my lady-governor; and my music and dancing masters came regularly; and I never missed any religious service nor my regular confessions.

So happy a summer! I liked sitting in my father's great chair heaped about with cushions, a high stool beneath my short legs. I liked seeing people and I liked the smiling faces turned towards me; and, most of all, I was glad my godfather Wolsey was across the sea with my mother and father. He was one to smile upon me, too; but it was a smiling I did not relish. Even then I knew the difference between false and true smiles.

I remember one day especially. Three great gentlemen of France were to be brought to me by my lord of Norfolk that acted as Regent.

'You have done right well, so far,' my lady Salisbury said, 'and I am glad of it; for my lord Cardinal requires daily reports of you.'

'He is across the sea and I would he would stay there!'

'Yet for all that, return he will; and he is a man to make a reckoning.'

'He is an ugly man and I do not like him.'

'He is truly an ugly man . . . to offend,' she said. 'And you owe him respect. He is not only a great prince of the church, but your father in God. Show him then the respect due from a child, princess though she be!'

'I will try.' I took her hand and kissed it. 'But still he is an ugly man!'

'If you truly try I have no fears. As for your visitors, they must be at hand, for here comes the household!' She lifted me into the great chair; and in came the procession—my marshals, chamberlain, knights and gentlemen; and with them my ladies to stand behind my chair. My lady governor took her place at my left hand, my lady of Norfolk at my right. And there I sat, a very little girl to take the place of the King of England.

Lady Salisbury praised me later that I had received them perfectly, bidding them welcome and enquiring first of their master, his majesty of France, of his young son the Dauphin—to whom I might or might not be betrothed—and last, of my father and mother. After some pleasant conversation they asked my lord of Norfolk if I would honour them by performing upon the virginals. And so I did, though fearful lest my fingers play me false; but they obeyed me perfectly whereat the French gentlemen paid me great compliment, saying it was a marvel to see such tiny fingers so sure upon the keys. The music being finished, I had the hippocras wine brought in together with dishes of wafers, strawberries and cherries.

'You have done excellent well,' my lady-governor said. 'Your parents will be proud of you and not even the great cardinal can fault you!'

Chapter Three

My mother and father were home again and lost no time sending for me. We were again a happy family—or so it seemed. They had brought me some pretty presents including some fine-worked smocks and a good jewel upon a chain—smocks and jewel a gift from the King of France to his *little daughter*. So I was, it seemed, betrothed to two grooms at once; a fact that did not trouble me since what betrothal might be I did not understand.

My parents made much of me, praising me for the good reports they had received. 'All France knows that we have a good, well-mannered child,' my mother said; and, beneath the scarlet cap, my godfather's yellow face nodded agreement. But such praise did not satisfy my father. He tossed me up in his arms, crying out, 'It is spread beyond France and throughout Christendom that we have the cleverest, merriest, prettiest, most delectable princess in the world!'

I delighted in his praise; I had yet to learn that one word from my mother was worth twenty of his—for let his quick anger ride and all your virtues were wiped clean away.

It was now I heard a name; a name that was to bring my mother to her death and darken my whole life. *Anne Bullen*.

My mother spoke it lightly, as of little moment. She had been telling her ladies of the splendour of Ardres, the kindness of the French King, the revels and the pretty girls that had graced them. I see it all very clear; the ladies at their needle and I, a little girl at her feet, sorting out the wools. 'There was a dark girl with a lively eye. I remember her name. Anne Bullen.' She turned to lady Salisbury and said something in so low a voice we others could not catch it. Years later, when I was fourteen, and suffering because of this same Anne Bullen, I asked my governor if she remembered the words.

'I remember them perfectly,' she told me. 'Madam, your mother said, *It is a name I must remember though I would prefer to forget!*'

My mother turned to the rest of us again. 'The girl is sister to Mary Bullen. Mary Bullen's prettier but the sister's merrier. She has a wit, they say, to set the table in a' roar. It is a wit overloud for my taste. She's maid of honour to the Queen of France and her mistress dotes upon her—so I am told. But I have the fancy that Madam Queen Claude would not be sorry to be rid of this wild, bright creature. She has, indeed, hinted as much to me; but we've had enough of Bullens here and Mistress Anne shall stay where she is!'

It was the simple life for me once more; back I went to Ditton, back to the one dish at every meal with pudding if I behaved well; back to my lessons. I sighed often for my indulgent parents and for the gay life of the court. I wished with all my heart I were back again—the centre of love and admiration.

'Stop your sighing,' lady Salisbury said. 'God is nearer to us in the quiet of the country.'

'He is everywhere alike—so you always say!' I answered very quick.

'But we hear Him better in the quiet.' And that I know now to be true.

I lived for the most part in the country but for the high festivals, for holidays and other especial occasions, I joined my parents. And now, child though I was, I began to understand—or rather to *feel*—all was not well between my father and mother. I would catch a word here and there I did not understand but which, nevertheless, troubled me. And I could see for myself that my father came less often to my mother's rooms and stayed but a few minutes; he had given up his habit of hearing Mass there—a thing I knew must grieve her. I thought she looked thinner, a shadow across her face. I did not know that, since my own birth, she had brought into the world two still-born babes—and one of them the longed-for son. I knew nothing of the anguish these bitter labours had cost them both—and that, in him, fear was already stirring lest he had offended God. But I felt the sorrow I was too young to put into words.

But one thing I did know—and beyond any doubt. She had begun to distrust my godfather; he frightened her. That surprised me. I had always feared Wolsey, but I was a child. How could he harm her—a woman grown and a Queen!

'Once he was my friend,' she cried out. 'Now he is my enemy!'

We were alone with her, my lady Salisbury and I; I had expected my lady to laugh the matter away. Instead she lifted her head from her stitching and said very low, 'Madam, he has his spies everywhere; and he is dangerous to anger.'

'He is all anger,' my mother cried out, 'all ambition, all pride; his pride—a sin against God.'

'Be sure, Madam, God will punish him!'

'Why should I wait upon God for so simple a thing? I have endured the man's insolence too long! I have made no complaint. But now he insults my friends before my very face. I'll endure it no longer!'

'Madam, he does it to anger you beyond endurance. He seeks to pick a quarrel with you, to embroil you with the King. I beseech you, Madam, be patient still.'

'Have I not been patient enough? As long as that man stopped short of insolence I kept silent. Now he goes further. He means to make an end of my friends—and if ever I needed friends I need them now! He knows Buckingham for my truest friend and so he seeks Buckingham's head.'

'And Buckingham himself will help him, Madam. Buckingham's pride is as great as Wolsey's—though with more reason. He has royal blood in his veins and Wolsey's base blood cannot endure it. And Buckingham talks wildly of a place in the succession; it comes near to treason. I, too, fear for Buckingham; I fear greatly.'

Her fears were justified. My godfather, too impatient to wait upon chance, made his own. In a court, gossip spreads to every corner and the littlest child may gather as much as his wits allow. Even I could piece together the tale.

My lord of Buckingham was in attendance upon the King; he was holding the basin while my father washed his hands. My father had scarce removed his hands when Wolsey pushed forward and plunged his own hands into the basin. It was as though he said, *You are my servant to stand at my pleasure.* The insolence angered Buckingham; he jerked the basin from those fat hands and splashed the cardinal's robes. Wolsey said nothing; not a muscle of his face changed.

Within a week Buckingham was dead. Wolsey had preferred charges of treason and witchcraft, and my lord's handsome head grinned from the Bridge.

'He was my friend, my true friend!' my mother cried out to my father come at long last to visit her; and neither remembered me sitting over my Latin primer in the shadow of the arras.

'Your friend! The man that with treason and witchcraft sought his King's life! You have strange tastes, Madam!'

'He never sought your life, not by treason nor by any other way. He was a true man! But this . . . this Wolsey! Insolent and lying. . . .'

'I would advise you, Madam, not to attack my friends.' My father's mouth pouted to a pinhead, was scarce to be seen in the scarlet of his face. 'It could be worse for you, let me warn you!'

She said nothing. She rose, very pale, and went down in her curtsey. He turned his back and left her kneeling. She went on kneeling, her face hidden in her hands. I do not know whether she wept or prayed. Thoroughly frightened, I crept from my place and put my arms about her bowed shoulders—whether to comfort her or myself I cannot say. But she did not know I was there.

She had said enough to deepen my own fear of the man. Now, whenever I saw that massive figure enfolded in scarlet satin, that heavy face with the cold contemptuous eye and the chin set like granite, my heart was troubled; I was afraid for my mother's sake and for my own. I never spoke of this fear; not to my mother, not to my lady Salisbury; but already it had begun to shadow my life. Children have a strength—and a wisdom—to keep their secrets and to hide their fears.

For all I had been twice betrothed, I was still too small to understand what betrothal meant. Yet something of the matter I did understand. I knew that I must give a ring and receive one in exchange; and I was bound to marry him that exchanged rings with me. But what marriage might be I knew nothing save that, one day, I must go away with him that had given me the ring of betrothal. I did not want to be betrothed. I did not want to go away, I did not want to leave my mother.

It was, I remember, a sweet morning in early May and I but three months past my sixth birthday when my mother summoned me to Greenwich Palace. After she had kissed me, she put me from her, very loving, that she might see me the better, and then drew me close again. 'My little daughter,' she said, 'I am very happy. Your cousin, my own sister's son to whom you are betrothed, is coming to England. He is coming to see *you*! He is the greatest King in Christendom and the kindest and the best. One day he will marry you. . . .'

'I do not want to go away from you, Madam,' I told her. 'I had rather marry my father!'

'You cannot marry your father,' my lady Salisbury said, 'he belongs to your mother.'

At that, I heard my mother take in her breath as though in pain.

'A pity!' I said. 'Very well then I suppose it must be my cousin!'

We were back again at Ditton. The homeward journey down the maytime river, the trees in Tudor green and white with blossom, the boats saluting as we went by and I, myself, waving and blowing kisses, put all other thoughts from my mind. Nor, settling again to my books did I think of my betrothal until my lady-governor said, 'Your betrothal gives your mother the greatest happiness. Your cousin is the greatest King in the world. He is called *the Emperor* because the lord Pope and all the princes of Christendom have chosen him to be their leader. It is a very great honour. Next to the lord Pope he is the most important man in Christendom. And, besides, he wears the crown of Spain, of Austria, of the Netherlands, of Naples. . . .'

'It is too many!' I put my hands up to my ears. 'And, besides, I do not want to go away.'

'You will when the time comes! It is a marriage to bring much good to this country and so it pleases your father as much as it pleases your mother. Your father is a great and strong King and this marriage will make him greater and stronger still. If he had to fight, the Emperor would stand by his side.'

'I would like to please my father, I would like to please my mother, but I don't want to go away; I don't want to leave them. But most of all I don't want to leave my mother—not at any time!' And I began to cry.

'You'll not leave them until you're a big girl; twelve at the least. Six years; that is a long time. A princess must marry you know! Some have to marry old men; or little babies—as you nearly did. But here's a handsome young man and your own family, besides. Why, it will be like going home!'

Even at that tender age I knew the truth of what she said. A King's daughter must marry; and to marry my cousin and go with him to Spain, would be, in a way, like going home. My mother had spoken so much about her own country; and since she did not seem very happy here, maybe she would come with me. Yes, since marry I must, nothing could be better than the Emperor . . . and no-one told me that he lived, not in Spain but, for the most part, in the Netherlands.

It was the beginning of June when my lady-governor said, 'Any day now you shall see your betrothed. He is here!'

I looked about me somewhat fearful and she laughed. 'Not *here*. Great princes ride with great procession; you should know it! He rides from Dover. Your father went with a great train to meet him. When the ships beached Wolsey himself went down to the water's edge to greet him; yes, scarlet satin, fine buckled shoes and all. And there he stood bowing himself in the wet sand. They are riding for Greenwich; and as they ride, the people everywhere turn out to cheer. So you see this is a match to please everyone!'

'Not the people,' I said. 'They don't like foreigners; you told me!'

'Well this foreigner they do like. To begin with he looks like one of us—English. And he rules the Netherlands; and on the Netherlands much of our wealth depends—and that you know well; I have explained it to you. And, best of all, he saves us from a match with France. Of all foreigners we hate the French most. We don't trust them and never did. And the reason's simple enough. France belongs to us.'

I lifted puzzled eyes. France belonged to its own King!

'France belongs to us,' she said again. 'We won it by war and we won it by peace. French princesses brought us great lands in their dower. You know what a dower is?'

I nodded. It had been explained to me.

'But more than everything—when our King Henry V married Catherine of Valois—and from her you are descended—her father promised, when himself should die, all France; a free gift to the English crown!'

'Then I should marry the Dauphin; it would give us the French crown again!'

'Never think it. It would give England to France; we should be ruled from Paris. Oh the French King would promise otherwise but never trust French promises! But Spain you may trust. Spain is your own blood.'

I did not understand the whole of this at the first telling: but she returned to it again and again until, at last, most of it was clear. Thus she sowed—and rightly—the seeds of my life-long distrust of France and strengthened my trust in Spain.

On a summer's evening in late June I stood by my mother at the great entrance of Greenwich Palace to greet my betrothed. Through the dark archway lawns and gardens glowed, the river flowed bright in the late afternoon sun. And, as we stood, we caught the distant sound of cheering that grew ever louder. I clutched at my mother's hand; then, knowing that to be childish, I let it go and stood upright, making the most of my inches as I had been taught.

In a roar of welcome from our servants and from the crowds upon the river bank, I saw three figures in advance of the rest—my father all in cloth-of-gold, Wolsey in his scarlet silks—and between them a young man dressed all in black, a chain of gold about his neck. Child as I was, I sensed the distinction of him walking between those two, his sober richness outshining their gorgeous figures. When, at last, they reached the gateway, he took a step forward and bent the knee to my mother. I saw the long, fine hand go up to the black bonnet, the fingers bright with jewels; the lifted bonnet showed fair hair bright in the evening sunshine.

'It gives me the greatest joy—' and he spoke in the Spanish tongue which afterwards she translated to me; for though he had sufficient Latin, it was a courtesy to her, 'to see Madam the Queen, my dearest aunt; and in especial to see my young cousin the Princess Mary.'

My mother raised him and clasped him in both arms and, *Welcome, welcome!* she cried out in that same tongue, her voice bright with tears. All this time he had not looked at me; it was not etiquette. Now he went again upon his knee; and I, as I had been told, stretched out my hand, the hand with the betrothal-ring, to touch it with his own.

I saw a tall young man with yellow hair, pale grey eyes and a heavy chin; a young man, neither shy nor forward but moving with a beautiful ease. He was fairer even than my mother, for he had the looks of his Austrian father, even to the Hapsburg chin. And it was these fair looks that had given rise to the rapturous welcome. He was, indeed, more English to look upon than many an Englishman!

There followed days of feasting and merry-making; but he was a solemn young man and did not care for such amusements. Once I heard him tell my mother that money might be better spent. That surprised me; how should a King not have money for everything? I asked her what he had meant. 'Even the richest King has not always sufficient money in his hand,' she said and sighed; and did not add that, with both hands, my father was flinging away his own father's hard-got treasure.

To me the Emperor was always kind. He would sit by me and listen while I played to him, though at best he had no love of music and his mind, no doubt, was elsewhere. He was teaching me to play chess. *We must guard the Queen well; without her the King is lost.* It was a lesson he must repeat more than once. He showed me, also, how a pawn may become a Queen. Another piece of wisdom; for I have seen more than one Queen move into that exalted but dangerous position. He was not one to pay compliments; but for all that he said I was the prettiest princess in the world and that he loved me dearly. And so he did—as a young man with heavy responsibilities may love an agreeable child. I liked him too, though he could not compare, this slow young man, with my handsome, vigorous, mercurial father.

Our solemn betrothal took place at Windsor. Even as a little child

23

I enjoyed the high ceremony of the church; but now, Wolsey conducting the affair spoilt it for me. I could think of nothing—not even the pleasant young man at my side—for discomfort of that scarlet bulk casting its shadow upon me.

Now England and Spain were pledged to war against France; and the war being won, France should return where she belonged—to England. And all this while I was still the Dauphin's promised bride. Well, it was all one—for neither my father nor my new betrothed meant to keep faith; each meant to play his own game—my betrothed to marry with Portugal where heart and pocket looked to be better served; my father to keep his pawn in his own hand for a more advantageous move. He knew well that a little daughter unwed, is of greater value than one already disposed of. Hand me over to the Emperor! My cousin might be the greatest King in Christendom now; but who knew what a few years might bring? Hand me over to anyone at all— his only lawful child and heir—and no likelihood, it seemed, of another, I was beyond words precious; *the* bargaining point in all negotiations with Spain, with France, with Scotland, with every prince in Christendom.

And Wolsey encouraged them—father and betrothed—both. He did not intend I should marry my cousin. The Emperor had not kept his promise; not Wolsey but the newly-elected Pope had received his support. My lord Cardinal was not to exchange the scarlet hat for the triple crown. Now he revenged himself my making mischief, slyly encouraging each in his duplicity. My mother—need I say it?—had no part in all this; her heart and her honour were in the betrothal.

The court moved to Westminster and I went back to Ditton. For five weeks my father did his best to dazzle the undazzled young man with the riches, the loyalty and, above all, the strength of London; and, the visitor still undazzled, my father carried him back to Windsor where I was commanded to make my Farewell.

I parted with my betrothed with as little emotion as I would have shown any other pleasant visitor. He knelt, kissed the hand that wore his ring, called me his lady and wife and departed; his manners and duplicity perfect to the end.

I never saw him again.

Chapter Four

The Emperor was gone, and back I went to my quiet life in the country; to my Latin, and my Italian, my French and my Spanish. The plans for my education had been drawn up by the Spanish pedagogue Vives, a man of some renown. It was a hard régime he laid down; long hours of close application to religious and philosophical writings, to suitable passages from the antique tongues—and no pretty tales whatsoever. He believed that the rod should be forever upon a child's back; but my mother softened his precepts as overhard for a little girl; so, unlike other children, I never felt the rod upon my back. She saw to it, also, that I had the gentlest of teachers,—for gentleness in a teacher begets gentleness and the desire to learn.

So I learned happily and did my lessons well enough; indeed the French ambassador was pleased to report that I was the most accomplished child he had ever seen. 'It is but the compliment paid to princes,' my lady Salisbury said. Most accomplished of women and most careful of governors, she saw to it that, though I bowed to discipline I was not crushed beneath its weight. She would read to me whatever my mother wrote about my education; and those letters I have still, treasuring them because they came from her beloved hand.

'Madam the Queen wishes you to pay especial attention to foreign tongues; both Christian and antique. I fear we do not always sufficiently apply ourselves!' my lady-governor would say; then I would work harder for fear of disappointing my mother.

'Madam the Queen enquires of your music and your dancing. For your music she need not fear; nor for your dancing. The Spanish ambassador told your father that you twirl so prettily, no lady in the world could do it better.'

I clapped my hands at that; I was a vain little thing.

'She enquires also as to your skill with the falcon.'

My happiness clouded. I could not endure to let the fierce bird fly, to see it strike down upon its victim; nor do I now.

'You must learn all the skills of a gentlewoman,' lady Salisbury said.

'When you are old enough you shall choose whether or no to use them. All accomplishments are needful but without them a man may live. But what he cannot live without is a heart pure and obedient to God. Madam the Queen writes that you must learn to serve and love Him first, from whom all grace flows.'

That lesson I have kept always in my heart. For beauty vanishes and health, also; but God's love is forever perfect. It is our hope and our anchor.

When I was a child I loved my mother because she loved me. It was only when I had lost her—too young alas—that I was able to understand her wisdom and her care for me. The things she despised, I despise; the things she valued, I value. And above all things I value obedience to my Faith—that obedience to which every child of God must hold fast.

Quiet years of gentle learning and country pleasures broken only by happy journeyings when we left for the court. My memories of those country days are all of a summer garden where I would sit stitching— a handkerchief for my mother, maybe, which she had rather have, she said, than any jewel; or a garter for my father that I never saw him wear. For though my stitches were neat and the colours sweetly chosen, he preferred a jewel upon that handsome leg of his.

Of Ditton I remember best the summer days; of the court, the high festivals and especially Christmas—the joy of gifts given and received; the delights of music in which my father played his so-admired part, the dancing in which, like him, I played my own. I remember the enchantment of the masque and the laughter aroused by the lord of Misrule. I was a child and happy; there's no happiness so sweet, no laughter so gay.

But more than the merrymaking I loved the Christmas services. Even then I had a deep tenderness for babes; it seemed lovely and right —as it does now—to celebrate the Babe's birth with high Mass and holy music while light falls soft upon angels and saints in glass and stone so that they seem to come alive and join us mortals in adoration.

My father continued to send for me to show me off to visitors; he was proud of me, then. And sometimes he would send for me to receive his instructions. I remember one such time. It was February and I but a few days from my ninth birthday, when I was summoned to Greenwich. My father and mother were not in residence but my godfather, the Cardinal, received me in his own apartments. My father's rooms were magnificent and himself served with every deference due to a King; but Wolsey's were yet more magnificent and he served as though he were God Himself.

When I, kneeling, had received his blessing, he held out a letter addressed *To my best-loved betrothed the Princess and future Empress.*

'It is to be answered at once,' he said.

I made to take it but, impatient, he waved me aside.

'No need for you to read it. I know its contents; that is sufficient.'

'My lord Cardinal, how can I answer a letter I have not read?'

'The answer is already written. You have but to sign it. It is to be sent with this ring.' And he drew from his thumb a great square emerald. 'You know what this stone signifies?'

'No, my lord.'

'It is a test of love, so they say! So long as the stone shines green as grass he that receives it is faithful; but let him prove faithless the stone shows yellow as hay.'

'Do you believe that, my lord?'

'It is a pretty conceit, but the ring shall be a token of his true love you when shall come together, husband and wife. Now here is the letter for you to sign.'

I brought it close to my eyes that I might see better and he *tschaed* his impatience.

It was a letter full of strange words. It seemed that I promised to be *continent* and *chaste* and desired the same from him.

'My lord,' I said, 'I do not understand the words.'

'*I* understand. It is enough!' And his red lips pouted like some horrid fruit.

The emerald, the letter said, was a test of my own devising, whereby his majesty might see my assured love confirmed by jealousy, this being one of the greatest signs of assured love. . . .

'My lord,' I began again, 'the last words I do not understand and I do not hold them to be true. Jealousy, I have been taught, has no part in love.'

'You're a fool to believe it. If you doubt me, go ask your mother,' he said brutal—the only man that durst speak so to me. But—butcher's son, butcher's breeding!

Well, butcher's breeding he may have had; but he had also a shrewd unpleasant knowledge of the world. I see now why he, old fox that he was, should send such a letter in my name—and I but nine! It was meant not as a token of my trust but of my father's lack of it—a warning that my betrothed must not dare break faith. Though still my father had no intention to honour his part of the bargain, he meant to frighten Francis with a show of brotherhood with France's implacable enemy —Spain. That game should continue as long as it pleased my father.

And no-one thought of a young heart thrown back upon itself, the humiliation of a child rejected. Nor did any give a thought to my mother whose whole heart and comfort hung upon the Spanish match nor of her fears at this sly shuffling on both sides.

Of all this I was, then, happily ignorant. I knew nothing but what my lady-governor chose to tell me.

It was later that same February when she said, 'The King of France grows bold; his eyes are greater than his belly! He means to have Milan, the Emperor's own city. He has crossed the Alps. He means to take Pavia first.' And she pointed out the places upon the globe.

'God will not allow it.' I cried out.

I prayed passionately for my betrothed's success; so it was no wonder to me that his forces had attacked outside Pavia and utterly routed the enemy. And, especial sign of God's Grace, the King of France had been carried—a prisoner—to Madrid.

'And there he may cool his heels and his pride!' I made a dancing step for joy.

'It is not so simple,' she said. 'For who knows what may come of this? For listen and note it! When one prince in Christendom rises too high—then there's trouble. There's a shuffling and reshuffling of friends and enemies to bring him down again. Look!' She went across to the balance we used for my lessons and placed a great weight upon one of the pans; the other swung high. She picked up some lesser weights placing them carefully upon the empty pan, now adding, now taking from them until both pans swung even. 'So it is with power,' she said. 'If there's not to be trouble, war, perhaps, the balance must be kept even. This balancing of power may well concern yourself. You are betrothed to the Emperor; but your betrothal to the Dauphin has never been broken. Spain rides too high; your father may find it needful to marry you in France.'

'I'll marry Spain or none!'

'You'll marry where your father chooses!'

'Spain or none!' I said again but I knew she was right. I'd no more dare gainsay my father than gainsay God.

In March I was sent for again to court. I found my mother troubled, my father hearty and gay. It was now I heard about the little boy so long hidden. It came to me in odd words and whispers and I did not believe it. I was my father's only child; I, and only I! And how could he be my father's son and not my mother's? And, if he were truly my father's son why was his name Fitzroy and not Tudor?

Some inner monitor warned me to hold my tongue and use my ears instead. I soon heard more than enough. The little boy was truly my father's son; he was handsome and clever; gifted beyond any child in Christendom and my father doted on him. And now to my bewilderment—jealousy. Jealousy I had never known before; I was stabbed through and through with misery and pain because the unknown child was handsomer than I, cleverer than I and my father loved him better than he loved me.

Jealousy sharpens the senses. I saw my mother and father no longer shared bed nor board nor prayer nor pleasure. They were never seen together, save on ceremonial occasions—at public prayers, on progress or to receive some ambassador. I saw that she was beginning to look old; older than he. That she was indeed, older, had never before entered my head; always she had been prettily plump and gay. But she was forty to his thirty-four; and, in his handsome prime he looked younger; now with all her bitter pregnancies and my father's coldness, she looked older than the six years between them. I know now what I did not know then; for some time he had been tiring of her and was taking his pleasures elsewhere.

The little boy had been brought out of obscurity. He had been acknowledged the King's son; he had been given princely establishments—far handsomer than mine. Now my father displayed him everywhere and did not spare my mother. For myself, I never, at that time, saw him; my father did not bring his son into my presence—he had yet some affection for me.

No end to the honours bestowed upon the boy. He was duke of Somerset; he was Lord High Admiral of Ireland—the six-year-old! I was increasingly jealous. The little boy was duke of Richmond—a royal title; it had been borne by my father and his father before him. I knew well that a King's son came before a King's daughter; and to the new pain of jealousy was added the new pain of fear.

'He wears the title of a royal prince; will he not, one day, wear the crown?' I asked my mother.

She cried out as though she had been stung.

'God forbid!' And then, very quick, 'The Council would never allow it; nor Parliament, neither. Still less the people. They have too much love for you; and for me, for me, also! They will never allow Eliza Blount's bastard near the throne.'

Bastard. I was nine years old and knew what a bastard was. But what a bastard might suffer—that I was to learn year after year with increasing bitterness.

Within a few days, I, myself, received a new title.

Princess of Wales.

Whether my father meant me to have this greatest of royal titles—unspoken declaration that I was his heir; or whether he yielded to the pressure of his Council, I do not know. I think it must have been the latter; for he said no word to me but left my mother to explain the matter.

'It is the greatest title next to the King's; and never before has it been given to daughter of any King. Until now it has been borne by the wife of the King's eldest son—in her husband's right. We have no son—' and she sighed a little. 'But God in His goodness has given us a daughter worth a dozen sons, so now you are to be Princess of Wales—in your own right. So tremendous, so unlooked-for an honour —you will have to deserve it!'

The honour I understood; but deserve it—how?

'It must be worked for,' she said. 'You will have your lessons as before, but there will be more of them; lessons learned not only through books but through people. A great title brings great responsibilities; and these responsibilities you must learn to carry. You will hold your own court, you will administer justice. . . .'

'Administer justice. *I?*'

She smiled. 'Not you. Your Council. You will have your own Council; your father has chosen it.'

My own Council? I stared at her.

She nodded. 'Yes. And at once. You go to the west country where the people have never seen you. They will learn to know you and love you and accept your high position. You will hold your court at Ludlow—where I, myself, was Princess of Wales; but only in my husband's right. You go as Regent for the King.'

Quite suddenly there came to me the dark side of all this glory. I was to be sent away from those I loved; from her I loved best of all.

'I don't want to go.' And I heard my voice tremble. 'I cannot stand in my father's place. I am not old enough!'

'That is why you must go—because you are not old enough. Not old enough to stand in your father's place but old enough to begin your lesson—how you may fit yourself to rule when the time comes; may it be long in coming! You will be advised in every matter by your Council. In small affairs it will act of itself; in great affairs it will take instructions from the King. But all documents, great or small, will be signed with your name, sealed with your seal.

'But though you stand Regent to the King, you are still a child, obedient to authority. So in public you will give no opinion, utter no word but what your Council decrees, and, in private, you will in all things be obedient to my lady Salisbury; you will make no move but by her consent, for she will speak with your mother's voice. *Your own obedience.* Never forget it, though at times forgetting will be only too easy; for you will be surrounded by every mark of royal authority. Everywhere you will be received with reverence—England's future sovereign. Queen Regnant. Such a thing, I think, has happened in this land but once before. You must learn to walk humbly before God; yet proudly, also, because He allows you such greatness.'

Thereafter she spoke to me often of my duties. 'You must learn to be gracious though you be sick or sad. Never let anger ride because you cannot contain it. If you show anger let it be because you *will* to show it—a warning; and, like all warnings, to be used sparingly. Show kindliness when you can; if you do not find it in your own heart then look for it in the heart of others that it may grow in your own. So you will come to understanding; you will learn like a good physician to take the pulse of the times. Kingship is a craft to be learned. You must think of yourself as an apprentice that one day you shall be master of your craft—Mary the Queen.'

'It is very much to learn; I will go and do my best. But not without you, Madam. You must come with me!'

'You will go because it is your duty. And I must stay here because it is mine. You will have for your comfort, my lady Salisbury. But I—losing you, my little daughter—am left without comfort.'

I saw tears brighten in her eye, felt tears prick within my own. So, lest I distress her further—for I was ever an easy weeper—I asked permission to withdraw, made my curtsey and was gone.

Tailors, glovemakers and shoemakers; jewellers, embroiderers and furriers; and when at last a little new crown was fitted upon my head and the mantle of state put about my shoulders, I began to feel the weight of my responsibilities.

Now my father sent for me to instruct me as to my conduct. He never spoke of the high duties of a King but only of the deportment of one that carried the weight of his authority. And all the time he spoke I sensed his regret that it was I who was going to learn the art of kingship, who should stand in his place and not the little boy, his bastard.

'You must be proud—but not too proud; familiar but not too familiar; distant but not too distant. You must learn when to smile and when to frown; when to be gracious and when to shut your ears to mercy.'

Truth and justice; of those he said never a word; maybe he took it for granted that the need had been sufficiently impressed upon me. To be truthful I should not find it hard; I am by nature truthful. To be just; it was a thing to learn and to practise. But expediency; to weigh to measure, to give so much and no more—it seemed to me, as still it does, well-nigh impossible. But to him it came natural as the air he breathed; he had with it magic to bind men to him, a magic that can never be learned; and a terrible majesty to make men tremble before him.

As the days drew nearer to my departure I would seek my mother whenever I might. I would sit drawing comfort from her nearness, listening while she spoke of the faraway days in Ludlow when she, herself, had been Princess of Wales.

'We were both so young, my husband and I; I was but seventeen and *pretty*; God forgive my woman's vanity! I hadn't liked England; after Spain I found it cold and wet; some days you couldn't see the sun. But Ludlow and the sweet border country! Gentle hills and rivers flowing clean—not like the Thames that stinks for miles; and rain falling warm. You could see the sun, *feel* the sun warm as at home. And the people were kind, heavenly kind—and so you will find them!' She stopped; she said on a sigh, 'But soon it came to an end. A few weeks—and my husband was dead and I was no more Princess of Wales. I was nothing; and for all my dowry, very poor. And then— the miracle. Your father married me and I was Queen.'

I had always known that my father was her second husband. She had come from Spain to wed the King's heir Arthur, Prince of Wales. And, he dying within a few months of their marriage, bride and dowry had been kept in England. Later she had been betrothed to the King's new heir, his second son—my father. There had been a papal dispensation, a great public wedding and a double crowning. That was all of sixteen years ago; old history. One would as soon have questioned her right as Queen as my father's as King.

Yet, already he was questioning the rightness of that marriage to his brother's widow—though as yet none knew of it; none save Wolsey. She herself had no suspicion. She had been sad because my father no longer loved her, because she had not given him a son and because she was losing her pretty looks. Now she had another cause for sorrow; I was going away.

Yet it may be that her heart knew the future—for the heart needs no reason; knew it and feared it.

Chapter Five

Drum, trumpet and fife; pennants waving, men-at-arms in new livery of my own colours, Tudor green and white, the great procession set forth. Kneeling, I had taken my Farewell of my father with some affection and awe; to my mother I had already said my true Farewell, weeping both of us, and holding fast one to the other. Now, as they stood together in the great doorway at Langley I thought my mother had a thin and forlorn air; but the August sunshine, falling upon my father, gilded him rose and gold so that he looked like a god. I longed, at this last moment, to dismount, to run back, to protect her. But, lest I shame us both, upright and smiling, I sat the mare and, looking neither to right nor left, took the road.

A very great procession and a gay one. The servants, commanded by my stewards, had ridden ahead to make all ready against our coming. With them had gone the wagons that carried beds and tables and other furnishings; and, protected by men-at-arms, the packhorses carrying chests filled with gowns and furs, plate both silver and gold, pots and pans and other kitchen requirements. Yet those that rode with me now, filled the country roads as far as eye could reach. There rode first my Masters of the Falcon, the Horse and the Hunt; and with them a full court of ladies and gentlemen above three hundred. There rode with me, surrounded by men-at-arms, my Council together with my Chamberlain; this last I mention, for it was that same Dudley who later, swollen to madness by ambition, strove to snatch the crown from my head to give to his son's wife, Jane Grey; but now he rode humble enough. There rode with me, also, my Treasurer, with his clerks, my priests and some half-dozen physicians, chief among them, good Dr. Butts that was to be my life-long friend. I had with me my tutors whose names I cannot now recall save only Master Fetherstone that so gently led me in the antique tongues; and that, for all his gentleness yet had strength to go to his martyr's death. But chiefest of all, my dearest governor, my lady Salisbury.

As I rode through the blue-and-gold summer, I had but one grief—

parting from my mother. Her last words rang in my head. *Do not be over-quick to give your word; but the word, once given you must keep— though it be hard and injurious to yourself. The word of princes is their pledge. Scant not your prayers nor any duty that you owe to God. He comes first; the King second—but second only to God.*

So I rode grieving; but, so lovely the journey with everything fresh and new to my eyes, grief soon lessened. In every village the people waited with gifts, in every town waited the mayor with his officers to bring me within, and from every great house the lord and lady came forth to receive me with reverence because I rode in place of the King. As we rode ever westward, the country grew more lovely; its beauty fell upon me like a blessing. The west country has for me an especial magic—a warmth, a kindliness in its very stones. I understand very well my mother's love of Ludlow and its marches.

Never such golden days. I was Princess of Wales and kept royal state. Everywhere bent backs and smiling faces; every day folk coming with gifts—lords and squirelings and farmers. And I would talk to them all, learning a little of their life and their problems. I sat with my Council and listened to their deliberations, I signed their documents though I understood little. I travelled from town to town; Gloucester, Bristol and Shrewsbury, I knew them all. I sat quiet with the judges and paid attention to the working of the law. I worked at my lessons, I made progress in music and dancing, I learned to take pleasure in my growing skill with the needle that I might make gifts for those I loved. And I gave my lady Salisbury my complete obedience.

I missed my mother still but now it was not a grief in my heart. She did not seem so far from me after all. She wrote often to my lady-governor forever careful of my health—soul, mind and body; she watched over my duties, my lessons and my pleasures.

'Madam the Queen forgets nothing; nothing at all!' lady Salisbury looked up from one such letter. 'You are to ride and to take all other exercise; but in moderation. You are not to tire yourself. You are to walk only in sweet and wholesome places and we are to keep ugly and harmful sights from your eyes. She is concerned, also, with your food. It is to be simple and pure; mark you, Madam, *simple!*'

I hung my head. There had been some argument on my part about the plainness of what was set before me.

'Simple, Madam but beautifully prepared; and that is the best of all food! And it is to be eaten in pleasant, merry company; not, I take it, with your eyes upon a book! And she does not forget that young people may be wilful or lazy, even the best of them; and a princess beneath

35

her fine clothes go dirty, and her bedchamber be unfit. So we must look to both; Madam, I read her very words, *everything to be clean and wholesome as to so great a princess shall appertain. . . .*'

To me she wrote often, also, my sweet and careful mother—her chief and earnest desire that I must never forget God and to love Him from Whom all mercies flow. She was happy, she wrote, that kind Master Fetherstone, that good scholar, should instruct me; she asked that sometimes she might see my work.

. . . for it shall be a great comfort to me to see you keep your Latin fair writing and all.

And so it was that, though I longed to see so kind a mother, I could not, in this magic land, long be sad.

The happy year moved on. At Christmas we had great festivities—masques and games, mummers and tumblers. We had a great gilded boar's head carried in to the sound of carols, the tusks wickedly gleaming in the light of a hundred candles. 'My lord Chamberlain grumbles more than a little,' lady Salisbury said. 'Christmas festivities are one thing, he tells me, new year entertainments, another. And this one, he says, beats all! All those masks; and mittens and tails of catskin for the mummers, and new coats and silver bells for the dancers. . . .'

'And gunpowder for fireworks to make a joyful noise unto the Lord! Let him not forget the gunpowder!'

The new year of 'twenty-six came in. And soon it was spring; for in this sweet country spring comes early. In March when our own trees are bare, here hazel is already out and under the hedges you can smell violets.

I remember that March well; for lady Salisbury brought me some news.

'You know,' she said, 'France and Spain have made peace; that the King of France is home again and that he's sent his two sons in his place—hostages?'

I nodded. I was not much interested—the news was two months stale.

She said, careful, yet making little of it, 'The Emperor is married.'

I looked at her unbelieving, yet I believed it too. For I felt in my heart the sharp prick of betrayal; a small, sharp wounding. I had been happy in my betrothal. I loved my betrothed; but it was the love of a child, a good child, for a kind father. Yet even a child may feel the pain of love thrown back in her face; and the humiliation of being rejected. Nor was humiliation any less that I had been forced by

Wolsey to send my betrothed protestations of jealousy as proof of my love; I, the Princess of Wales that held my own court.

My first humiliation. I was to know that bitter taste too well!

'That emerald must look pale,' and I felt my smiling lips shake.

She said, very gentle, 'It is not an easy thing for you, yet not too hard, neither. Pride not love is hurt. Never tell me, Madam, you desire to wed—and you but just turned ten and small of your age! The Emperor's a full man; he needs a full woman. He needs to get him an heir, as soon as may be. When there's no heir there's quarrel among the lords and disquiet among the people!'

'He should have thought of that before! He has behaved with some deceit.'

'There's some would call it policy. And, indeed, there was no help for it. Emperors no more than princesses are their own masters! Isabel of Portugal is the bride; it was part of the peace treaty with France. And, Madam, your father signifies his goodwill in this.'

And seeing me still hurt and disappointed, she said, 'I will whisper a secret. Had the Emperor not broken the contract, your father would have done it himself. He'll not lightly give you away; the Princess of England is a jewel to be kept for a worthier setting!'

'Until we find a higher bidder? Does no-one think of me, myself; Mary Tudor? What does my mother say to this affair?'

'She grieves deeply for you and for herself; this betrothal was her dearest wish. But mothers have no say in such affairs—not though it be Madam the Queen, herself. It is the price of royal blood. But come now, Madam, my darling; do not keep this thing too long in your heart. The Emperor is own nephew to your mother; there is good friendship between them. Do not let this come between them; one day she may need a friend.

A friend? How should my mother need a friend? But when I pressed her on the matter she only said, 'We may all need a friend; who knows?'

In one thing she was right. Though I tried to keep my anger hot, it cooled, soon enough, I was glad not to be contracted in a marriage that should take me forever from my home and from my mother. And, since the Emperor was my mother's friend I must learn to look upon him as my own.

My father commanded my return. I was to be betrothed once more; and once again to France. My lady Salisbury told me that; and no more. But still I gathered the details with a sick heart. I was sitting over my book within the window-seat catching the last of the evening sun when my governor and my Chamberlain came into the ante-room. They were discussing the move to London.

'So!' she said, 'another betrothal! A gentle child; a heart of gold. But they toss it about like a tennis-ball! This time it's to be the King of France himself!'

I heard Dudley take in his breath so that it whistled.

'The old man himself! He's older than her father and rotten with lecherous living!'

I did not know what lecherous living might be but I gathered it was nothing pleasant.

'It is not quite sure!' she said. 'If not the father, then the son—the second son. She's lost her chance with the Dauphin.'

'She'll not lose much there—a sickly creature! But little Orléans—he's another matter; tough as a riding-boot and sharp as a needle. Formidable, young as he is! If ever he rules in France, God help us all!'

'And God help her also, tossed between a sick and wicked old man and that frightening child.'

Back went the great procession through the keen March air; and though I was joyful at seeing my mother and my father, I was troubled at this new betrothal, having no mind for marriage in France whether with unpleasing father or unpleasing son. I wished with all my heart they had let me stay at Ludlow where winds and hearts are warm.

I found the court at Greenwich; the French ambassadors, already arrived led by Monseigneur the bishop of Tarbes. My father, golden as ever, moved with all the energies of youth; yet he seemed not so gay. We would hear that great laugh of his booming through the rooms, see him snatch an instrument from the player's hand and himself strike upon the strings, his fine voice breaking into song. And then, for no reason it seemed, the gay mood would break into sudden rage. I sensed an unease in him, an unhappiness; he was brittle with it. My mother looked thinner even than I had remembered; pale lips in a pale face, the cheeks fallen into folds. I could not, now, for very pity, sit with her when the women were about her toilet; could not endure the moment when they removed the coif to uncover her hair, her beautiful red-gold hair, all streaked with grey.

His heart was no kinder towards her, though her own was gentle and loving. It was a love that no unkindness could kill. Dying she blessed him that had brought that death about. But still they were seen together upon occasions; for, admired and acclaimed though he was, he was less welcome without the good Queen the people loved.

My father and my mother made much of me; and, although I lived quiet in my own apartments with my lady Salisbury, he would interrupt my lessons that I might show off my talents. I must speak to the French ambassadors in their own tongue; to all others, make a show of my Latin. I must sing, I must dance, I must play upon whatever instrument he should command. As a little child, knowing no better, I had been pleased enough to obey him in this; but growing older, I found it an increasing embarrassment. He expressed great satisfaction in my looks; and every visitor echoed his praises or invented new ones. Never let it turn your head, my lady Salisbury told me. Nor did I, nor indeed, could I. My looking-glass showed me a small, thin child, whose grey eyes had already the earnest look of short-sight; a pretty enough complexion of pink-and-white and truly beautiful hair, red-gold and sweetly curling. *The Pearl of Christendom* they called me, but I needed no reminding that a royal princess, though she be plain as a dumpling, may yet, in her father's court, be lauded on the tongues of men or shine in beauty on the canvas of painters.

Yet looking back upon old letters to refresh my memory for this writing, I come upon a letter written to my god-father Wolsey by one that knew me well; staid Dr. Sampson was not given to eulogies, and for very vanity, I that am no longer pretty nor merry, copy it as testament that I was once both.

. . . My lady princess is surely of her age as goodly a child as ever I have seen and as of good a gesture as of countenance. Few persons of her age blend sweetness better with seriousness, or quickness with deference. She is, at the same time, joyous and decorous in manner.

And as I write tears blur the pages for the merry child that knew nothing of grief to come.

Though neither my father nor my mother was happy, all was hid beneath festivities. I was betrothed to little Orléans that later, as King of France, was to cause me so much fear and grief.

St. George's Day we celebrated by a splendid masque. At one end of the great hall a cave was set up, all hung with green and set about with sweet herbs. Four steps led up to this cave; and, either side of each step, stood our handsomest young men, eight in all, clad in cloth-of-gold, holding, each one, a flaming torch. Within the cave

39

waited eight girls—our prettiest; need I say that, right or wrong, I led them all?

We were dressed alike in cloth-of-gold, our hair gathered within a golden net beneath a cap of amber velvet; and, holding the cap, a garland of jewels. To the sound of music, out we came tripping and the youths put their torches by to lead us in the dance. Now ten masked figures appeared, all clad alike in cloth-of-silver, and all wearing black velvet slippers.

My father was among them; he had hurt his foot and, unable to wear a shoe, had commanded all alike to wear slippers. It suited his vanity that, himself masked, should win the highest praise in the dance: a curious conceit, since, masked or not, he stood out above all men by his height, his elegant proportions and the shapely legs of which he was, not surprisingly, proud.

Each masked dancer took a lady by the hand; my father choosing me, we danced together. Soon we could not hear the music for the sound of clapping and the cries of admiration. I raised my head; and there we were, he and I, dancing alone while the whole court stood and watched. I think it was not only that everyone knew the masked dancer but because he did dance with extreme elegance; and I, myself, was no mean dancer.

He was a man forever eager for praise; and now the applause exciting him—or maybe it was the wine he had taken—he snatched cap and net from my head so that my hair fell about me to my waist. Amidst cries of adulation I stood, hanging head and scarlet cheeks. 'Why, sweetheart,' he cried out, 'you are now only betrothed; you'll show more when you're wed. Come, hold up your head!'

I felt command beneath the jest and did as I was bid; but, as soon as might be, I went over to my mother and stood by her side and danced no more that night.

Chapter Six

Coming back to my father's court after so long an absence, my wits sharpened by the life I had been leading, I was no longer the child I had been. I was eleven now and able to understand some of those things that at nine I had seen and not truly understood. Thus, before I left home I had seen my father's coldness and my mother's uncomplaining sadness; now I realised that something between them was broken never to be made whole again. I saw clearly that beneath the courtesies he paid her as Queen, lay frustration and anger; beneath her sadness—fear. Once I found her weeping and it frightened me; a high courage she'd always had. Even when she had lost her last hope of a son she had smiled out of pale lips declaring a daughter worth a dozen sons. So now when I asked her why she wept she smiled saying it was a weakness of the eyes, the sun being overstrong.

One other thing I noticed. Wolsey had further enlarged his grandeur. Ambassadors and courtiers alike fawned upon him; and, I have no doubt, pressed bribes and gifts upon him—and not overmuch pressing, neither! All feared; none loved him. But though the whole court bent servile backs, with my father he was fast wearing out his welcome.

'He is like a rotten fruit, all swollen with his pride and like such a fruit, must fall!' lady Salisbury said. Since our return from Ludlow she spoke daily to me of men and affairs. She was preparing me to understand events and their importance; I think, too, she was preparing me for evil to come.

That May we heard that a son had been born to my cousin the Emperor. My mother received the news with joy; but she must have measured the young wife's good fortune against her own, for the babe's mother dying shortly afterwards, my mother said, 'Would God it had been so with me. I should then have died happy!' Afterwards lady Salisbury said to me. 'You see the Emperor needed a son; he could not marry a little girl!'

'I am not a little girl!' I told her. 'And the matter does not concern me.'

But it did concern me—the birth of Philip of Spain. And how deeply the whole world knows!

At the end of that same month the Emperor's forces sacked Rome. Sacked! The holy city where the Pope lived! It shocked me profoundly. Of the cruelty, the bloodshed, the burning and the horror lady Salisbury said little, but such tales cannot be hid; when I asked her about them she said, 'It is war!' And when I pressed her about the Pope himself, she said, 'He has fled to St. Angelo. He's safe enough as long as he stays there. Let him put a foot outside—and he's the Emperor's prisoner.'

'God's Vicar—and a prisoner of the Emperor, God's own holy Emperor? How can that be?'

'Pope Clement is not always a wise man. In the matter of the Spanish possessions in Italy he shows overmuch friendship with France.'

'But—he is *Pope!*'

'He's old and sick; the old and sick are often frightened. But do not fret; he is better under Spain's thumb than France's. It is all part of God's plan.'

Now Wolsey carried himself more arrogant than ever—if such a thing could be. The bulky scarlet figure looked, indeed, like an over-ripe fruit ready to burst.

'Once more his heart is set on his great ambition,' lady Salisbury said. 'Now that the Pope is to all intents imprisoned and reported sick to death, Wolsey hopes once again. How he would love to brandish the whip over all Christian Kings; and above all over your father who loses no chance to humiliate him. But let Wolsey beware. He is not Pope nor like to be. Let him keep his eyes on the ground beneath his feet lest he fall never to rise again!'

Let Wolsey beware . . . lest he fall never to rise again. She spoke true; I knew that for myself; with my own ears I had heard my father's insults, with my own eyes seen the great Cardinal curb his arrogance and all but grovel. That he ran to sweeten his master, losing no chance, I also saw for myself, and could not blame him until he seized the last chance of all; and for that I must blame him to my life's end.

I tell the story as I know it now, piecing together the things I, myself, saw and heard. The things I was too young then to understand, I understand now; letters, documents and conversations have shed light upon Wolsey, upon my father and upon the woman herself—if light be the word.

And so I come to her I had not as yet seen, though some talk of her I had heard. Now I was to see and hear only too much.

Anne Bullen.

Even now, after the long years, and though she paid, God knows, for her wickedness, my hand trembles, writing her name. Anne Bullen that danced on the day of my mother's burying, all in a yellow gown.

She was niece to my lord duke of Norfolk on her mother's side: daughter to Sir Thomas Bullen, come from tradesmen that knew how to drive a hard bargain, to make money, to buy themselves titles and great houses that belonged to their betters. And from these forebears she inherited that same gift—if gift you can call it; and with her seeming virtue bought more than a title or great house—bought the crown itself.

At first sight I did not like her; and thereafter I grew to hate her with all the bitterness of a young heart that, for the first time, sees wickedness flaunting itself and goodness trampled underfoot. She was of middle height, slender and not in any way voluptuous. She was light and graceful, her every movement flowing like water. That was the first thing you noticed; that and her eyes. They were large and brilliant; they were black as onyx and as hard—no softness in them; clever eyes, watchful to take their chance. And her hair was as dark as her eyes; soft curls flowing below that small waist. She wore it free-flowing, announcing a virginity of whose value she was aware but which, even then, was doubtful.

And that is the full sum of her beauty. The nose was long, the mouth wide, the skin sallow. Those black eyes set in a sallow face gave her a foreign look; she looked more foreign by far than my Spanish mother. And lest you think that, for unkindness I deny her looks, let me set down what the envoy Sanuto wrote of her.

She is not the handsomest woman in the world. She has a swarthy complexion, long neck, wide mouth and a bosom not much raised. She has, in fact, nothing but the English King's great appetite and her eyes which are black and beautiful.

I wish I might not copy those words about my father, but I am pledged to the truth as I know it; and indeed, that particular truth all Christendom knows. But if I must tell the whole truth I must add that her mouth, if large and proud, could smile seductively beneath its bright paint. And she had another gift, to women inestimable; she knew how to set off her best points and to hide her worst.

'She learned that art at the French court,' lady Salisbury said. 'She

43

went, as a little girl, to join Queen Claude's demoiselles in Paris—in which school they were moulded into the form of fashion, and to make the most of such wits and graces as they had. And there she remained—lady to two Queens and the bright star of the French court.'

Certainly she knew how to hide her worst points. It was she that introduced the wide hanging sleeves from Paris; a pretty enough fashion. And she had her reason. For such a sleeve casts a shadow upon the hand. Others might forget what that shadow hid but I—never! I sickened lest those hands touch me. They were long and delicate; but, at the base of each little finger was a tiny budding as though another finger should grow. Witch's hands. I do not know how any Christian could endure those hands upon him.

And there was another fashion she introduced, to hide yet another blemish. That throat of hers, so long, so slender, was fuller near the base than any throat I have ever seen; it drew my eye with a horrid fascination. She never appeared without a jewel or a riband upon that place where the throat swelled. A pretty fashion and much copied—she was ever one to set the mode. But in her case, behind the jewel—*what*? I had heard more than one murmur—for she was not much liked—of a witch's mark; a wen or a pap where a familiar might suck.

Women did not like her; but men did. She had that secret of her sex; as it were an essence, an emanation, a challenge, to call out the passions of men—and not the best passions, neither.

My father was in love with her. At eleven I was old enough to know it. I saw how he looked for her, casting his eyes about until she came and how he followed her every movement seeming to eat her with his eyes. And I saw how she encouraged him with smiles from that wide painted mouth; but never a word the whole world might not hear—her tongue and eyes alike watchful. She was careful, the lady Anne; like her tradesmen forebears she gave nothing away.

My mother was as courteous to Mistress Bullen as to all her ladies; though, at times, Mistress Bullen scanted her courtesy to the Queen. Once I asked lady Salisbury why my mother did not send the woman away. 'My lord the Cardinal desired the place for lady Anne,' she said. 'He asked it a favour of the Queen!'

Wolsey had done this! Wolsey that called himself my mother's friend, that professed his love for me—his godchild; Wolsey that knew my father's passion for the woman!

Do her justice, Anne Bullen had, at first, no intention of ensnaring the King; to be any man's mistress, even a King's, was not for her—she set her sights too high. But to be a Queen never entered her thoughts; she was too clever to waste her charm in improbabilities.

'Why did she come back to be a plague and a grief to us all?' I cried out to lady Salisbury. 'If she shone so bright at the French court why didn't she stay there? Maybe she shone too bright!'

'She came back for two reasons. We seemed on the outbreak of war with France. And, besides, she came home to be married!'

'But she is not married!'

'No. That's an old story; five years old. She'd been betrothed to her kinsman, a betrothal to end a family quarrel—land or titles or some such. She was content with her match—and good reason. The Butlers are nobler than the Bullens, richer, too; and her betrothed's a personable young man. She didn't come to court at first; she stayed in the country till she could burst on us in all the glory of her fine match.'

I remembered now, she'd been at Ardres at the famous Field of the Cloth of Gold; my mother had mentioned her—a lively girl with noisy tongue.

'I fancy she came to court once or twice with her father,' lady Salisbury said; if she did she didn't make much impression. The first time your father actually noticed her was, I believe, in her own home. He'd arrived at Hever all unexpected, heated from hunting nearby and with a raging thirst.'

Well, hunting he may have been; but was he on the scent of a young lady new-come from France? Hot and thirsty? Did he burn and thirst for that same young lady? And had he been truly unexpected when he found her alone in the garden? Certainly when he left Hever the heat and thirst for her was in his blood.

It was after the first meeting at Hever, my lady Salisbury told me, that Wolsey, God's archbishop, came smiling and bowing into my mother's presence. 'Madam,' he told her, 'you are sad and that grieves us all. There is a lady new-come from France—a lively, witty lady. If, Madam, you would send for the lady Anne Bullen she would please you well; and, pleasing you, would please the lord King, also.'

My mother knew nothing of the King's passion: it was not yet on any tongue; but she did know he was thinking of breaking his marriage. It was that made her melancholy; a melancholy none but the King could lift. If she could please the King, it was enough. So Anne Bullen became one of the Queen's ladies and the court took on a new gaiety; when my father was pleased all went well—for all but my mother. Now she had more cause for melancholy than before.

Anne Bullen had become the leader of a new and fashionable set. She was admired, she was envied but she was never liked; her arrogance was too crushing, her tongue too wounding. Yet there was not one of the younger sort but longed to be admitted into that company where, with her brother George, her double in looks and wit, her cousin Wyatt, Bryan, son to my dear Margaret—poets all—and a few favoured familiars, she shone like the sun. They made music and poetry, they invented daring dances, and somewhat doubtful games. The court rang with the sound of their laughter. To be admitted into this set was the topmost feather of your cap; to be out of it—failure. There were some that would have given their very eyes to be admitted.

She pretended to be a madcap; but she was no madcap, not she! Those black eyes of hers watched for her own advantage. I thought that, for all the noble relatives on her mother's side, there was a boldness about her, a noisiness that savoured rather of her father's stock; certainly it did not become a well-bred woman.

And yet there was more to her than calculating ambition. For she fell in love—and not with her betrothed. Head over heels in love; I think, for the first and only time in her life. Had she been let to wed her love she had become a kinder, happier person and certainly my mother and I had been spared much grief. For she came out of that affair harder and more calculating than ever. With her it had not been heart alone; head, reinforcing heart, had told her that this was a match dazzling beyond even her expectations. Her lover was young Percy, Northumberland's heir; she of a parvenu house, he of an ancient, noble line. Do her credit, the greatness of the match had not been her first concern—though certainly it played its part. Nothing counted quite so much as the kind, charming, rather weak young man himself.

Quite suddenly Mistress Anne had left the court. My father had sent for her. 'Mistress,' he berated her in front of all, 'your behaviour is not honest—you are already contracted. It is not such conduct as we look for here. Go home until you come to a better mind in the matter!'

It was Wolsey that had brought about her disgrace. Wolsey had seen the King's jealousy and Wolsey knew how to deal with it. Young Percy must be sent away. The King must be allowed to amuse himself with the girl—as he had done with her sister, and with her mother, too, if rumour spoke true—and no harm done. He would tire of her soon enough; she had a vile temper that so far she had managed to hide. But meanwhile the King was besotted and talking of divorce—let him play the fool as much as he chose, there could be no divorce. Never! One Pope had declared the marriage good; how should any successor declare it wrong? He himself was a cardinal; he had hoped for the triple crown and still did hope. Allow any King to strike at the roots of the Pope's infallibility. Never. It could not be.

'Fool! Fool'! he shouted meaning all, even the lowest menial, to witness the young man's humiliation. 'Fools the pair of you! And for such foolishness you are like to pay dear! It is not only your father you have offended, dishonouring his betrothal for you and seeking to match yourself with one to whom he could never consent—so low her station beside your own. But you have offended your King; your King also. It was your bounden duty to consult him in the matter. But not you! Not you! You have chosen to go your dishonourable way offending those two to whom you owe your first duty. But take care; take care! The one will have you in the Tower, the other cut you off from your inheritance. Sue, sue for pardon before it is too late!'

So a weeping Percy left the court and home went Mistress Anne all bitter with her wrongs—her heart wounded, her great match ruined and her humiliation. For this she would never forgive Wolsey.

It was the greatest mistake of his life. He had underestimated my father's passion for Anne Bullen; he had underestimated Anne Bullen's power. That the passion could not last he had been right in thinking; but its strength and length—there he had been wrong. It lasted long enough to destroy him. The breaking of her match had brought her that for which in her wildest dreams she had never hoped—the crown itself; but it made no matter. Once her enemy always her enemy.

Meanwhile, her place empty, I looked to see the cloud lift from my mother's brow. I was too young to know that she had even greater cause to fear; for now jealousy possessed my father utterly. So at Hever Anne Bullen brooded over her wrongs and my father and the court languished for want of its bright star.

Chapter Seven

But not for long. Anne Bullen was back.

My father, himself, had gone seeking her. At first his quest, it seemed, was hopeless; not one glimpse of her did he catch. She sent praying forgiveness of the lord King; she was ill and dared not leave her chamber. He left Hever a disconsolate man. She knew well how to play him—the fish upon her hook. Now he sought to please her every way; honours fell thick upon her family; and upon my mother sorrow sat heavier. For though my father had not yet spoken to her on the matter, tongues were busy. The King's desire for divorce—his *secret matter*—was secret no longer. And now my mother understood what before she had only suspected—Anne Bullen's part in the matter. Yet, when the woman returned to her place about the Queen, my mother remained courteous and gentle.

And now, since it was more or less in the open, and I might hear of it from anyone, my mother talked to me of the matter.

'It was I, and only I, I myself, that was not willing for marriage with my husband's brother. It was your father wanted it; his heart was set upon it. His sacred duty he said; and his own heart's wish. He wanted my dowry; and he wanted me, with it. I was a pretty thing then; it is not vanity to say so—my pictures show it. And I was, besides, bred to a throne and educated beyond most princes. And of my disposition men spoke well. Between a well-grown youth of eighteen and a young woman of twenty-four—especially if she be young and small of her age, there's little difference to catch the eye. But the difference is there; *it is there*. Time will not be cheated. Between a man of thirty-seven in the full of his strength, and a woman broken by tears and grief, the difference is more than six years. The gap widens, grows ever more!

She caught at my wrist and I noticed how thin her hand, how little strength to it.

'Ah well!' and she drew a sigh from the bottom of her heart. 'Pretty and young I might be; and he lusty, already a full man . . . but still

I was older than he! A woman should not wed a man younger than herself—never mind how small the difference. I pray God, child, you be not made to wed such a one! Princes may not be choosers in their marriages, yet I pray God you be not overborne as I was!'

Had she forgotten I was already betrothed; and to a groom younger, by some years, than myself?

She had not. 'Do not trouble your heart about Orléans. Your ather will never betroth you in France! And so I say again, do not be overborne as I was. For my marriage was made at the deep desire of our two fathers—the King of England and the King of Spain; and two wiser men never lived. And more; it was made by dispensation of the Pope. So what could I do—a young creature in a strange country—but obey? But I swear to you child, upon my soul's salvation, I never slept with my first husband as a woman sleeps with a man, to lie with him and to bear his children. I must speak plain and I think you understand.'

'I understand.'

'There are some to question that a man and woman may share a bed and lie together like brother and sister. But so it was with my first husband and me. He was never truly my husband. He was young of his age and delicate; during those few months of our marriage he was never well, fever burned in his flesh and at times he would spit blood. But sickness he would never admit. He would ride and hunt and give himself to sport daylong; at night he'd come to his bed too weary for man's work. Good nights he'd fall asleep at once and lie like the dead; bad nights he'd sit up coughing his heart away. He was too sick a man for pleasure in bed or out; and so his physicians warned me. Had I lain with him as his wife, not King of England nor King of Spain, nor Pope himself not with a hundred dispensations, had made my second marriage.'

I believed her then; and I believe her now. Gentle she was, but one to stand firm upon a principle. And she was incapable of lying. Fear of offending God must have kept her from a second marriage.

And once she said, eyes haggard in her thin face, 'Your father has been troubled in our marriage this long time. Son after son . . . and never one to live! And then—you! A healthy child. A *living* child! Disappointed he was, a little, at the first; but then so proud, I thought him easy in his mind. But not so. *A son. A son. For the country's sake, a son.* . . . The words were forever on his tongue. So once more—one infant and then another; and always the same sad pattern. And all the time doubt was growing in his mind; he was remembering something he'd read in the Scriptures—that a man who beds with his brother's wife shall never beget a son. He searched for the passage and found it; he said never a word to me but left the book open for me to see, the passage marked. It is marked forever on my heart.'

And so I knew, beyond doubt that, before ever he set eyes on Anne Bullen, my father's conscience had begun to prick.

'Why does he need a son? he has *me*,' I asked my lady governor.

'He fears a woman's hand will not be strong enough to keep the country in peace when he is gone. He *meant* you to have the crown; he made you Princess of Wales. Now he believes it will need a man to keep the country at one; a strong man!'

'I shall have a husband. . . .'

'That helps nothing. Wed an Englishman—and you split the nobles with jealousy. Marry a foreigner—and he'll put his own country first; besides we do not like foreigners. Either way there would be trouble; and it is that your father fears. You see,' she said slow and earnest, 'we are but one generation from civil war—new Tudor against old Plantagenet. It was then your grandfather won his crown. Civil war; thank God you do not know what it means; please God you never shall! Of all wars it is the most cruel, the most bloody. Your father means to keep the country in peace. Right or wrong, he says he must have a son!'

That he felt this deep in his soul there is no question. For it was now he sought a royal match for his little bastard son, his ambassadors hinting in the courts of Christendom, the greatest of all honours for the boy; the crown itself. In his mind he knew well Parliament would never sanction such a thing; it is easy to see how his mind took the next step.

Why a bastard son?

The words look quiet enough upon the page; yet, even now, as I write, I shake head-to-foot in remembered grief.

Why a bastard son? There was Anne Bullen healthy and young with her dark hair and her dark eyes and her witty tongue and her vaunted virginity. But even if there were no Anne Bullen he would live no longer with his wife. On that he was determined. He'd not bring down upon the country the curse inherent in his sin; the curse of civil war.

Divorce. The only way. And divorce he meant to have.

Wolsey had changed his mind. A divorce; certainly a divorce. But not to wed the Bullen girl. She was not worthy; her birth was too low; and he was none too sure of her virtue. She was disliked; and, most important of all, she was his own deadly enemy. He would make the King's new marriage—he, Wolsey; a marriage to advantage the country; and himself. Marriage with France. Strengthen France against Spain and forever earn Francis' goodwill. When the time came for Pope Clement to give up the ghost—and surely it must come soon—why then Wolsey, with the votes of England and France, would step into the longed-for, most glorious place.

But gaining with one hand, he had no mind to cast away with the other. Spain's vote he would need also. How then a divorce without making an enemy of the Emperor, the Queen's nephew?

He thought he knew the way; a way to offend none—not even the unhappy Queen. She should enter a convent. She was deeply religious; beneath her glittering court gown she wore—so he had heard—the habit of a religious. And she was easy to persuade—if thereby she might please the King. Witness the way she had received Anne Bullen among her women!

Meanwhile he courted Anne Bullen, flattering her shamelessly and sending her costly gifts. He did not, for a moment, believe my father would be fool enough to marry her—a match too low even for Percy! Let her lie in the King's bed till he got the itch for her out of his blood. So reasoned my lord Cardinal, archbishop of York that aspired to be God's Vicar on earth; that would kneel to the devil himself if he could pluck therefrom his own advantage.

And still he underestimated a hatred not to be won by flattery or gifts; and he underestimated the uprightness of my mother that, for love of husband, child and God, could admit of no divorce.

And now my father found good reason to make public his *secret matter* that was no secret. Indeed, he could do no other; for the matter affected me. It arose, he always said, from my betrothal. Monseigneur, bishop of Tarbes and chief envoy in the matter, had raised the question of my mother's marriage. If I were not legitimate, not my father's heir, not the Princess of Wales—then I was not for the royal house of France. I was nothing; my father's bastard.

Bastard. For the first time the hateful word was flung at me; but by no means the last. And here I must add that later Monseigneur swore on behalf of himself and the other envoys, the question had not been raised by them; but by my father; my father himself!

It was towards the end of June that same year of 'twenty-seven that my father raised the question of divorce with my mother herself.

He could do no other. Already Warham, archbishop of Canterbury and Wolsey were holding a court to determine the matter; a court —need I say it?—at my father's request.

A sweet summer's day it was when he came into her closet. My mother sat in her great chair reading in her book of devotions; Anne Bullen stood at her back and I, myself, in my favourite window-seat to catch as much light as I could upon my sewing. As my father came in, the sunshine struck arrows of light from the jewels on his doublet and about his neck and upon finger and knee. My mother's gown of grey silk, rich and plain, carried no jewel save the great collar of gold with its hanging cross which she had brought with her from Spain and always wore.

As he came in I saw the quick glance fly between him and the woman at my mother's back. Anne Bullen was dressed finer by far than the Queen; she wore a gown of green satin—pure Tudor green, I noted— with raised flowers of gold. Long, loose sleeves hid the hateful budding at her little finger; as always, a jewel lay upon the swelling of her throat. Her dark curls flowed with some impudence—considering her reputation—from beneath a cap of lawn sheer as water and edged with gold; the little hood that fell from forehead to shoulders, was sewn thick with jewels. Yet, for all that, there was no doubting which was Queen.

My mother rose and we went, all three, down upon our curtseys. My mother, having risen, gave Anne Bullen the nod to withdraw; and when I would have gone also, she said, 'Stay child! I fancy this concerns you, also!'

I could see her poor heart beating beneath the silk of her gown and I guessed this visit came, a climax, to her fears. Yet, maybe, there was release also, to have the matter out in the open at last.

'Madam,' he said, 'there is enquiry concerning our marriage.'

'Enquiry, sir? We have been wed these eighteen years. What enquiry?' And her voice was steady.

'The enquiry is not of my making. But when Christendom asks a question, it must be answered.'

'There can be no question!' And she held him with steady eyes. 'We were married with the Pope's blessing, and with the blessing of our two fathers. Since then no circumstance has altered.'

He threw out his hands delicate as silk and strong as steel; and still he kept his voice gentle. 'Do not make overmuch of the affair; for I, myself, rate it at a pin! We do but search out the truth for the honour of us all—you, myself and this dear child!' His hand fell in a caress upon my head. I stood between loving father—for I swear he loved me then—and loving mother whose love had never failed. How could I doubt but that all must come right?

She would have spoken then, but his lifted hand forbade her.

'It is right to search out the truth, to remove every doubt. And Kate . . .' I saw how his eyes could not meet hers, 'until the truth be clear to the eyes of all men, we must not come together—husband and wife!'

I saw her whiten at that. He came seldom to her bed but never had he spoken so plain in the matter. She tried to speak; one long sigh escaped her—and then silence.

'It is not for long!' And still his eyes could not meet her face of anguish. 'This enquiry!' and he shrugged. 'It must turn to good; your good and mine; and to the good of this dear child—this heir to England. For be sure, God will not send us another and with her I am well content. Come now, Sweetheart, do you think I'd part for long from so true and loving a wife? As God hears me, let me search the whole world through, I'd not find such another!'

And for all his infatuation for Anne Bullen, he half-believed himself for I saw tears start into his eyes; and it was then, for the first time, I noticed how small they were, how secret. And I found myself thinking, if he swears by God he'll not part with so true a wife, what is Anne Bullen doing queening in it at the court?

My mother sent for Fisher, my lord bishop of Rochester; good man, good friend.

'They smear my marriage with the sin of incest!' she cried out and wrung her hands. He cast a look upon me that stood by her side and she said, 'My daughter is eleven; old enough to understand. It is right she should know the truth of this affair and that, I fear, she'll hear from none but me. Lies already she has heard; lies aplenty. This smear they put upon my marriage, what shall it make of this child; and what shall it make of me? You do not answer, my lord, so I must answer for you. It makes her a bastard; and me—the King's whore, his incestuous whore!'

'The Queen's grace shall pardon me; but such words are not fit for a child's ears. She is too young, God be praised, to have understanding of them. But, indeed, there's none, Madam, believe it—least of all the lord King—that seeks to cast a slur upon the Queen nor yet upon my lady Princess. Nor could they; not he or any man. He seeks only to clear your name of every doubt in the eyes of Christendom.'

'Eighteen years wed—and he seeks to clear my name!' she cried out bitter.

'Madam, if there be some trickery; if any man—though it be the King himself—hold this enquiry for any other purpose, be sure that I and all men, shall stand for the right.'

So he said and so he believed.

'When good men are blinded,' she cried out when he was gone, 'where shall I turn?'

And reason she had to cry out; for Fisher, when at last he understood what lay behind the enquiries, did speak out and was to suffer imprisonment and death in her cause.

As for myself, he was only part right. *Bastard and whore*; I understood both words. I had heard them in such context, I could not fail to understand. *Incestuous*. That word I did not know. I asked my lady governor and she, too, held it unfitting for my ears. But soon enough I learned the meaning of that, also.

And still my mother behaved with courtesy to Anne Bullen; but Anne Bullen did not behave with courtesy to the Queen; rather she carried herself in a manner that, if it were not insolent, came very close to it. Now, the tale of the insults cast upon her marriage being spread abroad, the kindness of the people increased so that they loved her not as a foreigner, Queen by marriage only, but as one of themselves—Queen by right of inheritance. As for Anne Bullen that meant to lie in the King's bed—if already she had not made it her own—her they abhorred.

'It is not a poor spirit that allows Madam the Queen to conduct herself with courtesy to that woman, it is a great spirit; greatness of birth and breeding,' lady Salisbury said.

'And the woman returns it with all the meanness of her nature,' I told her. 'A lack of breeding for all her schooling in the fine French court!'

'Nature will out! She flaunts herself as though she were Queen—though I never saw any Queen, ever, carry herself so!'

Only once did my mother's courtesy wear thin. To ease her melancholy she had sent for her playing-cards—a handsome set made in Spain. As a child I loved to handle them enchanted by the gay figures all set within borders of flowers; to those cards I owe, I think, my own love of gambling.

My mother, shuffling the cards, smiled to me to join her; but already

Anne Bullen had thrust herself forward, her witch's hands seizing upon the cards meant for me. Even now my mother's courtesy did not fail; she allowed herself to play with the woman that had already taken her husband and sought to take her honour and her crown also.

My mother was a clever player, but now, use what skill she might, she could not win; her opponent held all the cards. Anne Bullen played with both skill and bravado, throwing away, reckless it would seem, cards of high value. Yet she reckoned with care that her loss was less than her gain.

Rivals at play; and for more than cards. Beneath my mother's quiet and Anne Bullen's bravado I sensed the duel.

At length the play ended; a smiling Anne Bullen swept up her winnings. That smile was too much. My mother said—and her voice was level, 'Mistress Anne, you have cast away valet and chevalier; but you stop at the King, holding him fast in your hand. You will, it seems, have all or none!'

The red came up staining those sallow cheeks; for the first time she was at a loss. Even that quick tongue of hers could not, or dared not, find an answer.

'We will excuse you, mistress,' my mother said.

Anne Bullen went down in her curtsey—as scant a curtsey as she dared; and I saw her face. There was hatred in it. Till now she had disliked my mother as one dislikes the person one has wronged. Quite suddenly hatred flared—hatred that did not stop at my mother but reached out to me, to me also; nor did it stop at my mother's death but increased, rather, to shadow my life.

Chapter Eight

And now it began, the bitter, hateful struggle that was to drag on for six long years; and, in those years, my mother was thrust from her rightful place and Anne Bullen commanded the Queen's honours. Keeping herself from his bed until such time was expedient, she whetted my father's appetite, and, little by little, reaped her incredible harvest. By the end of those six years she was going everywhere with my father, in every royal house, the Queen being absent, she had the Queen's rooms; and, in the end, while the Queen was actually in residence, Anne Bullen had them too. She commanded every ceremony that belonged to the Queen; she had her own court and from her Presence chamber men walked backwards. She had her own Council; she had her own great household all in her livery, together with every officer, high and low; Chamberlain, Treasurer, Master of the Horse, the Hounds, the Falcon; captains and men-at-arms, she had them all. And though still on needful occasion my father and mother were seen together, everyone knew that the mistress was Queen.

And all these long years my mother upheld her rights, with dignity and complete lack of bitterness; that last I could not understand. She would never allow one word against my father and seldom against his mistress. When she rode abroad with the King she gave no sign of the differences that sundered them. But, for all that, the people knew; and everywhere she was greeted with love. It both angered and troubled my father. 'It is treachery!' he said it everywhere. 'The Queen steals the people from me!' But let his harlot ride forth all glorious as on a royal progress, the people stood sullen as she passed. Yet my mother's was a losing battle; she knew it and grew ever more sorrowful.

Those six years I grew from childhood to girlhood; and days begun in sunshine grew ever more overcast to end in storm and darkness. From my birth I had known only love, admiration and respect; courtiers—even old and honoured men—addressed me on their knees. Tongues could not sufficiently praise my virtues, my talents and my beauties—flattery offered to a princess but none the less sweet to young ears. In dignity I stood next to the King and Queen; and in the marriage-markets of Christendom—sure sign of value—I was second to none.

Mary of England; Princess of Wales.

Little by little, incited by his witch, my father turned against me; she was forever at his ear with her tales—I was stupid and obstinate, I was ungrateful and wicked. I was disobedient, holding the King's Majesty light; I blasphemed against God, so that not He nor any man had use for me.

Where the King leads, the court follows; whatever he felt in his heart no man dared praise me. But that was towards the end; at first I scarce noticed the diminished chorus of praise. For one thing I was less often at court. Quiet in the country, surrounded by my own household and with my dear lady Salisbury, I was happy enough with my books and my music. I was troubled, at times, remembering my mother's sadness but at eleven, one cannot always remember. I prayed, putting my trust in God, as she had taught me, and was confident right would prevail. God is just. Since my father so rarely sent for me now. I did not understand how hatefully the climate had changed until it was too late.

Six years of struggle and ever-increasing misery for my mother and me, beginning that summer of 'twenty-seven when I returned from Ludlow, and my father—a court of bishops, already enquiring into the matter—opened the question of divorce with my mother. And though Wolsey bullied the court without mercy; and the archbishop of Canterbury, Warham the tired old man, was willing to give the King his way for the sake of quiet and peace, the bishops did examine the matter with careful honesty.

My father had expected a clear answer in accordance with his desire; a desire so ardent that he was willing to appear before the court and plead guilty to the charge of incest—he, the King's majesty. But Fisher—true man, true friend—would have none of it. Dispensation had been granted and the marriage was good; others argued that not even the Pope's self could grant dispensation against God's laws. So a divided court gave no decision and my father showed his anger in no uncertain manner. The brunt of it fell upon Wolsey who judged it wise to put himself out of the way till it should cool. He departed for France to stir up mischief against the Emperor, to make a fresh alliance with Francis, and above all, to gain support for the divorce.

'Wolsey is not clever to leave England now,' lady Salisbury said. 'The King's confidence in him is stone-cold and his anger red-hot.'

And that was true enough. My father's passion for the witch had grown so hot that she shaped him as iron upon a hot anvil.

'I pray he may never come back; he's my mother's enemy! But come back he will; he cannot be spared. My father, for all his anger finds the man too useful, too clever!'

'It depends who's cleverer—Wolsey or Anne Bullen. We shall see; as you say he cannot stay away for ever!'

He came back on a golden day in late September; he went direct to Greenwich where my father and his mistress held court. In the Queen's rooms my mother and I sat alone—for courtiers if they would come to harvest must bend the head when the wind blows. To us came lady Salisbury, all breathless.

'Madam, Wolsey is back; he went direct to the King but the King refused to see him. It was that woman! She cried out in that high voice of hers, *Does he expect the King to go to him? Let him come where the King is; but first let him cool his heels!*

'So, Madam, there he sat, the great cardinal, in the ante-room, waiting his turn with the humblest; and his face, so they say, grey as muttonfat. And when, at last, he was let into the Presence, he found the King with Anne Bullen and the whole court. It was as though the King announced publicly that whatever the man had to say was unworthy of his private ear. So Wolsey made his humble obeisance and murmured a few words and left. I fancy he reads the writing on the wall.'

In November, the Pope signed a treaty with the Emperor.

'His Holiness gets his freedom in return for friendship with Spain,' lady Salisbury said. 'Friendship—another word for obedience. Now we may see why God allowed His Vicar to be defeated. Now he'll not dare give your father his divorce. No! He fears the Emperor!'

Christmas came with all its preparations for merrymaking—for those that could be merry. My father sent for me and I remembered how last year I had spent the festival at Ludlow amidst true merrymaking. But now, beneath all the preparations, we felt the sting of his anger—he was not a man to be crossed or delayed in his desires. My mother's presence he had commanded, also, but he visited her not at all save to fling cruel words at her. 'You hold to your shame; you disgrace yourself in the eyes of Christendom!' This was his only theme; then, seeing me large-eyed and tearful, he would speak to me kindly telling me not to grieve. 'I speak for your mother's good; but she, being mere woman, will not have it so!'

On the last day of the old year the Pope, under pressure from France, granted a commission to examine grounds for divorce.

'God's Mouthpiece is a shuttlecock tossed between France and Spain!' my lady governor said.

'I'll have no part in the matter!' my mother cried out. 'Appear before a commission. Let men discuss whether I be the King's whore and my child unfit to inherit! Never, though I die for it!'

The new year of 'twenty-eight came in; my father held wassail with his mistress; and all the Bullens looked with confidence to a good year. Especially merry was Norfolk, the witch's uncle; he was strengthening a party to make an end of Wolsey—Wolsey and any man that threatened his own power. But good folk everywhere knew sorrow for my mother and shame for my father. Put away his good wife for a strumpet! The common folk of England stood solid against it. But those that dared not oppose him or meant to snatch advantage with a show of goodwill—his Council, the most part of his Parliament, some lords and bishops, stood by the King. Abroad the Emperor stiffened the Pope; but King Francis could not be relied upon—except to act to his own best advantage.

Anger in my father had a way of hardening into cruelty; and of that cruelty my mother bore the full weight. To me he still showed himself affectionate; he would send for me from time to time, he showed concern for my health and education—though never, I think, for my happiness. He gave me pretty gifts until Anne Bullen put a stop to it. For now, so besotted he was, he bowed to the lift of her eyebrow; when I stood before him in her presence I felt her spite like a bitter wind upon me.

The early months of 'twenty-eight moved on; my twelfth birthday came and went. My body thin and small gave no outward sign of quickening womanhood; yet within myself I knew a deepening sensibility, a richer capacity for joy and sorrow, an awareness of life unfolding about me and I, myself, part of it.

There was no further word of the commission. When I went to Westminster or Richmond or wherever the court might be, I found things always the same.—My mother quiet in her rooms and Anne Bullen urging my father to further humiliation. Before my mother's strength and courage I felt humble; but I felt angry too. Her patience was a thing I could not understand.

'Where does she get the strength, the courage to bear it all—and without complaint? It is as though she does not *see* the humiliation; but she sees it; she *sees* it!'

'It is not only strength and courage; there's a nobility in her, also. No man can humiliate her, nor woman neither. She is all goodness!'

'But not to allow one word against my father; nor against that woman, neither.'

'She has discretion, also! God grant that you, Madam, learn it too!'

But that is a lesson I have never learnt. I am a Tudor. I love and I hate. And even now, though turned of forty and having learned many a hard lesson, I have never learned—either in love or hatred—to hide my heart.

At times I would speak my bitterness against Anne Bullen. I was afraid of her. I thought she was a witch. How was it that my father before whom all trembled, obeyed her every whim, endured the lash of her tongue? I was too young to know that a woman may enchant a man—and not by witchcraft. At times I tried to speak my fear but always my mother forbade me. Should some word reach my father there was no knowing what punishment he might put upon me; in his present mood he would stop at no cruelty.

But I was growing up and could not always be stayed.

'She is a witch, Madam, a witch. She has the marks. Why does she forever cover that neck of hers with a jewel? What is it she hides?'

'Nothing, you may be sure!' my mother said. 'It is a fashion—and a pretty one.'

'But *who* set the fashion? And why? It is to hide a witchmark; a wart or a wen where she suckles her familiar!'

My mother's face moved in disgust. 'Child, you should not know such things.'

'If we are not to know the devil's marks how shall we keep ourselves from him and his?'

'For Mistress Bullen I have no love. But this tale of witchmarks—never believe it!'

'Madam, it is true. I had it of my Bet that had it from Moll, a wench of that woman! This wench, being told to take up her lady's combs to wash them, comes into the chamber expecting to find it empty. And what does she see? She sees the lady, the lady herself and her neck all bare. And in the middle of the neck where the swelling is—a place all red and wet as though something has sucked upon it. The wench sees the lady; but the lady does not see her, so away goes Moll on soft feet. She told my Bet and my Bet told me.'

'Then both wenches had best hold their tongues! I take it for a lying tale. Never repeat it! My daughter should know better than to repeat servants' talk.'

'If I may not speak about those things I have not myself seen, is it permitted to talk of those I *have* seen?'

'It might be wiser not!'

'Her hands then; that budding by the little finger. That, also, is a witchmark.'

'On that matter, too, I forbid you to speak!' Her voice came out sharp. 'Not to me, not to my lady Salisbury, not to anyone at all! It is not your mother that commands you but your Queen!'

Never had she spoken so to me before, my gentle mother. I understood her fear for me, for what my careless tongue could bring. I went down upon my curtsey. 'I understand Madam the Queen and I will obey.'

And still from Rome no word of commission or commissioners.

Anne Bullen appeared in ever more splendid jewels; some my father had made for her, bearing her cypher intricately worked; others were my mother's personal ornaments. My mother said nothing; so much had already been taken; a jewel more or less—what did it matter? She had not been commanded to give up those she held in right of the Queen; this was to come. Of her own jewels she kept back only the collar with the crucifix and some small ornaments she had had as a girl.

Those that called Anne Bullen *strumpet* were wrong. If she went awhoring with the King, it was, as yet, only in her mind. She had not as yet gone to bed with him—she was playing for the highest stakes of all. *Stop at the King, holding him fast in your hand; you will have all or none.* For all his passion, his love-songs and his gifts, she had not, at that time, yielded her body. This is certain. One of his letters I have seen; it found its way by secret messenger to Rome and stiffened the Pope still further in his refusal of divorce.

It is a long, impassioned letter. He tells her that for a whole year he has been wounded by love; he minces no words. . . .

> If you choose to do the duty of a true and loyal mistress and give yourself heart and person to me, I shall be, as I have been, your most loyal servant—if your rigour does not forbid. . . .

If your rigour does not forbid. Clear testimony that, so far, she had denied herself. And *rigour*; there's an interesting word! For all the fascination streaming from her like an odour to attract men, she was cold. A cold woman. And though he goes on to promise he will cast all other women out of his life to serve her only, cold she remained. Cold and clever; too cold, too clever to trust to promises. Her answer was always the same. *I would rather lose my life than my honour.* Well she was to lose both—and sooner than she looked for.

To say that I disliked my father would not be true. How should I, twelve years old, dislike my father and my King? Moreover my mother forever told me that, after God, my first love and duty were for my King. But I was angry, I was puzzled; I did not know then how flesh may hunger for flesh to the edge of madness. I saw only Anne Bullen— brilliant eyes, brilliant gowns, brilliant jewels; and my mother that had been both pretty and gay, sad, neglected, and aging. At times I thought my heart must burst with grief.

My father's anger against Rome and the Emperor was forever growing. In London the Emperor's ambassador was set upon and his luggage examined; maybe he deserved it. Maybe he knew how my father's letter had found its way to Rome. But nothing was proved against him; and to search an ambassador's baggage was a deadly insult. My cousin the Emperor said nothing; but it did not make him and my father better friends.

And still from Rome no word of commission or commissioner.

Behind Wolsey's back my father was forever sending his own especial messenger to Rome. This I know because that messenger himself told me—Stephen Gardiner that was to be at first my enemy and then my trusted friend. Master Stevens he was called then; a man in his mid-thirties and looked ten years older. He was no bishop at that time but a humble clerk. Do I say *humble*? There was nothing humble about Master Stevens. Tall and hawk-eyed; sharp witted and sharp tongued; a scholar and shrewd lawyer. My father, that judge of men, had noted in him a keenness that would let no point go by, a clarity of mind and tongue to make the most obscure point clear, and a subtlety to carry his will against his master—Wolsey himself; and all this with an application that would not let him rest until a piece of work was finished—and finished to his own satisfaction. Plain Master Stevens had, as yet, no outward authority; but he had the authority of his strong will and did not hestitate to use it.

Now he was to prove himself in Rome. Clever, choleric and persuasive by turn, he harried and cajoled the Pope until the sick old man named his legate at last. Campeggio was to sit with Wolsey at the head of the commission to examine the case. For long years I hated Stephen

Gardiner that had worked to break my mother's marriage. But he, at least, was honest in the matter; and honest I found him at my need—a man incorruptible. I thought he had no heart—until I found it well-hid in his sleeve.

Now Anne Bullen carried herself as though already she wore the crown; my father's satisfaction was immense. Soon the affair would be settled. Soon!

But spring moved into summer and the legate did not come. Excuses were many—all relevant documents had not been received; the Pope was sick again; the legate himself had fallen ill; winds were contrary. And for such delays my father blamed not the harassed Pope shuttlecocked between France and Spain, but the unfortunate Wolsey. Do I say unfortunate? I think we have such fortune as we make for ourselves!

That June Anne Bullen fell sick of the sweating sickness. One of her women had first contracted it and my father hating sickness and fearing it, too, broke up the court. His mistress he sent home to Hever and removed himself to a safe distance at Hunsdon. Desire her he did; but he'd not have her near him until danger of infection was passed. So my mother and I were left together at Richmond and happy we were out of that woman's sight. I was glad of Anne Bullen's sickness and I hoped she would die. I thought, being young and ignorant that, she being out of the way, all would come right again.

'Please God she may die!' I told my mother. 'I do pray for it!'

'Such prayers hurt none but yourself!' my mother said. 'Be satisfied to leave all to God!'

But alas! My father sent his own physician; all too soon Anne Bullen was well again and she and my father back together at Greenwich. And now, since he had nearly lost her, her power over him was greater than ever. And Wolsey felt it—as she meant him to feel it! Oh she was gracious enough in her smiling and in acceptance of his gifts; costly gifts given by a desperate man. But behind his back she lost no opportunity to put him down—it was common property. She ridiculed the man himself, fat, pompous and servile; she distrusted him as chancellor, she trampled upon his rights as archbishop to make church appointments, persuading the King to give them to her friends. She accused him of bribery, corruption and fraud, pointing to the man's vast possessions—and especially to York House and to Hampton Court, palaces both and more magnificent than anything the King could afford. And always and upon every occasion, she harped upon the divorce. It was Wolsey with his especial obedience to Rome; Wolsey the Pope's cardinal that stood between the King and his desire; that robbed England of its heir.

Now the King would openly rebuke the man that held such proud positions—archbishop, cardinal and chancellor; and Wolsey, that had once been the King's master, would abjectly apologise even when there was no fault in him. Yet in my father's eye there was fault and fault enough! Wolsey had not been successful in the King's *great matter*; he had kept the King from Anne Bullen's bed.

And still I held to my hope. Any day now the legate would come. In the rightness of my mother's cause I put my trust. God would not permit the sin of divorce.

Chapter Nine

Campeggio had come at last. He had been delayed by the Pope himself believing that my father's passion must cool. Now, though there seemed little hope of that, the legate had his orders to delay the examination as long as possible while he strove for reconciliation between my father and mother. It was the only solution his Holiness could with Christian honour, see.

It was at the end of September that Campeggio arrived. Anne Bullen had been sent from the court lest her presence affront his eyes; and my father received him with every high honour and a heart full of hope.

I remember the day well—a bright, warm day that might almost have been summer. I was visiting my mother at the Bridewell Palace and our own hopes were bright as the day. 'Now we shall have justice!' my mother said.

Towards the end of October Campeggio and Wolsey came together to visit my mother; Campeggio because he longed to help her, Wolsey that he might help himself. He was desperate. He saw nothing for it but that Anne Bullen who hated him would be Queen and hoped to placate her by persuading my mother into a convent.

That day, too, I remember. A melancholy day, lacking all sun, the river heavy with sodden leaves and no wind, so that the water scarce moved beneath their weight; in the garden a few flowers hung upon blackened stalks.

They found us at our needles, my mother at her frame, myself stitching, eyes close upon a strip of cambric. Shirtbands for my father— he liked his linen finer than bishop's lawn. For all her grief my mother never dressed less than queenly. She was wearing a gown of dark blue velvet opening upon a petticoat of silver; from her jewelled cap hung a mantilla of black lace, Spanish fashion. She wore no other jewel save the Spanish collar and crucifix. Pale and anxious she was, but an un-doubted Queen—as the Bullen woman could never be. My own gown I remember too; I have always loved fine clothes. It was of satin damask of Our-Lady blue stitched all with bright flowers. I wore a light jewelled coronal as befitted my father's heir; for that I was his heir my mother bade me never forget.

When the gentlemen came in, my mother rose and made to bend the knee to Campeggio but he would have none of it. I would have withdrawn but my mother held me fast by the hand.

'This concerns my daughter as much as myself. She is going on for thirteen—old enough to understand the matter.'

'Madam,' Wolsey said and he did not address her as Queen, 'I bring a message from the lord King. If you will submit to a divorce between you, he offers you whatever you may in honour ask and promises that, in honour you shall receive it. As for the lady Mary—' and he did not name me *princess*, 'she shall be named next in succession after the issue of his second marriage.'

'Second marriage!' she cried out, stung. 'While I live there can be no second marriage!'

Wolsey went on as though she had not spoken. 'Madam, you have but to agree and the King shall hold you—and name you—his dearest sister.'

'A sister that has lain in his bed and borne his children!'

'You shall be Princess of Wales, Madam; second only to the Queen herself.'

'Here is the Princess of Wales!' and she took me by the hand. 'And' —her hand went up to her breast—'here is the Queen. As long as I live there can be no other.'

'Madam,' Wolsey began again; she turned her back on him.

'Eminence,' and she went down upon both knees, 'help me. Spain is far away and there's none in England dare advise me as to my rights; nor the rights of this child. Eminence, for the love of God, I pray you, help me!'

He raised her before he spoke. 'Madam the Queen knows I am here to sift out the truth. From such papers as I have seen I hold your marriage to be good and yourself a blameless wife. All the papers I have not yet seen; and whatsoever the examination shall prove—' he shrugged, 'so it must be! As for my brother here, do not blame him overmuch; he swims in a bitter sea!'

My eyes went to Wolsey. I thought I saw pity softening those hard eyes of his! He, even he, seeking to ensnare my mother for his own ambitions was, for the moment, softened by her grief, by the rightness of her cause and by her gentleness.

'Madam,' Campeggio said, 'I am told that you would enter a convent, to offer the rest of your life to God!'

66

'Eminence, whoever told you so, lies!' She turned to face Wolsey and I saw the hardness come back into his eyes. 'Nor could it help anything. I am still the King's wife.'

'The Pope could, in that case, give permission for a second marriage.'

'Two wives? It is against the law of God. About the laws of this land I say nothing! But let us not waste breath on the matter. I consent to nothing that makes my daughter a bastard. As for offering the rest of my life to God, I serve Him best in that station in which He has placed me. And from that station and the lawful bonds of matrimony nothing shall move me but death; and for death—so I see my daughter lawfully accepted—I am not unwilling.'

'Madam', Campeggio said, 'it is a thing I have not understood. That a man put away his blameless wife if their marriage be lawful, may not be. A Christian man must remember his vows to honour them; how much more, a Christian King?' And, she kneeling, he gave her his blessing.

When my father heard of my mother's pointblank refusal he could not contain himself. Refuse this honourable way out—a way for which she was perfectly suited! Nothing for it now but the public examination—the washing of dirty linen! Nor could he be certain of the outcome; Campeggio had not only stated his intention of seeking out the truth but had expressed some kindness for the Queen. Anger rode high against the legate; higher still against Wolsey that had raised hopes only to dash them; highest of all against his Queen that delayed his satisfaction, deprived the country of its hoped-for heir and brought the majesty of England into open court.

He went raging to his Council. 'The Queen shows no love to me nor to God, neither. She'll not make right the sin we unwittingly sinned together!' And still he accused her of riding abroad to win the people and steal their hearts from him with her piteous looks. And that last, at least, was not true. These days she went abroad only when he bade her accompany him. She remained, for the most part, in her own rooms lest she meet her triumphant enemy; and, for the same reason, when she took the air, walked only in the Queen's private garden. She had never attempted nor would attempt to win the people from the King.

This year of 'twenty-eight my own position had not changed. I was still Madam the Princess of Wales, still my father's heir. I had still my full household, I had still my friend and governor lady Salisbury. I lived, for the most part, quiet in the country; my father did not send for me—he was too angry; maybe too, he was ashamed. Of my mother

I was allowed to see little but we had continual news one of the other. She had full reports of my health and my progress from lady Salisbury, who brought me back news again.

From the outside my life seemed peaceful enough; but heart and mind alike, I was forever on the rack. I was no longer a child; events had forced me to be in understanding beyond my years. Now I was forced to see my father with new eyes. As a little child I had loved him with a perfect trust; I loved him still—but I trusted him less and feared him more. My mother I loved ever more tenderly; I longed to protect her and knew my uselessness; my love for her was pain. The first thing as I woke, the last thing as I slept, I prayed beseeching the blessed Virgin to intervene and make all good between my father and mother. Then I might come to love him as once, for, not loving him as I should was a grief and a guilt in me.

The matter of the divorce scarce moved. Campeggio obeyed his orders to delay as long as possible, while the Pope, increasingly wretched beneath pressure from Spain on the one hand, and pressure from France and my father on the other, sought some way out. He must have been desperate when he suggested a quite different solution. My father wanted a son to succeed him; he had a son, a bastard son. Why not marry young Richmond to the Princess of Wales and so pleasantly settle the affair. Brother and sister to come together as husband and wife. There was incest, indeed! My insides crawled with disgust.

'Never fret yourself,' lady Salisbury said. 'The Pope is a very sick man and a very frightened one. Your father would never consider such an idea—for how would it stand then with his own marriage? And if he did, the people would soon make him change his mind.'

'When did anyone or anything change my father's mind once it was set?'

'He'd never go against the expressed will of the people, not when they speak with one voice—he knows his own limits. And in such a marriage their voice would swell to such a roar, he'd be forced to listen. And besides . . .'

Her voice stopped; but I knew her thoughts. *Nothing will satisfy him but a second marriage; and no wife but Anne Bullen.*

My father was a harsh man these days, overbearing and often unjust. His voice high with fury echoed through room after room; his eyes sparked red. Nor did it sweeten his black mood that Anne Bullen must keep from the court. He missed her laughter and her saucy tongue, her rages even; he missed her intolerably.

And still Campeggio delayed. My father meant to have his divorce;

he meant to have it *now*! And he meant to have it with the goodwill of the people—he knew well how to win the unwary heart. He must make a show of justice and conscience, of regret and love for his Queen. At the Bridewell Palace he called a great gathering to represent the whole country—princes of church and state, Council and judges, the lord Mayor of London together with all his officers. He addressed them with tears in his eyes, so we heard; and being the man he was, I doubt not that, though shortlived, the tears were genuine. He could always convince himself!

'If it should be judged that the Queen is my lawful wife nothing could give me more happiness. She is a woman of great gentleness and humility. In all noble qualities she has no equal. If I were to marry again I would choose her of all women.' By the time he had finished he had not only himself but the whole assembly in tears.

The speech had not lightened my mother's heart, lady Salisbury told me, whereat I wondered. For, if marrying again, my father would choose one like my mother, then clearly he did not mean to marry his witch. And, surely, my parents would come together in love once more. The young are always ready for a miracle!

Still the days passed and still my mother sat lonely while my father feasted and hunted. At times he would absent himself for days on end. Since he must not flaunt his mistress beneath the legate's eyes he must seek her in the country. So away he would ride to hunt, to dance, to make music—and what else they did together I can guess. If she did not permit him that last freedom she permitted him all else; and though it was said—and not softly neither—that the last freedom she had permitted also, I doubt it. She was not one to forget that her maidenhead was priced with the crown itself.

That Christmas my mother sent for me that we might, as usual, spend the festival all together at Greenwich. I found her looking drawn and tired; but the sight of me, she said, made all well.

'Will my father join us?' I asked lady Salisbury; my mother I could not risk to wound with such a question.

'Who knows? The Bullen woman is in residence at Suffolk House, your father may join her there. He has given her the house—a gift. And there she lives in royal state aping the Queen with her levees and her presence-chamber, her trainbearers and her ladies-in-waiting.'

I bit upon my lips lest I fault my father for this further insult to my mother.

My father did come to Greenwich—but he had done better to stay away.

I was sitting with my mother, the short afternoon beginning to fade into evening, when I heard the bustle of arrival. I went over to the window.

'Madam!' I cried, 'it is my father; my father has come! Now he will be with us as we used to be and all will be well!'

'God grant it!' She did not sound hopeful.

I turned again to the window and my heart all-but stopped. That woman had come with him, Anne Bullen with all her train. I could scarce breathe for anger and for shame that she had come to profane the holy season.

Well, Greenwich is a large house; my mother kept her rooms—but they were no longer the Queen's rooms. She had been removed from her apartments; and who flaunted herself in the Queen's rooms, the rooms adjoining the King's; who but Anne Bullen? When I would have spoken my anger my mother bade me respect the King's wishes. But gossip did not hold its tongue. The whole court—save for the friends of Anne Bullen—was angered; but none dared show anger nor yet love for the Queen.

If I must not speak I could, at least, keep to my mother's rooms; I did not join in the festivities save at my father's command. At my mother's request I showed courtesy to Anne Bullen, but I showed no more than I must—the courtesy I paid to any other; no more. Anne Bullen did not hide her anger. 'When I am Queen,' she cried out in rage, 'that girl shall pay for her insolence She shall go hungry or full-fed as I choose. She shall be my serving-wench and I will give her in marriage to one of my serving-men! As for her mother that encourages such insolence, would I might see her hanged!'

She had spoken where I could not but hear and I went raging to my mother. 'Anger helps nothing!' she said. 'Pity her, instead!'

'Pity—*her*, Madam?'

She nodded. 'Your father endures her vulgarities because they are new and amuse him. But novelty grows stale, especially when joined to a spiteful tongue. But she will pay for it one day never doubt it!'

But *how* she was to pay my mother never dreamed!

It was a wretched festival; though I grieved to part with my mother, I was not sorry to find myself again in my own home.

The new year came in; new year of 'twenty-nine.

Four whole years since my father's conscience had begun to prick; and every day of every year reminding him of his chains. And now, it seemed, he must wait longer still for release.

'The lord Pope is so sick,' lady Salisbury said, 'he may die—which

God forbid; for he favours the Queen's cause. If he should die the case cannot be heard until a new Pope gives his consent; and which side he may favour, who knows?'

'Pray God keep him in life! They say Wolsey works for his place—and then God help my mother!'

That spring—and I just turned of thirteen—I fell sick of the little pox. Brought low by distress, I was too sick to understand anything; yet all the time anxiety dragged upon me like a chain. I wandered in a maze of fever where misery forever pursued me—misery I could neither remember nor understand. My father's physician Dr. Buttes and lady Salisbury nursed me with devotion; yet, for all the care, it was feared I must die. But, little by little the sickness left me and I moved slowly towards life. I remember lying, one day, eyes closed so that lady Salisbury, thinking I slept, spoke of her fear lest I be marked for life. For myself, I cared nothing; but as I grew stronger, I feared it, too, and would not, at first, look into a glass for fear of what I might see. But the scabs fell and the raw places healed—and there I was clean, as apple-blossom.

And now I longed for my mother. Lady Salisbury told me that, in the worst of my illness I had cried her name again and again. She had begged to be allowed to come to me but my father had forbidden it.

'And you can understand it,' she said, 'the little pox is an ugly thing and your mother not strong. She might herself have taken it; she might have carried the sickness back with her!'

So much I understood. My father had a horror of sickness and of death an even greater horror. His own death none, save by his permission, might mention. Indeed, later, he made a new law: let a man but speak of the death of the King—and the penalty was death.

I understood why she must not come when I was sick; but why not now? Now I was well! And I would sit tears of weakness and longing pouring down my cheeks.

The truth is, as I found later, that when she had asked, 'Go!' my father said, 'but never come back!'

Clearly she could not go, could not leave the field to her rival. She was fighting for my rights and for the honour of my name—both dearer to her than her own.

Chapter Ten

Spring had slipped away in my sickness. Since Christmas I had not set eyes upon my mother; my father had forbidden it. I understood, with grief, there was not only cruelty in him but a meanness, also.

The Pope had recovered somewhat; he was a sick man but no longer a dying man and there was no more excuse for delay. The last week in May my father commanded Campeggio and Wolsey to begin their work.

The court opened in the Blackfriars Hall; and, in the third week of June, my father and mother were cited to appear. Scarce recovered in strength and deeply troubled, I wandered the summer gardens at Richmond beseeching the Mother of God for my own mother.

Lady Willoughby, my mother's oldest friend—a Spanish lady come with the young Catherine long ago and married here in England —attended my mother that day, and from her we had an exact account.

The two cardinals in scarlet robes and caps sat in chairs hung with cloth-of-gold; upon a table before them lay their hats, symbols of their authority. To their right a throne with canopy of estate awaited the King; and next to it, a lesser chair without canopy for the Queen. Both chairs were to remain empty. My father, confident in the court's decision, remained at home, awaiting his happy news.

When Madam the Queen entered the court, every man rose and bowed his head. Salute to a Queen! And royal she looked. She was robed and crowned. Behind her walked her ladies, two-by-two; at her left hand two bishops walked, and at her right hand, two also. She had always the royalty that attends a Queen; today she was supreme.

She did not so much as look towards the waiting chair. Standing she addressed the court. 'Sirs—and her voice was clear and steady—'I am not here to make an appeal. One judge here is not my friend.' She turned her eyes full upon Wolsey who stared ahead, unseeing, so it seemed. He might have been a man of stone, save for the tightening of his mouth; it was the mouth gave him away. 'Neither do I recognise the right of this court. No! I appeal to the court of Rome; from that court, alone, I take my answer.' She bent the knee to both cardinals in virtue of their office, and so, in her own splendour, departed.

With neither principal to testify, the court could give no judgment. When my father heard the news his head went down sideways like a bull; his eyes glared red. He swallowed in his throat and no words came so that they feared he had taken a fit. Then the words came bellowing out. *I will be master in my own house!*

For three days the court sat while learned men pleaded my father's cause; my mother made no appeal—she had spoken. At length, unable to make any progress, the principals being still absent, the court ordained a new sitting and summoned my father and mother both, to attend.

July twenty-first, in the year of grace fifteen hundred and twenty-nine, in Westminster Hall the court met once more; but this time, a full court—cardinals and bishops, lawyers and a host of witnesses. And this time, in their great chairs,—the King and Queen. At the last court those chairs had stood side by side; now—ominous sign—they were separated by the judges, he on their right hand, she on their left. Sweet Christ knows what she suffered there, knowing the King bitter. Wolsey implacable, the court uneasy and fearful!

Here is the tale as I put it together from those that were present, from my mother, from my father himself when he was dying, and from the writings made in the court itself.

When they called my father's name he cried out, quick and impatient *Here!* When they called my mother she rose in her place. 'I am here to obey your summons. So far I go and no further. I take judgment from the court of Rome and no other!'

'This court, Madam, is ordained by the Pope and by it you shall be tried!' Wolsey's voice came heavy with authority.

'It is a court of my enemies!' she told him. Then in a hushed and astonished court, she walked to where my father sat. Never a Queen so queenly with her pale sad face. When she reached my father down went her proud head, and, upon both knees like a suppliant that begs for life—and there was grandeur in that humility—she spoke in a low voice that reached every corner of the great room.

'Sir, I beseech you, for the love there has been between us, give me right and justice. Have compassion upon me—a poor stranger in your land.'

A stranger in a strange land. Twenty years my father's wife, bearing his children—those sad, dead children; and now his rejection had made her a stranger once more.

'Sir,' and surely the gentle voice with its pretty foreign accent must have pleaded for her, 'you are the head and fount of justice and to you I appeal!'

My father made no answer; I think he could not. He sat silent and would not look at her.

'Sir—' and she was kneeling still, 'I take all Christendom to witness that I have been a true and humble wife, ever conforming to your will and pleasure. For twenty years I have been your wife and borne your children. That it has pleased God to call them out of this world is no fault in me. I came to you a virgin; search your conscience if you can deny it.'

He sat stone-still and still he would not look at her.

'Sir, if you have found dishonour in me, then I am content for this divorce. But, if there be none, I beseech you, humbly kneeling, to keep me in my proper state.'

And now, seeing he was not to be moved she said, both hands outstretched, 'Then most humbly do I beseech you, for the love of God, to spare me the sentence of the court, until I may be advised by my friends in Spain which way to take.'

And when still he sat dumb as stone, staring above her head with little, bitter eyes, she said, 'If you will not grant me, even that, then let your pleasure be fulfilled. To God I commend my cause.'

She rose to her feet and one of the King's gentlemen—God reward him!—put out a hand for she was all shaken. She made a deep reverence to the King and, on the arm of that same gentleman, left the court.

Catherine, Queen of England come again into the court. The cry followed her, calling, it would seem, upon deaf ears.

'Madam, you are called back!' the gentleman told her.

'I hear it!' she said and went resolute from the court that would never give her justice; and all the time her own name following, *Catherine, Queen of England. . . .*

So they judged her contumacious—she, gentlest and humblest of women! It was too much, even for my father. For then occurred the strangest, the most unlooked-for thing. He cried out in praise of her he was putting from him.

'My lords, she is the most obedient, the most virtuous, the most comfortable wife as I could, even in my dreams, desire!'

It was as though some voice inside him spoke in spite of himself, he told me later when he was dying. 'Maybe it was shame putting away so good, so loving a wife. But it was not lust that drove me. Anne Bullen; she was pregnant with my child before I married her.

City or woman; I never stormed one or other in vain. And I *had* to have a son. The country needed that son to save it from bloodshed and destruction.'

All through July and August the case dragged on. A dry picking-over of legal bones. But for my mother—honour or shame; the one meant life, the other death. Few dared to speak for the Queen; but bishop Fisher, good man and true priest, spoke his mind and suffered for it.

At the end of August Campeggio was unwell and at his wits' end. Whichever way judgment went, disaster must follow—England torn by political strife, or worse still, civil war. War with the Emperor too, perhaps—the Queen was his aunt! All three evils together, maybe. And worse; beyond all evils, evil—it could cause a split to destroy the unity of the church itself! *I will be master in my own house!* What did that threaten but disobedience to Rome?

There must be decision; but not now and not in England. Campeggio summoned the full court to dismiss it.

'My lords, this court is now closed. It is the custom for every papal court, wherever it may sit, to close from now until October. This is a papal court and must conform to rule.' And in the stunned silence that followed he announced, 'This court is to meet no more. The lord Pope has revoked the commission. He will, himself, hear the case in Rome.'

This was a great and unexpected joy to my mother and to me. God had answered our prayers. We need fear no longer; so in my innocence I thought. I had not yet taken the full measure of my father nor of his witch, neither!

My father sent for Wolsey publicly to revile him. To make more solemn the occasion the King sat in state, his Council all about him. From a face already growing heavy, congested now with anger, his reddened eyes glowed. By his side, in a great chair scarcely lower than his own, Anne Bullen sat; behind him stood Master Stevens, once Wolsey's man, now the King's; the same that had pleaded the King's cause in Rome. Now, seeing the woman's arrogance and malice, he was already doubting his wisdom in the matter; he told me so himself, long after.

'Traitor and coward!' my father cried out, Wolsey all-but lying at his feet. 'You have betrayed me! All Christendom knows you work against me, favouring the Queen. You have spun this matter out to the peril of my soul; for still I am held in an incestuous bond—marriage I'll not call it. You. . . . You . . .' he choked in his throat; and only the cardinal's scarlet saved the man from the hand uplifted to strike.

'The lord King knows well that the matter was not in my hands. Campeggio that sat with me, the Pope named my senior. And from the Pope he had his orders, the King's grace knows it. And, for the case being heard in Rome, it is for the Pope to judge; the Pope and none other!'

'For me . . . for me and none other!' the King shouted. 'To Rome—I'll not go!'

'Then let me go, sir. As Cardinal I have some power. . . .'

'A fig for your power! You'll act no more for me in this nor any matter!'

'Sir, consider. I have fought to the uttermost in the King's cause. I will go on fighting. . . .'

'Not you!' my father cried out, savage, and struck out with his foot. But still the wretched man implored.

'Let the lord King consider. There was never a matter like this! The dispensation was granted by Pope Julius. In its wording there is no fault. We could not break it in any court of law. One person alone can revoke it—Pope Clement; and that he cannot easily do. Revoke a dispensation granted by his predecessor—and what becomes of the Pope's infallibility? Yet break it he shall; I swear it! Have but a little patience.'

'Patience!' Anne Bullen cried out, passionate. 'Before God you should lose your head!'

'Better I lose my head than the King the people's love!' Wolsey answered very quick—too quick; for, losing his wits he spoke the truth. The people no longer stood silent but hissed when the King and his mistress rode abroad.

'Liar and fool!' and my father addressed him neither as archbishop nor chancellor; but as one may address a thieving butcher-boy. 'Never was King so loved!'

The last of Wolsey's wits went flying. 'Sir, the people love the Queen and pity her.'

With a vicious kick my father sent his footstool hurtling. 'Get out before I use your head in a like manner!'

Wolsey managed to get upon his feet. He went humble enough, but such was his pride he had still good hope of winning his master again.

My father's rage against Wolsey burned yet hotter because, declaring the people's love for my mother, the unfortunate man had spoken the truth. My father judged it wise to make some public show of affection for her. The cardinal's court having come to its abrupt end, he took her on progress. In spite of Anne Bullen's noisy complaints they were to be seen everywhere together—he very courteous, she accepting his courtesies with a pale, smiling face.

So the people began to hope again; but my mother had no hope at all. This progress was designed to throw dust in their eyes—nothing more! Hope my mother had lost but never courage. She had the hero's courage to fight when all hope is gone. Wolsey, too, had lost all hope. He had not been invited to ride with the King on this progress—such a thing had never happened before. He had gone to bid my father Godspeed in hope of a last-minute invitation; but so far from any invitation my father had roughly bade him begone. And, by as much as their hopes were down, so the hopes of Anne Bullen rose.

The progress ended, my father returned to resume life with his mistress; my mother to her solitary life. Now, Anne Bullen's anger riding high and her confidence in the King's passion for her being great, she began to berate him with her shrew's tongue. Her confidence was not misplaced; he was hopelessly bound in her witch's spells.

Anne Bullen kept him at fever-heat; he burned with anger and itching flesh, both. She forever cried out against my mother, not caring who might hear or see. *That woman who calls herself Queen is a traitor; traitor that would rob you of your immortal soul! Send her away; banish her and her byblow with her! Shall you wait till I am too old for childbearing?*

She would fling her question, striking herself upon the belly, sharpening his appetite for her young and supple flesh, increasing his torment that he had no son.

And against Wolsey she cried out, also; nothing could appease her spite. For failures my father had no use, but because of the man's long and faithful service was inclined to let him go without punishment. Wolsey was archbishop of York; that office none but the Pope could take from him. Let him confine himself to his duties at York. Let him come no more to court nor meddle in the King's affairs. But this did not satisfy Anne Bullen's spite. If he might not be stripped of his priest's office he should be stripped of everything else. She would not rest until he had lost everything—self respect, wealth; livelihood and life itself.

She began with Wolsey's great palace of Hampton Court, with its wide lands, its priceless pictures and tapestries, its fine French and Italian furnishings. Was it fitting, she forever pricked the King, that a subject should live better than the King? And where had one born so poor found gold for such a mansion? It was a point my father appreciated. Within a little, Wolsey was offering Hampton Court with all its treasures to the King—a loving subject's gift. This *gift* was followed by another—Wolsey's London mansion York House. It was a gift Wolsey had no right to give nor my father accept. The house belonged not to Wolsey but to the see of York for the use of its archbishop. Yet given it was; and accepted.

My father gave the house to Anne Bullen who cried aloud for joy—as well she might! Yet even in this joy there was spite. *My house; mine. The woman that calls herself Queen has never lived in it. Nor shall she ever. I shall be its first Queen, I and I alone!* She cried it everywhere and, together with my father, set to work pulling down and building up, furnishing and refurnishing until York House was born again—Whitehall.

Wolsey must meddle no more in the King's affairs. The King had said it; yet in his heart the man believed the King could not manage without his great chancellor. My father showed him his mistake. Already he had taken Master Stevens—the Reverend Stephen Gardiner now—to be his chief secretary and confidant. Gardiner had shared many of his old master's secrets and—shrewd lawyer that he was—had given him sound advice. Secrets and advice both, he brought to the service of the King.

Yet still Wolsey might have struggled back to power but for Cromwell. Thomas Cromwell the most able, the cleverest, the most unscrupulous of Wolsey's advisers; his fingers were on every one of the chancellor's strings, he alone knew how to tangle and untangle them. And this man my father took into his own service; Wolsey's last treasure—if a lying trickster can be so called.

At this time Thomas Cromwell was some forty-five years old. Lowborn, he knew all the crooked ways by which a trusted servant may feather his own nest. He had followed, God knows, what dirty trades in his youth. Beneath an air of breeding aped from his betters, he was a coarse and ruthless bully—as I, myself, was to find later. Treacherous, greedy, completely unprincipled, he stepped not into his master's shoes but into richer shoes than even Wolsey had dreamed. They say that when Wolsey fell, Cromwell wept. Maybe he did—where all might see; weeping done, he lost no time in serving his new master to the utter destruction of the old.

Stephen Gardiner and Thomas Cromwell. Obscure men, yet each rich in experience. But in experience as in character, poles apart. Gardiner was a hard man but honest to the core; a man content to die for what he held to be the truth; satisfied that, for the good of the community, those denying that truth should die. Cromwell was not hard, he was merciless; and dishonest to the heart's core. All that stood in his way, guilty or innocent, must die.

Two men hating and fearing each other; and both to shape the fortunes of England and my own fortunes—misfortunes is, perhaps, the better word.

Between Gardiner and Cromwell, Wolsey's occupation was gone. My father saw him never again but once when, in the autumn, Campeggio made his Farewell to the King and Wolsey went with him. My father received them, all gracious smiling, but Wolsey was not deceived. He knew well that, beneath that smiling lay hostility to hound him to his death; hostility forever sharpened by Anne Bullen's spite because but for himself she would now be Queen. She would not have to hear when she rode with my father the voice of the people: *We'll not have Nan Bullen for Queen. We'll have no Queen but Madam Catherine; no heir but our lady the Princess Mary!*

Chapter Eleven

I went back to the country, sometimes I would be at Beaulieu, sometimes at Richmond; at Greenwich my mother lived her solitary life. Once or twice a week my father visited her—a sop to public opinion; and these scant visits were a light in her sorrow. Whatever he did, whatever he might do, he was the husband she loved. Longer than half-an-hour he dared not stay—he knew his mistress took note of the minutes; knew also the sharpness of her tongue. He might rule England but she ruled him.

These days one heard more and more the name of Thomas Cromwell; even in the quiet of the country we heard the sinister sound. My father did not like him; no-one could—a man without humanity. Yet my father forever sent for him; Cromwell had his hand in every affair. He was *the* coming man; no-one could doubt it. But the power he was to wield no man could foresee. At one time this lying low-born churl was to be considered for me—the King's daughter—a husband! I had died rather.

The dreary year of 'twenty-nine wore on. In the autumn my father appointed a new chancellor in Wolsey's place. Sir Thomas More was a man well-liked, he was genial, witty and wise; and he was utterly honest. 'He'll not last long,' lady Salisbury said. 'Too honest, too godfearing!' And that was true enough. Faithful to his King he was; but first he was faithful to his King in heaven.

That same autumn brought my mother and me some consolation; for it brought us the best friend we ever had. Towards the end of September Eustache Chapuys presented his credentials—ambassador of the Emperor; the Emperor, my mother's own nephew. A comely man, Chapuys, well-versed in the ways of courts, a watchful man, anticipating events, letting nothing go unnoticed, calculating to a nicety which way the cat should jump. To my mother he was like a good son; to me a good brother, though later, he came to love me— I sensed it though he gave never a sign—as a man loves a woman.

That winter the Bullens rode high, high, high. Anne Bullen's father, plain Sir Thomas had already stepped up into the rank of peers —my lord viscount Rochford; now he was to step higher still—my lord earl of Wiltshire and Ormonde. And it was not only—as some thought—because of the King's passion for the daughter; the man had all the acumen of his tradesman forebears and all their lack of honesty. A useful man. At this same time her brother stepped into his father's place—my lord viscount Rochford. As for the lady herself, shameless she acted the Queen. She received my father's guests; and, at a banquet to honour the French ambassador, it was she that sat in my mother's place.

Whether it was because Monsieur Chapuys had remonstrated at this dire insult, or whether my father made a last effort to gain my mother's consent before he, himself, made the final break, I do not know; but after this he was kinder to her than he had been for some time. To me he had never shown anything but kindness—when we met, which was not often. When we were apart he showed himself indifferent; maybe to keep the peace with that woman.

At Christmas he came, as usual, to join us at Greenwich. There were festivities and diversions; and in all these he saw that my mother took her rightful place. And of me, too, he made much, leading me in the dance and seeing I was paid every honour. I was still Princess of Wales.

I was a pretty girl. Visitors told me so; my own looking-glass told me so and—in her warnings against vanity—lady Salisbury, unwitting, told me so. There were ballads aplenty written about me; one, though rhyming and scansion are vile—I treasured and remember to this day. It was written upon the occasion of this Christmas dancing.

> I saw a King and a Princess
> Dancing before my face,
> Most like a god and a goddess
> I pray Christ send them grace.
> So jocund fair was she to see,
> Like to none of her age,
> Without God's grace it cannot be
> So young to be so sage.

What girl nigh on fourteen would not rejoice that men found her fair? How should I know that even then—whether my mother submitted to divorce or no—my father meant to disinherit me?

It was shortly after this dancing that he again raised the matter of divorce. But though she blessed him for the kindness shown of late, nothing could move her. To Rome's judgment, alone, would she submit. In one of his furies he flung himself out of Greenwich to join his sweetheart at Whitehall.

And so the year of fifteen-thirty came in. For my mother and me, a wretched year, for Wolsey too, most wretched—a year of fear, to end in his death; for my father hounded him without respite. Yet since God is merciful to the broken-hearted, a year of blessing too.

'Now he is stripped before the world; now we may see the man he might have been, had not ambition driven him in strange paths,' lady Salisbury said. 'For the first time he works for others; for the first time wins love and true esteem. Let him make the most of it, his time is short.'

'Short? Is he sick? Or will my father punish him further?'

'I fear he will. The Bullens, the Howards, the Norfolks and all their hangers-on mean to have his blood. With Anne Bullen as Queen they see no limit to their ambitions. But she is not Queen; and for that they blame Wolsey. They accuse him on several counts, the chief being that he gives preference to foreign courts of justice before our own; in other words he obeys the Papal courts first and our own, second.'

'But a priest must obey the Pope.'

'By our laws—no! Wolsey has offended against the state and the King!'

Wolsey had offended against the King that would be master in his own house! For this he stood to lose everything—offices, goods, freedom—and lucky if he escaped with his life! My father would forgive him never!

'But a priest's first duty is to Rome—and especially this priest's—Cardinal and Legate, and chosen to preside over the court not only by the Pope but by the King himself.'

'Your father thought Wolsey clever enough to arrange things to his master's liking—his master being not the Pope but the King. I think ...' and she spoke slowly, 'this is a challenge to Rome itself.'

Challenge to Rome. Challenge to God Himself! My blood ran cold.

The most part of this year I spent in the country. I should have been happy enough with my lessons and my music save that not once did I see my mother. Once my father rode over to see me but all ease was gone; my mother stood between us.

In January we heard of a great ball at court with Anne Bullen queening it in all but the crown. Again she received the guests, together with the King led the dancing, sat at table in the Queen's place. As for her father, he received fresh honours. He was made Keeper of the Privy Seal, he was accredited ambassador to the Emperor's court—a piece of defiance that!

And now there came into my father's service a man I learned to hate; and, with reason, hated all my life. Though he is dead and paid for his sins, God forgive me, I hate him still.

Thomas Cranmer.

A slight, tall man, about forty I should judge; very elegant, with his thin scholar's face and thoughtful eyes. The mouth, though, told a different story; mouth of a man that likes overmuch the good things of life and means to have them. And both eyes and mouth spoke the truth. He had not, at first, meant to enter the church; he had been married—and to a low woman. Black Joan she was called, niece to a tavern-keeper; niece and tavern alike frequented by the young men of Cambridge. Lucky for him she died. For then he set about preparing himself for the church. Yet still he lusted after women; for after he was ordained he made yet another secret marriage. And what sort of priest is it that affects to give his soul to God when already he has given his body to women! And this was the man that was to become Primate of England!

How had he come to my father's notice, this unknown young man? To the Bullens we owed yet one more grief laid upon my mother and me. He had been heard to say—one of the Bullens eagerly reporting— *In the matter of the King's divorce there is no need of the Pope. Let the universities be asked and their opinion taken.* 'By God!' my father cried out, 'he has the right sow by the ear!'

So Cranmer came to cast his baleful influence upon my mother's life and mine. For favours given and favours promised, he supported the divorce with all his heart. He expounded its rightness and its need before the universities of Oxford and Cambridge; he had copies of his speech sent to all the universities of Europe. And these copies he followed in person, his pockets filled with gold—sweet persuader to those that might doubt his wisdom. His headquarters were Durham House where the Bullens kept him on the fat of the land. Yes, he was doing well for himself—and would do better!

The opinions of the universities began to come in. Cambridge had decided in favour of the divorce and Oxford followed Cambridge.

'Courage,' my lady Salisbury said. 'This is but the beginning. The universities of Europe have yet to speak!'

'What shall they answer!' I said, despairing. 'This Cranmer has a golden tongue and a golden purse.'

In April came a gleam of hope. The universities of Angers and Poitiers held the marriage good. But the King of France being all set, for the moment, on friendship with my father, it was not surprising that the university of Paris spoke for divorce. Agonised we waited for the full results; yet we might have guessed them! They had little to do with faith and much to do with policies. In a country that feared the Emperor, the universities voted against the divorce; where a country feared Francis, its universities, by and large, voted for it. There were more for the divorce than against it.

And now the Pope's commands went forth. The King of England was summoned to Rome. Meanwhile he was not to live with any woman save his wife. My father laughed at both commands; and still Anne Bullen kept the Queen's place at board—and some said, in bed, too.

The sad year ended with the death of Wolsey. A wretched ending to so much glory you might say; yet you might say wrong. For, since his fall he had, indeed, given himself to the poor, the sick and to those that suffered injustice. In early November sick, old and broken, he was arrested and brought south under guard, followed by the blessings and tears of those he had learned to serve. At Leicester he died; and all Christendom knows his last words. *Had I but served my God as I served my King, He had not left me desolate in my old age.* But God had not forsaken him. God had given him a little space to love others and to serve them; and to die in the gentleness of his bed and not by the rigour of the law.

I grieved for Wolsey more than I could have believed.

'Why should I care?' I asked lady Salisbury, the tears running down my cheeks.

'Because he was once your friend and your mother's friend, and because, in his heart, he was always, I think, your friend. And because he was your godfather—your father in God. And because he died, I think, redeemed of God. When pride is taken from some proud men they rot at the heart; with Wolsey it was not so. The tree of his pride was cut down and put forth shoots of true faith and service to God.'

Well that was true enough! But it was less grief with me than missing his actual presence, that magnificence of his. I wanted him back because I feared, without fully understanding, the brutal cruelty that lay beneath those fine manners of Thomas Cromwell. Wolsey, with all his faults, had humanity; in Cromwell, less imposing to the eye, I sensed no humanity, nothing but a dark, implacable power.

In all that long, sad year I had seen my father but once, my mother not at all. And now it was the year of 'thirty-one and I, almost upon my fifteenth birthday. I had wept more than a little with fear and longing for my mother, I was experiencing not too happily my growth into womanhood and altogether I had lost much of my natural spirits. I tried to content myself with my studies and with my music—both a sure refuge. And so I continued, in spite of lady Salisbury's protests. 'Learning is good, but we learn not from books alone. Do not spoil your eyes with weeping and working. Look about you and learn to laugh again!' But still I continued, being able to do no other. I wish I had listened to her, for I did my eyes no good.

Again the Pope uttered his warning. Better he had not spoken. For each warning angering my father still further, robbed my mother of what remained of his kindness. Friends that dared speak for her were sent from court; to Chapuys, whom he could not dismiss, my father turned a deaf ear and sullen face.

More than five years had gone by and still my father had not married his witch; still he had no legitimate son . . . and a man grows no younger—as Anne Bullen never ceased to taunt him. He would endure it no longer; he swore it. If Rome would not cleanse his conscience, if the Pope still refused his heart's desire to breed a lawful son, then he was finished with the Pope. The King was the supreme head of temporal affairs in his own kingdom, now he would be head of spiritual affairs, also!

Challenge to Rome. Challenge to God!

I heard with anguish of this deadliest heresy. Now I must grieve not for my mother alone but still more for my father. 'He cuts himself off from God's Vicar on earth; he will lose his immortal soul.' My voice came out in a whisper, unable to take the weight of those terrible words. 'And those that obey him, will they not lose their souls also?' I asked my lady-governor.

'Cranmer makes all easy. He has himself sworn on oath to obey the King—as long as conscience shall allow it. Cranmer's conscience! And all priests will be required to take that same oath; but to some conscience will come first.'

'Cranmer cannot command the clergy,' I said. 'That is for the archbishop of Canterbury!'

'Maybe the King will wait for Warham to die—it cannot be long now. Then Cranmer will find himself in the position to command!'

'An archbishop that betrays God and the Pope! God help England!'

In the spring unlooked-for happiness came to me. I was let to stay with my mother. So long, so very long since I had set eyes upon her. I could not contain myself for joy. 'Now you look yourself again!' lady Salisbury said. I had still further cause for joy; as we rode the country-side, crowds gathered to show their love, and to send messages of good hope to my mother.

I found her looking pale; but she brightened when she saw me. She had, of late, taken little exercise save to walk within the Queen's garden, now she exerted herself to come riding with me; and, the wind whipping colour into her cheeks, she would look almost well. But when the colour died then the thinness of her face showed clear. Yet never a word of complaint passed her lips, nor would she allow any complaint from me on her behalf; nor must I speak, even to her, of her weakness.

Towards the end of May my father received yet another summons to Rome. It was Chapuys who told us how he received it.

'The King received the nuncio in public; he did not honour him, as was proper, with a private audience. First he laughed at the Pope's message; then one of his rages fell upon him. He brought his fist down upon the arm of his chair so that I thought the bone must crack. "I'll marry when and how I choose, though it be in the face of all Christendom!" he roared out. "Go tell your master so!" '

But for all that he sent the most skilled of his Council to Greenwich in an effort to persuade my mother. I was with her when they bowed themselves into her presence. These days she kept me always with her; she had a presentiment, maybe, that we'd not be together long. I listened, sick at heart. How could she argue against these men skilled in the law?

I need not have feared. There she sat, little and pale, listening with courtesy; she interrupted with no word, not even when Cromwell, forgetting his genteel manners, sought loud-mouthed to bully her. Only when they had made an end did she speak. 'I am my husband's true wife, unless Rome say otherwise.' That, and no more.

'When she knows herself to be right,' lady Salisbury said later, 'there's nothing can move her. She would die first!'

'Why so she may!' and I began to cry.

'Come now,' she said, 'don't wash away your looks with tears! Do you know what the Venetian ambassador wrote of you? His secretary showed me the letter. . . . *The princess has a pretty face and is well-proportioned with a very beautiful complexion.* Shall you make him to be a liar by spoiling it with tears? He commends your French, your Latin and your Italian. He admires your singing and your dancing. Well we must strive to deserve these compliments; for your Italian is less than your Latin and your singing less than your dancing!' She had said nothing, I noticed, about my Spanish. I had made no progress of late—indeed I was in danger of forgetting what I had learned; for, to my sorrow, I had been forbidden to study my mother's tongue.

But no compliment, not even upon my looks, could raise my spirits. That my father should desert my good and gentle mother, that he had no wish to see me, his daughter, was a burden upon my heart. Once he had been proud of his girl that never cried. Well she had cried enough since; enough and enough!

And yet that early summer brought me a little hope. I had been let to stay with my mother for the festival of Trinity; now, most unexpected, my father joined us and I again began to think that our prayers had been heard and all would be well again.

I was not let to think it long. He had brought the witch with him and I saw for myself how she took possession of the Queen's rooms, my mother being turned out to make room for her. That she had taken the Queen's husband and the Queen's jewels I had heard; things heard are hurtful enough. But, seeing with my own eyes was another matter; it stabbed me to the heart.

Those two did not stay long. I was standing by my window, early one morning, looking out upon a summer world all green and gold and blue. So sweet a day—how could one not be hopeful? And so standing, I heard a bustle, as of departure. I ran to another window that looked upon the courtyard and there I stood, fighting down my tears. Baggage was already loaded upon carts, servants were running, horses neighing and pawing impatient, while the grooms finished their business; for all my short sight I saw my father's favourite mare stand ready, esquire at the stirrups. And now my father, himself, came forth. No mistaking those great shoulders, those handsome legs, the royal stance; nor yet the grace which, in spite of increasing girth, he swung himself into the saddle disdaining the outstretched hand of his esquire.

And now came Anne Bullen in a riding-habit of Tudor green; and still she played the virgin for her black hair floated free. My father bent down, caught her at her waist and lifted her on to his own mare. There was a clatter of hooves and they were gone—he laughing and waving his feathered bonnet, she black hair afloat, wide red mouth lifted above white teeth and laughing . . . laughing.

He had gone; and not a word of warning nor farewell! Half-blinded by tears I stumbled to my mother's closet. She was sitting there, half-dressed, her hair hanging loose; and that was added pain for I could never see, without grief, the grey hair that should have kept its brightness. She was not old enough for grey hair; not old enough. I thought of the witch with her long black hair and my heart all-but burst.

At the sight of me she managed to smile, though I saw the swelling throat all-but choked her.

'I know,' she said. 'He is gone . . . and I must go, too; but not with him. He has sent his commands. I am not to be found here when he returns.' And then, since she was but human, and of a high spirit that misfortunes never broke, she cried out, 'An old wife is like an old shoe—to be cast out. But new shoes pinch—and so he shall find! But, before God, send me where he will, I am still his wife!'

I had no word to answer her. I knelt and took the grey head upon my breast. I said, 'We are together, we have each other!'

And now I saw the tears rain down her cheeks.

'I am to leave you here!' she said.

'I'll not stay.'

'You must obey your father!'

'Even when my conscience says *No*!'

'Are you sure you know the difference between what you truly think right and what you *want* to think right?'

And when I did not answer, she said, 'Listen; for God knows if we shall meet again. If any command you against your conscience, you must refuse—even though it be your father, himself. Every other order he shall lay upon you, you must obey. It is my command to you; maybe my last command. So now you must stay here until your father order otherwise. Come now, it is not so very hard—' and her smile all-but broke my heart, 'we have had our separate houses this long while, you and I!'

That was different; quite different. And we both knew it. *God knows if we shall meet again.*

She said, very gentle, 'We shall not truly be parted; nothing can part us in spirit. I shall write to you and you to me. You still have lady Salisbury, God be thanked. You must not be so sad. It is not the end of the world!'

But it was the end of the world; her world and mine.

Chapter Twelve

My mother was sent to The More in Hertfordshire, a house isolated and much in need of repair. In summer it was pleasant enough, in winter desolate, dark and damp. The palings were broken, deer wandered where they would, and the roads were such that no carriage could come up to the door; visitors must alight and walk knee-deep in mud. It was midsummer when she arrived and she appeared to be cheerful; sun shone, grass was firm and clean beneath her feet and though she tired easily, walking was a pleasure. With such small pleasures she had taught herself to be content; of misery she had enough.

As for myself I was commanded back to the country before my father arrived; he had no wish to see me. I had, it seemed, lost father and mother both. My mother I was never to see again; but mercifully I was not to know that then. I was fairly cheerful for we had our letters she and I; hers were brought to me in secret, and in secret my answers delivered. All of us involved in the matter—my lady Salisbury, the messengers, myself, and most of all my mother, ran great danger; but there was no other way. I had written to my father imploring that we might write to each other my mother and I; I would welcome any one of his secretaries to read my letters before despatch and hers before they came into my hand. He did not so much as answer; so the secrecy must continue, news of her I must have.

There was but one comfort in the whole miserable affair. Though The More was unfit for a Queen, yet my mother kept a Queen's state; she had not yet been forbidden her rightful title. When she dined thirty maids-of-honour stood about the table and fifty servants served her on bended knee. Her court numbered some two hundred; and every heart loyal and loving. Neglected by her husband and banished the court, she was still—the Queen.

That autumn brought a visitor to Richmond—Reginald Pole, lady Salisbury's son. She had talked of him a great deal. 'He is so good and so clever; and handsome! In Padua, where he lives they call him not *Polus Anglius* but *Polus Angelus*. And, indeed, goodness shines from his face.' I put it down to a mother's partiality and could not blame her; it was so very long since she had set eyes upon him. I was glad for her; and, for myself, I was pleased too. In the quiet country a visitor is always welcome. I was curious, about him, besides. At my birth my mother had wished me to marry him, partly to atone for his brother's blood, shed to make more secure the Tudor throne—an ugly tale; and partly because he was of royal Plantagenet blood. Such a mingling of Plantagenet and Tudor, she had thought, must strengthen the throne better than any bloodshed.

As the time drew nearer for his coming lady Salisbury grew anxious. 'I hunger for the sight of him. If ever you have a son, Madam, you will understand. Yet I am afraid; afraid for him. If the King should discuss this bad business of divorce, my son will speak out, fearless!'

'Then let him come as quick as he may!' I cried out. And then, 'No, but you are right. Keep him away!' For we knew, both of us, that my father was a frustrated man; plain-speaking on this matter could end in prison or in death.

It was early autumn when he came at last. And he was everything his mother had said. He was then some thirty years old: he was handsome; and goodness did shine from his face—a pure commanding goodness that gave strength to a fine-drawn, somewhat delicate appearance. I knew, as soon as I set eyes upon him that this was no husband for me —or any woman. He had taken the Church to wife; this was God's servant, holy and dedicated. But as a brother he was perfect, wise; understanding and loving.

Our time of happiness was short. My father sent for him and, in return for support in the matter of the divorce, offered the seat of York left empty since Wolsey's death. To so devoted a priest the bribe was great. Pole refused. 'The King's marriage is good and every true man must find it so!' he said and asked permission to return to Italy. 'For, sir, should I stay and the matter be raised in Parliament, I must stand for the right!'

'The lord King refused; and with so ugly a look, fingering his dagger the while, that I judged it wise to go without permission!' he told us, having come in the dark of the night to say Farewell. His mother could scarce bear to let him go. So long since she had seen him; and now, how long before she should see him again? She held him in her arms and blessed him. He took my hand and kissed it. 'Madam,' he said, 'I foresee many good heads must shortly fall. One day you may need head, heart and hand for your service. When that time comes send for me. I am now and forever your servant!'

'God bless and reward you!' I said; and reached up, for I was small and he tall, and kissed him upon both cheeks.

Autumn wore away to winter. At The More my mother ached in every bone; yet even in ill-health and sorrow her abounding charity flowed out to those in need. And news of her gentle kindness, being carried by countryfolk into the market-place, whipped up anger against my father and for his witch; *the great whore* they called her.

Christmas passed sadly. It was the first Christmas in my life we had not spent all together at Greenwich. My father sent neither gift nor greeting; not to us nor to our servants—a thing that had never happened yet. My mother sent him her own gift—a gold cup. He would not receive it but sent it back with bitter words. He never visited her nor enquired of her health—nor mine, neither. He was too busy; he was riding with the lady Anne, hunting with the lady Anne, dancing with the lady Anne . . . and now he was sleeping with the lady Anne.

The New Year of 'thirty-two came in with sleet and biting winds; next month I should be sixteen. The More had become a death-trap for my mother; she coughed; she could scarce use her swollen hands. She sent asking permission to leave this house and my father commanded her to Bedfordshire. Ampthill was no better and in some ways worse. It was not so pleasantly situated; and, first sign of increasing pressure, she was allowed less state, the number of her servants was cut by half. Ampthill suited her health no better; yet she uttered no complaint. She was one that, when she must, spoke her mind; all other times she held her peace. Yet even here she knew some happiness; for the tale of her charity and forbearance had spread and the countryfolk —gentry as well as peasants—came to pay their respects and bring her their gifts.

In spite of Anne Bullen's malice I still kept my state and title. It did not seem right to me that I should receive full honours and my mother have hers clipped. For now began those humiliations that, increasing, were to bring her to her death. It was not, as yet, actual privation nor any threat to her life; but the lessening of her state wounded her proper pride and the desolation she endured fed upon her heart; and upon mine, upon mine, also.

The break between my parents was undermining my health. It was not only my mother's unhappiness; there seemed nothing stable in my life, nothing enduring. It was now I began to suffer from the migraines that were to grow upon me; and I, myself, encouraged the condition by constant study—a way of escape from the burden on my heart. In music and in books I could, a little, lose myself.

It was at this time that the Pope, making a last effort, summoned my father to Rome. His reply? To send Cranmer—Cranmer so eager in the divorce—as ambassador to the Emperor, my mother's own nephew. Defiance without words. Another thing—smaller but sinister enough: he made Cromwell Keeper of the Royal jewels; Cromwell, my mother's enemy, Anne Bullen's friend.

For me life though sad was not unendurable; not yet. I had lady Salisbury; and, though I never saw my mother, her messages and advice showed her loving care of me. Above all I had her letters. She bade me at all times please my father, obey him with a willing heart and never, at any time, utter a word of complaint. I had—and still do have—fierce affections and a hasty tongue: and she feared for me.

'How can I obey him with a perfect heart when he puts my mother from him; when he will not let me see her, ever? I cannot nor I will not!' I cried out, rebellious.

'Obey him you must!' my governor said. 'However your heart rebel, make a show of grace for her sake. She endures sorrows enough; do not add to them!'

'How can I add to them? She is ill and she's lonely and I am not let to see her. What can he do more?'

'He could punish you—and that, for her, would be the worst. Madam, dear child, believe it!'

'I will try; but it is hard!' And hard it was; and though I prayed for a heart loving and obedient to my father, things grew no easier. I would lie awake weeping, remembering my mother's words, *God knows if we shall meet again!* Why? What had we done, she and I, that he should so punish us? Sometimes, lady Salisbury hearing some restless movement, would come bringing her candle to sit by me until I fell into troubled sleep. Yet she had troubles of her own. One did not speak plain to my father, deny his expressed wish and not suffer for it. Her beloved son had escaped . . . but she had other sons. Yet the days went by and my father made no move against either of them and she lulled herself into peace. But my father was biding his time; and when that time came at last—but of that I will not think until I must.

My mother was a sick woman; her letters said no word of it but her handwriting showed it plain. She sent asking my father that I might visit her; and was refused. I worried about her until I, myself, lay sick of a melancholy. Again my mother wrote begging she might come to me or I to her. And was again refused.

'Why?' I asked lady Salisbury. 'Why? Why? It is right we should be together. What harm could we do?'

'The King's mistress forever speaks against you both! She says you encourage each other in stiff-necked obstinacy. She tells him that once you are together the people will rise in your defence.'

'She does not know my mother; nor me, neither. Let the King do what he will we'll lift no hand against him!'

'It is not so much spite in that woman; it is *fear!*'

'Then I am never to see my mother again?'

She made no answer.

Now the melancholy truly fastened upon me. I would lie in my bed, tears raining down my face. I would not rise, would not allow myself to be dressed; I took no more pleasure in my books nor in riding, nor even in music. I wanted my mother, I wanted her so desperately I thought I must die.

'It is the witch . . . the witch. . . .' I heard my voice sharp and high.

Lady Salisbury put a quick hand upon my mouth. 'Madam, my darling, have a care! Who knows where she plants her spies?' She came close to whisper in my ear. 'That woman means your death; yours and your mother's both! She has said it. *I would sooner see them hanged than call the mother my Queen or the girl aught but the bastard she is!* Spite and fear in her are bitter!'

'She dares . . . the *concubine!*'

'That is no fit word for you!'

'It is no fit thing. But everyone calls her so and well you know it! I have heard Monsieur Chapuys. . . .'

'It is still an unfit word for you; and worse, it is a dangerous word. Madam; Mary, Mary have a care!'

That she called me by my baptismal name showed me the measure of her fear.

'A heart loving and obedient to my father! God Himself cannot expect it!'

'Leave God out of this! Your father expects it—and will have it, too!'

My heart was hot against my father. Yet, like others older and wiser than myself, on the rare occasions that we met, I was taken by his charm, unwilling to believe that so godlike a man could, of his own will, be so cruel.

During this year and the next I saw him but twice; once he came to Richmond to take me hunting. We said no word of my mother but when he left he kissed me very kindly and promised to send for me soon. He never did; the concubine saw to it. The second time was by chance. I was walking in the woods of Beaulieu; he had been hunting and did not know I was there. As always, in the chase, he rode ahead; and now, seeing me, drew rein and alighted. Walking together, an arm about my shoulder, he enquired of my health; and while I wondered whether I might entreat to see my mother, two of the witch's spies rode up, for she kept them ever about him. It was long before he knew it; but by then he was out of love!

So he swept his bonnet and mounted again and I was not sorry, even though I had not been able to ask permission to see my mother; certainly he would have refused. I had no mind to see the woman, herself, ride up, commanding my father with her bold eyes. I had no mind to endure more of her pride, neither. We hated each other, she and I. She hated me because she had wronged my mother; and because, though I might not speak a word, my bearing showed my own hatred I was too young to dissemble, and it is a trick I never since learned. It is less a trick than a thing born in us; my sister Elizabeth had it before she could speak.

In May, my father commanded my mother from Ampthill; there, also, she had won much love. She was removed to Bugden; a dreary place and a worse house, set in the marshes of Cambridgeshire. The house I have seen, making my pilgrimage later, for her sake. It stands upon the high road between Huntingdon and Cambridge. The red walls and towers give it an appearance of warmth; but her rooms are small and dark, catching the winds that blow without let or hindrance across the wet marsh. There is no view from them of the garden nor of the road; nothing but high walls and the lonely marsh forever stretching. Now she was more than ever tormented with pain in her joints; on bad days, could scarce walk and even then upon sticks. My father kept her short of money and short of servants; she went short of blankets, short of warm clothes. No more queenly state.

Even here, in this most desolate place, she found loving hearts and willing hands. Since, her bills unpaid, her household ill-fed, she could no longer give to the poor, the country folk came bringing her what they could—eggs, butter and cheese, ham and salted beef; and once there was a length of home-woven wool for a cloak. To such a pass was she come, the Queen of England; yet never so much a Queen! And still I had her letters, full of wisdom and love; and never a word of complaint.

My father, for all his defiance of Pope and Emperor, was uneasy in his mind. He knew well that the people held his marriage true; that they loved his wife and hated his mistress that daily grew more arrogant and bold. Nor were the best of his clergy silent. Friar Peto preached against the divorce both at Greenwich and St. Paul's and was forced to flee the country; bishop Fisher of Rochester, that staunch man, spoke out for the truth, and was cast into prison where he all-but died of poison. Archbishop Warham, for whose shoes Cranmer so ardently waited, spoke for the dignity of priests and their obedience to Rome; he was too sick a man to dare anything but the truth. And Sir Thomas More resigned the seals. Good, wise man, he would not swear allegiance to my father as head of the church; would not accept my father's marriage as anything but true.

'Now it begins, it begins!' my lady Salisbury told me and fetched up a sigh from the depths of her heart. 'My son said many good heads would roll! God be thanked he is safe from England!'

'There are many,' I said 'to take the first step towards his death.'

My father resolved to take his whore into France; that she might go with every honour he could bestow he created her my lady Marchioness of Pembroke—the title to be borne by the heirs of *her* body, hers and hers alone. And that, I think, is clear proof that already she had become his harlot. That she might go in greater splendour, she was to have the crown jewels; nor was it possible for my mother to refuse them—Master Thomas Cromwell had them in charge.

'Yet another stroke of the lash!' I told lady Salisbury.

'Jewels. They've never meant much to her; she'll not care!'

'She will care; and greatly. Personal jewels mean little to her—save the collar and cross she brought from Spain. But the crown jewels —that's another matter! It is as though the witch wore the crown itself.'

The concubine was to go in greater state than any Queen. Careful instructions were sent to France with regard to the etiquette expected for her household—herself, her ladies, her gentlemen, her very servants. Her royal state as yet unlicensed, he was determined she should meet no slight.

'Let her go with a great title, with a royal train, yes, with the crown jewels, also,' I cried out to lady Salisbury, 'She's still the King's harlot and no honest lady of France will touch her hand!'

And so it turned out. The Queen of France, her husband would not insult by asking; and no other lady would offer save the duchess of Vendôme—and her reputation so scandalous that to meet her would be an insult. So since Madam Anne could not appear alone, she stayed in English Calais, while the two Kings hobnobbed in Boulogne. And there she remained with her fine title and crown jewels and all her court! Francis himself, not too particular where a fine woman was concerned, to please my father did visit her once and gave her a jewel. Maybe she was not as fine as he remembered, for he went but once; and with that she had to be content. I was not sorry when I heard it.

My father was more than ever bent upon marrying his harlot; he had—for him—the best of reasons; to my mother and me the most dire. That she slept in his bed was now an open secret; any day might find her pregnant with his heir. Yet still the people were bitterly opposed. Let him beget his bastards if he must! In this he was no worse than any other King in Christendom, not excepting the Holy Roman Emperor himself! But let him not declare his whore his wife! Let him not declare his wife his whore and his true-begot daughter a bastard! Now when he rode through the streets, even though he rode alone it was in silence; those that had once cheered him stood dumb. As for the new-made marchioness, she dared not go abroad save in a closed carriage, all curtains drawn; and even then the people hissed, crying out *Shame! Shame! We'll not have you for Queen!* But still she took to herself every attribute of Queen—even to the blessing of the cramp-rings.

'It is for the Queen, the Queen alone to bless the rings for the sick; in all others it is blasphemy! Yet still she dares . . . she *dares*. And God does not strike her dead!'

'Be content to leave it to God!' lady Salisbury said.

But everything seemed to be going my father's way. Already the most part of the clergy had sworn to regard him as supreme head of the church—*as far as the law of Christ allowed*; and who should interpret that law for them but Cranmer? For Warham dying—his death hastened by the insult put upon the church—my father put his tool in the archbishop's place. Now it was for Cranmer to show his priests and all England that Christ's law was the King's law.

Chapter Thirteen

My father had married his harlot. So secret the marriage not even Cranmer, ardent in the divorce, had known until she had been two weeks my father's 'wife'.

'No! No!' I cried out at the news; lady Salisbury's stricken face spoke the truth clearer than words, panic took me. *What shall this do to my mother? And what to me?*

'This will kill my mother. I must go to her! Now he must let me go!' And I stood wringing my hands.

She came to me and put both arms about me. It was as though I were no longer Princess of England, *the* Princess, but any young girl that needed comfort. Never, for all her love, had she permitted herself an embrace; and the very embrace that should comfort me, frightened me the more.

She said, 'Say nothing, do nothing, till the King himself speaks. As for Madam the Queen, she has great strength, great courage.'

'Enough for this?'

'God will make it enough.'

The need for this hurried, secret marriage soon became clear. Anne Bullen was pregnant; she must have guessed at the matter, being scarce one month gone with child. Yet in that little time she had made the most of her condition with her uncontrolled behaviour—her noisy fits of weeping, her high laughter, her inordinate craving for green apples; there was no shame in her. Before the court she carried herself with pride; but in the privacy of my father's closet, it was another matter! She wept, she tore at her long black hair, careful to do herself no hurt—this I have from Jane Seymour that, at this time, waited upon her. She threatened that were the child born and she unwed she'd make an end of herself and the child together.

My father needed not these unbraidings, these tears, these threats. The child she carried would be a son—so the soothsayers prophesied. The long-desired son. There must be no question but that the child was legitimate.

Secret the actual marriage might be but the whole court had known my father's intention. With considerable courage Chapuys had tried to turn him from that resolve.

'I must have my heir!' my father said; that, and no more.

'Sir, you have your heir. You have the Princess Mary.'

'I need a son.'

'How shall you be sure that the lady shall give you a son?'

My father's face deepened to purple, Chapuys told me later. He roared like a bull. 'Am I not a man like other men? A man, a man a *man*! By the body of Christ she shall be married and crowned at once!'

In the dark of a winter morning, towards the end of January, in the year of grace fifteen hundred and thirty-three, those two went through the blasphemy of the marriage service. A chaplain had been summoned to the King's private chapel to find groom and bride and two witnesses. Rome had sent, my father said, a last-minute dispensation; and what humble chaplain dare question it?

A fortnight later, Anne Bullen aglitter in gold tissue and my mother's jewels took her place next to the King in the royal chapel at Windsor. The Queen's place.

The witch-concubine was Queen.

There followed banquets and balls, masques and music; every ambassador attended to pay due honour, save Chapuys only—he was indisposed, he said.

And now the Pope must move and move at once.

The King's first marriage was good. His Holiness declared it again. The King of England must put away his mistress and receive his own true wife again. This he must do no later than June on pain of excommunication.

Breaking-point with Rome; breaking-point long prepared.

My father sent for Cromwell his Privy Seal, and for his archbishop of Canterbury that had not yet been consecrated and never would be, unless he obeyed my father without question; Cromwell that knew all Wolsey could teach and more, Cranmer that feared God less than he feared the King.

Together they received their orders.

Repudiate the Pope. Repudiate him utterly. There must be one supreme head in England. The King. The King that ruled the state should henceforth rule the church also.

Repudiate the Pope. I sickened with fear; and the fear was all for my father. He sought eternal damnation and to that damnation sent the souls of all that obeyed him. In spite of the griefs he had put upon my mother and me I prayed for his soul.

Cromwell and Cranmer did their work thoroughly. In Parliament Cromwell introduced a bill denying the Pope's authority. Convocation, summoned by a hastily consecreated archbishop, denied obedience to the bishop of Rome. Cranmer, spiritual leader, was the first to take the oath; and, for very fear, the most part of the clergy followed him. But here and there good men refused. Fisher, that fearless, upright man, found himself once more in prison.

And what of my mother, in these, her despairing days? My father had sent her, as yet, no news concerning his new 'marriage'. What she had heard she heard like the rest of us—by hearsay.

Now Chapuys visited her; he told her of the people's grief and anger. If she were willing, the Emperor should bring war into England and the people would rise in arms to join him in restoring their good Queen. But she would have none of it. 'I am my husband's loyal wife,' she said. 'I'll have no part in rebellion against him!'

In the first week of April, lord Mountjoy, her own chamberlain, was commanded to tell my mother, officially, that she was no longer wife nor Queen; and that I, her daughter, was a bastard, unfit in blood to be my father's heir. He went unwilling to his task. Like all that served my mother he knew her goodness, knew it more than most—for he was father to Eliza Blount that had borne my father's son. Yet my mother had said no word of it ever and for that he loved her the more.

He had seen her twice on this most unhappy business and of his own goodwill came to tell me what had passed.

But first I must know of her condition—her spirits and her health.

'Not well, Madam, not well at all! Her spirit is strong but her body . . .' he shrugged. 'She was lying upon a couch—she had a poisoned foot; she had pricked it upon a thorn or a pin. I think she guessed my mission, yet she smiled and gave her hand to kiss.'

'Madam,' he had told her, 'bear with me and the news I bring, the lord King is married. You are no longer his wife and Queen and none must call you so. By right of your dead husband you are a widow and dowager Princess of Wales; that and that only. You are free, Madam, to marry where you will!'

It seems she smiled at that, the smile lying faint upon her mouth. Marry again, she that was still a wife and loved her husband!

'Sir,' she told him, proud yet gentle, too, 'I am the King's true wife. I am Queen of England hallowed and crowned. Our daughter is the

Princess of Wales. By the name of Queen I will be called and to no other will I answer so long as I live.'

'Madam,' he warned her, 'do not for mere vanity of glory anger the lord King. If you, yourself, fear nothing, remember your daughter; for her you may fear much. How if the lord King visit his anger upon her? Madam, that should move you!'

And move her it did. But not in the way he had hoped. That they should thus cowardly threaten her through love of her child stiffened her anger.

'I hold to the name of Queen not in vanity of glory but in right of conscience. I will never brand myself the King's incestuous harlot nor my child a bastard. She is the King's daughter true-begot in lawful marriage. God gave her to us. I give her back to her father to do with her what shall stand with his pleasure.'

I cried out at that. Had she abandoned me; she, too?

'My lady Mary—' and he no longer addressed me as *Princess*, 'Madam your mother answered with great wisdom. She declared your rights as the King's true daughter. She puts the King's duty to you where it belongs—upon the King's own shoulders.'

The next day he had gone to persuade her once more. She would not even discuss the matter. 'Yesterday,' she told him, 'I spoke my mind and you set my words upon paper. Did you write as I spoke them, neither adding nor omitting any word? Let me see!'

Unwilling, he brought out the paper. He had referred to her—according to command—as *Princess Dowager*. 'She went white with anger; a white hot anger—like ash beneath which the fire still burns,' he said. 'She spoke no word, save to call for pen and ink. Her hand, unfaltering, struck through the offending title wherever it occurred; and above it she wrote *Queen*. She drove the quill so that wherever the word stood, there is now a hole. She handed it back to me and I felt like a whipped dog.' I am glad, even now, after all these years, that the world has clear proof of her mind in this matter. Sick, abandoned and threatened, she kept her courage and her royal pride. Any courage, any dignity I may have—such as it is—comes to me through her.

She was very quiet, Mountjoy said, when once more he held the paper in his hands. 'I will never admit,' she told him, 'that I have been the King's harlot this four-and-twenty years.'

'Madam,' he said, 'it is all useless. You are no longer Queen and no man, on pain of dire punishment, may call you so. It is treason; see to it, Madam, that all your servants are told!'

At that she bade him summon her household; so in they came, himself leading them. He was her own chamberlain. He had commanded these same servants and, like them, he loved her. There they stood, crowding the narrow chamber and the room beyond. They looked at her bewildered while, very steady, she told them the King's command. 'So you see I must do without servants; for I'll not put any one of you in danger.' And she dismissed them all; and weeping they went—all save some half-dozen that would not leave her; being, as they said, dogs too old to learn new tricks.

This my father had done! While she lay sick abed and wretched that he had abandoned her, he laid upon her yet another indignity. Was there no end to the miseries she must endure?

It seemed there was not.

In early May when all is burgeoning to hope, and even my sad heart a little lifted, she was commanded to appear before Cranmer's court. She refused. She would recognise no court but Rome. So once again sentence was given in her absence. My father's first marriage was declared incestuous, null and void. My mother had never been his wife; and I was a bastard.

She had expected it; and so, I suppose, had I. But I had hoped and prayed, believing that, at the last, God would speak. I was tormented body and soul, and the torment in my soul was the greater; through my head the blinding pain of migraine, and in my heart the bitter pain of hatred. Hatred of my father. There, it is out—the thing I have never admitted yet to my secret heart! To hate my father's harlot was right and proper; but to hate my father whom God and my mother, and my own duty, all exhorted me to love! It was too heavy a load for a young soul to bear. Hatred was a pain so agonising, I thought I must run mad with the torment of it. Yet, had he made the smallest movement of kindness towards my mother, hatred had melted quick as snow beneath the sun.

My mother. She was never out of my thoughts. I longed to be with her. Within that poor and gloomy house with few to do service to Madam the Queen of England, we might be a little happy together. I thought I must die of the longing to run to her, to kneel, my head in her lap, to hide from the eyes that must either scorn or pity me— for all eyes held the same accusation. *Bastard*. And soon I was to hear it put plain. I was no longer Princess of Wales, I was no longer any princess at all. I was a *bastard*.

I carried my head high—I was my mother's daughter; but my spirit fainted within me. I spoke little, save to my lady Salisbury;

and but for her loving understanding must have fallen into a melancholy and thence to my death. *Bastard*. It can never be an easy name to bear; but to one born royal, heir to a great King, suddenly fallen to that base estate, there is no word can tell my suffering. My disgrace, mirrored clear in the eyes of others, engendered in myself an inner sense of degradation. I seemed to myself another person.

My father had no more kindness for me. I would not, could not accept the concubine in my mother's place; and his heart, so long indifferent to me, hardened with his anger. And, as if this anger were not already sufficient, Anne Bullen kept it hot with spiteful tales of my pride, my contempt, my disloyalty for my father and King. It was as though she could not wait for her crowning to savour her full triumph, but must like a spiteful dog pursue me with her spite. My mother she contrived to wound every way, be it large or small. I remember one such piece of meanness that sent me raging to lady Salisbury.

'It is not enough she has stolen from my mother the name of Queen, not enough to have me a disgraced bastard . . .' and I choked over the word. 'No, but she must have everything, everything! She has taken my mother's own barge—did you know that? She has had my mother's emblem painted out and her own painted in. The white falcon replaces the pomegranate; the bird of prey the sweet fruit. No it is not enough she has my mother's husband, my mother's crown, my mother's jewels, my mother's place, but every last little thing . . . everything!'

'Dear heart, so small a thing! I am very sure it does not grieve your mother! Let it not grieve you. It doesn't matter. It doesn't *matter!*'

But it did matter; it mattered. Every sly, small meanness was an extra thorn to fester in my heart.

Chapter Fourteen

Towards the end of May my father solemnised with public splendour that marriage the true church holds to be no marriage. And, losing no time, he summoned his peers, together with their ladies, to give attendance on the first day of June at the crowning of his *dearest wife Queen Anne*.

Spirit working upon flesh there was, these days, no ease to my physical distress. I could not eat without vomiting, migraines were constant and intolerable, I grew very thin. I was, alas, sowing those seeds of ill-health that were to shadow my whole life.

To quiet Beaulieu came news of the celebrations. Lady Salisbury tried to keep the tales from me but every tongue was busy and I could not help but hear. I did not want to hear; yet with a hateful fascination must listen.

For a full week before the crowning London was gay with ribands and flowers, crowded with citizens, with folk come in from the country, with visitors from abroad—and all in holiday clothes. There were pageants and masques in the streets, torchlight processions and dancing by night. And all the time, music; music sounding over the sunlit river by day and upon the lantern-lit river by night. And, day or night, you could scarce see the water for boats all hung with flowers; and on board there were countless pretty conceits—golden dragons bowed fire-breathing heads on to the new Queen, heroes both pagan and Christian laid their arms at her feet while little boys sang sweet as angels. When the barge with the white falcon appeared, the lord mayor's barge led it and those of his aldermen followed—and every barge hung with scarlet and gold.

Money poured away like water! And all the time in Bugden my mother could scarce manage to live from hand to mouth. My father had cut off her allowance as Queen; her allowance as Princess of Wales she refused. It was not hers, she said; rather than touch a penny of it, she'd go beg in the streets! Her gowns were growing shabby and her linen hard to replace; jewels and furs she had none save pieces of little worth. But the countryfolk saw to it that there was food enough and no tradesman pressed his bills. And if all London paid lip-service to the new 'Queen', in quiet Bugden the villagers gathered together, and horsemen rode in from Cambridge and Huntingdon to cry out *God bless Queen Catherine!*

'My father stuffs all mouths in London with cakes and ale; he deafens and blinds folk with shows and music so that they forget their anger. But when the sun goes in and the torches go out; when cakes and ale turn sour in the stomach—what then?'

'The end of Anne Bullen!' my lady Salisbury said.

On the twenty-ninth of May, Anne Bullen left Greenwich for the Tower; according to custom, before a crowning, she was to ride through London to show herself to the people. Never such a glorification of mortal woman! It was as though my father sought to cover up all baseness with trappings of unmatched splendour.

Platforms had been set up tier upon tier that the people might behold their 'Queen'. Cornhill was all hung with scarlet and gold, and the Chepe with cloth-of-gold. At the great gates of the Tower stood my lord Mayor with all his officers to await the concubine's procession and lead it into London. Out it came, my lords the archbishops riding in front, the bishops following—mitres and croziers flashing with jewels, copes bright as the sun in patterned gold; monks and priests chanting; their crosses raised. The church giving its blessing! So all was well—save that at Bugden my mother was breaking her heart, and I was too racked with pain even for weeping. Following the princes of the church, came princes of the state led by little Richmond; foreign princes and ambassadors came next, the French ambassador leading with his train, all in yellow and blue; there was no Imperial ambassador—Chapuys was confined to bed we heard; and little wonder! Upon the heels of the ambassadors came the knights of the Bath all in royal purple and miniver; and after them, two esquires bearing upon cushions the ducal crowns of Normandy and Aquitaine —my father's feudal rights.

And now, heralded by so much majesty—the woman herself. She sat upright in an open litter drawn by eight white matched palfreys. The litter was hung with white satin embroidered with raised flowers of gold; it moved slowly beneath a canopy of cloth-of-gold carried by four knights. She wore a gown of pure silver tissue and, lined with that same tissue, a mantle of ermine. No edging of ermine upon velvet for her, as befits most Queens, but the whole great cloak. They say she outshone the summer sun itself! Her long dark curls fell

free from a crown of rubies. Decency should have confined her hair—
she was six months gone with child—and showed it. But decency was
not in her. She carried the King's bastard—and carried it with pride!
And I wondered if, now the devil had given her her heart's desire,
the witchmark was wet beneath the jewels at her throat.

'They say,' lady Salisbury sought to comfort me, 'that not all the
splendour of crown and gown, nor all the high painting could hide
the dark skin, the heavy eyes and the long nose. And, Madam; the
whole great procession passed in silence. Not a single cheer! Already
the cakes and ale are sour! The people stared silent and sullen. She
marked it, they say, and the colour drained from her face so that it
showed greenish. They say, too, that the men-at-arms along the
route, being commanded, raised a cheer; their voices and theirs alone
breaking the silence!'

'Let her be glad it was no worse!' I said, bitter.

Of the great pageants for that crowning, I have not heart to speak.
But there was a white falcon sitting upon a nest of red and white roses—
her emblem uniting York and Tudor; for on her mother's side she
boasted some thin drops of Plantagenet blood. There were muses, all
nine of them, bowing low before her, there were angels offering
crowns, and to my mind, sweetest of all, children singing her praises;
and of these little ones she was not worthy.

Well she had her day of glory—if not the people's love. And all
through the night beer flowed in torrents and folk drank themselves
silly, hiccoughing *Long live the Queen!* Which Queen they were too
fuddled to know. But good, sober folk remembered their true Queen
to bless her in the silent heart.

I heard all the tales of that crowning with a still face, neither weeping
nor complaining. But when I heard that at Bugden, the stone upon
which my mother knelt to pray was found wet with her tears, I could
no longer keep silent. '*God save Queen Anne.* It is blasphemy. God is
just and she is forever damned!'

'God is merciful!' lady Salisbury reminded me.

'But the devil is not; he will see to it!'

'Do you hold the devil greater than God?'

And when I made no answer but stood blazing like a wild cat, I that
was for the most part quiet, finding relief for anger in tears, she said,
'That is a question that needs no answer.' And then, a little stern,
'Do not wish her ill. Ill-wishing, you hurt yourself—your own soul.
Madam your mother has told you so. Once, when one of her
women cursed Anne Bullen, Madam the Queen said, "*Do not curse*

but pray for her. The time will come when you shall find reason to pity her!" '

For the moment I could not speak. My mother had said those same words to me, myself, and they brought my childhood suddenly back. But the past was past and this was the bitter present. Yet I knew her well enough to wager that even now, had she occasion to speak of Anne Bullen, it would be without spite. That she, poor, abandoned and sick, could yet speak with pity of that woman in all her glory, shook me to the heart.

'My mother's a saint,' I said, 'and I am none.'

'She would not have you a saint; that's a way too hard for young feet. But a good woman—that she would have you be; and goodness is not to be had for wishing—it must be worked for.'

'Goodness comes from prayer. And how can I pray for the concubine that sits crowned in my mother's place, that walked from the palace to the abbey upon fine silk that her shoes be not soiled—she that cares nothing for the soiling of her soul?'

'Hush, oh hush!' she said.

'How shall I sit silent when the bishops that should lead us to God are deaf to the Pope that speaks with His voice, and lend ear to the devil? No!' I cried out in sudden passion, 'I'll not be stopped. I see her day and night, the concubine sitting crowned in the abbey and bowing herself before the high altar, while Cranmer, my lord arch-bishop of Canterbury no less, prays for her well-being . . . and no fire comes down from heaven to blast them both!' I was silent for a moment; then I said:

'Maybe God stayed His hand because He saves fit punishment for such blasphemy. Maybe my mother was right!'

'That is not what she meant. Your mother spoke in gentleness and pity; you speak in anger.'

'I cannot think but in anger; I cannot pray but in anger. Even while she offers herself to God she cannot wait to sin with my father—the harlot he calls *Queen*. But for all that he knows her unworthiness. When they sat at the crowning feast there was no knight to cry the rights of the "Queen". That challenge is the custom . . . but my father did not dare; or maybe no challenger could be found lest God Himself answer it!'

'Hush!' she said again and wrung her two hands. 'Your father's an easy man to rouse and his wrath could be terrible. Let some word of this be carried to him—who knows what spy listens?—and it could be, God forbid, worse for you; and for your mother, worst of all!'

And while I stood gritting jaw upon jaw lest further words burst from me, she said, 'Walk carefully, Madam . . . if you would walk at all!'

The summer dragged for me; long, weary days in which I prayed that the child Anne Bullen carried might not be a son; that she might bear no child at all: that she might miscarry and, miscarrying, die. Did my mother, I wondered, make that same prayer? She might well pray that the woman should not bear a son to inherit, but for the rest—no! there was never any spite in her.

And yet she had an even greater reason to wish Anne Bullen dead. She feared—as all about her feared—that someone unsuspected and not to be guarded against, might, to please the concubine, poison the true Queen.

'Madam Queen Catherine is afraid and rightly afraid!' Monsieur Chapuys said, come with news from Bugden. 'Yet still she utters no word against the concubine that calls herself Queen; on whose account she is in constant fear of death—and such a death! There is in Madam, your mother, a strength and a belief in God such as I have never met!'

When Monsieur Chapuys that was no man's fool feared such an end for my mother, then I must fear it, too. Now there was a burden, heavier than all the rest put together, upon my heart. If my mother should die of poison, I could not endure to live.

Anne Bullen's spite still pursued me. Yet had she offered me friendship it had been worse; for I must have refused her and so brought down my father's anger yet more heavy upon my mother and myself.

The slow months passed. The Pope and all his cardinals declared my father's new 'marriage' no marriage at all; they censured him and his concubine, both.

'Much they care, those two junketing at Hampton Court!' I said, very bitter, to lady Salisbury. 'You'd think Wolsey's ghost would haunt them—and would to God it may.' And later, when they betook themselves to Greenwich, 'Pray God memories of my mother, and of me that was born there, may soften his heart!'

But neither ghost nor memories troubled either of them; all was gay with balls, with masques and with music.

Anne Bullen sat in the Queen's place, wore the Queen's crown but, for all that, she did not savour her full triumph. There were many to look upon her as upstart and usurper; I was not the only one to call her *concubine*. She was her own worst enemy with her pride and her sharp tongue and her light behaviour. Even in those early days there were tales about her—the way she conducted herself with men, young men; and the familiarities she allowed.

'She is much disliked,' lady Salisbury said. 'She sits in the Queen's place but she cannot command the respect due to a Queen. Some, old enough to be her father, she insults; others, she neglects. Her arrogance offends those she should repect, and her over-free behaviour with those she calls her friends shocks the rest of the court.'

'They say she's such a shrew, my father already tires of her!'

'It may well be true; but to gossip and scolding tongue alike he must turn a deaf ear . . . she carries his child!'

All that summer we heard tales of Anne Bullen. She was wasteful, a spendthrift; when my father did not, at once, give her the thing she wanted, she let him, and everyone within earshot, know it. The truth is that he had always been a lavish spender, and, of late, with her jewels and her furs—the ermine cloak alone must have cost a King's ransom—with the expenses of her crowning and all its festivities, the fortune his father had left was all-but gone and he scarce knew which way to turn. Taxes fell upon the people heavy as hail and more continuous; and he himself must make his economies.

And I must make mine. Once I had danced with the King in a golden gown and golden slippers. Golden Princess. Now, for above three years I was to have neither new gowns nor new shoes. I must wear my gowns with care lest the faded silk crack; I knew what it was to wear a darned petticoat and patched shoes—not golden shoes, alas! I was no more any sort of Princess.

All through that long summer, I at Beaulieu and my mother at Bugden, waited with fear for the birth of the concubine's child. We had been forbidden to write to each other, but let punishment be what it might, write we must and write we did. Without those letters full of love and wisdom I do not think I could have lived. I must never, she wrote, let go my trust in God. I must obey my father with a cheerful heart, for grudging obedience is worth little. God is always good; and though things seem to work for our ill, He would see to it that, so we deserved it, all would turn to our good.

Towards the end of the summer she sent me a letter that disturbed me more than a little. It began with a warning. She had heard that my father was about to send for me. I was to carry myself with care and answer with few words, obeying the King your father in everything, save that you will not offend God and lose your soul. Wheresoever and in what company you shall come, obey the King's commands and meddle nothing. . . .

What did she know? And why should my father that had abandoned me, send for me now?

Then followed a curious piece of advice.

Keep your heart with a chaste mind and your body from wanton company.

Why had she said that? I was not inclined to unchaste thoughts; my mind was, for the most part, upon her—our troubles; and upon my books. Did she consider Anne Bullen's wantonness a threat to me?

She wrote, she said, with good cheer for she knew I should see a very good end to my troubles, since God, she was sure, loved me. Then followed a piece of advice that troubled me yet further. She warned me to keep possession of my own keys. Clearly she did not trust those I should find about me. And so she ended, saying yet again that she was in good heart, since when enemies have done their worst, then good must follow. She sent her greetings to lady Salisbury. . . .

pray her to have a good heart, for we never come to the Kingdom of Heaven but by troubles.

Well, if that be true, we all three deserve our heavenly place!

Not a reassuring letter. I was going among enemies, I must keep a careful tongue, I must guard my keys.

I carried it to lady Salisbury.

'Madam Queen Catherine fears what I, myself, fear,' she said. 'You will be sent for to witness the birth of Anne Bullen's child!'

The blood left my heart. 'I'll not go. I cannot be expected to go!'

'It is expected and you must go!' And when I would have argued the matter, she said, 'Your father commands it. It is your duty!'

'To see that woman's bastard born—my duty? No!'

'It is the custom,' and her words came slow and careful, 'for the heir-apparent—that is you, Madam—to be present when the Queen gives birth.'

'She is not the Queen. Nor am I heir-apparent. I am the heir. I! There is not, nor there cannot be, any heir but me!'

She made no answer to that. She said, instead, 'Madam, it is not only your tongue you must watch but your face, also. It is tell-tale of your private thoughts.'

'I have no thoughts that shame me!'

'Then you are luckier than most! But consider. Because your thoughts are right and proper, and because you are young and innocent, you may fall into some danger.'

'I am still my father's daughter. If he send for me, who shall hurt me?'

'Madam; dearest child, I must speak plain—as your mother would speak were she here. *Keep your body from wanton company*. Why did she write that? Because she fears for you; she fears Anne Bullen. She—' and she would never call Anne Bullen *Queen*, if it might any way be avoided, 'may take you in a trap. You have a most loving heart; you could be guiled by false words, by lies. That woman—spiteful and wanton—might have your maidenhead taken by force.'

The sickness came up in my throat. 'She would not dare! Such useless wickedness, how could it serve her?'

'It is far from useless; and it would serve her very well! Such a piece of wickedness, which God forbid, would cut you from the crown forever. For then Parliament must declare you corrupt in blood; you could never inherit, not though your father have no other child. No! The crown would go to your cousin the King of Scots or to the issue of my lord of Suffolk or to some other with Tudor blood in his veins!'

'I am not afraid,' I said, though still I sickened with loathing at the thought. 'Not that she could not be so base; but she would not dare! My father may love me no longer—' and I took in my breath lest I weep at the thought, 'but still he has a use for me. I am still of some value in the marriage-markets of Christendom. Let any rob me of my maidenhead—and the value's gone. It could mean her death and she knows it!'

She looked at me in some surprise.

'It is not a hard piece of arithmetic,' I said. 'But—' again the loathing took me, 'let any man try to take my maidenhead before marriage and I'd kill myself!'

'That could not comfort your mother!' she said drily. Her eyes went back over the letter. '*Take heart, and take heed*. Your mother does not speak for nothing!'

Chapter Fifteen

I was for London; my father had commanded me. In spite of my brave words I rode in fear; for I had been commanded to leave lady Salisbury behind. To whom should I turn for advice; who would stand my friend? I rode not at all like the King's daughter but very sober—a waiting woman and a couple of men-servants. My father had commanded that I be not gaily attended and that I ride in a closed litter. 'The order comes, no doubt, through my lady concubine,' lady Salisbury said. 'She fears lest you be seen! She knows the people love you but her they hate. They hate her, not for herself alone; but because, on her account, the King breaks with Rome. And, above all, they blame her for the heavy taxes. That, at least, is not her fault. Your father has always been a spender; but when the people see her—all those jewels and furs; when they hear about all those great houses, they visit their anger upon her. Everywhere there's bewilderment and discontent. One word from you—and they would rise. A careless word spoken in all innocence could trigger off an explosion. Remember what Madam Queen Catherine writes, *Guard well your tongue and meddle nothing*.'

Poor my escort and poor my gown; neither could give me confidence. They seemed a symbol of that situation to which I travelled. I felt like a servant—and not an upper one, neither!

My father and his harlot were in Greenwich; and there, in an obscure part of the palace I was lodged. Some of the servants, not knowing me, treated me, at first, with scant ceremony. But I am my father's daughter; such behaviour did not last long. I stayed within my poor chamber not daring to stir abroad save to walk in an unfrequented part of the gardens. I was not sent for to pay my respects to my father and his 'queen'; nor did my father, whom I saw but once before the birth, show much joy in the daughter he had once loved. It was the first time we had met since his 'marriage'; he greeted me with a cold and calculating look that warned me to have a care how I carried myself to his new 'wife'.

Anne Bullen was near her time when she sent for me, at last, to attend her in her closet. I bent the knee, but, it seemed, not low enough, for she did not acknowledge my greeting. She bade me kneel behind her chair as though I were the servant she had promised to make me. I remembered the warnings of those two that loved me; I commanded my face to quiet and went as I was bid.

But my thoughts I could not quiet. I knelt there willing her to die— she and her child together, that like cuckoos should thrust me from my place. She kept me there; knees shaking beneath the strain, I examined my thoughts.

Pray God she may die, she and her child together—and not because I want the crown. Had my father a true-born son I should rejoice. I want the thing all women want—to respect my husband, to love my children, to order my household. And with that, to take my proper place—the King's daughter. Nothing more; save, God willing, that my husband love me. To welcome the child of this woman that names my mother incestuous and myself a bastard—it is not possible. . . .

I came from my thoughts back to find myself alone. She had gone softly away with all her women and left me to kneel like a fool in an empty room.

These days before her delivery I was passionate for her death. Why should she not die? She was small-boned and nigh on thirty. My mother I knew would fault me for this but I could not help myself—I am, after all, a Tudor. I spoke to my mother in my mind. . . . *Many women die in childbirth; better women than she! She would gladly see us dead, both you and me—she has said it. You live in daily fear of poison by her command and as for me—who knows?*

I had no fear she would contrive aught against my life at the moment; she needed me. She'd not forgo the royal custom; and she delighted in flaunting before my eyes her great belly. She commanded me with less courtesy than she would command her meanest servant; I was sent to fetch and carry, to do this and that, though half-a-dozen waiting women stood by. She was shrewish and, for all her royal air, vulgar; in her there was no generosity. She was forever complaining of me to my father who bade me carry myself seemly lest I cool my heels in the Tower. I knew that he, himself, bowed before her shrewishness lest, crossing her, harm come to the child she carried.

Anne Bullen was in labour. They had drawn aside the bed-curtains that she might breathe more freely this close September day. In the great canopied bed, bearing her initials entwined with those of the King, she turned and tossed. Upon a stool in the ante-room I waited and prayed, *Let her die; her and her child together*. I was cankered with bitterness because my presence here acknowledged her Queen; an even deeper bitterness that I must attend upon the birth of my rival.

All that day and through the long night she twisted and groaned and cried aloud. Through the open door of the bed-chamber came heat from the brazier that forever burned; nor could aromatic vinegars hide the stink of sweat and pain. Once I caught sight of that yellow face aglisten with sweat, the long nose, the wet dark hair—for she had cast aside her bedcap. But the riband from her throat she had not cast away; the hidden place was hidden still.

Night gave unwilling way to dawn; and then through early-morning mist the hidden sun gave promise of a glorious day. I knelt upon the window-seat to watch, through thinning mist, the green of the garden come clear and then the blue of the sky. And, as I knelt, drowning the song of birds, I heard the bells summoning folk to prayer and remembered it was Sunday.

Sunday, the seventh day of September, in the year of grace fifteen hundred and thirty-three.

Throughout the long bright day I sat while she twisted and groaned in the room beyond. I had no pity for her; she was bearing the King's child. And for that my mother would gladly have given her life.

But this child the woman laboured to bring forth, was it truly the King's child? She was far too free with her friends—and those friends men, young and well favoured; gossip had long said it. Now, in the King's own house, gossip named them—Wyatt the poet, her kinsman; Rochford, her own brother, that was fonder of her than any brother should be, that came into her bedchamber and up to her very bed . . . and into that bed, some said. And there'd been other men, too! Had the tales reached my father? I judged not; for who would so far dare? And were they true? True or no, they were not such tales as should be breathed of any woman—especially if she partner the King of England.

And now it was noon. I knew it without any clock by the deep shadow lying upon the bright grass.

It was one o'clock, it was two, it was three. . . .

All through the long hours of these two days my father had not visited her; he had sent often to ask how it fared with her but none of us about the Queen had set eyes on him. He kept his rooms, biding the time; but I doubt not he strode about irritable and impatient, making those that waited with him to shake in their shoes. And, I doubt not, he prayed also—but his prayers, how different from mine!

Four o'clock. And a cry of agony tearing the air. And then a cry, small, thin and bleating. It brought me to my feet, my whole being, from clenched fists to knotted belly-muscles, crying out in protest.

Cry of the new-born.

Presently they brought me the child smeared still with the slime of birth. Beneath my schooled face the thoughts shouted. *Not a son! She has not triumphed over my mother. Thank God not a son!* The moment of relief turned to revulsion. Give up my place to this morsel of flesh, this creature, like myself a female! A son had been less mortifying. In the flesh of this infant God had chosen to mortify me!

Yet, *God loves you,* my mother had written. *You shall see a good end to this business.* What love did He show? And what good end should I see? And I remembered once again what she had said of Anne Bullen: *Do not curse her; she will be in a lamentable case.* Had she been right? Did God lift up this spurious Queen to hurl her to a bitter end?

It did not seem so. For all his grievous disappointment, my father was kind. He told his concubine, as once he had told my mother, 'Do not weep. We are young. There will be other children!' And when her tears fell faster he said, 'Come now, sweetheart, I had rather beg from door to door than forsake you!' And this he had never said to my mother.

His gentleness did not last long. His disappointment was most bitter and he was not the man to hide it. Soothsayers had deceived him; heaven, well-bribed, had tricked him. He had been made to look a fool in the eyes of Christendom. Letters announcing the birth of a prince had been prepared for all the courts of Europe; now with a bitter heart he must make his alteration. His *prince* was a princess.

Weeping done, Anne Bullen tried to cover disappointment with a jest; but it was no jesting matter, with fear she knew it. She had committed the unforgivable sin. She had borne the King a daughter.

And reason she had to fear. My father's eye was already straying; it was whispered about the court with some pleasure. Chapuys, also, whispered it in my ear. 'It is true. Two months ago he sent the concubine his richest bed; he had it from the Duke of Alençon, part of his ransom. Well for her she had it then; be very sure she'd not have it now! The King is weary of her; he'll no longer endure her rages now the child is born. He told her—with my own ears I heard it—she must shut her eyes and mouth to his affairs, as her better had done before her! Her better . . . we know well whom he meant!'

Yes we knew . . . we knew.

'He warned her, also—and not in private neither—that, though he had raised her high, he could humble her again and lower than he had found her!'

Do not curse her. . . . Maybe my mother was right; maybe I should see a better end than I had looked for. But . . . *you shall see a better end*; I—not we. . . . If she did not see it, also, all would be dust and ashes.

These days I was not admitted into the presence of Anne Bullen. I had done my duty. I had still another duty—to be present at the christening of her child. Till then I must remain within my poor chamber; then, duty done, I should be sent home. My father sent for me once; and, for that once, treated me with less coldness. He had lost nothing of his disappointment but something of his anger—he liked all children; and me, as a little child, he had loved.

There will be more children he had told his concubine as once he had told his Queen. But the pattern of his first marriage was to repeat itself; from this second union there would be no other child.

Anne Bullen, reassured by my father's surprising kindness, and with all Christendom kneeling with gifts, was her own, old self. Let the King's eye wander where it would, she was still the Queen and the King meant to keep her so. *There will be more children*, it was a promise.

Certainly Anne Bullen was herself again. Preparations for the christening going forward, she wrote to Bugden, demanding the christening shawl my mother had brought from Spain. This shawl was sacred to my mother and father, both. It had been used once, only; to carry to his christening the little son that had breathed so short a while and died. My father had not allowed it to be used at my own christening; it was meant for his son and for his son alone. From the one she had taken everything, Anne Bullen demanded this last thing, sacred to a dead child and to dead hopes. She wanted it to show that her own child stood higher than my mother's; that the new-born girl, ranking equal with a son, was the King's heir. A piece of behaviour both subtle and coarse which perfectly showed her quality.

My mother answered with one word. *No!*

So the infant went to her christening in a mantle more splendid than the shawl but lacking its significance. And such a christening! Fitter for the son of God had he been born again. From Greenwich palace to Greyfriars church, the covered way was hung with rich tapestries; and the church, itself, hung with yet richer tapestries and sweet garlands. The silver font brought from Canterbury—as seventeen years ago it had been brought for me—stood benath a canopy of estate, all crimson and gold. About it stood the noblest peers of England, their robes ridiculously protected by aprons; hands, more used to carrying swords, now carried towels—a sight to make one smile, if for heartbreak one could smile. At the church door stood my lord mayor and his officers in state mantles of scarlet and fur.

I sat in the shadow of my lowly seat; I had not been asked to take part in the ceremony; my presence was merely to acknowledge the usurper. I was glad to take no part, I had no wish to honour the child; yet so are we made, my heart burned at this slighting of me—the King's elder daughter.

Now there entered two processions. From the great door came the lord mayor and all his train; from the palace entrance, the peers and their ladies, each in his degree, the boy Richmond leading. My lord earl of Essex carried a golden basin, my lord marquis of Exeter a lighted candle of virgin wax; lady Mary of Norfolk, that was to wed young Richmond, carried a jewelled chrism. I thought how different Richmond's position and mine this day. He was my father's undoubted bastard, yet here he stood, endowed with every high honour; and a good chance of the crown—if he lived so long; he was a delicate boy. Neither father nor mother of the babe was present; it was not the custom. She was being dressed for removal to the ceremonial day-bed to receive congratulations; he was watching from a window that gave on to the church from the cloisters. So he had watched at my own christening; so he would watch when, at last, his son was born.

And now, the whole congregation standing, in came the cause of all the furore. Beneath a golden canopy of estate borne by four knights, in the arms of her great-grandmother, the dowager duchess of Norfolk —the infant. My gorge rose at the sight. She was wrapped in a mantle of royal purple lined throughout with ermine; so great a garment that my lady countess of Kent and my lord earl of Derby must follow to lift it from the ground. I knelt in my poor gown unable to pray for anger at all this high ceremony for my father's bastard.

The great service began; and ended. It had, for the most part, passed me by. I was brought from my bitter thinking by the voice of garter King-at-arms. *God send a prosperous life and long to the high and puissant Princess of England, Elizabeth.*

Princess of England. She!

With a flourish of trumpets the processions swept out. I stayed a little to pray—first for my mother's return to health; and then that my bitter heart might soften towards the innocent child. When, at last, I stumbled from the dark church the night sky was red with light; a thousand torches had been kindled to keep Londoners mindful of this day.

Myself, I needed no reminding.

Chapter Sixteen

Shabby, insufficiently attended, as I had come I took my homeward way; and since the September days held much of summer warmth and light, and my father had given no order, I rode my mare taking my pleasure in these last days of summer. The fallen leaves added to my melancholy at first; but soon, the people coming from house or shop or from the fields to greet me, cheered my drooping spirit; and many a lord and bishop that had not the courage to speak before my father, came also with every good wish. *God bless our Princess Mary. God bless the Princess of Wales.* I heard it on every side, so in spite of myself, my spirits rose, and now, as I neared Beaulieu, my spirits rose higher still. I was going home; home to the house I loved and the kindness of my dear lady Salisbury. I could not get home fast enough; I set the mare at a gallop.

But even as the grooms led the mare into the courtyard I found downcast faces, eyes that could not meet my own.

What now?

Lady Salisbury, unwilling and grieving, gave me my answer.

'These have been hard weeks for you, Madam, dearest child. . . .' Her voice, faltering, filled me with foreboding. Was harder to come; harder still?

'Madam, as soon as the infant's title was proclaimed, your own was denied!'

'No!' I cried out. 'She was proclaimed princess; but not Princess of Wales. My title was not denied me.'

'It will follow; Parliament will see to it. Already we have received our orders. The King's messengers came galloping express.'

It was not, I suppose, entirely unexpected but my father had said no word to me; and the blow expected, and the blow fallen, are two different things. The first may never come; the second crushes hope for ever. Tears started in my eyes, rained down my cheeks. I could not stay them; I did not try. The last weeks had been all too much.

'Do not cry so terribly, Madam, my darling!' lady Salisbury said.

'This state of affairs cannot last long. The King wearies of that woman. Not only can she not hold her tongue but she is losing her looks. And worst of all—for her—she is not clever. Witty she may be and accomplished; but she is not *clever*!'

'Clever enough to keep all she's worked for! And, let us think what we may, he's *wed* according to the law of this land. Fast-bound. Weary he may be, but there's nothing he can do about it, Nothing!'

'You do not know your father! When he can bear the yoke no longer, he throws it off. His conscience will show him the way.'

'Conscience?' And did she make a jest?

'Make no mistake,' she said, 'it *is* conscience with him—though, perhaps, not all the time. With him, conscience is apt to sleep until desire prick it awake again. So it was between him and your mother. So it will be with him and Anne Bullen. For still he has no son; if she does not give him one—and quickly, she'll find her head lightened of the crown.'

'Will it put my mother back in her true place? No! Still he'll leave her to eat her heart out in Bugden—or some worse house.'

A little later, that same day, lord Hussey my chamberlain came to me.

'Madam, my lady . . . I have the King's orders. We must not, under pain of death, address you as *princess*. It is treason.'

'Your orders, let me see them!'

He held out the paper, shamefaced, as though he, himself, were to blame.

The paper showed, very plain, my degraded position. For it styled me, *the lady Mary the King's daughter*, that and no more. I was not even the equal of young Richmond, for he had his great title.

'And, Madam; I have my orders to reduce your grace's—' he corrected himself with a swift look over his shoulder, 'your ladyship's household.'

Decidedly less than the bastard son with his princely retinues!

'Then you must obey your orders, my lord.'

I went straight to my closet. I asked no advice. I wrote to my father. I had received his orders, I said, and had . . .

desired to see the letter which was showed me, whereon was written *the lady Mary the King's daughter*, leaving out the name of *Princess*. Which when I saw I could not a little marvel, trusting verily your Grace was not privy to the same, for I doubt not, your Grace does take me to be your lawful daughter, born in true matrimony. If I, myself, should say to the contrary, I should, in my conscience, run into the displeasure of God. In all other things your Grace shall command me as humble and obedient a daughter and handmaid as ever child was to father.

I signed it,

Your most humble daughter, Mary, Princess.

I had done better not to write. With no loss of time came my lord of Norfolk, uncle to Anne Bullen. Without permission or any ceremony he thrust himself into my chamber where I sat with my lady Salisbury. In plain words he informed me that I was not the King's lawful daughter but his bastard only.

But worse was to come: worse than she or I could have imagined.

'My lady Mary,' he said, 'you must leave this house. It is no longer yours.'

Turned out of my house! I stared as though he or I were crazed.

'My lord,' lady Salisbury spoke as one amazed, 'do you not, perhaps, mistake your errand?'

It was as though she had not spoken. He did not even look at her.

'You must make all haste, lady,' he told me. 'My lord Rochford takes possession at once!'

George Bullen to have my house! A blind man could see Anne Bullen's spite in this. I kept my eyes steady; I would not let him see how this thing hit me. 'My lord,' I said, 'I will give my orders.'

'I have given them; they are simple enough. Your household is to be dispersed to go where it choose—so long as it be not with you!'

My household broken up! Faithful friends all; some had been with me since, at the age of four, I had been given my own retinue.

'Madam, you will not need them. You will join the household at Hatfield!'

At that I let out a sharp cry and I heard lady Salisbury take in her breath. *Hatfield!* Where Anne Bullen's infant lived surrounded by every symbol of royalty.

'Madam Queen Anne graciously appoints you waiting-woman to the Princess of England!' He spoke the words short and sharp as though to be done with his errand.

Bereft of home and household! Waiting-woman to the concubine's child! My mother will break her heart for this!

I turned from the sight of lady Salisbury's stricken face; I doubt not my own was as stricken.

'How many servants go with me?'

'You will find sufficient where you are going!' He was evasive, unwilling, I thought upon this errand.

For all he was Anne Bullen's uncle, he liked neither her nor her manners. Beneath her arrogance he smarted still, he, great Norfolk! He had made her what she was; had brought her beneath the King's eye. That meeting at Hever had been his work; and, in those early days, he had advised her as to her behaviour. He had intended her for a strong bulwark for the house of Norfolk against all parties. Now she went her wilful way that, without him, had never been Queen! And, for myself, standing there, he had, I think, some pity—the King's daughter thus degraded! There I stood small and thin and younger than my seventeen years—a child, almost in his eyes, smitten to the heart, yet holding fast to the one thing I had left—my dignity.

'How many, my lord?' I pressed him further.

'Two.' And now he did not look at me.

'Two! Two servants for the King's daughter!' Lady Salisbury's voice came out sharp, indignant.

'Make no argument, my lady,' I told her, 'of what use?' I turned to him. 'My lord, will you, of your courtesy, see that my servants—now thrown upon the world through no fault of their own—be paid a year's wages?' At that he nodded.

Then came the most horrible, the most unexpected thing.

'Of course I go with Madam the Princess,' lady Salisbury said; 'and I will take with me sufficient servants for her needs; I take them, naturally, at my own cost.'

He turned upon her then, glad to vent some of his discomfort upon her. 'Madam you have already made sufficient mischief; it is you that stiffen the obstinacy of the lady Mary, here! And she is no more *princess*; note it. You do not go with her!'

She whitened and her jaw dropped; she looked like a dead woman. And I doubt not I looked the same! That she should ever leave me had never entered our heads. Next to parting with my mother this was the direst thing that could befall me; for she was my second mother, dear and loving, true and wise. To her I could speak my heart, listen without fear. To whom should I speak now, whom trust?

She made a step towards me. 'No, my lady,' he told her quick and rough, 'you do not go to Hatfield; but you may go elsewhere! Have a care lest it be the Tower!' He turned to me. 'Make ready, lady; we should be on our way!'

Of a sudden he turned him about, rage sparking that cold eye. Hussey had come into the room.

'What is that?' Norfolk's finger thrust at the badge my chamberlain wore upon his breast; my badge. 'You have had your orders. No-one within this household—or anywhere else—may wear this thing!' He tore at it roughly so that the stitches cracked. 'See to it, Hussey, that you, and all within this house, remove the lady Mary's badge!'

Hussey came to my chamber where already the women were packing—*my* women no longer. 'Madam,' he said, 'forgive me. Your jewels, your furs and your household plate must be left behind!'

'So there is less trouble for us all!' and I made my mouth to smile. 'We are finished!' I looked at the scant baggage that held my shabby gowns, my books and the few treasures saved from childhood— Wolsey's gold cup, the pomander, the Book of Hours. And suddenly, I know not why, there came clear to my eyes the little tree of gold— the tree that had first shown me my father as an angry man; and I could have wept for the little tree, for my childhood, and for my father's love; gone, all gone.

The baggage being corded and carried away, I stood looking about the empty room.

What now?

The door opened and lady Salisbury came in. We ran to each other and she took me in her arms. She held me as a mother holds her unhappy child; and such a child I was.

She said, 'I should have expected this. My son spoke plain about the divorce. This is my punishment. It comes late but it comes sure.' She lifted her face and I saw that these last hours had put the weight of years upon her. 'Madam Princess, I grieve at this parting and fear for it.'

'For me?'

She nodded. 'Listen to me, listen as though I were your mother; for I speak in her name. You have great courage; and discretion sufficient for your age. But—sufficient for where you are going? It is not to be expected; yet such discretion you must somehow find. Guard your face, your eyes and your tongue. Let no-one provoke your too-quick spirit. You go to a house of enemies.'

'I will remember.' I knelt by her and took her dear face between my hands and kissed her upon both cheeks as is courtly fashion, and then upon the mouth, in daughter's fashion. And I went out of the door and I never saw her again.

Either side of the great doorway my household stood, greatest to least, bright patches showing where the badge had been ripped. They stood heads bowed; I bowed my own, unable to look into those faces some of them grown old in loving service. I tried to speak my thanks and could not speak. I lifted my hands as though to bless them; but my lord of Norfolk, his own hand impatient upon my reins, dragged me away.

In the cold December weather I rode out upon my journey towards sorrow, humiliation and danger that was to last two years; two cruel years. And, as I rode, people stood bare-headed in the bitter wind and cried out that I was their true, their only Princess. Norfolk rode beside me, his face of stone, making himself neither to see nor hear; he had no mind to punish these simple folk—whether to preserve his own image in their eyes or because of some good in him I do not know.

And now, for the first time in my life I felt completely alone; alone as never before. I was not yet eighteen—and my years sheltered. I was being taken to a house of enemies controlled by kinsmen of my arch-enemy Anne Bullen.

No sooner had I set foot within the house when Norfolk, allowing me no moment, addressed me without ceremony. 'Lady, you must pay your respects to the Princess!'

I looked at him; and though my heart beat to shake my whole body, my voice was steady enough. 'My lord, I know of no Princess in England save myself. As for the daughter of my lady Pembroke—' and I would not name her Queen, 'Princess she is none. But since the lord King acknowledges her his daughter, as I call young Richmond *brother*, so I will call her *sister*.'

His bleak face went bitter; I had made clear the child's bastardy. He lifted a hand as though to strike me; had he but touched me, I must have fallen, being weak with fear at my own daring.

Before he rode for London Norfolk came to me again. 'Madam, have you any message for the King?'

'Only this. The Princess of Wales, his daughter, asks his blessing!'

He looked at me, for the first time, with some respect. 'Before God, Madam, I dare not take such a message!'

'Norfolk is no coward; he will take it. And one more kindness, my lord, I do entreat you. I have written to the lords of the Privy Council. Will you deliver my letter? You may read it, if you will!'

I watched his face as he read.

. . . I protest before you all that my conscience will in no way suffer me to take other than myself for Princess, or for the King's daughter born in holy matrimony. And I will never willingly do aught whereby any person may think I agree to the contrary. Nor do I say this out of any ambition or a proud mind, as God is my judge. If I should do otherwise I should slander our mother the Most Holy church and the Pope in this matter. I should also dishonour my father, the Queen my mother and falsely confess myself a bastard, which God defend I should do. . . .

'Madam,' he said, 'I had rather some other take your letter; yet, for all that, take it I will; aye and see it rightly delivered.'

'Then God shall bless you, my lord; and I, also!'

He bent to my hand and there was, I swear, kindness in him. I was sorry to see him go; there was a rough justice in him.

And so began two wretched years for me; years that all-but broke my spirit and completely broke my health. And yet Hatfield was bright and pleasant and healthy; a handsome house, well-found. Different, indeed, from Bugden with its small, dark rooms and the bitter winds sweeping across the flats.

If Bugden was a death trap for my mother, so Hatfield was for me. Here I must watch every word lest it be misreported to my father. The household was commanded by lady Shelton together with lady Clere; and each of them aunt to Anne Bullen. She had commanded them to bring down my proud stomach if they killed me for it; they made no secret of it.

Those two years I dragged out my miserable existence—life, I cannot call it—in anguish of mind and body. My father's harlot—wife nor Queen I'll never call her—saw fit to humiliate me with her mean commands. Her orders were constant. Lady Shelton was to see that, every way, the babe took precedence over me. I must not leave a room where the child was until she had been carried hence; I must not enter a room save at the tail-end of the infant's train. The servants treated me with rudeness and the two women harried me every way. My letters were opened before ever they reached me—if ever they did reach me. In all those two years I never received a letter but the seal was broken. Letters I, myself, wrote, I did not seal, knowing full well they would be read before ever they left the house—if ever they did leave the house. But my two maids, though they were kept from me so that I saw little of them, now and again smuggled a letter in or out. My papers, my books, my few possessions were fingered; they were left torn and dog-eared and out of order. And every scrap of paper about which they were not certain was sent to Cromwell—

even a prayer I had put into English that I might not forget my Latin
and also while away my sad time.

Lady Shelton obeyed her commands with relish—all save one. 'If
you do not show a sufficiently humble spirit I am to beat you, for the
accursed bastard you are. Madam the Queen has written it! And I
will do so, too!'

'Then obey your orders!' I beat her down with my eyes. To strike
me was the one thing she never dared, not then or ever.

Save as a little child I was never strong. Grief for my mother had
brought me low in my growing years; now persecution and threats
brought me lower still. Shelton and Clere had been told to bring down
my proud spirit if they killed me for it; it looked as though they meant
to carry out those orders.

I had been used, at my mother's wish, to eat my food pleasantly
served in pleasant company. Now I must eat at the common board—no
high table for me! I must manage with coarse food and coarser company. Never was I allowed to eat in the privacy of my own room;
were I sick abed I must drag myself downstairs or go without food.
I preferred the latter. It did not help to build up my strength.

Whether their kindness to me in the matter of letters was suspected,
I know not; but within a little, my two maids were taken from me.
But God does, indeed, remember the broken-hearted; to this household
of enemies He sent a friend—lady Bryan. She had governed my infant
years and was now come to govern the nursery of my father's bastard.
Of Margaret Bryan I must speak a few words. It had been told me
that she was of kin to Anne Bullen—her aunt, they said. She had been
my own dear lady-mistress—but then the name of Anne Bullen was
unknown. Now she performed those loving duties for Anne Bullen's
child in this household of Anne Bullen's devising. I could not, in that
first moment, look at her nor speak with her.

That first night she came by stealth into my bedchamber, and
whispered gently in my ear. 'I am not of her kin. I am my husband's
second wife—it was his first was aunt to Anne Bullen. He is of kin
through marriage, only; I, not at all. My lady Mary, you may trust
me!'

'When I was a child,' I said, 'I loved you and trusted you; and so it
shall be now. To this unhappy place you bring comfort and friendship.
I trust you in all things.'

And love and comfort she brought. Through her I had news of the
court that otherwise I had never known. Her son, Sir Francis, was
much-loved of my father—a comely young man that could tune a lute,

and turn a line of poetry. He was a soldier and well-versed in diplomacy; he served my father openly as ambassador to France—and on secret missions, too. His finger was in every pie. 'The King favours him; and the concubine casts a favouring eye—she likes a handsome man,' lady Bryan said, 'no more than I has he love for Anne Bullen. He likes neither her nor her behaviour!'

Between Sir Francis and his mother the tie was strong; he would whisper to her any news that concerned my mother or me, and so I had news I could trust. Bryan was trusted by those that governed the house—for Anne Bullen, herself, had set her there; but to me she never swerved in kindness and loyalty. She would manage to smuggle my letters from the house, and, in secret, would deliver those writ to me. Through her I would receive the most precious of gifts—a letter from my mother written in her own hand. I would hear also from my lady Salisbury or from Chapuys. She was careful not to show herself my friend; she would scold at me for some disrespect shown to her little one; but when the household slept, she would come into my bedchamber with words of good cheer. Let me be patient and all would come well; so she promised, sweet Margaret. But for her I had died of a melancholy.

My mother was a very sick woman. She could not see food without nausea nor eat without vomiting. Chapuys thought she was being poisoned—and he was not the only one! If it were truly so, my father would have no knowledge of the matter; but his harlot it would please very well. My mother, herself, feared poison, and was thereby still further weakened. To add to her pains she was twisted with swellings in the joints so that she could not, in any comfort, sit nor stand nor lie long in her bed. There needed no poison to put an end to her. Bugden was killing her by inches. Very humbly she wrote to my father begging some other house; and he, no doubt, urged by his harlot, chose Somersham in Ely. If Bugden was slowly making an end of her, Somersham could be relied on to do it more quickly. It lay not so much on marsh as in water; a desolate spot from which rose evil smells of stagnant water and undrained marsh.

She refused to go.

'Madam the Queen holds fast to her refusal,' Bryan whispered to me in the dark of my bedchamber. 'My son writes me the whole story. Lord Suffolk went with the King's command. She locked herself in her closet and would not speak with him save through a hole in the wall.

He dare not break in to take her by force, for the countryfolk stood without—pitchfork, spade and scythe to the rescue. Besides, he did not relish his orders—he told the King so!'

My mother had her way—the country-folk saw to it! She went not to Somersham but to Kimbolton, some few miles away. As she lay within the litter, being too weak to sit upright, men, women and children crowded about her kissing her hands and blessing her. For poor as she was, she had looked to the needy sharing more than she should of the food good folk had sent her—for her own stores were scant and her purse empty.

Kimbolton was a little better than Bugden, for it stands somewhat higher; but not much better. And carrying her there in the depths of the winter was not like to do her much good. The Bullen woman saw to it that I had news of her when it was bad . . . and it was always bad.

Chapter Seventeen

The New Year of 'thirty-four came in and I was all-but eighteen. Had things been otherwise between my father and mother I should have been at the court; I should have been dancing, taking my part in masques and merrymaking. I should have been betrothed; married perhaps. But marriage hung fire for me—I had lost value in the marriage-market; and moreover my father was cautious lest a husband make trouble in respect of my rights.

At Hatfield there was merrymaking enough; the lord of Misrule presided over the morris-dancers, the music and the feasting. I would sit alone in my chamber, the tears stealing down my cheeks. To weep was natural enough in the circumstances. If I must not speak how else to relieve my soul? Tears took the place of words; it is a habit that has grown upon me. But I was not often let to weep alone; I would be commanded below and there I must sit, laughter all about me and bitterness in my heart.

And yet, in the midst of my abandonment—a little hope. My father was coming to Hatfield to see Anne Bullen's child. Surely he would see me, too—his other child whom once he had loved. I would kneel to him, pray his kindness for my mother and me, win his kindness. I prayed beseeching God in the matter; I did not think I could fail.

In the second week of January my father came; and he came alone. The concubine he had left some twenty miles away and I thanked God for it. I was sure now he would see me; I was sure.

He would not see me.

'Anne Bullen has forbidden it!' Margaret Bryan said. 'She fears that when he sees you so good, so gentle and so pretty, his heart will soften. And though he cares for her no longer, still he hopes for a son. When she is crossed she rails like a madwoman. He obeys her not through love but to be rid of her and her tongue.'

That he, proud King, should obey his concubine, was added pain. Truly she was a witch!

He stayed but one day at Hatfield, going straight to the babe with whom he played for some time. Thereafter he questioned the women Shelton and Clere, listening to their tales of my wicked obstinacy to the King's will. I did not see my father; but I saw one I had done better not seeing. Cromwell. Anne Bullen had sent him posting after my father lest he attempt to see my face.

Cromwell, without so much as by your leave, thrust himself into my private chamber. He barely saluted me but pushing his formidable face close to my own said, 'Madam, if you do not freely and willingly renounce the title of *Princess*—to which you have no right—the lord King will humble you to the dust. He will, he bids me tell you, break your pride if he must break your neck with it!'

'Was it your master that sent this message; or, perhaps your mistress?'

'You had best not bandy words,' he said. 'I speak for your good.'

I sat there obstinate and dumb. He stood over me, the big, powerful man, and there was no pity in him. He stood for a while, pressing upon me with all the weight of his will. But my will is strong, also, and since I sat there and uttered no word; he turned upon his heel and went.

I sat there while all the things I had planned to say to my father turned useless in my head—words that implored his love, his forgiveness, while I, humbly kneeling, swore obedience in everything—save one thing only. I could not admit his marriage to my mother, no marriage; could not admit myself a bastard. I thought, maybe, he would remember that once he had loved us both. I prayed through the long hours that he would send for me; that he would not leave me utterly abandoned in this house of my enemies.

He did not come.

I heard the bustle of departure. Like a mad thing I flew from my room. I ran upon the terrace where, if he would not look upon me, I might at least look upon him. He no longer loved me, he was cruel; but he was still my father. Surely some natural tie remained.

I knelt upon the stone of the terrace; through my gown the frosted ground bit like steel; across my head and shoulders the wind whipped —I had not stayed for a cloak. The outriders came forth; out came the company, and at last—my father.

I bent my whole will upon him, my Tudor will. I saw someone— whoever it was may God bless him—touch my father upon the arm. He raised his face. What expression it wore I could not see; but I saw him raise a hand to his bonnet, the feathered bonnet he affected. All faces swung towards me; each man's hand went to his bonnet . . . and they rode away and I was left alone.

The sad year moved on. News of my mother was forever bad. I

feared for her and I feared for myself; Cromwell's words had left their mark. Now my life was not only one of insult and misery, but of poverty, too. If before I had felt the pinch of having to manage, I now knew the crueller pinch of going without. I lacked money, I lacked clothes; I could buy no books and—last piece of malice—virginals and lute were taken from me. I was to have no comfort, no alleviation. Mewed within the house and spied upon, I was the most unhappy lady in Christendom.

I was to be unhappier still; soon I must fear not for my mother and myself alone; I must fear for all those that loved my church. For once more the Pope spoke against the union with Anne Bullen. It hardened my father still further. He hoped still for a son and she was pregnant —she said. He knew well how the people hated her, holding my mother to be the true Queen. Now an obedient Parliament bound the whole country with two new laws. The first invested the crown in the heirs of Anne Bullen. The second declared the King supreme head of the English church. Convocation had commanded the clergy alone; Parliament commanded every man and woman in the country. It was the law; and like every other law, disobedience carried its penalty.

Two laws; and so interwoven that acceptance of my bastardy and the King's supremacy were one.

And now the King's officers rode the countryside to punish any man that offended against the new laws. To deny my father absolute and supreme head of the church in England was treason—and no more nonsense about *as far as the law of God allows*; no more nonsense about conscience—that saving clause for which Fisher had striven and suffered that men might save their souls. To address me by my rightful title was treason. And as treason both should be punished; a traitor's death, the slow strangulation, the tearing out of bowels from the living body.

Peer and peasant, archbishop and humblest priest, judge, sheriff, magistrate, every citizen—all must swear to accept in perfect obedience the new law. To make good a marriage of which already he tired, my father must pull down the church of Rome. Or, maybe, the converse is truer. To pull down Rome—and nothing less would satisfy him now —he must keep Anne Bullen. For let him repudiate her—and he acknowledged the ruling of the Pope.

All through sweet springtime, through summer, autumn and winter the officers went about their business forcing people to take the oath; and everywhere folk accepted it because they must, save for those few brave men that refused and went to their death.

Early in spring a terrible thing happened; it sickens me even now, as I write. They took a poor crazy woman nun in Kent that would not swear the oath; Cromwell, himself, went down to question her and thought it no sin to mislead her with sly words. He might have spared himself the trouble; so simple she was, she did not know what it was all about. But for all that they took her and tortured her and thereafter dragged her to Tyburn.

Elizabeth Barton, the first woman in England to suffer the full rigours of a traitor's death—and she astray in her wits. To my father fell the distinction of beheading the first woman, and of condemning the first woman to a traitor's death. There were some, countryfolk as simple as herself, that followed her, believing her to be God's holy fool; and many of these died that same cruel death.

The hanging of Elizabeth Barton sickened me because she was simple; and because there was no mercy shown. If I might choose the thing to be remembered for I should choose mercy. Justice I would—if I might —leave to God. But mercy we all can show; it is an attribute of God.

Nor did the matter end there. For, on her account, Fisher was accused of high treason. He considered her guiltless because of her simplicity—and that was treason. He was sentenced once more to imprisonment; but there was no fault in him—even my father must see it. So, for this, time he contented himself by confiscating all the bishop's goods and driving him penniless from his see. Would to God the good bishop had left the country like many another priest.

In April he was once more arrested. Against both new laws he had turned his face. To the oath of supremacy he refused to swear—the cutting-out of the soul-saving clause had made it impossible; nor could he swear to the oath of succession. Let the King choose whomsoever he would to be his heir, but Fisher would never admit the King's first marriage unlawful or the Princess Mary a bastard. So old and very poor and staunch in his faith, to the Tower he went.

That same April, More, good Sir Thomas, chancellor, refused the oath of supremacy; he was tried, judged guilty of treason and to the Tower he went also.

'More and Fisher are in the Tower!' Shelton said with a wicked glance at me, and, as though they were felons, refused them their titles. 'And there they shall stay until they declare the King's pleasure—or until they come to their death. And I pray, for Fisher, especially a cruel end, for he'll not admit a bastard to be a bastard!'

'Oh Bryan, Bryan!' I whispered in the darkness when she came to comfort me that night. 'Two good men; men worthy for their goodness to be loved. And both must die because of their truth to God. For the good bishop—because he'll not admit me a bastard I feel the weight of guilt here!' And I laid a hand upon my heart.

'Hush,' she said, 'hush. There's no guilt in you!'

'And Sir Thomas. How many true men dwell in high places that we can spare one? And how shall England fare lacking him? I used to see him about the court, walking, my father's arm about his shoulder; and many a merry jest he passed with me—the pleasant gentleman. I cannot rest for thinking of his wife and children; Margaret is my own age, or maybe a little younger. Like me she is a scholar—but a better one. Some of the children are very young; what shall they do lacking a father?'

'They have a Father in heaven. . . .'

'Little ones need a father on earth also; and older ones, older ones, too!'

Hearing of true men come to their death and of others rotting still in prison, added further to my melancholy; and the Bullen women perceiving it, forever tormented me.

'Never think to escape us!' Shelton would taunt me. 'Certain it is you'll not escape through marriage. For who would marry you, bastard that you are? No marriage for you, unless my niece the Queen, of her goodness find some varlet that, being paid, will lower himself to mix his blood with yours.'

'Why talk of marriage?' Clere would laugh that neighing laugh of hers. 'She'll not last so long! She'll go the same way as her friends—to the block or the fire.'

And all the time both women persecuted me with cruel tongues, watched me with cruel eyes. They forever goaded me to answer back that they might make evil report of me to my father; but I remembered the warnings given by those that cared for me—my mother, lady Salisbury and Margaret Bryan, so that I clenched my teeth upon my tongue and answered nothing.

I was poor, I was shabby; I could not digest food eaten at the common table. The migraines were constant and laid me low; my monthly periods were painful and irregular. I was mocked at, despised and spied upon. Save for Margaret Bryan there was neither help nor kindness.

Dear, good Chapuys worked hard for my better comfort. My father roughly bade him hold his tongue. 'My daughter is well enough; I shall deal with her as I see fit!' All this Shelton repeated to me, Clere standing by.

'Madam the Queen says that when the King crosses the sea—and he's soon for France—she will make an end of you. Oh it will be very quiet—a little poison or a pillow perhaps!'

'She'll not dare! I am still my father's daughter!'

'He'll not miss you! Madam the Queen says die you shall, though she burn alive for it afterwards!'

'It is no more than you deserve!' Clere joined in. 'No-one can say that my niece is not tender-hearted. When her little dog died she wept fit to break her heart.'

She will make an end of you . . . very quiet . . . a little poison or a pillow . . .

What way then? I slept little at nights, waking in terror for a pillow to come down upon my face, a hand at my throat.

They had taken away my food-taster. Poison then. Nothing now between me and death.

'It is their malice to frighten you!' Bryan whispered in the dark of the night. 'Have no fear for all their threats. I sent to Monsieur Chapuys; he wrote at once to the Emperor and the Emperor has replied. He will demand the death of that person whoever it may be—man or woman, high or low that shall offer you injury. Monsieur Chapuys has seen to it that his master's words are known to the Queen and all that serve her. Man or *woman* . . . *high* or low. That should give her pause; for all her wicked talk she'll not risk her skin!'

But for all Bryan's comfort I was still afraid; for still they kept my food-taster from me. And still I was always on the edge of nausea. I think that already they had begun their murderous work and that the Emperor's threats halted them. Should I now die beneath their care my father would not hold them innocent and not the concubine herself could save them.

But if they held back from poison, still the insults continued; insult after insult; they stopped at nothing short of striking me. I remember the day when they laid upon me, the bitterest, the most degrading insult of all.

It was late spring; a golden day and the sun was high and a little breeze blowing. Hatfield was to be cleansed and the infant to be taken to her mother at Greenwich. All stood ready—litters, horses, wagons; every member of the household in his place; all save me. What madness took me I cannot say. I think it was the culmination of all my miseries, all the insults and shabbiness of hy life. I saw the fine coach where already the infant sat upon Bryan's lap; I saw the miserable litter assigned to me.

Anger swept over me. I stood rigid in the doorway. I refused to move. Not for all the world would I budge. If I did not choose to go, no-one could make me . . . so I thought. I was indeed a fool! I had laid myself open to the last, the unspeakable degradation. Four low fellows laid hands upon me; upon Mary Tudor, Princess of the royal houses of England and Spain. They carried me bodily to the waiting litter. I lay stiff upon their hands like the effigies they place upon royal biers. I lay like the dead, save that the dead feel no shame. They thrust me into the litter amid coarse laughter . . . and I wished that I were truly dead.

But the litter took its way by budding hedge and ploughed field . . . and I sat there and, for all my wishing, did not die.

Chapter Eighteen

Things were no better save in one thing. Though my food-taster had not been restored, I lost, little by little, my fear of being poisoned. Lest the Emperor's threat be not sufficient, Chapuys, himself, informed Shelton that, should I die beneath her care, her own death should pay for it. She pretended to be amused, taunting me in the matter. 'Your great little Emperor lifts no finger to help that mother of yours; why do you suppose he shall help you?'

But for all that she was not amused. Now when I lay sick abed my meals were carried to me and she, herself, stood in my presence tasting before I ate and trembled till I was well again.

Anne Bullen, her spite increased that I had not died, despatched her uncle Norfolk with threat of still harsher treatment. I was sent for and made to stand while those three sitting, Norfolk said, 'Madam the Queen desires to know why the girl has not been beaten for the accursed bastard she is? The Queen commanded it; why have you not obeyed? My girl—' and he turned to me, 'If you do not mend your ways, your father will have your head. This I am to say in your presence that you may understand the matter.'

Suddenly, surprising us all, Clere cried out, 'It is not right! Whatever the girl may be—even though but the bastard of some poor gentleman —she deserves respect, aye and kindness, too! She is a good girl!'

I trembled and all-but fell with the shock of it.

'Hold your tongue!' Shelton commanded when, taken aback, she could find her own. 'Quiet she may seem but she's sly and deep as the sea!' She turned about to me. 'Wait, my girl, my *good* girl! Your father will send his commissioners to you—to you yourself! Then your pride will tumble! For you shall swear the oaths—both of them. Yes, you shall swear to your base birth and your mother's incest. If not—' her hand made a cutting movement at her neck.

Norfolk said nothing. He made me a curt salute; but I thought his face wore a look of distaste . . . and the distaste was not for me.

Now I lived once more in dread. It was worse than the fear of death;

for to swear the oath could mean death to the soul. I could not sleep, I could not eat. Write to my father I could not; they had taken away pen, ink and paper. Comfort myself, a little, with music, I could not, neither; they had taken away my instruments.

What must I do if my father send?

Conscience must be my guide; but when one is young and sick and alone, fear may drown the voice of one's soul.

The days moved on and it was June. And now nightmare became reality. Norfolk came to demand that I swear the double oath.

'I cannot do it, my lord!' Faint voice echoed the faint heart within me. 'One act stains my mother's honour and my own birth; and the other is heresy to damn my soul!'

That last touched him. He supported the King's supremacy over the church from policy and not from faith. He said, 'Madam, I do beseech you, sign. If not, the King will make an end of you. So he has sworn; and Parliament cannot save you, for to refuse the oaths is treason!'

I put out a hand to steady myself. Death to the soul is worse than death to the body. But we know not the soul as we know our body. It is always with us; we wash it, feed it, touch it, feel its pains. It is our very self. To the young, violent death is terrifying.

I took in my breath. 'My lord, I cannot do it.'

He shook his head at that and called for Shelton; pushing me before her she jostled me back to my chamber. Four men stood on guard. And while I stared wondering what this could mean, she thrust me within and I heard the key turn in the lock. Within all was darkness—windows bolted and barred, black stuff nailed to cover the glass.

I sat alone in my prison and knew not whether it was night or day; nor how many days had passed. I tried to reckon by guessing at the time between meals; but Shelton was not regular in coming. Every time she brought me the coarse food, she stood over me with insult; and, between times, her voice came shouting through the door. *You shall lose your head for this! Were I your father you had lost it long ago! It will make a fine football to be kicked this way and that!* Or changing her tune. *Beheading is too good for you! You should be hanged, drawn and quartered for the traitor you are!*

I was sick, I was frightened; I sat there in the darkness while outside summer was bright—and I would not yield. When at last I was loosed from my chamber, I must be led by the hand until my eyes should use themselves again to the light.

Norfolk motioned Shelton away. 'Lady Mary,' he said when we were alone, 'I grieve with all my heart that you will not sign. For, believe me, whether you sign or not, you cannot hold back the tide. I have stood your friend with my niece. If you will sign, and if you will acknowledge her *Queen*, she will reconcile you with your father; and you shall stand in greater honour than before!'

'My lord, I thank you for your gentleness; but I know of no Queen in England but my mother.'

'Then I am to say that proud Spanish blood of yours lies upon your own head!'

He had spoken in a clear voice; now he came near and whispered, 'Yet I will do for you any good thing I may. And Cromwell, though he be harsh, is in his heart your friend; we pity you, both of us!'

'I thank you, my lord, with all my heart. I will never forget your goodwill towards me.'

When he was gone I gave myself to despair. Things looked black indeed when Anne Bullen's uncle pitied me; when Cromwell, heart of stone, pitied me. If they would do aught they must hasten; for myself I could see no future but the block.

But God remembers the broken in heart. I had a visitor—and a more welcome, never stepped. It was Dr. Fetherstone, dear tutor of my happier times. He was to be allowed to talk to me on one condition—Shelton must be present. She stood there, all smiles; I think she hoped he would persuade me.

Greeting him, I saw concern upon his kindly face; he would have kissed my hand but I put my arms about him and kissed him upon both cheeks; and even as I embraced him I knew how to use my God-sent chance.

'Sir,' I said, 'I am right glad to see you and I would you might stay awhile. I fear I have forgot my Latin. I can scarce put two words together!'

He was a man quick of wit. 'Then speak with me in Latin; let me hear for myself.'

'I am in danger of my life,' I told him in the Latin tongue. 'If I do not swear the oaths the King will have my head—he has sworn it. What must I do? Ask my friend'—and I dare not say *Chapuys* lest she put two-and-two together—'to advise me.'

He perfectly understood; he shook a deprecating head. 'Madam, it is poor Latin and makes poor hearing. Now let us practise it while we may!'

Shelton would have interrupted. She feared—and rightly—this speech in a foreign tongue; but smiling at her, very friendly, he went serenely on—in Latin. 'Your friend works for you, both with your father and with the Emperor. I have brought you a letter; I shall pass it when I can.' And now he spoke in English. 'Madam, since your Latin is no longer good, I will translate it in the vulgar tongue. Your friends advise you—Monsieur de Chapuys, himself, advises you—when the King commands, you must obey!'

I stared at him unbelieving; over my head Shelton sent him a satisfied smile.

'Well, Madam,' he told me, 'look well to your Latin and listen to your friends. And so Farewell!'

He bent the knee, stumbling a little, as an old man may, and, as I went to raise him, he slid a paper beneath the hem of my gown. He and Shelton went out together.

I drew the bolt and opened the paper. The hand was disguised but still by the great C I knew it for that of Chapuys. He said I must hold out as long as I could; but I must not put my life in danger. Should my father send again, with threats, I must sign. Folded within was a letter for me to copy in my own hand. It said that I, Mary Tudor, signed by force; and that never by deed or word, would I willingly agree to anything that should rob me of my rights. His own writings, I must for the love of God, destroy; my own I must put in some secret place to witness for me in time of need.

The Lutheran whispers were more than mere whispers; they had hardened into solid fact. Now there were three forms of worship in our country. The true Catholic church that owed no obedience except to Rome; the new Protestant faith; and in the middle my father's church of England—the only safe path for a man to tread. But no true Catholic could ever tread it, nor no true man of the new worship. Protestants were willing enough to take my father as supreme head of the church in England—they had turned utterly against Rome; but they were riddled with heresies, utterly denying the blessed miracle of Bread and Wine made very flesh and blood. And for this they must suffer death.

So on the one hand stood true Catholics, traitors in my father's reckoning since they would not acknowledge the King supreme head of the church, Protestants on the other, steeped with their heresies. Make but a step to right or left from my father's middle way and it was death. For Catholics, the traitor's rope, for Protestants the heretic's fire. In heretic countries Catholics must suffer, in Catholic countries, heretics. It was left to my father to punish—for the first time in our country or indeed in any country in Christendom—heretic and true believer alike. It was as simple and dreadful as that.

So the long summer passed. My father continued stubborn to punish all that disobeyed him, More and Fisher languished in the Tower. The bishop was sixty-five now, Sir Thomas ten years younger —and both aged beyond their years, made feeble by their cruel prison.

Would they ever see daylight again? They were but harbingers of suffering to come—of prisons overflowing, of friars thrust forth from their houses to beg their bread, of men and women put to the torture, to die a traitor's hateful death; good people that asked nothing but to serve God.

When would my father strike at me?

For me, myself, the summer was long, sad and full of fear. All this time my mother continued sick; Chapuys had set out to visit her but was prevented; my father forbade it. I grieved for her most bitter disappointment. She must have so longed for the sight of this true friend, longed even more for news of me.

In September the Pope died and Pope Paul, harsh and imperious, sat in his place. My father cared as little for him as he had done for Pope Clement. Still he would be master in his own house. *Junker Heinz would be Pope and King in one*, the German Luther said.

'Even a heretic may speak the truth!' And my father roared with laughter.

And now it was October. My mother's health grew steadily worse. I awoke every morning sick with fear; she would die—and I not see her ever again.

In the fine autumn weather we set out to carry the infant Elizabeth to Richmond where the concubine was in residence. I had no intention of having another unseemly scuffle over precedence, nor had I any mind for Londoners to see me walking like a waiting-maid behind Anne Bullen's child.

The Comptroller had promised that I might go on horse-back if I drew my hood—I must not be recognised. I was glad to be riding in the crisp autumn air; gladder still because a litter must go slow, but a mare as fast as you please. And so it was that, riding ahead with the servants, I reached Greenwich a full hour before the others. And there I found someone I had not seen all these weary months—Monsieur Chapuys waiting to see me pass.

He knew me for all the concealing hood; off came his bonnet and he stood bareheaded, telling me without word—for he had been forbidden speech with me—that he was forever my friend. Having no mind to be seen upon the river in a place unfit for the King's daughter I took my proper seat, and the wind blowing shifted the hood; so there I sat plain for all to see. And now, the word passing, there came a crowd down to the river to bid me Godspeed. Presently all came aboard; Shelton dared not risk a brawl; so there I sat amid the cheers in my rightful place; and there Monsieur Chapuys stood, bareheaded, never taking his eyes from me and waving his bonnet until the bend of the river hid us one from the other.

He wrote of this meeting to his master. It was a great joy, he said, to see such excellent beauty, accompanied by so brave a bearing; it all the more increased his pity to see me thus ill-treated. Gossip goes to and fro among the ambassadors at any court and Sir Francis retailed it to my drear Bryan, that it might pleasure me. To know that sorrow had not yet marked me was comfort, indeed. But—excellent beauty, brave bearing! I put it down to Chapuys' kindness for me. Pretty, I think I was, but a beauty—never; nor was I ever brave. But still I treasured his words; long and long indeed since any had set a value on me.

At Richmond I kept out of Anne Bullen's way and she did not send for me. She was out of favour and left much to herself, my father's fancy having turned elsewhere. He was even now disporting himself at The More with his new mistress leaving Anne Bullen to sulk, alone.

'A very pretty young lady,' Bryan told me, 'and prettier still in the jewels Monsieur Chapuys has sent her!' I must have shown my surprise for she added, 'Oh he has paid her well to speak for you!'

'I had rather a friend spoke for love of me.'

'It could not help so much as her pretty face. Monsieur the Ambassador is no fool!'

And help me she did, as I was soon to know.

From Richmond I, together with the infant and her train, was summoned to The More. Anne Bullen accompanied us—uninvited. I kept my distance from the litter where she sat sullen. She could not but note that bonnets swept the ground as I rode by and people cheered, but there was no movement while in silence her litter passed by; she might as well not have been there.

At The More roads and fences had been repaired, the gardens set in order, the house fresh-painted and furnished to the King's taste—a house busy with the coming and going of folk and gay with music. But for all that I must remember that this house had been my mother's first step to martyrdom.

I had not seen my father since he had saluted me as I knelt upon the terrace at Hatfield in the cold of a winter morning. Now he greeted me with kindness; and this kindness I found reflected in the manner of the court. His new mistress I looked for to thank, but she was not there; my father had no mind to expose her to Anne Bullen's spite. Nor did I see her ever in my life but—whether she was paid for it or no—I thank her for her kindness. Her name I never knew—she did not last long.

But Jane Seymour I did see and right glad I was, for she had been among my mother's ladies and I had liked her for her quiet and gentle ways; and she, for my mother's sake, had a kindness for me. For Anne Bullen that she now served, she had none; the concubine was a harsh mistress, arrogant and suspicious—that last, perhaps, not without cause.

Mistress Seymour was in her mid-twenties; she was pale—skin, eyes and hair; she was elegant and her manners were exquisite. Never such a contrast to Anne Bullen. At this moment my father had no eye for her, his fancy being otherwise engaged. All the time I was at The More she spoke little to me; but that little was both courteous and kind. Indeed, she spoke little to anyone, being careful in her words; over-careful some said, secretive and sly; but I never found her ought but honest. She was the first to pay her respects to me, the others following, ladies and gentlemen, to kiss my hand. Though neither she nor any other dared bend the knee nor address me as *Princess*; some pale shadow of my former position being a little restored, I took hope for the future.

Anne Bullen sat in her closet and bit upon her finger-nails. My father cared not whether she came or went but he sent often for the little Elizabeth. She was just above a year old; a quick and merry child, with every whit of her mother's nature—high rages and overbearing will. But what we cannot tolerate in a grown person we often find charming in a little one; my father was charmed with her—as once with me. He would toss her into the air while she crowed and gurgled; he delighted in showing off her little tricks—as once with me. But sometimes I saw his eyes gloomy upon her—this small, bright creature that was not a son.

Of this child I have, so far, scarce spoken. *The little bastard* Chapuys called her—as many another did beneath their breath; and, as indeed she was. In that moment I heard her first cry—cry of an infant new-born into life, like no other cry in the world—the heart had melted within me; and at once hardened again. For this babe I had been put from my place, my birth sullied, myself humiliated. This creature must have precedence over me—at all times and everywhere; to her I must play waiting-woman, carrying her train. For her they prayed in all our churches; for my mother and me, never—unless in the silence of the heart. For her I had been persecuted to admit myself bastard and heretic—and, no doubt, would be again. For her I had stood in danger of my life—and still did stand. How could I help but compare our states? How help hating her with all my heart?

I have always loved children; but this child I could not love. I never saw that infant face but I saw her mother. She had Anne Bullen's eyes black and brilliant, she had that same sallow skin. But her hair, black at birth which had made the likeness uncanny, had rubbed off; now it showed reddish-gold. Tudor gold. Or was it? Was she, indeed, my father's child? There were many to question it. During those early months of her life I would not touch her, save I must; for whoever had fathered her, she was all her mother's child, the concubine's child, the witch's child, and I could not do it.

On my father's new-found kindness I dared not count. There remained between us, for this little while unspoken, the matter of the oaths—oaths which he must demand, and I refuse. And, besides, who knew when the witch might not attack again? She had sworn to bring me to my grave. Though he had little love left for her, it was easy enough to prick him in his pride, to rouse his anger. His anger against me slept at present but not too soundly. So I walked on tip-toe and within me a pale bud of hope began to stir.

Once more back at Hatfield, I found his kindness to continue. He had given orders that some few serving-maids and waiting-ladies of my own choice were to be restored; also I might walk at will within the gardens. More freedom meant more news; and soon I heard—and not from Bryan alone—that which Shelton would fain have kept from me. Norfolk's long anger against his niece had broken into open quarrel; he was now her bitter enemy—and so was likely to remain. My bud of hope began to unfold.

Shelton blamed me for this break and blamed me bitterly. She wrote to my father lying tales of me. With my wheyface, my tears and my lies I had turned Norfolk's heart from the Queen; with traitorous promise of future favour I had dishonourably won him. If I could steal Norfolk's loyalty from his niece, what loyalty might I not steal from my father?

When my father came again to Hatfield to visit my sister, he would not see me nor send any greeting. So all was back where it had been before.

Chapter Nineteen

The new year of 'thirty-five came in and I was a month from my nineteenth birthday. My life was wearing away, and to the wasting there seemed no end . . . years of sorrow are long years, especially to the young. At Hatfield there were the usual rejoicings but in these I took no part nor did any constrain me. For I was ill; I was very ill and confined to my bed. I seemed to be slipping from life, I had no strength in my body. My monthly periods, often irregular, had stopped altogether; migraine attacked me with the old weapons, I vomited continually, pain speared eyeball to eyeball. Sometimes I must bite into my pillow lest, in spite of myself, pain have its way with me, and I cry aloud.

Shelton was troubled; she had not forgotten Chapuys' warning. She wrote to my father and he sent his own physician, Dr. Buttes. My mother that had asked nothing for herself, now asked that she might be allowed to send her own physician; and to this my father agreed—upon one condition. I must ask no question concerning my mother; and I must speak no tongue but English. Shelton had learned her lesson!

Both physicians were much concerned at my condition.

'The lady Mary has undergone a quite needless strain!' Dr. Buttes said, his eye accusing Shelton; and he so far forgot himself to add, 'She would be better with her mother!'

My heart leaped. Could I be with her—were it but to die—how welcome then, would death be!

My mother, frightened at her physician's account of me, wrote to Chapuys begging him to implore my father to let me come to her. Years after, Chapuys, himself, sent me her letter and I count it among my greatest treasures. It shows so perfectly her love for me that, even now, all used to sorrow as I am, tears fall to stain the paper.

She desires him to ask my father, of his charity . . .

. . . to send his daughter and mine where I am; because treating her with my own hands and by the advice of other physicians and my

143

own, if it please God to take her from this world, my heart will rest satisfied; otherwise in great pain. You shall say to His Highness, that there is no need of any other person but myself to nurse her; that I will put her into my own bed where I sleep and will watch her when needful. ...

To this piteous letter—refusal.

'He fears lest Madam your mother smuggle you out of the country,' Margaret Bryan said. 'It is all the talk!'

'Would to God it were possible! Let me stay here much longer and I shall die.' And that was no idle threat so sick I was!

My mother wrote to Cromwell—and that shows the measure of her distress; he had never been her friend nor yet pretended to be. Moreover, should I die, how easier his own life then! Yet he—himself harassed by my father and the concubine—did his best. I see that now, though then, hating and fearing the man, I did not believe that from him any good could come. But for all that, he wrung from my father a first step towards permission. I might go to a house near my mother; but we must make no attempt to see each other.

For this scant kindness she wrote to Cromwell her heart's deep thanks; and I was content also. For if we might not live together in one house she and I, this would take me from the house of my enemies. And if we might not meet, it was comfort to each to know the other near. As to our meeting, she reassured him. Even had she not promised, it was impossible for her to visit me. Though I should be but a mile away she had no strength to walk—and she had no carriage.

No carriage for the Queen of England!

She implored him to soften my father's heart still further that we might not be parted.

... the comfort she would have with me would be half her cure. My request was so reasonable and touched so greatly the honour of the King I did not think it could be denied me. Do not forbear I beseech you and do what you can. ...

As for my father's fear that she would smuggle me out of the country,

... I offer my person as security that, if such a thing be attempted he may do justice upon me as the most treacherous woman ever was born. ...

To offer herself security for me! It was the measure of her love. She knew that, either through sickness or from Anne Bullen's spite,

144

Chapuys feared for my life. She knew that my father would send again and again demanding obedience in the matter of the oaths. She feared for my body; still more for my soul. Could I have fled the country she knowing, I think she would have shut her eyes and paid the price. And that price was not her life; she must have known her time was short. To break her word; there lay her punishment. So great her integrity that, breaking her word must break her spirit as no cruelty had ever done. She could not then endure to live with herself even the short time she had left. I am forever thankful she was not called upon to make the choice.

The plan to live near her was abruptly broken. Anne Bullen—her spies everywhere—had got wind of it and commanded us all to Greenwich; the entire Hatfield household. I had no choice but to obey and at Greenwich I celebrated my nineteenth birthday—if celebration be the right word for so unhappy a life. The concubine looked haggard and ill; I thought maybe she was pregnant.

'Not a bit of it!' Bryan said. 'She'd give both those black eyes of hers to be with child. She is in great fear lest she does not conceive again. If she does not give the King a son it will be the end of her and she knows it. For the King wearies of her and the people hate her—it is you they love; and she knows that, too. She is in such fear she would be glad of friendship with you now.'

'From such a friend God preserve me!' I said. 'Does she expect me to forget my mother? And for myself—she has ill-treated and humiliated me; she has forever egged on my father to do the same. Does the leopard change his spots? I will not, nor I cannot, trust her!'

At Greenwich my sickness increased; I cannot suffer in the spirit but I must suffer in the body, also. When the Hatfield household left and Anne Bullen was gone with her retinue to Westminster, I could not be moved but must be left behind. And now tongues wagging more free, I found my suspicions confirmed about many things.

That there was a discontent and anxiety among the people I had known; but it had not hardened, as yet, into anger or fear. Discontent was widespread because of the burden of ever-increasing taxes; anxiety because when you have been bred to obey the voice of the Pope as the Voice of God, suddenly to cast him off is a shock and a heresy. And for this new and frightening heresy, good men lay in prison, and a few already had come to their death; there had not, as yet, been any burnings. In this country no heretic had died at the stake for above one hundred and fifty years. But burning was a common enough practice in Europe. My father found it an excellent way of disposing of his enemies. Between death by the rope or death in the fire he made his careful distinction. He was a man of conscience.

Did I say there was as yet no anger? I was wrong. Anger there was, a direct, personal and bitter anger against Anne Bullen. *The great whore* they called her, and *the common stew harlot*, that lay in the King's bed while his true wife lay in prison. A show of kindness from me would sweeten her position. It was plain enough, the reason for Anne Bullen's offer of friendship.

Did she suppose, for one moment, I could ever take her hand in mine, or ever give her countenance? These days I had no desire but to be well again; to be where God's religion was no crime. I wanted to be safe and free; free from the eternal spying, eternal fear.

Chapuys came to see me; he found me looking so ill he feared I might die. Within a few days he came again with a plan for my escape. It was simple enough. At night I was to creep down to the river where a waiting boat should take me to Gravesend; there la Renterie, good captain from the Netherlands, would be waiting to take me across the sea and there I should find welcome from my cousin. Would I go?

Would I go?

I dreamed of it throughout the April days. Such a chance could never come again. Everyone here wished me well; even Anne Bullen's spies did not look too close; I was too weak, it seemed, to take more than a few steps across the garden. But those few steps were all I needed, for the garden ran down to the river; and take them I would if I had to crawl on hands and knees. I would die, if need be, in the attempt.

My few possessions made ready, I waited for the word; in growing distress, waited. The precious days of my freedom were passing . . . passing. Chapuys had said we must await the Emperor's final word; that word had not come.

'Affairs in Europe are uneasy for my master—and the King of England is the cause. Your father intrigues with France—well, that is nothing new! But now he intrigues with Denmark and with the Lutheran princes. He raises enemies against the Emperor everywhere —Catholics and heretics alike. Your rescue could cause an explosion to blow Europe sky-high!'

'Then I must pray for patience—but patience comes hard. I live only in hope of escape. The moment you send, I will come; you need tell me nothing of the plan beforehand—I trust you utterly. I would go to sea in a sieve should you ask it. I have a sleeping-draught all ready for my women, it is safer so—for them and for me; I can manage very well by myself, I am small and light on my feet, I can steal by

the guards; the lighting is poor at nights—my father makes his economies. I know my way very well in the darkness; there's a wicket leads
down to the water. Send me word and you shall find me waiting.'

'Madam, I pray, as you do, word will come soon!' And, indeed, he
looked a troubled man.

The visits of Chapuys had not gone unnoticed. Without warning I
was moved to Hunsdon. It is a house some forty miles from the
coast; a long and hazardous journey. But even then I did not give up
hope. Such a removal could not be kept secret; Chapuys would know
what to do. But the days went by and there came from him no message
nor dare I attempt any.

I am not one to give up. I had my own plan; very simple. I would
walk a little way into the country with my ladies, all very innocent;
then, being set on by a band of riders—Chapuys' men—I should be
carried to Gravesend and across the sea. But for that I needed Chapuys.
But still the days passed; I could not move without eyes watchful upon
me and, disappointment being too much, I fell sick again. So sick I was
my physician thought I had been poisoned; and, for myself, I feared it,
too. But it was not poison; long disappointment working upon a
body already weakened, brought me so low I scarce had strength to
hold a cup to my lips. When I was a little recovered my father had me
carried again to Hatfield.

To come again into the house of my enemies! It is not possible to
imagine my despair as I stepped once more across that hateful thresh-
old. All the miseries I had endured, the disappointment I had just
suffered, rose again to engulf me in a monstrous wave. But it was all
nothing to what I must now endure. For Shelton's daughter being at
this time in favour, there was nothing to curb her mother's spite. She
might go as far as she pleased—to my very death, if I might believe
her. She continually mocked at my fears for my mother, prophesying
with jubilation her early death; every word that could distress me,
every insult she could devise, Shelton flung at me.

'You know the marriage of Madam the Princess Elizabeth with
Monsieur le duc d'Angoulême is being discussed. The French ambassador, Monsieur Gontier, said the King of France must know before his
son is contracted, that the Princess is her father's heir. And what do you
think your father answered? *My brother of France need have no fear.
Everyone knows Mary for the accursed bastard she is!*'

And when my face remained quiet, though my heart nigh broke
at that piece of cruelty, she cried out, 'You are the thing, the cause of
all our troubles. So says the King! When your precious Chapuys

enquired of your health the other day your father—if indeed he is your father—cut him short. *Would to God she were dead!* Those were his very words!'

I shrugged as though I did not believe her.

'Yes!' she cried out angry that I gave no sign. 'Your father wishes your death; and Cromwell wishes it—as all true friends of the King wish it. And no wonder! For my niece the Queen declares that so long as you and your mother live, she cannot bear the King a son—a wise woman has said it! Well for your mother's death we'll not have to wait long; as for you—we shall see; we shall see! God willing we shall see you both in your grave!'

I made no sign that I had heard. She'd get no satisfaction out of me. But in the quiet of my closet I lay outstretched upon the floor praying the Mother of God to intervene for my mother's life. If God should let her live I would make myself content, whatever miseries be heaped upon me.

To punish heretics was my father's duty; there was no personal anger in the matter; but to punish those that could not and would not deny obedience to the Pope was something quite other. It was a matter to raise his bitter anger. It was treason. It held my mother's marriage lawful and myself true-born; it held the union with Anne Bullen unlawful and any child by her, bastard. It threatened *his son*. She had not given him a son—as yet. But the time would come; it *must* come. And when it came the child must be acknowledged the King's undoubted heir. That any man should account him otherwise aroused not only my father's fury but his fear. He had sworn to be master in his own house; that vow he was now keeping. In dead men there's no disobedience.

That year of 'thirty-five was a cruel one. The pain of those that suffered increased my own pain; *was* my pain.

The spring sun shone, the birds sang, life was quick in field and byre; quick in men and women . . . and of those last all too many came to their cruel death. In April the Charterhouse monks, following their prior, refused the oath and came to their death; some must be carried to the gallows so twisted and broken they were with torture. Their great house was closed until I, myself, opened it again.

The higher a man stood in public esteem, the more needful it was that he take the oath, and in the Tower, having lain there above a year were two such men; men of honour, of grace, of distinction, well-beloved and well-regarded. Again they were called upon to swear obedience; again they refused. My father would have given much for their obedience; such men he *needed*. To Fisher, poor and old and ill, came Cromwell with all his Council. Weak in body, strong in spirit, the old man refused. He was, Cromwell told him, the only bishop in the country that refused; in obstinacy, he stood alone. Obstinacy—that was a word Cromwell understood; strength of spirit was beyond his understanding. To Sir Thomas More, aged beyond his years by rigorous confinement, came Cromwell and Council also, tormenting him with threats and bribes. Threats and bribes—those, too, Cromwell understood.

Both men refused. They were given six weeks to consider of the matter. They needed not to consider; they were steadfast.

To honour the bishop the Pope bestowed upon him the cardinal's hat. A great honour and a great mistake. *We'll send his head to Rome to fetch his hat!* my father cried out and exploded into furious laughter.

On a sweet June day bishop Fisher was condemned to a traitor's death; but not even my father dared countenance that sentence. It was commuted to beheading—an honourable death; and to that death the good old man went steadfast. But they took the venerable head and they set it upon London Bridge where it rotted and was cast into the water.

A few days later More followed him to the scaffold. He was not only steadfast but gay; he took his death with a jest. 'Help me up, friend,' he told the executioner, for he was weak from his prison, 'I'll need no help in getting down!' And that to me is the high point of courage; as my father's jest was the high point of cruelty. His head, too, they stuck upon a pike on the Bridge; thence it was taken by night under her apron by Margaret Roper—worthy child of such a father.

And still it went on—the tortures, the beheadings, the hangings and the burnings. There was, I think, a streak of cruelty in my father which my mother's gentle influence had curbed and the concubine's spite inflamed. These days there was a madness in him to break every will that opposed his own.

Chapter Twenty

Rain fell, sun shone. Roses blossomed, apples and plums took their first faint flush of colour, corn ripened . . . and on the Bridge, with many another, Fisher's head rotted. Everywhere God showed His mercy; but my father showed none. Condemning good men to die in torment because they would not deny their God, he was himself confident of God's mercy. God would grant His zealous servant a son. And I? Ill and frightened I waited at Hatfield for the King's officers that should command the obedience that must corrupt my soul.

The summer months passed and with it my mother's strength. As autumn closed in, her hold on life grew ever weaker. Had Anne Bullen ill-wished my mother or had she commanded poison? Poison the resource of witches, for which in the Latin tongue they are named; the word *witch* and *poisoner* being one and the same. And, indeed, my mother feared poison; she would touch no food but what was cooked in a pot in her own room upon the fire.

Were we as sure of your death as we are of hers we should be right merry, Shelton continually said. Well she'd not have to wait long for her merriment! My thoughts were forever with my mother locked within Kimbolton lacking all those comforts even a strong man needed in that winter-bound, wind-swept place. And she was so poor; even the smallest comfort she could not afford to buy. For still the Queen's incomes were withheld; and still not a penny of the money due to the dowager Princess of Wales would she ever touch. *The Title is not mine nor the money neither!* she had said. I doubt, had dire necessity made her willing, they would have given it now, for they had taken everything from her—jewels, great furs and court gowns. Bedingfield, governor of Kimbolton, was the King's man, so was every servant within it—save for the handful of faithful women that would not forsake her they held to be the true Queen.

From that gaunt house she wrote to Chapuys; that letter I have seen for myself—and the words are those of one about to die. Chapuys thought so, too; for he wrote to warn me how desperate her case.

Shelton, herself, brought it, the seal broken, she smiling the while. I sent at once to my father praying that I might see my mother one last time before she died.

He refused. I could not, at first, believe it. In spite of all his unkindness to us both how should I believe it? Even a criminal is allowed Farewell to those he loves. But I was worse than a criminal. I was my mother's daughter. Shelton took care I should know the reason for this refusal.

'Madam the Queen is with child; and this time, please God, it shall be a boy! But still she weeps, swearing your mother ill-wishes her. The child in the womb will die, the wise woman says, unless the Spanish woman die first. Why then should we give her comfort to prolong her life? No! The sooner she dies—and you with her—the better for us all!'

I bit upon my tongue. I went to my chamber and there Bryan came seeking me.

'It takes a witch to think out such a piece of wickedness!' I cried out, bitter.

'Never fear it! The King knows her for what she is! He endures all her humours—she is with child. But if she lose it—finished Anne Bullen. The King has found a new friend.'

She answered my question unasked.

'Jane Seymour.'

'Jane Seymour!' I could not believe it possible; she was so pale, so quiet, scarce even pretty!

'The very same. She rests him. He longs for peace and true affection —and that she can give. And if she is not high-coloured, she is elegant; and if she is quiet she is gentle and discreet. Madam she is your friend; she works for you!'

'Pray God she work fast; else my mother will die and I go the same way!'

'To work fast is to mar all. Madam, your mother is in God's hands and you must be content to leave it there. As for yourself—Mistress Seymour is steady for your advantage. She went upon her knees—I had it from one of her women—to beseech the King bring you back to your rightful place.'

'Then may God bless her, as I do!'

And now it was November. Fog enshrouded Kimbolton and the winds blew bitter. Jane Seymour might, with time, do me some good; but for my mother she must be too late. That month our household was summoned to Eltham and there the concubine came to visit her daughter. She looked very thin, her condition apparent only in the dark-circled eyes and the sallow skin blotched with brown. And now the unlooked-for happened; she once more made an offer of friendship.

I had attended prayers in chapel; and, the service ended, made my curtsey to the high altar and left. I did not see her standing there; but she believing—or, as I think, affecting to believe—that, curtseying, I showed at last, the respect she craved from me, sent asking that we might be friends.

It was the woman Rochford, wife to George Bullen, that came bearing the message; and the messenger alone must have forced me to *No!* the corrupt and lying creature.

'My lady Mary, Madam the Queen thanks you for your courtesey in chapel this morning. She says you need pay her no other mark of respect, not so much as to hold up her train. If you will but acknowledge her the King's lawful wife, there is no good thing she will not do for you. You shall take your place the King's undoubted daughter; save for herself, and the Princess Elizabeth, none shall stand higher. She will be a mother to you. . . .'

She! a mother to me! She that had brought disgrace and sorrow upon my own mother; she through whom my mother even now lay dying—and could not die fast enough for the woman that now asked my friendship!

I all-but laughed save for the sickness in my throat.

'Tell your lady that I bent the knee not to her but to God's altar. As for my being the King's undoubted daughter—I need no word from her; all Christendom knows it. With her I have nothing to do!' I feared afterwards for what I had said; it was not courage that had moved me but an angry spirit. Yet we are as we are; and had the thing to be done again, so exactly would I have answered.

'But why should she wish for my friendship now?' I asked Bryan all amazed. 'She carries the King's hope. She has no need of me.'

'She fears she may miscarry—she is not well,' Bryan said. 'Or the child may be another girl. And, moreover, she's sick with jealousy of Mistress Seymour—and not without reason. She knows the lady's kindness for you; now she wants to show her own good-nature, her own goodwill. But, above all she wants, if not goodwill, then, at least respect from you. She has always wanted it; now she is desperate for it—insurance against ill-fortune!'

I had made my answer; I had thought it the end of the matter. But not so; for there befell the oddest thing—mark of a twisted mind. Upon the floor of my private oratory I found a letter dropped it would appear, by some mischance. It was written to Shelton in Anne Bullen's hand and deliberately placed—neither of those two women was careless with private correspondence. I read the letter as I was meant.

The writer asked her aunt to make no further move to bring me into my father's favour; her offer of friendship had been mere charity, since neither she nor he cared what road I took.

> . . . for if I have a son, as I hope shortly, I know what will happen to her. Considering the word of God to do good to one's enemies, I wished to warn her beforehand; because the King's wisdom is not to esteem her repentance of her rudeness nor her natural obstinacy. I beg you not to think to pleasure me by turning her from her wilful courses, because she cannot do me good or evil. Do your duty about her as I am assured you will. . . .

So much for her friendship! I copied the letter for Chapuys and returned her own to its place upon the floor.

Back again at Hatfield, I suffered the old persecution. *Do your duty about her as I am assured you will.* Shelton had been given carte blanche; and as my mother grew steadily worse, the persecution worsened, also. Merciless they mocked both her and me.

'Your cousin the little Emperor has written the King that he likes not the way your mother is treated. Well then, he must lump it! For the King told Chapuys—and the whole court heard it—*There is no wrong offered my sister!* His sister; do you mark it?'

Yes I had marked it. Even to a dying woman there was no respect shown; for still she was smeared with the sin of incest.

Christmas came; the last Christmas of my mother's life. And still I was not let to see her. At times I prayed that if I might not see her, we might leave this world together. But even as I prayed I knew the prayer to be wrong; she would wish me to live; and, for all my unhappiness, I was young enough not to wish to die. She was now so ill that, at last, Chapuys had leave to visit her; towards the end of December he rode out.

It was New Year's Day when he reached Kimbolton. 'The best New Year's gift I ever had!' my mother told him. Well, if it was the best it was also the last.

Three years since he had set eyes on her; and at first he did not recognise the woman in the great bed, so thin, so grey, so *small*!

'Oh,' she said—and her voice no more than a thread, 'now I have a friend to close my eyes. Now I need not fear to die alone like a sick beast!' And by the sound of that voice with its pretty foreign accent—though but the ghost of a voice—he knew her.

He sat with her, he told me; and she laughed with him . . . last flicker of the dying flame of her spirit. It was a flicker that deceived them both. When next day he rode away she let him go with a smile; and with a smile he promised to come again. And each believed her case not so desperate but that she might mend.

Yet still God had one last kindness in His Hand. She did not die, as she feared, alone and friendless. Lady Willoughby, born Maria de Salinas, that had come from Spain thirty-five years ago, a girl to serve her young Princess, served her at the last. For she came to Kimbolton hard upon the heels of Chapuys; all drenched with rain, her skirts bespattered with mud, she asked for shelter in the name of God.

So fine a lady could not be denied; and, once within, she made no bones of the matter, asking at once for the Queen's bedchamber. And Bedingfield allowed it. He was not soft-hearted, God knows; but even he could not refuse—the good, sweet Queen was dying. He said, afterwards, he believed the lady to have had the King's permission. Well, whatever he believed, he let her go to my mother; and for that, in spite of his harshness, I thank him.

So Maria de Salinas that had shared my mother's girlhood, sat by her side and, in the dear language of home, those two spoke together. It was Maria de Salinas that held the dying hand, heard the last words, *in manus tuas,* closed the world-weary eyes.

The seventh day of January, in the year of grace fifteen hundred and thirty-six, my mother died. She was fifty years old.

She had written a letter to my father; I found it, after his death, among his papers. It begins, *My most dear lord and husband*—and that was no mere greeting but the exact statement of her heart. She writes, she says, in the hour of approaching death. Because of the love she bears him she must advise him to look to the health of his soul which he should put before all desires of the flesh; for which desires

> . . . you have cast me into many calamities and yourself into many troubles. But I forgive you all; and pray God to do likewise.

She loved him so that her first thought was for his soul dearer to her than her own.

> I commend unto you our daughter Mary, beseeching you to be a good father unto her . . .

She thinks next of those servants whose love she is too poor to requite. She entreats him to give the younger ones

> ... in marriage, which is not much—they being but three; and to all other servants a year's pay besides their due, otherwise they will be unprovided for.

Her husband, her daughter, her servants! And then, before she closes her eyes in death—once more, her husband.

> Lastly I take this vow that mine eyes desire you above all things. ...

From first to last she speaks the exact language of truth. He was her heart's love; and, sick or well, she wearied for the sight of him. And her forgiveness, like her love, was pure and full, true and perfect. In her there was no spot of meanness or spite.

Her Will was pitifully short—so little she had to leave, royal Queen of England. Gowns in good enough condition were to be cut up for the use of the Friars-Observant—I think she did not know they had been driven out; but the fur trimmings were to be removed and sent to me. This, with the Spanish collar together with a gold chain that carried a splinter of the true cross was all she had to leave to me, her only child. The fur I never had, nor yet the collar of gold, but the chain, being light in weight and the sacred relic unvalued by an unbeliever, Cromwell sent to me. I wear it always upon my heart; it shall lie with me in the grave.

My mother's body lay awaiting burial; and even then I was not let to see her. Perhaps it was as well; I must have broken my heart. She lay in such state unfit for a Queen; and for that I cannot blame Bedingfield. *Sir, I have no money, I beseech your aid with all speed* he wrote to my father. I must suppose none was sent; for a groom of the chamber cered her and a common plumber enclosed her in lead—Catherine Queen of England, Princess of the royal house of Spain.

My mother was dead. Desolation and grief worked upon me. For above three years I had not seen her; yet there had been messages and there had been hope—hope that one day I should see her face again, touch her hand. Now she was dead. My father cared nothing for me; the Emperor was too engaged in war for the love of God to have love to spare for me. Jane Seymour, then? There was kindness there; but it had done my mother no good. And—since my father's mistress she would not be; and his wife she could not be—she was in no position to do anything for me. One true friend I had: Chapuys; he did his uttermost but it was little enough. The Emperor, avoiding trouble, had tied his hands.

And now to add to my grief—horror. There were whispers everywhere that the concubine had had her way; my mother had died of poison. The truth of this I cannot say. True it is that she had feared poison to the point of eating nothing but what she saw cooked in her own room; but there's more than one way of poisoning; and when her physician came to speak with me after her death, he was not let within the gate. Did Shelton know more than she should? Who can say? But the tale was everywhere; certainly Chapuys, that shrewd man, believed it, for he sent me a message to look to my own food; but how in that household was it possible? So the old fear of poison being once more upon me, I went in fear and trembling.

Desolation and fear; hatred and anger; heavy burdens for any young heart to bear alone—and I had cause and cause enough. I had a sick, cold anger against my father that had treated my dying mother so ill and took her death so light; and a hot, bitter anger against the concubine that had turned a not unkindly man to such cruelty.

Shelton saw to it that I should hear how my father had taken my mother's death and cared not at all whether the tale were false or true.

'When the lord King heard that his encumbrance was dead, he cried out *God be praised!* and gave orders that the court dress itself fitting the occasion. And so it did! For he, himself, and Madam Queen Anne and every lady and gentleman down to the smallest page appeared in . . . *yellow!* All very gay to befit the occasion; and your father wore a yellow feather in his bonnet!'

'Never believe it,' Bryan said afterwards, 'I hear otherwise. About Anne Bullen it is true enough; but the King and the court were in mourning.'

God grant it was so! I never enquired for fear of what I might learn . . . that yellow feather bore the touch of truth.

'The concubine is a spiteful woman. To show such spite against a dead woman that never harmed nor wished to harm her—I had not thought it possible even in *her!*' I cried out.

'Spite's a mischief there's no plumbing,' Bryan said. 'She's spiteful because she did the good Queen great wrong; and the more spiteful because she's frightened—and it isn't only lest she lose the child she carries. She has further reason, greater reason.'

'Can any reason be greater?'

Bryan nodded. 'There are tales about to blacken her name.'

'Are they true?'

Bryan shrugged. 'That such tales go about is enough!'

'Has my father heard them?'

'There's none dare repeat them to his face save, perhaps, Cromwell. But the King knows; he knows everything—and says nothing. Let her give him his son and she's safe enough. He'll find the way to quiet wagging tongues. Live with her again he will not; but she keeps crown and reputation. He'll not slur the birth of his son!'

'And if she have no son—as I pray God she may not—will he use the tales against her?'

'Who knows? If his anger be greater than his pride, he may well do so. If his pride be the greater, he'll put an end to the marriage, decently for his own sake. With him you can never tell.'

Chapuys came down to see me. Shelton made no trouble; already she foresaw trouble enough. We walked in the garden that we might not be overheard.

'We may look to changes,' Chapuys said. 'The concubine's crown hung upon two chances. One chance, through her own spite she has lost, the other, by her own rash humours, she may also lose.'

'The chance she has lost?'

'Your mother's death put an end to it; God is just. As long as Madam Queen Catherine lived your father would not declare his union with the concubine unlawful. He'd not humble himself before the Pope, nor again set Catholic Europe by the ears; he's wise enough to let sleeping dogs lie. So, if she miscarry or give him a girl—he'll end the marriage.'

'But he is fast-wed by law; the law he himself made.'

'He'll find a loop-hole, trust him! So he will please everyone. He'll please those of the true faith that have always held his union with the concubine null and void; and he'll please those that acknowledge the marriage and hate the woman. Joy will be beyond all bounds. So pleasing himself, he'll please everyone.'

They buried my mother at Peterborough; not at Windsor where my father should one day lie; and they buried her not like a Queen but like a poor gentlewoman—a plain black pall with a silver cross upon a plain coffin. But there were crowds to follow her funeral that bitter January day; gentle and simple, great and small, rich and poor to weep at her burying.

But in the stillness of my chamber I wept alone. Up to the last moment I had not believed my father would forbid me to show a last token of love.

'Why? Why?' I cried out to Bryan.

'Because the King fears to let the people see you stand by her coffin knowing, as they do, her sorrows and yours. He fears their love will cry too loud against him!'

But God is not mocked.

That very day they buried my mother, Anne Bullen was brought to bed of a miscarriage—a three-and-a-half-months child—a boy.

My father had lost his son, his prince, his heir.

And she? She lost not only her honour and her crown; but her life, her life, also.

The whole of Christendom heard how my father's rage exceeded all human reason; how he strode into the chamber where she lay wet with the sweat of her labour and the blood of her pain, and cried out against her, swearing she'd get no more boys out of him! It is known, too—for such tales cannot be kept secret—how she begged for his pity, tears joining the sweat upon her face. 'Sir,' she had wept, 'it was love for you brought me to this pass; love and fear. It is two days since you fell from your horse. You made nothing of it, but the fall was heavy—should not I, your wife, fear for you!'

He made her no answer but turned and went limping from the room.

Afterwards she told a different tale. She had come into the King's closet to find Jane Seymour in his arms—pale hair tumbled, pale cheeks flushed . . . and she, his wife, standing there, all heavy with his child. Should not the King, the King himself and his sly paramour, take the blame of her miscarriage?

I think it was not true. In the King's closet Jane Seymour may have been; but not clipped fast; and not alone. It was a thing she had never allowed, having regard to her reputation. I think Anne Bullen owed her miscarriage to her own violence. She had been heard that same day berating the King like a fishwife. Her voice had been heard from the inner closet to the last ante-room of the King's suite.

For my father I tried to grieve; my mother had commanded me to love him. But love is not to be commanded and I was glad. For myself I wanted no crown; I am a simple woman. But I could not have endured Anne Bullen's bastard to sit upon the throne. Had I seen her with my own eyes maybe I had pitied her. Bryan heard that these days the King never saw her; he walked and talked with Jane Seymour; but though the whole court knew his passion for the quiet, pale lady, she carried herself so that there was not a single hair upon which suspicion might hang. Always when she was with the King her brother or Cromwell went with them. Once he sent her a purse of gold; kneeling she received it, and kneeling returned it. 'I cannot with honour take this purse!' she told the messenger. 'But if it shall please the King's grace to send me a gift, let it be when God shall send me a husband.'

A sly hint that; or the honest truth?

Anne Bullen had no doubts.

'A *husband* says she! And she with both eyes on the King! Well, him she shall never have—save it be over my dead body!' And did not know that she spoke her own doom.

Chapter Twenty-One

Things looked black for Anne Bullen. I knew it by the look in Shelton's eyes; and by the way she cared not whether I came or went. She no longer persecuted me—maybe she had no heart; maybe she was afraid. I began to hope for a happier future. Jane Seymour continued still in kindness towards me. Bryan told me this: she had it from her son who had been present. 'Mistress Seymour went down on her knees to beseech the King restore you. He was peevish, though not angry. For who, my son says, could be angry with so sweet a lady?'

'"Madam," the King said, "you have lost your wits! You should think of your own children." She did not pretend not to understand. She said, "Sir, I do think of them. Unless you do justice to the lady Mary there'll be no content in this land nor any peace."'

'May God requite her!' I said. 'I pray my father may marry her and that heaven send them a prince!'

Bryan sent me a sidelong look.

'Before God I mean it! She loved my mother and she has a kindness for me!'

'Yet Anne Bullen puts it about that Mistress Seymour is sly, that she wrongs her mistress the Queen!'

'I think it is not true. But, if it were, who showed her the way; who but the concubine that wronged her own mistress, the King's true wife? But Jane Seymour wrongs no-one. If she marries the King she'll be his lawful wife; he has no other . . . now. To my father's son, lawfully begot, I would gladly give up the crown.'

'Marry the King she will. Cromwell will find the way. He means down with Anne Bullen. She hates him and he doesn't mean to end like Wolsey. And besides, his son's married to Jane Seymour's sister —that counts with him more than a little! And there's another reason. He wants peace with the Emperor.'

'*He*—peace with the Emperor; it cannot be!'

She nodded. The wool trade makes gold for us; and whence comes that trade but from the Netherlands? And who rules the Netherlands but the Emperor? And who stands in the way but Anne Bullen? She'll have no friendship with the Emperor; first because he's your own cousin, and second because she favours France against Spain and works for it underhand. With France her friend she believes herself safe. She stands between Cromwell and his plans—and so she must go!'

The concubine put from her place and Jane Seymour the Queen; friendship with the Emperor, and myself restored! 'Oh that God would grant it!' I said.

'He will grant it.'

The King sent Jane Seymour to her father's house Wolf Hall lest scandal busy itself with her name; for from Greenwich Anne Bullen was crying out her accusations. But much good it was keeping his sweetheart from London, when he rode every day to see her. Edward Seymour, her brother, he made gentleman of the Privy Chamber. 'Sure sign of favour to come!' Bryan said. 'My son whispers that the King is questioning the rightness of his marriage with Anne Bullen. He's set Cranmer to work in secret, on that business. The King is talking of witchcraft too. She has bewitched him, he says, into marriage with her black arts.

And I remembered how, long ago, I had accused her of this same thing and my mother had said, *Not her black arts, her black eyes!* Which of us had been right? And *Pity her*, my mother had said, *soon she will be in lamentable case*. It looked as though she had been right there! Cranmer was already at work; the archbishop that had been so eager about that marriage would be even more eager to find it no marriage at all.

'Then my father will have three bastards!' I said, bitter.

'Young Richmond is a sick boy. I doubt he'll last long!' Bryan said.

'God grant him health. He's over-young to die.'

Things might promise to look rosier for me; but still my father held me a bastard. The Emperor proposed me in marriage with the Infante of Portugal. A good match; I should, in the course of nature, become Queen of Portugal. But . . . my father must declare me true-born; like France, Portugal wanted no bastard bride.

Declare me true-born he would not. He had no wish to marry me at home or abroad. An English husband might lead a revolt for my rights. But a foreigner! Declare me true-born, and, if my father had no son I must succeed. He did not relish the notion of England under a foreign King; nor would his people, neither. Well the reasoning was good!

So the match was off and I irretrievably stamped *bastard*. That the match was broken I cared little. True I was twenty-one, and more than old enough to be married; but I was small-made and ill-health had slowed my ripening. My pride would have welcomed marriage but my body was glad of respite.

'Now you may see where you stand!' Shelton summoned enough spite to taunt me. 'Any day the commissioners will come and you'll be made to admit yourself the bastard that you are! With your own hand you will sign it!'

Chapuys must have feared it, too; for he repeated his warning through Bryan—to sign only under fear of death and to keep safe my paper declaring that I signed under duress, 'He says, Madam, you must not put your life and claim in danger; or what becomes of the true faith then?'

In Greenwich Anne Bullen had stopped weeping. There was, as far as she could see, no more talk of nullity or divorce. Cromwell was against both—he had told her so himself; and she had told Sir Francis, holding him to be her kinsman and her friend. 'Madam,' Cromwell had said. 'There shall be no divorce. I shall advise the King.' So she took heart of grace. But what Cromwell was preparing for her she did not know.

Cromwell did advise my father against divorce or nullity. Sir Francis knew about that, too!

'To try a second time, sir, is unwise. How will it look in the courts of Christendom? We know the King's wisdom; we know the mischances of both his marriages. But your enemies will discount both mischance and wisdom. And they'll not be slow to say so!'

Christendom will hold you a fool and make the most of it! My father read the blunt meaning beneath the courtly words.

'And besides, sir—divorce or nullity is a long process of law, as you well know. The King should marry as soon as may be, the country desires it. Sir, I know a quicker way—and no-one to fault the King!' And he whispered in the King's ear.

This I know, because long afterwards, my father himself told me.

Anne Bullen had not only stopped weeping; she was smiling. The King and court were come to Greenwich for the annual tournament. *I am here, and he is here; and Mistress Wheyface is sent from the court.* She had but to show herself smiling and handsome to win the King again; he was tired of Mistress Wheyface. She said it openly.

But then there were so many things she did not know. She did not know that already she had been named adulterous with five men and one of them her own brother; that already the Privy Council had met and decided her guilt and drawn up their indictments. She did not know that two of those named lay already in prison—and one of them Smeaton her favourite musician. She had not missed him; he had had leave of absence and they had taken him at his home in Stepney. All these things she did not know.

Mayday in the year of grace fifteen hundred and thirty six. High-painted and handsome Anne Bullen moved well-attended to the tourney ground. Wyatt her kinsman—and her lover, too, maybe—said afterwards she walked that Mayday morning sweet as May herself. Well, he was a poet and we must allow him some licence. If she had no notion of the blow to fall, neither had anyone else—except the King, except Cromwell, except the Privy Council.

What did befall that May morning all the world knows; how my father, in courtesy, took her by the hand and led her to the Queen's place so that folk believed all was well between them. But those that stood near the King said his eyes were red and sunken in his head and that his mouth twitched. And there are some to say that the Queen, sensing his unease, was uneasy, too. So many tales! They said she dropped her kerchief into the ring, that Norris, already named for adultery, picked it up, and having wiped his face all wet with exercise, lifted the thing on the point of his lance and offered it to the Queen. Such a piece of madness I cannot believe; but that people spoke of such a thing shows only too clearly the familiarity between those two.

All the world knows, how, suddenly, in the midst of the jousting my father rose suddenly and flung himself from the place leaving the Queen to sit there alone, and how he rode furiously for London, six gentlemen, only, in attendance—and one of them his closest friend Norris; and how within an hour of reaching Whitehall, Norris lay in the Tower.

What did Anne Bullen make of it, sitting there abandoned and alone? Had she been innocent she must have sat perplexed and shamed; guilty she must have died a thousand deaths.

It must have been a long, long night for her; nor did morning promise any better. For there came to Greenwich her uncle Norfolk and sundry privy councillors to question her close and long. And now she knew there were charges against her and what they were—all except one; the darkest. A pity she had quarrelled with Norfolk for he handled her roughly; so she told Kingston, Constable of the Tower.

The Queen was in the Tower; and in that same Tower, on her account, some half-dozen gentlemen, including her brother, my lord Rochford.

When the news reached us at Hatfield, it was for the household, as though the heavens themselves had fallen; to me, it was as though the angel Gabriel himself had trumpeted her ill-fame. And yet it shocked me too. That she, hallowed Queen of England, should lie in prison—and on such foul charges! I was shamed for my father; I had thought that, for very pride, he would do all decently, permitting nothing of scandal.

In the dark of my chamber and below our breath Bryan and I discussed the charges. They were too horrible to be spoken aloud in the light of day; yet people did speak of them—and of little else wherever men met together. And soon they were to be spoken louder still in the pitiless light of a public trial.

'They have been collecting evidence this long while,' Bryan said. 'They charge her that she is guilty with Norris and Brereton, with Weston and Smeaton. They lie in the Tower and I doubt they'll ever come out again! Wyatt is mentioned also. They say she has lain with Smeaton—a low-born fellow but a pretty one. That I do not believe. But if it be true, one thing is sure: he had never dared lift his eyes to the Queen but she seduced him.'

'There is yet another charge,' I said.

'Madam it is not fit . . .'

'No need to name it. I know it.'

And, indeed, something of it I had heard when I had been at court for the birth of the child Elizabeth; yes, even then, they were saying she had lain with her brother—her own brother. Whatever she was, could one believe *that* of her?

'There are other things . . . treason,' Bryan said.

'Adultery in a Queen and with a Queen *is* treason.'

'There's yet more treason. They say, Madam, that she and her lovers have conspired to kill the King; that they have forecast his death and discussed, between themselves, which one shall wed her. And Monsieur Chapuys says—he told my son so—she is to be charged with poisoning Madam your mother; and also with trying to bring about your own death and that of young Richmond.'

'Chapuys certainly thought my mother had been poisoned and her physician thought so too. As for me, she had them take away my food-taster.'

'They'll not press those charges, my son says, there's enough against her already.'

'I am glad of it. I would not have my mother's name or my own mixed in this affair. It is so foul it smells to high heaven.'

Chapter Twenty-Two

All the news I have now about Anne Bullen, until her end, I had from lady Kingston, wife of the Constable of the Tower, that was in attendance upon her. She came to me afterwards with a message I did not want to hear and yet—words from the grave—I must listen.

Anne Bullen's head was high when they carried her to the Tower; with her in the barge was Mr. Secretary Cromwell, my lord Chancellor Audley, Norfolk and others of the Privy Council. Five o'clock it was of a golden afternoon when she went up the steps of the Water Gate which men call the Traitor's Gate; and that head was low enough seeing the grim Tower that was no longer a palace but a prison.

When she went up those steps she trembled so that a gentleman each side must support her. Kingston, at the head of the stairs, received her with a cool courtesy to conduct her to her lodgings. She had thought it must be a prison cell but she took courage, a little, when she saw it was the Queen's own rooms—those very rooms in which she had spent the night before her crowning. She cried out now, *It is too good for me!* That is a thing to remember. And then, I suppose the difference between her state then and now must have smitten her to the heart—as how could it fail to do? It shook even me that had no love for her. She threw out her hands and but for lady Kingston, quick to catch her, must have fallen.

That day she was troubled for her brother; she did not, as yet, know that already he lay in that same Tower; but still she was troubled. *Where is my sweet brother?* She kept asking Kingston until at last she had the truth. When she heard of the charge against him—the foul charge of incest, with her, his own sister, she laughed aloud. 'Incest! It works in the King's head like a maggot! Well, he's an old man and age will have its way with him!' And this being repeated to my father poured no oil upon her troubled waters.

Everywhere now, like a foul miasma the dirty stories spread; and everywhere folk believed them—and were glad to believe them. And my father seemed content it should be so.

ever did prince wear his horns more lightly they said of him and it was true. And this, I think, was a fearful thing. My father had loved the woman; he had made her his Queen and the mother of his child. Now she lay in prison on the most shameful of charges; though not yet come to trial, already she had been judged. Her blood must be the sacrament upon my father's new marriage. So he laughed and feasted and wore his gayest clothes; he filled the royal barge with musicians and with ladies and did not care—or perhaps meant it should be so—that the sound of their music should reach the desolate creature that had once been Queen.

The truth about my father is this. He had a warm way with him but a cold heart. I doubt there was ever one person in all his life he truly loved, except his son; his true-born son. I understand how, after the bitterness and the noise of his life with Anne Bullen, he would turn to Jane Seymour as a thirsty man to water in the desert. But that thirst being quenched, I doubt he would have remained faithful. He would have kept her in high dignity—the mother of his son; but she was too quiet, too gentle, too devoid of passion to hold him long. Faithfulness was not in him.

Anne Bullen did not believe she would ever come to trial; not at first. Norfolk had given her the rough edge of his tongue and she was confined to the Queen's rooms within the Tower; and that would be all. She would proclaim her innocence; and the King's pride satisfied, he would set her free to go whither she would—so she kept her distance.

'I am well rid of the old man,' she told lady Kingston, 'I will take myself to France, to the gay life and the favour of King Francis—we are old friends, he and I!' That she must lose the crown she knew; that she would lose her life never entered her head. She had reckoned without Cromwell; she had reckoned without that wound to the King's pride which—though he bore it lightly—festered inwardly, turning him to cruelty.

The charges are false. She said it until she wearied of the words.

'False they are and the King knows it. There will be no trial. He cannot, for his dignity, put the Queen of England on trial!' And she laughed so long and so loud that Kingston must reprove her for unseemly mirth. But I think it was not the laughter of mirth. Had she not laughed she must have given way to fear; and that she knew she must not do.

When she heard that the date of the trial was fixed, even then she laughed. 'There can be nothing found against me!' she said. And when they reminded her that already Smeaton had spoken she said, 'He admitted nothing until they racked him! and then, like his betters before him, he said whatever they put into his mouth. There was nothing he *could* confess—save a few kind words for his sweet music; and a few silver pence because he was poor and liked to go fine!' And she sighed that for so small a thing a lad must come to the rack and to his death.

My father had sent her a message through Cranmer. Confess and he would show her his mercy. But even then she was confident that there would be no trial. Her answer, in a long letter, stood by her innocence. That letter I have before me as I write.

> Try me good King but let me have a lawful trial. Let not my sworn enemies stand as my accusers and judges. Let me receive an open trial, and then you shall see either my innocency or my guilt openly declared. But if you have already determined of me that not only my death but an infamous slander must bring you the joying of your desired happiness, then I desire of God that He will pardon your great sin herein, and that He will not call you to a strait account for your cruel and unprincely usage of me.

Then she made her request; and whatever wrong she did my mother and me, that last, useless request still catches at the heart:

> My last and only request shall be that myself, only myself, bear the burden of your Grace's displeasure; and that it may not touch the innocent souls of those poor gentlemen that are in strait imprisonment for my sake. If ever I have found favour in your sight, if ever the name of Anne Bullen has been pleasing to your ears, then let me obtain my last request.
>
> From my doleful prison in the Tower, the 6th May.
>   Ann Bullen.

I give the letter that it may stand in her favour, for I, myself, can speak no good of her. Whether it be the letter of innocence I cannot tell; I leave it that others may judge.

To this—no answer; nor did she write to him again. She had her own courage, her own pride. She would need them.

On Friday May 12th Norris, Weston, Brereton and Smeaton came to their trial. They were found guilty—all four—and condemned to a traitor's death. She wept for them all; and especially for Smeaton that, not being a gentleman born, could not be expected to suffer with fortitude; and yet for that same reason must be the only one of them all to suffer the full rigours of the law.

But there was little time for tears; on Monday the fifteenth she must face her own trial. Even then she was confident. Smeaton, it was true, had 'confessed' to ill-conduct with the Queen; but who would believe she had misconducted herself with so low a fellow? Who would believe a poor lad crying out under the rack? Brereton had withdrawn his confession and neither of the other two had said a word to her undoing. But when she heard that Norfolk—her dire enemy—was to preside over the court, then her courage drooped.

Yet when she came into the King's Hall of the Tower, lady Bullen wife to her uncle on the one hand, and lady Kingston on the other, she carried her head, so they say, as though it wore the crown. The great court was crowded by such as managed to find a place, having waited all night to see a Queen of England tried for adultery, incest and treason . . . and among them all not one heart to wish her well.

Yet still she carried her proud head high, and so held it, even when she saw Norfolk in his place beneath the canopy of estate, High Steward of England for this day; and twenty-six peers to sit as judges. A picked company these; there was not one but her own tongue had made him her enemy. Yet had they been chosen with utmost honesty still they must have been, for the most part, her enemies; there was scarce one she had not offended.

She had asked her husband, direst enemy of them all, for a fair trial. And, in its procedure, the trial was fair enough. Everything according to law; with, by especial order of the King, the lord Mayor of London sitting with his officers to see justice done. But, with all men knowing the King's will in the matter, with her own light behaviour to witness against her, and in this court of her enemies, asking for justice was like crying for the moon.

Did her eye rest upon Northumberland; did she wonder whether he remembered the love that had been between them once? Did she herself remember that but for the King she had been this great earl's wife, honoured and respected?

Pity her my mother had said; *for soon she will be in lamentable case.* In lamentable case she was, but I could not pity her. Her cruelty towards myself I might forgive; the cruelty that had killed my mother—never. But if I might not pity her, admire her, in that moment, I must. For that day she carried herself, a true Queen.

Down the great hall she went until she came to the chair that was set beneath the judges' bench; and, she standing, the indictment was read. She knew the charges by heart; Norfolk had not let her forget them. But all the same she listened courteously and with care.

... that you, the lady Anne, Queen of England, having malice in your heart against the King, and following your carnal lust did falsely and traitorously procure divers of the King's familiar servants to be your adulterers. ...

That you the Queen, on the first of October in the twenty-fifth year of our lord the King Henry VIII did procucre and incite one Henry Norris. ...

Henry Norris had maintained his innocence. That indictment she could deal with. Her voice was steady, pleading *not guilty*.

At the second charge in the indictment she felt shock and distaste run through the hall like a great wind.

... that you the Queen, on the second of November procured and incited George Bullen, Knight, lord Rochford, your own natural brother to have intercourse with you. ...

She took in her breath on a great sigh. There was no witness against her but one; her brother's wife mad with jealousy—and everyone knew it—against those two that had stood close within their own magic circle. What the woman had said was so little, but it was enough.

The lord Rochford would come into the Queen's room and come up to the bed where she lay and he would kiss her and finger her. ...

It was little enough . . . but enough; enough.

Her voice low, unsteady as she denied the charge, gathered power with her most urgent need. It was not her life, alone, she defended; should she be found guilty then her dear-loved brother, that matched her as two halves of one apple, must die too; upon her trial hung his own. Her voice rang out true and pure. One might well believe her guiltless. Norfolk, seeing how well she impressed the court, cut her short.

On and on the indictment.

That you . . . that you . . .

Name and date given. As is usual in such a case, she saw no witness; but with each charge, was read what had been witnessed against her. And still she stood steady to her defence.

Nor were these charges of adultery the whole of it. My father had charged her with witchcraft; by her black arts she had bewitched him into marriage. That did not surprise me; I had always held her to be a witch. There were other charges of treason, also, apart from her adultery. She had sought the King's death, she and her lovers together.

There remained one more charge; she had slandered the King. The thing she had said was not read aloud; it was written down. But the King's Privy Council had read it, and the bench of peers had read it; and someone had copied it, and though unspoken, yet the words were heard as clear as though shouted through that hall. . . . *The King is impotent.* Words of devilish cunning to wound the King that once had cried out in anguish *Am I not a man . . . a man . . .?* And again, it was the Rochford woman alone that stood as witness.

Whether Anne Bullen had said them or not—those words were her death. All other crimes the King might have punished short of death. If she had said those words she had killed herself. If she had not, then the Rochford woman had murdered her as surely as though she had strangled her with her own hands.

The Queen's verdict all had expected. Expected, yet horrible when it came at last; each lord rising in his place from least to highest and the word of death repeated . . . repeated by all save one alone. Northumberland had not forgotten; grey-faced and weeping he had stumbled from the court.

And then the sentence.

You shall be burnt within the Tower of London upon the green; or have your head stricken off at the King's pleasure.

'I think, Madam,' lady Kingston told me, 'she did not take it in; her mind was too full of her brother—what must come to him now? For when we were come again into her chamber she said, 'For myself, I have no fear; but I grieve for those innocent gentlemen that must die for me.'

When she had been taken away her brother was brought to trial. There had been no witness against him but one; and that one, again, his own wife. 'Riddled with jealousy as with wormwood,' lady Kingston said.

Her sentence all had expected. So many indictments and each one carrying the death penalty. For her; but not for him. Against him nothing but this; and the only witness a lying, spiteful wife. But, true or not, the words had been spoken; and for that he must die. As truly as the executioner's sword, his wife's tongue had killed him.

Chapter Twenty-Three

The trials were unjust; yet through injustice, justice had been done. If Anne Bullen had not been adulterous, had not been incestuous, had not bewitched the King, she had brought about my mother's death, had sought my own; sought young Richmond's too—if my father is to be believed. Yet such justice sticks in my throat. . . . I had rather she had not come to her death.

For a full twenty-four hours she did not believe she was to die. How should she die—and life quick within her? This bad time would pass. She need not even go to France; the King would send for her again. 'Madam Wheyface can never hold him. There's no woman ever can but me . . . me . . . me!' So she laughed and she joked and was in good heart—save that now and again fear touched her with a cold finger and laughter stopped, soon to break forth again.

But the next day she understood something of the King's implacable bitterness against her. He had commanded that, with her own eyes, she see the death of those condemned to die. Smeaton they had already hanged at Tyburn—he was not a gentleman; they had carried him to the gallows, his racked limbs unable to bear him. She had wept for that. 'For so small a thing as a feather to his cap or buckles to his shoes, A lad comes to such a death!' But to see those others go to their death —that death she, herself, must die did she not suffer the more hateful death in the fire—it was cruel, cruel! Yet she had, in some measure, brought it upon herself. She knew the man my father was; yet she had driven him well-nigh to madness. She had laughed at him with her friends for a clown and a senile old fool; she had accused him of impotence—speaking, maybe, his own fears. She had goaded him, until like a maddened beast, he had turned to savage before the kill.

So now she must stand to watch them, those gentlemen with whom she had played—Brereton, Weston and Norris—lay their young heads upon the block. They died for her. If she had, indeed, been guilty with them, what were her thoughts then? And if they died, innocent? Then still she was not free of guilt; her own light behaviour had cast death's dark shadow upon them.

'And yet,' lady Kingston said, 'she neither flinched not wept. She stood there very still; I think she was praying. When she spoke at last, I saw a bead of blood upon her lip. "Poor gentlemen," she said, "It grieves me to the heart that they should die for me." And then she said, "Wyatt; I do not see Wyatt!"'

'The King is not yet determined on his death,' lady Kingston said. 'At that, she lifted her hands in prayer, weeping a little and saying, "God have mercy that this dear companion of my childhood be spared!" And there, at least, she had her wish.

'That same day—and she shaken to the heart at what she had but this morning been forced to witness, Cranmer visited her and spoke with her alone. *She has confessed her sins,* he told the King. But, *I confessed nothing to him, nothing at all and I never will—there is nothing to confess!* she told us.'

Well, I suppose her word was as good as his!

The next day she was brought from the Tower under guard to Lambeth palace. There, in the presence of the Lord Chancellor, of Cromwell and the Privy Council, my lord archbishop, time-server and turnabout, declared hers no marriage; she had never been the King's wife—for she had not been free to wed. Ten years since she had been contracted to Percy that was now my lord Northumberland; and had in secret married him.

But there had never been a contract; much less a marriage. She had loved the man and desired the match; but before ever it came to contract my father had parted the lovers for lust of her.

Now she was no longer a wife, nor ever had been; and her child was a bastard. No more a Queen she must put off the crown, lay down all insignia of royalty and every honour the King had bestowed upon her. She had come into that hall a Queen; she left it, Anne Bullen—no more than that!

'Yet, Madam, in that moment her worst enemy must admit some greatness in her,' lady Kingston said. 'She left in majesty; majesty learned too late.'

And now she had good reason to believe she would not die.

'If I was never the King's wife, then however many lovers I took—though I took not one—then I committed no adultery. What husband did I cuckold? And what treason was there? I have not endangered the title of the King's heir—for my child is made bastard!' and at that, lady Kingston said, she wept. But soon she was laughing again. 'They cannot kill me!' she said and twirled upon her toes.

'Lady Anne,' lady Kingston told her, 'hope is a witch. Pray to God

while there is yet time!' But still she talked and still she laughed . . .
until the night before the dreadful day. And then Kingston came to tell
her of her death. She was not to die in the fire. It would be the block;
not the axe but the sword. 'The King of his grace has brought the
executioner from St. Omer; a man of skill and very quick!'

And now she knew the truth of it; and now she could hear the
hammers strike as they put up the platform for her death.

'It was like a great slow heart-beat,' lady Kingston said, 'but for
her the heart beat for death.

'Then she knelt to pray; she prayed long and with all her heart. And
then, Madam, she spoke of you!'

'I will not hear it!' I said. And why should I be made to pity her—
and my mother but four months dead? But still the women begged
leave; her honour stood in the matter, she said. And still I refused.
'Through Anne Bullen the noblest woman died, and some half-
dozen men come to their death. Now she herself is dead, let it be the
end. I'll hear no more!'

'It is a promise made to the dying. Madam, I beseech you!'

'Then speak!'

'Madam, having prayed, she commanded I should sit in the Queen's
chair; for Madam she had the royal lodgings to the last. Sit I would
not; I had not been good to her—to my shame I say it. To her grief
and fear I had, God forgive me, added torments of my own, taunting
her that first comes pride, then follows the fall. For, like her, Madam,
I had not till then believed they would take her head. There was no
woman, ever, in this country came to the block. That she who had
been Queen should be the first—no man could believe it!'

*I believed it. I know my father. He sought my own death, his own daughter
that never offered him wrong. . . .*

'So, Madam, I was ashamed. In those few hours before she died I
must treat her as the Queen.

'I must not sit in the Queen's chair,' I told her. She smiled at that;
and, for the first time, I saw that a sort of charm she had.

'"I am no more a Queen but a dying woman," she said. "I pray you
sit." So I sat in the great chair—as you sit now, Madam. Then she most
humbly knelt upon two knees, as I do now.' And lady Kingston
went down upon her knees, both hands clasped—a suppliant. "I charge
you," the lady Anne said, "as you shall answer for it on the Day of
Judgement, to kneel, as I kneel now, before the lady Mary's grace
and ask her forgiveness for all the ills I brought her and all the wrongs
I did her. Until I have your promise I cannot rest, neither this short

night nor in the eternal night." So, Madam, I promised; and this promise I have, through your kindness, kept.'

I said nothing to that. I bit upon my lips lest weakness betray me.

'After that,' lady Kingston said—and now I must, out of some odd respect for the dead, listen—'she prayed again; then she lay upon the bed but she did not sleep. She lay there, eyes upon the ceiling, and the tears wet upon her cheeks and lips. Shortly before daylight she rose and sent for her confessor—not Cranmer. "He played me false," she said, "I never confessed to him nor never will!" Madam, she confessed herself in the old manner of the true faith—she, herself, told me so.'

She had torn Holy church in sunder; through her, men that stood by their faith had come to their death; yet God in His mercy had, in that last hour, brought her back to His truth.

'She sent for my husband, Madam. She swore upon the Host her innocence. Could she have done that, facing her death and knowing herself guilty? Madam, I was not good to her and I am ashamed.

'She was content to die. She was weary of living. She had but one wish—that the thing would soon be over. And even that last wish was not granted. For, Madam, you know there were delays. "I fear I shall not die before noon as I was told," she said. "I am sorry for it. I had thought to be dead by this time and past my pain," and fingered her neck as though to comfort it.'

Did she still wear the ornament to cover . . . what?

' "The pain will not be much," my husband said. "It is a very small, subtle pain."

'She laughed at that and could not stop. "To bring Master Headsman all the way from France for this! I have a little neck. See!" And she spanned it with two small hands.'

Witch's neck, witch's hands with the budding fingers.

'Madam, she sent a last message to the King; even in that hour she had not lost the wit she had. "Tell him he has ever been constant to advance me. From a private gentlewoman he made me a marchioness; from a marchioness—a Queen. Now he raises me to a martyr's crown." '

I cannot think that Kingston had the courage to tell him her words; but this I do know. My father dying, it was her death haunted him to the end; *hers!*

'And, Madam, there is one thing more. That morning, when we dressed her for her death, she said, "Of all the wickedness they hold to my account, and for which I am to die—I am not guilty. Before God I swear it. Yet there is much to repent me of. And, of all the things I repent me most is the wrong I did to her Grace the Princess Mary." '

My rightful name long unheard hit me like a blow. She, in her last hour, she, of all people, had named me so; she had begged forgiveness. My hard heart a little softened; I could listen, I could pity.

'Madam, when at last she was called to her death—her aunt and I at either hand, her ladies behind her and all of us in black—my husband came to lead her to the scaffold.

'Standing there, Madam, she wore a fearful beauty. Very pale she was, her mouth very red where she had bitten upon it. She wore a gown of grey silk upon a petticoat of damask, red as her mouth; the long dark curls were caught within a net of gold. Whatever she was—and *what* she was God and her confessor alone know!—to put an end to so much beauty, it seemed wrong. The crowd that had come to jeer fell to silence.

'And in that silence she spoke; she said, as near as I can remember it, "Good Christian people, I come here to die according to the law. I come to accuse no man; nor to speak of what I am accused. It could not help me. I come here to die; and humbly I hold myself to the will of the King. If any person would enquire into the cause, let him judge as best he may. And so I take my leave of you and desire you all, pray for me."

'They will tell you Madam, that she spoke of the King, calling him a gentle, merciful Prince. It was not so. Of him she spoke no word. For we stood close to her, lady Bullen and I, she to take the gown and I to take the kerchief at her throat.'

Her throat. Her naked throat. Did those that stood near see it at last —the witchmark? Or was there nothing but a slender neck innocent of blemish? I do not know. I never asked. It seemed the last insult and I could not do it.

'Madam, she turned to her women that stood white as she herself. "I cannot reward you for your loving service," she said; and then, "I pray you be comforted for my death. Hold your virtue dearer than your life; and, in your prayers, remember my soul." To me she said nothing; me she could not thank for loving service. But she gave me a long look. I think she was asking me to remember my promise.

'Then she knelt and laid her head upon the block, her eyes unbound, for she would have it so. Those eyes upon him, immense and brilliant-shining, unmanned the executioner. Facing them he could not do his work. He stepped behind her and lifted the sword.

'She knew nothing; neither stroke nor pain; and so she died. He was, indeed, a master.'

I thanked the woman but I made her no gift. She had tormented a dying woman. When she was gone I thought long upon Anne Bullen. Young—scarce above thirty—she had come to a bloody death; and come with courage. The first woman to die upon the block. Let me not waste tears upon that last; I should have been the first—had she her way. Yet I could not so easy rid myself of guilt. I had had no hand in her death . . . but I had wished for it, prayed for it.

Had she been guilty? Had she suffered, innocent?

I walked the room arguing this way and that.

Upon the Host she had denied her guilt. Yet, dying, she had said no word as to her innocence; and why had she, in that last moment, entreated her women to hold their virtue dearer than their life?

Guilty? Innocent?

With Smeaton, I am sure for all his 'confession', she had not sinned; she would hold him no better than her lapdog. And those others; Weston, Norris, and Brereton; not one of them, dying, had admitted guilt. I think she was neither guilty nor yet innocent. I think she behaved without discretion. I think she teased their manhood, exciting herself and them; I think she went with them as near the ultimate as she dared. She wore the crown and meant to keep it. She'd not risk the legitimacy of the child she had, nor of the son she meant to have; no, nor a charge of high treason with it. Foolish then and indiscreet; no more than that!

Her brother; there was another story. Carnal love between brother and sister—it is not unknown. And these two, in all the lust of youth, had met almost as strangers. From childhood she had been bred in France, he in England. Suddenly they stood face-to-face—man and woman. They had burst upon each other without warning. Each had thought himself unique; now, in the other, each saw himself—good to look upon, musician and poet, young, ardent, gay and quick with life. Each loving his image in the other, like the boy in the Greek tale, loved himself. Two halves to make the perfect whole.

Driven by so strange, so unforeseen a passion, I think they were guilty. Maybe she thought suspicion could never touch them— brother and sister; maybe, carried on the tide of passion she never thought at all. And, maybe there was no guilt in them at all. The evidence of his wife was spoken clearly in malice; and other witnesses there were none. Yet who knows? After his sentence he said he'd no longer plead his innocence. Why? Why had he allowed her honour and his to be forever spat upon? Would he not—being guiltless and on the point of death—have protested his innocence, endeavoured to keep her name and his clean?

I do not know; he died silent. So we are back at the beginning. But one thing I do know now, which then I did not know—the unrelenting force of love that can drive one beyond all sense, all accepted custom, all goodness even.

But, innocent or guilty, she had asked my forgiveness and I prayed for her soul.

Chapter Twenty-Four

The blood was scarce dry within Anne Bullen's nameless grave before my father married again. The very morning—while she waited to be summoned to her death—he had demanded, and Cranmer given, dispensation to marry Jane Seymour; there was a tie of kinship through the Plantagenet line. Nor did he wait for the guns to signal his freedom before he was off to Wolf Hall, all clad in white like a bridegroom to sup with Jane, to betroth himself to Jane; and this much is certain. For who went galloping ahead to tell the news of Anne Bullen's death, but Francis Bryan that knew everything! Ten days later the King brought Jane to London for their marriage. It was Whitsuntide; and there were double festivities for the two occasions. Again my father was clad in white top-to-toe.

No-one seemed to find his haste indecorous; his purpose had long been known. And the marriage was acceptable; it took the taste of Anne Bullen out of all mouths. Parliament, indeed, commiserated my father upon the misfortunes of his two marriages so gallantly borne; of the true sufferers from those marriages—his children—no-one appeared to think. He was thanked for marrying again. 'Our good King sacrifices himself for the welfare of his people,' my lord chancellor told Parliament assembled, 'let us pray for a fair issue of this marriage,' and they proceeded to repeal the Act of Succession. The crown was to go to the King's children by Jane Seymour male *or female*.

Now the little Elizabeth, too, was a bastard; she and I, bastards both.

Anne Bullen was dead; but the ill she had done did not die with her. Shelton still remained mistress of the household; no-one, as yet, had thought to remove her. She was no easier to live with. Badly frightened, harassed by uncertainty, she would ignore me for days on end and then suddenly lash out with her tongue, sharp as ever. To the little one, she showed herself indifferent; there was no loyalty in her to Anne Bullen's child. Elizabeth, not yet three, was not old enough to understand the hateful word *bastard* but old enough to feel the cold wind blowing—the loss in position, in respect, in affection.

I found myself pitying the little creature that played all unknowing;

and pity, striking with so sharp a pain, made, as it were, a breach in my defences. I felt an outrush of love towards the child. *Princess* I had refused to call her; but the name of *sister* I had never denied. Now we were truly sisters in adversity. But I was twenty years old and she so small, I felt towards her as a mother might feel. Poor, and myself out of favour, there was little I could do; but I could, perhaps, give back to her some of the love and consequence she had lost. For that little time I loved her with a true heart; by Almighty God, I swear it.

We had removed to Hunsdon. I went down to the little one's apartments to see that all was well. Already neglect was clear—both with regard to attendants and to furnishings. There was no-one with her save Bryan, quiet at her stitching. I should not have been surprised; the shabby cortège that had carried us from Hatfield ought to have been warning enough! Bryan rose at once and went down in her curtsey; she had never, when she might, stinted to give me due deference.

The child was there; a thin child with her mother's sallow skin and black eyes; and the bright hair of . . . my father? Of George Bullen? She looked up and came running; even then, baby as she was, she moved with grace unhampered by the weight of her skirts. I lifted her up and held her close; too close, for she fought at me with small, fierce fists to be free. So I set her down to play upon the floor.

'It is always so with her,' Bryan said. 'Little as she is she trusts no-one, save me—and then I must tread careful. I do my best to play a mother's part. I am all the mother she ever had—or is like to have!'

'I will be mother to her—I am old enough!' And I sighed. It seemed to me that this little one was all the child I was like to have. Of late there had been nothing said of my marriage. It looked as though I must wither on my virgin stalk in the sour soil of this household.

'If you concern yourself with this little one, you court danger,' Bryan said. 'For you, Madam, there's danger enough already!'

'My danger lies with Anne Bullen in the grave!'

She said nothing to that.

'And you!' I asked. 'Shall you join your husband in the country? Or your son at court? You have sighed enough in this sad house.'

'I shall stay here—as long as I am let!' she said. 'I have been honoured with the charge of two royal children. I have not been found wanting at any time; nor shall I now!'

I bent to kiss her cheek—dear nurse of my childhood, faithful friend of my girlhood.

She had spoken no less than truth. My ill-treatment and my danger were no less—as I was soon to see. Anne Bullen had set both in train;

now, it seemed, they must, of their own impetus, bring me to my end. I was as poor, as humiliated, as threatened as ever. My father's anger against me—rubbed raw by Anne Bullen—was a wound not yet healed. I doubted it ever would be.

I had expected so much from Jane Seymour's kindness—if not direct, then through Cromwell; not from his own kindness, he had none, but because, ambitious as he was, he would strive to please the new Queen. Two things alone sustained my little courage—the memory of my mother; and my certainty in the true faith. The two, indeed, were one.

'Have patience, Madam,' Bryan said. 'The King knows the Queen's kindness for you!'

'She interceded twice for me and risked his anger; will she dare it a third time? And why, indeed, should she risk herself for me?'

'Because of the love she bore your mother and now bears you. And because she has a sense of rightness; and that rightness demands justice.'

'I wish to God I might believe you! But what after all do we know of her? Nothing but that she is quiet and elegant with a gentle manner; that her family bears a great name and that she brought my father a rich dowry. Yet—twenty-five before she was wed! Women, especially if they be heiresses, are not wont to wait so long! The concubine held that she was sly; beneath that untouched look, shop-soiled.'

'Of all ladies, Madam, you should know how to value Anne Bullen's word. Mistress Seymour's sense of propriety I judge sufficient to have guarded her virginity.'

'Virgin without passion,' I said.

Virgin without passion. It describes Jane Seymour perfectly. And it was this, I fancy, that drew my father after the violence of Anne Bullen; that, and the sense of propriety with which she arranged all things. This propriety would, of necessity, include a sense of justice. She would wish to see justice done; but she would not pursue it with passion. There was no passion in her.

I had waited a few days after my father's marriage in some hope; but he sent not a word, good or bad. Since he had sent for me to The More some two years past he had not set eyes on me; he had left me to my enemies. He had not been a kind father to me; yet he had loved me when I was a child.

If now he should send for me . . . *if!* I would earn his favour with humble obedience in all things—save what touched my mother's honour and my faith.

The days went by and I dared wait no longer. Now was the time—if ever; now when my father was in love with his new wife. It could not last long; she was too pale, too passionless to hold him. Cromwell might help me but I shrank from the thought of him. He had never been my friend; nor yet my enemy neither. He knew the Queen's mind towards me; there might be help in him.

Towards the end of May I took my courage in both hands and wrote to him. It was not a long letter and the salutations to his greatness took up a great deal of it—he was a vain man. At length I came to the heart of it.

> . . . I desire you for the love of God to be a suitor for me to the King's Grace to have his blessing and leave to write to his Grace, which shall be a great comfort to me, as God knows—Who have you forever more in His keeping. . . .

I prayed him to forgive my poor writing, since for above two years I had not been allowed pen, ink or paper. I signed myself, *Your loving friend, Mary* and dated my letter, At Hunsdon, 26th May.

I had not written in vain. Cromwell moved in the matter and moved fast. I had my father's permission to write to him. So down I sat, the pen shaking in my hand.

> In as humble and lowly a manner as it is possible from a child to her father and sovereign lord, I beseech your Grace for your daily blessing which is my chief desire in the world.
> I acknowledge all the offences I have done to your Grace since I first had discretion to offend, until this hour; I pray your Grace in the honour of God, and for your fatherly pity to forgive me. Next unto God I will submit me in all things to your goodness and pleasure to do with me what you will, humbly beseeching your Grace to consider I am a woman and your child, who has committed her soul to God and her body to be ordered as it shall stand with your pleasure. . . .

I begged him to accept me as his humble daughter; I told him of my joy in his marriage. I asked his gracious permission to wait upon the Queen.

> . . . and do her such service as shall please her to command me. And this, my heart shall be as ready to fulfil as the most humble servant she has.

I ended my letter with my true wish that for his happiness. I dated my letter and signed it,

Your Grace's most humble daughter and handmaid.
From Hunsdon, this first day of June.

I waited long and long but there came never a word. Hour by hour I looked for his answer; the thought of it, I am ashamed to say, came between me and my prayers.

The long summer days were slipping by; and my life, it seemed, slipped with them. I had lain too long beneath my father's displeasure.

The meadow-sweet hung like scented lace upon the meadows, pale roses lit the hedges. Elizabeth had learned to make a daisy-chain; even then I noticed how elegant her baby hands, how deft. She would crown herself with daisies, hang them about neck and arms . . . maybe they were the only ornaments she would ever have. I vowed if ever I came into favour she should share it; for to whom might she turn if not to me?

Anxiety, as always had its way with me. I waited racked with pain—eyes, head and teeth, alike aching; and with the pain my old enemy—nausea.

I had done better to let things be. My letter was the spark in the haystack. I had angered my father yet more. I had promised to submit myself *next to God*. It would not do. It questioned his supremacy. I must submit myself entirely—and no nonsense about God!

Cromwell wrote to tell me so; he enclosed a letter for me to copy and send to my father.

I do most humbly beseech your Grace to pardon me, most humbly prostrate before your noble feet, your most obedient subject and humble child, that has not only repented her offences hitherto but also desires simply and from henceforth and solely to put my state, conscience and living in your most gracious hands. . . .

I sat staring at the copy. I could not do it. My body I could put into his hands; my conscience, never! Befoul my mother's memory and my own birth—and she but five months dead! Blacken my soul with heresy by denying God's chosen Mouthpiece, the Pope! I had rather die; might, indeed, very well die! Refusal was now accounted high treason; nor need I think to escape the penalty. Anne Bullen's death had pointed the way.

I wrote again to Mr. Secretary Cromwell. I urged him.

. . . by the passion of Christ which suffered for you and me, that you will find means in your great wisdom that I be not moved to agree any further in the matter than I have done. For I assure you, by the faith I owe to God, I have done the uttermost my conscience will allow me.

Cromwell's reply was commanding, threatening, altogether ugly. If I set any value upon my life I must copy the draft of the letter that he once more enclosed, and send it, at once, signed to my father. It was my last chance. How long I sat there I do not know; nor how many times I took up my pen only to lay it down again. And then, as though he stood with me there in the room, Chapuys' words came very clear, *For the sake of our blessed faith you must not put your life in danger. . . .*

I picked up my pen again and began to copy word for word; but when I came again to the vow of absolute obedience, body and soul, my hand began to shake. Necessity drove me on.

. . . to put my state, conscience and living in your most gracious hands. . . .

next to Almighty God. I stared at the paper. God Himself had spoken. Without my own will my hand had written it. I dared not unwrite it.

With this letter I enclosed one for Cromwell himself. I thanked him for his goodness and all the pains he had taken on my account. I said I had rather lose the life out of my body than offend the King's grace; but I could do no other. The letter to my father I left unsealed; for whether I did so or not, Mr. Secretary would surely read it.

I was sick with fear when, my letter gone, I went to find Bryan; maybe she would ease me of my fears.

'Madam you are too young, too forsaken; you cannot stand alone.'

'What else can I do? My body I put into my father's hands; his every wish I shall obey save where it offends my soul. My soul I cannot surrender.'

'It is no true surrender. There is no other way. You must live to do God's work. As for the King—it is not all unkindness in him. Need drives him. He stands between devil and deep sea. It is the people's wish that you be restored—his first-born, true-begot child. He knows it and he cannot do it. For so he admits himself wrong and both Popes right—and that he'll never do!'

'So I must forever be a bastard, born of an incestuous union!' I cried out, bitter.

'Forever is a long day, Madam. When we are young we are wild to cut through the knot though it bring the world in ruin about our heads. When we are older we learn to untie the knot thread by thread, and little harm done.'

'How long must I wait; have I not waited long and long enough?'

'Until the lord King have a son. Then, I think, having his heart's desire, he will bring you back to your rightful place. It will please the people and it will please the Queen; and he himself will lose nothing thereby. Meanwhile, Madam, you must show yourself patient and obedient. . . .'

'*Obedient!* Again! Again! The word will be the death of me!'

'God forbid!' And crossed herself.

I waited, as it were, between life and death for Cromwell's answer. I waited in vain. But if from him I had no answer, I had my father's reply from another quarter. My lord of Norfolk appeared at the head of a commission to demand utter submission. And this time I found no hint of kindliness in him. He had saved his own skin by harshness towards his niece; had he put himself about he might have saved Anne Bullen from death. He was not like to endanger his life for me.

'Sir,' I told him, 'I cannot put my father on earth before my father in heaven!'

'Chop me no logic, Madam, and do as you are bid!' His voice was edged with menace.

'The Scriptures tell us . . .'

'Leave the Scriptures to your betters!' he interrupted, contemptuous and rough. 'I'll have no words from you! Bastard you are, but before God, I scarce believe of the King's begetting, so unnatural is your behaviour towards him! By that same God, were you my own child, even though first-born and true-begot, I would kick your head from wall to wall till it were soft as a baked apple. You are a traitor, Madam; and as a traitor shall be punished!'

Fine words, indeed, from a King's servant to a King's daughter! Yet not without their use; they showed me in what danger I stood.

To whom might I turn now? There was none but Cromwell. Kindness of a sort he had shown, small, mean and grasping, but for all that—kindness. In my extremity I wrote to him again. His answer, when it came, was worse then even my fears could have imagined. Nor was it pleasanter because of the messenger that brought it. It was delivered by the hands of his secretary Wriothesley—a man grown fat on church lands and persecution of the monks, I was not like to get much tenderness from him. I scarce knew him as yet, save as my father's useful tool. To my sorrow I was to know him better.

He was all courtesy; but he watched me with keen eyes. I took the letter, kneeling, and kissed the seal. No fault to be found with me there! I went over to the window and stood, my back to him so that he should not see my face.

A cruel letter. It was as though I stood defenceless while, repeatedly, Cromwell struck me across the face. Blow after blow. I began to tremble. With mock courtesy Wriothesley led me to a chair; and all the time he watched me.

'Sir,' I told him, 'I will leave you; when I am ready I will send for you.' And took my unsteady way to my bedchamber. There, in the quiet, I read the letter again.

He could do no more for me, Cromwell wrote; my wicked folly had put not myself alone but him, him, too, in danger.

. . . You undo yourself and all that have wished you good. It were great pity if you be not made an example in punishment since you make yourself an example in contempt of God, your father and his laws, by your own fantasy contrary to the judgments of all men. For you, alone, must profess to know and love God as much as you do; whereby you show yourself altogether too presumptuous. Therefore Madam, to be plain with you, as God is my witness, I think you are the most obstinate and obdurate woman that ever was; and one that deserves the extremity of punishment.

I dare not open my lips to name you, unless I have some ground that we have all mistaken you; that you are repentant of your ingratitude and miserable unkindness. And that you are ready to all the things you are bound to do by your duty and allegiance with every common subject. . . .

Extremity of punishment . . . every common subject. Clearly he was threatening me with death—a traitor's death; I was not to think my royal blood would save me.

He enclosed he said, a paper of articles I must sign.

. . . whereby you shall please God. Upon receipt thereof, I shall eftsoons venture to speak for your reconciliation.

But if I would not. . . .

I take my leave of you, forever and desire you will never write to me hereafter.

He ends with the cruellest words that could be written to one that sought to do her whole duty to her father but, first of all, to God.

I beseech God never to help me if I know it not to be your bounden duty by God's law and man's; and I must needs judge that person that shall refuse it, not fit to live in a Christian community. . . .

Not fit to live in a Christian community. He was threatening me not only with death of the body but death of the soul. Excommunication. Blow-hot, blow-cold Cranmer would not hesitate. I was to be cut off from God and man.

Chapter Twenty-Five

I stood alone in the silent room. If I did not sign I was outcast from God and man. So Cromwell had said; but it was not true. Cranmer, though he could excommunicate, could not cast me off from God. But, if I did sign? Would not God cast me out? If I signed under duress, God would not require it of me; nor the Pope, nor any good man—Chapuys had told me so. He had said, and more than once, that, when I had contended to the uttermost, then, at the eleventh hour, I must sign. I must not risk death. I was needed to hold the torch of the true faith.

I took up the paper Cromwell had enclosed. It was called *the lady Mary's confession*. There was a great preamble about my wicked obstinacy to a good and noble King—it was Cromwell's way to fawn upon the King and to kick all others into the dirt. I swore to be a humble, obedient subject in all things,

I do plainly and with all my heart, confess and declare my inward belief and judgment with due obedience to the laws of this realm; so minding for ever to persist in this determination without change. . . .

I swallowed in my throat, reading the words; I must now and forever throw my conscience to the dogs.

I do recognise and acknowledge the King's Highness to be the Supreme Head on earth, under Christ, of the Church of England; and do utterly refuse the bishop of Rome's pretended authority within this realm hitherto usurped; and do utterly renounce all manner of remedy, interest and advantage which I may, by any means, claim by the bishop of Rome's laws, jurisdiction or sentence at the present time, or in any wise hereafter by any manner. . . .

Cast off God's Vicar beyond remedy—now and forever! From so embracing, so eternal a vow could God Himself absolve me?

Nausea was beginning to rise in me, pain to attack my eyes. As well as I could, I made out the following words:

I do freely and frankly and for the discharge of my duty towards God, the King's Highness and his laws, recognise and acknowledge that the marriage heretofore between his Majesty and my mother, the late Princess Dowager, was by God's law incestuous and unlawful. . . .

How could I sign it—and I still in mourning for her that was, of all women, pure and innocent?

How long I wandered the room I cannot say. Now I fell upon my knees and prayed for guidance; now I lay upon my bed weeping. Conscience attacked me upon the one hand, expediency upon the other. I was alone and frightened and bitterly unhappy; but for all that I did not want to die. I was young and had known little of the sweetness of living; and upon my shoulders I bore the task of bringing back my country to the true faith.

The afternoon sun had set and still I knew not what to do. I lay upon the bed eyes closed against pain that the brightness increased. I must have afallen asleep; for I lay there in the darkness of my own making, quiet and dreaming. Or perhaps not dreaming. I knew my mother was there in the room; I saw nothing, heard nothing but I felt her presence. Her soul spoke direct to mine.

'Daughter, do not break your heart for this. You sign for God, that one day you shall bring this poor country back to His Feet. As for my honour—I am past all earthly cares. For yourself, you must, for this present time, take the stain of bastardy. God knows the truth; one day He will show it forth and the stain will be washed away.'

I opened my eyes to a darkness not of my making; it was the darkness of night. Calmer now, I knelt upon the window-seat; it had been raining heavily and there came up to me the fragrance of the garden—wet grass and roses and spicy picotees. Under the moon the garden lay bright and pure and quiet after the storm. I thought, it is a parable of my own soul; I have been beaten upon by storm, yet I shall come to hope and peace.

I lit my candle, the tinder shaking in my hand; yet my pen was steady as though my mother herself guided it to sign my name.

Secured upon the last sheet I found yet another letter to be copied and sent to my father. I did not read it; I knew Cromwell's style well enough. Sign it I must; copy it, I could not—I was weary to the bone. To his own handwriting I added:

From Hunsdon, this Thursday, at eleven o'clock at night. Your Grace's most obedient daughter and handmaid, Mary.

It was done—rightly or wrongly, I did not know. Had I, out of fear, deceived myself as to my mother's presence and so perjured my soul? Or had she truly spoken to save me that I might one day testify for God?

Sitting there I fell suddenly into the sleep of utter exhaustion and knew nothing until sunshine lay bright upon the room and the birds calling one to the other.

Without further ado and lest I should change my mind, I sent for Wriothesley. I did not speak, could not, indeed, speak; dumb, I thrust the papers into his hand.

He said, 'Madam, I am glad. You shall surely get good from this. I have a message from the King himself. Now you have signed you shall have your own household again; you shall yourself choose what servants to have about you.'

It was a thing I could not, at the first take in, but he nodded smiling the while. 'It is true. Master Secretary will write to you. And another thing that shall please you well—the lady Elizabeth is no more *Princess*; to call her so is insult to the King and to Parliament—an insult to be punished.'

I said nothing. I had known it must come—the pattern repeated. There was no pleasure in me; nothing but pity for the innocent child.

'And Madam—if I may make so bold—Master Secretary has laboured long on your behalf. It has not, you understand, been easy; he has, more than once, taken the lash of the King's anger. Some word of thanks would not come amiss—you are not yet out of the wood; for your own sake I say it!

I had betrayed my conscience and now I must thank Cromwell for it. Wriothesley's eyes were fixed upon me; without any word they spoke. *Between you and death—Cromwell; only Cromwell.* So much of humiliation I had suffered, so much of conscience laid aside; should I strain now at a hair? I bade him wait; he should take my thanks with him.

It was a letter hard and hard, indeed, to write! But if the thing must be done let it be done and properly done. Cromwell was not one to rest without fulsome praise. I put the seal upon my submission.

How much bound I am to you, good Mr. Secretary who have not only travailed when I was almost drowned in folly but also to recover me before I was utterly past recovery. . . .

And, having praised him as much as even he could expect, I wrote concerning the child Elizabeth.

Concerning the Princess Elizabeth—for so, I think, I must call her yet; I offered, at her entry to that name and honour, to call her *sister* but it was refused unless I would add the other title to it, which I denied then more obstinately than I am now sorry for it . . . now that you think it meet I shall never call her by any other name than *sister*. . . .

Princess. For the first time, in pity, I gave her that title. But, if in future I must call her naught but *sister* that name I should honour with a true and loving heart.

I came then to my thanks for a restored household. I could not risk my father's anger in this.

Whatever the King's Highness shall appoint, shall without exception be, to me, most heartily welcome.

And then, my heart yearning for some true friend in whose love I could rest, I named but three, among them Susan Clarencieux, this last old, experienced and wise. All others I left to my father's choice.

Cromwell's answer was unexpectedly kind. I did not know that even then his ambition had reached to marriage with me, discarding a faithful wife in the process. It was as well I did not know. I had rather died than wed with him, the common fellow with his gloss of courtly manners and beneath it vulgarity running deep. He had enclosed yet another letter for me to send to my father. If the one had been abject, this was slavish. Well, I had swallowed so much; this I must swallow, too. I was not yet out of the wood, Wriothesley had warned me.

I copied it word for word.

. . . knowing your excellent learning, virtue, wisdom and knowledge, I shall put my soul into your discretion . . . and forthwith direct my conscience as well as my body to your mercy and fatherly pity. . . .

I had given myself soul and body into his heretic hands; yet I felt nothing—nothing at all but blessed release from fear. It was as though shame were dead within me; I had lived with fear too long.

From my father, no acknowledgment nor any sign of favour. The promise of my own household seemed now an added cruelty to mock me by comparison with my present state. One week went by and another week, and a third; and now the numbness of shame wearing off, I understood what I had done. I had signed away my soul, slavishly thanking the father that had commanded it. I no longer believed I had felt my mother in the room; I had imagined it for my own purpose. These were, I think, the most anguished weeks of all my unhappy life.

Fear may in time wear away; but shame—never. Shame's bite is longer, deeper, crueller. Wretched and ill, my spirits at their lowest, I waited still. Shelton, trying to secure herself against the future, now sought to humiliate me, now to flatter me. Her flattery was more insulting than her insult. I kept my distance.

Bryan brought me a message from Chapuys, 'Madam, he says you have done right, and the Pope will absolve you. He bids you give me the writing wherein you swear you acted under duress; you may need it some day. I am to give it to him to keep safe.'

I did as he advised; but not all his kind words nor the Pope's absolution could lighten my shame. I swore, before God, that never again should I allow fear to drive me against my soul. I would take the matter to God and let Him be my judge.

I had given up hope when my father came.

Suddenly, without warning, he was there—himself, after the long years of desertion, taking me by surprise. It was his way to catch you off guard; he trusted no-one.

It was growing towards evening when, up to my chamber, came Shelton pale and shaken. Whether this visit forebode ill to her or to me she could not know. 'Madam,' and she bent the knee—a courtesy I had not ever had from her. 'It is the King. The King is here, *here!* And the Queen with him. They would speak with you at once.'

So down I went in my shabby gown; but had I searched I had found no better. And, as I went, I trembled and held fast to the balustrade lest I fall.

They were there, both of them, he striding about impatient; I saw he was limping a little. It was the injury he had sustained falling from his horse. The shock had played its part in Anne Bullen's miscarriage—if we are to believe her; and so in her death. He was to go limping from it all his life; and in his death, too, it played its part.

I scarce knew him from the back, so stout he had grown; and, when he turned about, it was little easier. His face had lost its fine shape; it was squarer, coarser—if I may use such a word of a King, older than I had remembered; and the once-gold hair of head and beard that framed it, now all streaked with grey, added to his altered look. A network of purple veins discoloured the fine white-and-red complexion the Venetian ambassador had once admired. The eyes, the bright blue eyes, looked smaller sunk into the folds of fat; and the small mouth looked smaller too—a child's mouth, almost, pursed and pouting in that large, flushed face.

He had come into sudden middle-age; and beside his wife, that slender, elegant creature, he looked old and soiled. But she—whatever they whispered against her virtue—looked young and innocent; untouched.

I was taken with pity for him so that I forgot his long unkindness. He was my father and he was growing old. I knew what that must mean to his vanity—he had been the handsomest prince in Christendom.

Something of my affection he must have read, for he smiled; and then I saw the old charm still there. For all the change, he was still the dear father of my childhood.

At the door I kneeled, and again when I came up to him; and, so kneeling, waited for him to speak.

'Daughter!' he said; that—and no more.

I bowed my head until it touched my knee—a suppliant's bow. I rose then and knelt before the Queen. She looked at me with kindness. I kissed her hand but she bent and raised me up and took me in her arms.

'Now my good, obedient daughter is at the end of her troubles!' my father said. 'We shall arrange a good marriage for her.' He looked at my shabby gown. 'You shall have incomes sufficient for your need —and more: more! Meanwhile, here is my writing for a thousand crowns.'

Jane Seymour took from her finger a good, clear diamond and put it upon my hand. 'My friendship goes with it!' she said.

'Come, sweetheart, to bed!' my father interrupted, while yet I stammered my thanks at these tokens of favour so unexpected. She was clearly tired; there were blue smudges beneath her eyes staining the white of her skin. I marked the desire in my father's eyes. It was little rest she would get this night—or any other!

Chapter Twenty-Six

I chose Hunsdon as my chief residence. It pleased me to govern this house where I had been held less than the meanest servant. Shelton was sent about her business and all her household with her. I had asked Cromwell and received permission for Elizabeth to remain with me. I would care for her at need; and need there well might be! My father had delighted in this child as once in me; now, like me, she was to suffer neglect. As long as she had been let, lady Salisbury had spared me the worst of it, to her I had always looked for comfort; this kindness I might do for the child. And for myself I did a kindness, also; for with Elizabeth came Bryan.

Cromwell was as good as his word. Besides the gentlewomen I had requested, I had my full household—chamberlain and steward, ladies and waiting women, gentlemen, physicians and chaplains. I had my Master of the Horse—I that so recently must thank Cromwell for the gift of a mare since horse I had none. I was lifted up to a place befitting a King's daughter—though a bastard!

Since I had been told I might choose my own household I asked for lady Salisbury to govern all. To my surprise, I was refused and no reason given. 'Do not press it,' Bryan said, 'it is better for her and better for you!' And when I enquired further she said, 'The lady is old; she has retired into the country. She is seldom seen at court.'

Well, if my old friend would not undertake the matter, I must content myself with Clarencieux, that wise and experienced woman.

But in spite of these honourable trappings, and though I might write and receive letters, invite what guests I chose, I knew better than to suppose myself free. No letter came nor went but Cromwell knew its contents, no visitor but he knew of it, I made no step but it was reported; the wrong word spoken—and death might still be my portion. The seeds Anne Bullen had sown sprang thick as weeds.

That summer of 'thirty-six I spent in the quiet of my own home, enjoying those things of which I had long been deprived. Long quiet days refreshing my Latin and Greek; Spanish, alas all but forgotten,

I would have begun once more but Bryan warned me against it. 'The King is much set against Spain; he could make it a cause of quarrel with you!' I read a great deal in French, and all I could lay hands upon in astronomy and geography. And since my fingers had grown clumsy from disuse, Master Paston gave me lessons upon the virginals, Van Wilder upon the lute. It gave me the most particular pleasure to hear music and to make it again after the arid years. I had a dancing teacher from Paris and a drawing-master to make patterns for my stitchery. In the evenings I would sit at my needlework enjoying the elegant patterns and the fine colours. Or we would play at cards, for which I had discovered a passion. I have something of the gambler in me; it was, as I have said, the charming cards my mother had brought from Spain—kings and queens and chevaliers all painted fine and true within borders of bright flowers—that, in the beginning, caught my childish fancy to set that passion alight.

A quiet life for a young woman of twenty but none the worse for that. To quiet Hunsdon came rumours of disquet and discontent. I shut my ears to these—I could do nothing. I needed peace to heal me of the past years.

My dancing-lessons I was soon sharing with Elizabeth. At the beginning she had stood wide-eyed, watching; moving now a small hand, now a small foot. Good dancer though I was, she, at her tender age, outdid me. Where I must learn she had the whole matter by nature. She was forever dancing. Let me but pluck upon the lute and there she was, at the first note, dancing, dancing, dancing; knowing, without teaching, not only the rhythm but the correct placing of little hand and foot. Or should I play a song—for I sang but little, my voice being over-deep for a woman—there she was, her little pipe lifted to the tune. She was, at this time, though a wilful little piece, a delightful companion.

My thousand crowns I laid out to their best advantage for I daily expected a summons to the court. Bryan chaffered for me with silk merchants, linendrapers and other hucksters; she bargained also with tailors and shoemakers. The thousand crowns that had seemed so much dwindled like snow in sunshine.

That golden summer when my sun was slowly rising, young Richmond's sank and died. As a child he had been, like myself, sturdy; then, like myself, had grown delicate. Like so many Tudors he died in early youth. Elizabeth was different. From sturdy childhood, she grew through girlhood to womanhood in perfect health. She must have had her childish disorders but I cannot remember her ever sick or ailing. It was, indeed, this superb health of hers that, later, quickened my suspicions that she might not be my father's daughter. But so long as she was small and helpless I was content to accept her—my sister.

I grieved for young Richmond dead at seventeen; I grieved for my father. But he? Did he himself deeply grieve? Had he done so the whole court must have known—he was not one to hide his feelings. He was a sanguine man, so he softened his grief with a magnificent funeral and contented himself with high hope in his new Queen.

Early that summer Chapuys came to visit me. 'Has your grace thought' —and he never failed of my royal title, 'that young Richmond's death may advantage you?'

'How should it? The Queen is young. As for me, I have no itch for the crown, unless it come to me by God's Will. Believe it!'

'I do believe it. But the King may not. And with some cause. There's discontent everywhere; even in this quiet place you must know it. But one thing you may not know—your name is in every rebel's mouth!'

'No!' I cried out pushing away the thought with both hands.

'But yes. Whether the rebels be honest men or rogues, whether their cause be good or bad, the excuse is always the same—*Justice for the Princess Mary!*'

'I am sorry for it.' And I could scarce speak for the dryness in my mouth.

'*Should* you be, Madam? You have but to say the word and the whole country will rise in your name!'

'God forbid!' Monsieur Chapuys; you are my friend as you were my mother's before me. So now I speak plain. You have already raised this issue with us both. My answer was and is, and always will be, the same as hers. I will never lift my hand against my father and King. It is impious; and it is treason. Let me hear no more of it!'

'Maybe you are wise,' he said. 'But it is hard to see this country given over to heretics.'

'God will not prosper traitors,' I said.

He bowed and left me to my troubled thoughts.

Risings in my name! Would not my father visit them upon me? Now I was glad, indeed, to have had no word from him. No news is good news.

My father had troubles enough. Discontent; the country rocked with it. The once-loved King had lost something of favour by his treatment of my mother and myself. He had lost more by his union with Anne Bullen, though that he had somewhat redeemed by marriage with Jane Seymour. Some favour he had lost, too, by turning his back on the Pope; but, on the other hand, many of the new sort of religion welcomed it—it had made themselves, as well as the King, rich.

But how had these riches been gained?

By the casting down of monasteries. My father had started, in Wolsey's time, to destroy the smaller houses; and for a while their treasure and their incomes had sufficed. Now my father, that lavish spender, needed more money; the treasury was well-nigh empty . . . and Cromwell had sworn to make his master the richest ruler in Christendom.

But how? You cannot squeeze blood from a stone.

It seems you can! Heavier taxes had been the first answer; an answer that did nothing to lessen growing discontent. The money raised was not enough and Cromwell was ready with his second answer.

There were scurrilous tales going about of life within monastery walls. Maybe some of them were true, or half-true; for the most part they were lies—but they served their purpose. Cromwell sent his officers to enquire into them and the reports were all he could wish! Tales of lazy monks battening on their house's wealth; tales of midnight orgies, of drunken feasts and seduced nuns. But of good men that, in many houses, carried out their duties like true servants of God—no word. The smear was enough to cover them, too.

At first Cromwell moved with some show of reason. Smaller houses that had outlived their usefulness he closed and sent the monks into larger houses where there was work for all. It was scarce noticed, at first, that the churches of these closed houses had been robbed and their treasure—God's treasure—carried away.

The people, especially in country places, were concerned with greater losses than silver plate. They had lost the prayers, the alms, the food, the nursing and the physic—once freely given for the love of God. And their loss was the more cruelly driven home by the sight of the holy houses they had known from childhood burnt and blackened, the stonework destroyed, the roofs stripped of lead, the gaping windows, the grass growing between the stones. And the loss was even more bitter when the buildings, left intact, were sold to the highest bidder, or given to those men my father found useful and wished to reward—men that cared nothing for the poor now so much the poorer. So the new people, jumped-up nobility, sat pretty in their great houses, or arrogant, rode the countryside, fostering discontent and hatred everywhere.

In the north the suffering was worse. The plight of the people was growing desperate. Landowners, and especially those now in possession of monastery lands, were enclosing great tracts to graze sheep, land that had been used to grow food—there's more money in wool than in food; golden fleece, indeed! So farmers and tillers that had never been rich in the hard north, now knew the pinch of real poverty. So many left workless; and, since less food was grown, what there was, scarce and high-priced. Nor did the heavy taxes make things easier; and the help that poor men had once had of the monks, no longer to be found.

These men of the north were bitter not only with their own wrongs, there was anger and pity for the monks that had been driven out. Men that had spent their lives within sheltering walls doing their duty to God, old men, now wandered the country turning their hands—when they were lucky—to work they had never done before. Or else they begged or more often starved—men that themselves had once fed the hungry; I had seen them for myself, old, sick and bewildered, dragging blistered feet in the stones of the road and my heart had broken with pity.

Cromwell had sworn to make his master the richest prince in Christendom; it looked as though he were going to make him the most hated. Already Mr. Secretary was at work destroying the last of the monasteries—the greatest and richest that so far he had not dared. Again it was the old story; buildings destroyed or sold; land enclosed, church plate and ornaments sent to the King.

But even this, it seemed, was not enough to fill an empty treasury. There were rumours of new taxes—taxes on weddings, on christenings, on burials. A man could neither breathe nor stop his breathing, people said, without he paid for it. To quiet Hunsdon came ever louder mutters of their anger.

No wonder there was discontent everywhere. I prayed there would be no risings; and, please God, not in my name.

Summer passed and drew on to autumn; and still my father did not send for me. If his cup of trouble had been full before, it was now overflowing.

In the first week of October discontent broke into open revolt.

In Lincoln the people rose; it was not only the common folk but gentry and priests, also. They demanded no further increase in taxes and no more destruction of monasteries. They asked freedom to

worship in the old way; and since the two things were intertwined—
a repeal of those acts that made my mother's marriage incestuous and
myself a bastard.

I saw now why my father had so cruelly forced me to submit—and
to make my submission known. All over the country, men true to the
old faith saw in me their only hope. But they were not always honest
men. As Chapuys had said—every malcontent, every rogue, every
criminal, fearing for his skin, stirred up trouble; and stirred it in my
name. I was the danger spot. It was this, together with a nature that
could brook no denial, that had forced my father to offer me submission
or death.

And now the Lincoln rebels were on the march. Their demands were
right and just; but however good the cause, revolt is treason. I trembled for them; I trembled for myself.

My father dealt with them in his own way. He sent out heralds to
declare the rumours false; there should be no new taxes. As for the
monasteries; only corrupt houses or those that had outlived their
usefulness had been and should be closed—*closed*, a word more reassuring than *destroyed*. He would consider their every grievance, and
there should be free pardon for all. So the rebels went home—and
Suffolk followed them with a sizeable army to see that they stayed
there. And all was peace.

But not for long. Scarce had the rebels reached home before a new
rising broke out in Yorkshire and spread throughout the north—the
north already starving, body and soul.

'It calls itself the Pilgrimage of Grace,' Bryan said. 'It carries on
its banner the Five Wounds of Christ; and beneath it march not only
peasants but merchants and gentry and noblemen. Yes, and high officers
of the King, judges, even; and with them priests and scholars. They
are led by one, Robert Aske, he's a gentleman, a lawyer and a man of
honour.'

'God help them all!' I said.

'They will need it. They are rebels; yet they declare their loyalty
to the King.'

'Their demands, I suppose, are much those of the Lincoln rebels.'

'Pretty much; but Madam, there's one thing more. They demand that
the King declare you legitimate; and, further, that he declare you his
heir until such time as he have a son!'

'Then God help me, too!' I said. 'This revolt could be my death-
warrant.'

At Hunsdon, we listened with fearful hearts for the news.

A very great army—all Yorkshire, Northumberland and Westmorland was on the march; an army disciplined, well-disposed and forbidden to pillage . . . but rebels still.

Pontefract castle fell. York opened its gates.

'The archbishop, himself, marches beneath the banner of the Five Wounds,' my steward said, come in with news from market.

My father sent forces under Norfolk.

'They say he cannot match the number of the rebels,' my steward said. 'Nor, as I hear, are Norfolk's men over-willing. For they march in the name of the King; but the Pilgrims in the name of the King of Heaven!'

At the end of October Norfolk declared a truce with the Pilgrims. The terms were reasonable; a deputation led by Aske was to lay their grievances before the King—a King, Norfolk promised, debonair and in good humour. So home went the rebels, hoping to be about their proper business; and especially the gathering in of the neglected harvest.

To London went Aske to put his head in the lion's mouth—a lion gracious and reasonable. Nothing further from this lion than snarls or bites. No! But promises to consider with favour all grievances, promise of free pardon for all. Promises . . . promises.

All Christendom knows how the Lancaster Herald read out the King's pardon; and how Aske tore off his Pilgrim's badge crying out, We'll wear no badge but the King's! And how, back home again, he bade the rebels lay down their arms, the good King would settle all.

The lion, for all his graciousness, is a drinker of blood; so shrewd a man as Aske should have remembered it. But a King's word is a royal word; and it was nearing Christmas, the season of goodwill, and he longed to be home with his good news.

And now it came—the long-dread summons. I was to go to Richmond for the Christmas festivities. At the thought of facing my father my heart all-but stopped in my breast. Had he truly forgiven the rebels? Would he punish me because he had not punished them?

The Queen had sent me thirty guineas, earnest of her goodwill; and though I laid them out to make myself fine I was not pleased with my looks. My father liked a handsome firm-fleshed woman; and I at my best, was nothing but pretty in my small neat way. Now I was scarce that; fear and ill-health are not conducive to handsome looks. If I did not do him credit I should anger him further. A small hair to add to the weight of my anxieties—but a hair may turn the scale.

On a bitter cold morning I set out wrapped about in a great cloak and hood to keep me from the worst of the weather. For all my fine household I had not the means to make a fine show; the promised incomes had not been paid. I travelled like a merchant's wife—and not a rich one neither—with some half-dozen servants. I was dressed sober, no fur to hood or cloak—the Queen's gold had not stretched so far. But though I rode humble, everywhere folk came out to greet me, to visit me in my lodgings, to put into my hands such gifts as they could afford.

I travelled between hope and fear. The *Pilgrimage of Grace* was over—and no bloodshed. Surely my father would not hold it against me that my name had been used . . . and the Queen had sent me thirty guineas; surely she had not dared had he been angry still.

London was gay; it had hung out banners to greet me. I could scarce see the well-known streets for my tears. So long since I had been let to ride through this beloved city. And so to Richmond but not by water; for the Thames was frozen and bright with skaters, with fires and with braziers of roasting chestnuts.

There was no bustle in the courtyard nor any greeting at the great door. A cold reception after the long, cold riding. My father meant not to make overmuch of me; my heart, never very high, sank. Yet expected I was; for within, my lord of Norfolk waited to conduct me, all travel-stained as I was, to the presence chamber. The doors were flung open and there I stood. Never throughout all my loneliness and fear had I felt so lonely, so frightened. My father was a man to strike terror into hearts older and braver than mine; how should I not be afraid? My name had been writ large in the rebels' demands . . . and I had lain long, too long, beneath his displeasure and the shadow of death.

Chapter Twenty-Seven

He was standing by the fire chatting to the Queen; he had his back to me and he did not so much as turn his head. Yet, for all that, he knew I was there. At the door I went upon both knees, and then, since he made so sign, came half-way to kneel again; and still he made no movement. The Queen made a step forward but he restrained her with his hand. He was not going to make things easy for me.

My third obeisance brought me to his very feet. Then he did turn about and I saw the smile that was his chiefest charm. It meant little; but so loving it seemed, my heart took grace. And, as I kneeled a suppliant, he laid a hand upon my head in blessing—he that so short a time ago had threatened to take it from my shoulders. He raised me up and turned me to face the Queen. I kneeled again while he stood satisfied and smiling; then he raised me once more, and, holding me by the hand, turned to Norfolk that stood near. 'Some of you would have had me put this dear child to death!' and his voice was accusing.

'Then,' the Queen said, 'you had lost the chiefest jewel of England!'

'No!' he cried out, 'here is our chiefest jewel!' and smote her lightly upon the belly. She smiled, shaking her head; he was in too much haste—she did not conceive until February.

I stood between the two, for the moment forgotten; and it came to me again, how nearly he had, indeed, put me to death, importuning Parliament in the matter. And I wondered, knowing his sudden changes and his swift cruelties, how long it might be before he again altered his mind concerning me. I was not yet strong after my sickness and I was weary with my journey; now all the years of misery and fear came sweeping over me. My hands and feet went suddenly cold; the great room began to move, to whirl and turn . . . there was a blackness before my eyes.

Madam the Queen must have spoken for me; for the blackness clearing, I came to myself in an anteroom with my father bending over me. 'Why, child!' he said, 'there's naught to fear. Henceforth nothing shall go against you.'

It was my happiest Christmas since faraway Ludlow. When I remembered the wretchedness of other years I dared scarce believe my good fortune, knowing that still I stood, as it were, upon a quicksand. There were masques and music, feasts and dancing. There was much gaming and stakes were high; sometimes I won and then there was gold in my pocket—for my father, in spite of his promise, gave me none. When I, alas, lost, the Queen would send me a purse and once it was as much as fifty guineas.

I was glad to be back at court—in currency once again, as it were. I was glad to walk in friendship with the Queen and to receive my father's favour, fickle though it might be.

I was anxious now to speak for my sister; but my father, though he spoke often with me, said never a word of her. 'Leave it awhile,' the Queen said. 'With the lord King we must work little by little. And for yourself—walk with care!'

It was good advice. I must not trust to the new-found kindness of my father; for he pressed me constantly upon this and that; and especially upon my faith. He would open a conversation, all sweet-smiling, so that I did not, at first, understand whither I was being led and might have fallen into a trap.

Chapuys, too, warned me to watch my every word.

'The revolts were, in part, religious,' he said, 'and both made use of your name. It could not fail to arouse the King's suspicions of you—always, alas, too ready! And never think that all who now smile upon you are your friends; believe me they are not! Some the new worship has brought into a high place, others have grown rich on church treasure. It is not in their interest that your father's favour continue; it could overthrow them and their policies.'

'They're more like to overthrow me! There's the Rochford woman.'

His face twisted in disgust remembering George Bullen's widow that had sworn away her husband's life.

'She's been raised to lady of the Bedchamber—for services rendered,' I told him. 'God knows I had no love for Anne Bullen; yet that woman's mouth seems to drip with blood. Once I asked the Queen how she could endure the creature about her and she smiled. *It is the King's wish. I obey him instantly and without question. Thus, when I express a wish it is granted also, instantly and without question . . . but I am careful what I ask, and when.*'

'What she wishes is to bring you back into favour; when she shall ask must be in her own good time,' Chapuys said.

'I know it. But still I sicken at the Rochford woman; and fear her too! Her tongue brought her husband to his death, why should she be more tender towards me? I keep my distance; but always with due courtesy!'

'Your grace is wise!'

'I have need to be. And it is time. I am nigh upon my twenty-first birthday!'

The new year of 'thirty-seven came in. Cromwell, showing himself more than usual friendly, sent me a new year's gift—a gold comfit-box set with jewels. I would have returned it had I dared. But I did not dare. I put it by and would neither look at it nor touch it.

All this time I had seen nothing, heard nothing of my dear lady Salisbury. I asked Chapuys, who knew everything, why this was so.

'The King blames her for what he calls your obstinacy—he cannot forget she was your mother's friend. And he cannot forget, either, that her son would not acknowledge that first marriage unlawful!'

'A man must speak the truth. And, besides, it is all so long ago!'

'It is sometimes dangerous to speak the truth—and your father has a long memory. Madam, the best you can do for your old friend is—nothing. Bring her to his mind and you harm her, and yourself; yourself, also! And, forgive me if I speak out of place, do not urge the King's favour for Anne Bullen's bastard. Do not, I beg you! She is a snake!'

'At four years old!'

'For all that dangerous; and will grow more dangerous with the years!'

'It is a harmless little one!' I said.

The month of January went by. My father was restless, uncertain in his moods. From words he let fall I feared he meant to break his word to Aske. Once I heard him roar out to Cromwell, 'Of course I am afraid, you dolt, you blockhead! The man that is never afraid is a fool; and a King that fears nothing, a criminal. Should I not fear lest the country be split, top to bottom by these damned Papists? By God I'd sooner hang those northern rebels than see rivers of blood flowing. Aye and I shall, too, give me the chance!' I know he meant me to hear, for he turned him about to where I sat. 'I'll let no damned Papist tell me whether my girl be bastard or no; nor who shall wear the crown after me. It is for me, for me alone to decide.'

I trembled for the Pilgrims of Grace; I trembled for myself. I longed to be out of his sight and home again.

So for all his gracious smiling, all his promises, he'd had no intention, ever, of letting the Pilgrims go scotfree. He'd been waiting his chance and soon enough it came.

A handful of rebels, in a spot too remote to have heard, as yet, of the King's promise, muttered still among themselves. The movement having been broken, they were harmless; but it was the excuse for which he waited. To men unarmed and pardoned, he sent Norfolk upon a bloody mission.

All over the north men hung in chains. Aske, that my father had so pleasantly entertained, Aske that man of goodwill, being the first. There were not sufficient gallows nor chains to hang them all and some must be cut down still breathing before others could be strung up. Nor could any man forget the good men betrayed; the stench of rotting corpses spread from the north to pollute the air of the south.

And so it went; day after day, week after week until summer saw the last of those that had trusted in the King's word. And all the time I must carry myself lest my father's watchful eye detect in me some sign of distress or disapproval. Things must have gone hard with me but that the Queen showed me the most loving friendship. There was no question of my going home; she would have me by her. So from Richmond to Greenwich we went, thence to Westminster and after that to St. James's, a smaller house, friendly and comfortable, where the Queen might rest. And all the time she did not cease to show me her love and I grew to value her in return—not for her gifts but for herself; she had a natural courtesy that never failed. In precedence she put me second, only, to herself, seeing to it that the whole court paid me due deference. At dinner and supper I sat opposite to her; and, my father being absent, she would take me by the hand that we might go in together and sit side-by-side. Her courtesy was heavenly balm to one so long humbled and insulted.

To my father she was perfect. He was not easy to live with; his angers that had been fierce but fleeting, grew ever more fierce, more lasting. He was quick even with her, and jealous. She gave him no cause; but she was half his age and queenship had added to her comeliness . . . and Anne Bullen had taught him a bitter lesson. Whether she loved him or not, I cannot say; but patiently, lovingly she performed her every duty. It could not have been easy!

In March of that bitter year of punishment the Queen knew she was pregnant. She gave me her news herself; I think she feared that, being cut off from the crown, I might, unwarned, show some distress and thus bring my father's anger down upon me.

I was glad for her and for him; for myself, also, I should rejoice—if the child should be a boy. That the King's son should inherit the crown was right and proper; any daughter but myself improper and wrong—an insult to my mother and to me.

I said, 'God keep the Queen in health and bring her safe delivery. I pray, Madam, it may be a son.'

'Why, so do I!' she said. 'But—it could cost you the crown!'

'Any child of the Queen could do that!'

'A son must put it beyond question,' she said. 'But a girl? You are still the King's eldest daughter; no new act can alter that!'

'But still a bastard, Madam. I do not want the crown if a son may inherit. How should I, being a woman, bear its weight?'

'You could bring back the old, true faith,' she said very low.

'For that, if need be, yes. I would persuade men back to God. There should be an end to hangings and burnings in His Name.'

She put a warning finger to her lips.

'But these things your son—being your son—shall do in God's good time; and do it, I doubt not, better than I. Madam, if you should give England a son, how good for us all. And for me, in especial; there might then be an end to my bastardy.'

'It is the first thing I shall ask when my son is born.'

'And, if it be a daughter?'

'Still I shall ask; it will not be so easy, but I think he'll not refuse. For what is a first child but pledge of others to come? Still, you might pray for me!'

'I will pray.'

In June the Queen quickened. *Te deums* were sung in all the churches and all over England bonfires flamed; there was dancing in the streets and free wine as much as a man could hold. That summer my father might have won back much of his lost favour but for the memory of those hanged men that had trusted in him.

Yet he was a sanguine man. The last of the rebels had been hanged and everything would soon be forgotten. He had given the country something else to think about; the Queen was carrying England's son. There was a new gentleness in him for Jane Seymour. I had never seen him cherish a woman before. To my mother he had shown, at best, a lukewarm kindness; to Anne Bullen, appetite. I importuned God that the child might be a son and I, honourably quit of the crown. I

205

prayed that, holding his son in his arms he might show mercy to my sister and me. But most of all I prayed because I could never accept a younger sister as his heir.

During these months at court I learned many a lesson, the chief being the wisdom of a still tongue, a deaf ear, and a blind eye; in which hard lesson I would sometimes fail—as for all my years I still do fail—for nature will out. It comes easier to me to speak plain truth than the cunning lie. These days I understood what I had merely accepted before—the luxury and spendthrift waste that surrounded my father and all the court. No wonder the people groaned beneath the taxes. No wonder there was revolt and violence!

It was full July when, at last, I was allowed to take leave of the Queen. 'I let you go,' she said, 'because you are to come again for my lying-in. It is your right; and, I believe, your pleasure. Meanwhile pray for me!'

'I will pray for us both. I will come when you send, and come with joy! But, Madam . . . what of my sister?'

'Bring her with you; and the good Bryan, also. She's been parted over-long from her son. He's in France now on the King's errand but he'll be back. They'll be happy to see each other again.'

It was like her to remember even those that were not of her household that she might do them a kindness.

'The King loves children,' she said, 'and being happy in the birth of his child—though happier if it be a boy—will surely take the little Elizabeth to his heart.'

'She is a gay child and forward of her age. My father might have much joy of her.'

'And in you; in you also!' she said.

And so in love and friendship we parted.

From the great doorway, across the cobbled yard, Elizabeth, red curls flying, ran to meet me. I knew better than to take her in my arms; I gave her my hand and together we went within. I had brought her some pretty ribands but the Queen had sent her a turquoise heart upon a golden chain. Even then she knew the difference in value between a riband and a jewel, for she put my gift aside and demanded that I fasten the chain about her neck; this done, she ran at once for a looking-glass and there she stood nodding and smiling at herself—the vain little thing!

'She is not fit to go to court,' Bryan said. 'Scarce fit, indeed, for this quiet house. I have no linen for her; neither shift nor kerchief, nor stockings nor shoes. I say nothing of petticoats and caps. I do what I can. I have cut up smocks of my own to make her shifts. I know not which way to turn!'

'You must write to Mr. Secretary Cromwell. He holds the purse-strings. To lay out a shilling without his permission is to court trouble. But I have something in my purse; enough to buy her silk for a gown. She goes with me for the Queen's lying-in.'

'I am glad of it! When the King sees my little one so gay, so charming and so *clever* his heart must soften towards her. I shall be sad, though, missing you both!'

'You are to come with us; it is the Queen's wish!'

Her face lit up; in the past four years she had not, at any time, spent more than an hour or so with her son, she being in attendance upon her charge and he, for the most part, here and there upon the King's business.

So, the pedlar being come, we chaffered for five yards of silk thick and glossy and yellow as buttercups. Elizabeth laughed and clapped her hands and would not stand still while the tailor fitted her.

'Mr. Secretary has sent me a signed order for my little lady's linen.' Bryan said. 'Now we shall go respectable!'

'We must make ourselves fine, also!' I said. 'There'll be processions and progresses and public prayers; there'll be feasting and dancing!'

And so we busied ourselves about our finery . . . and did not know how soon it would be changed for weeds of mourning.

I had thought to enjoy the quiet of the country; instead I took to my bed. The sudden return to favour—and that favour uncertain, the months spent beneath my father's suspicious eye, the distress for those Pilgrims whose rotting bodies yet hung in chains—all this working upon a constitution already undermined by years of grief and fear, overthrew me. The migraines, the nausea, the irregular periods I had suffered and from which I had, awhile, been free, now fastened upon me again. Again my father sent his chief physician, which was good in him, seeing his concern with the Queen.

'Madam,' Dr. Buttes said, 'with care you should enjoy fair health; but I must warn you—when you are distressed, or even anxious, you must expect such attacks. You may avoid them, for the most part, by a quiet mind.'

'And if circumstances are beyond me?'

'Then one must accept one's fate—and do the best one can!'

Accept one's fate and do the best one can! Homely words to stay with me for the rest of my life.

By the end of the summer I was well enough to walk in the garden, to sit with my ladies, to make a little music or to stitch upon my embroidery. We waited, all of us, for news of the Queen.

'All goes well with her, I thank God!' I told them. 'As soon as she is strong after her lying-in she's to be crowned.'

There had been talk of a crowning before this; but shortly after their marriage there had been cases of plague in London and my father had sent her into the country for safety; then had followed the trouble in the north. Finally, she being with child, my father had feared to put too much upon her; she had always a pale and delicate air.

'A birth, a christening and a crowning!' Clarencieux said. 'Such junketings. I would I were young again!'

October brought us a birth and a christening . . . but never a crowning and never a junketing!

Chapter Twenty-Eight

In September, the Queen went into a month's retirement—it is usual before a royal birth. She sent for me to join her at Hampton Court and to bring the little Elizabeth to cheer her seclusion. So through the countryside of falling leaves we went; the child atiptoe with excitement, Bryan all bright with joy and myself wondering what the future would bring. It was on this journey I told my sister of the coming child. 'It might be a little brother, or a little sister. If it is a little boy he will, one day, wear the crown.'

'Then I shall tell God not to send a boy!' she cried out at once. 'The crown is for me, when I am big!'

I wondered who had been talking to her; I suspected the Shelton woman. That this child should have so clear an understanding amazed me; she had only just reached her fourth birthday. I was startled, too, at the peremptory way she spoke of God.

At Hampton Court all was atiptoe for the Queen's lying-in. I had not seen the place since my father had carried me, a little child, to visit great Wolsey; and, as I passed through room after room into the presence chamber his ghost went with me. My father received me in benevolent mood; I enquired of his health and he said God be thanked, he was well. When I asked about his lame leg I knew, at once, my mistake; his brow darkened. Middle-aged, run to fat, hair streaked with grey, he still found it hard to forget he was no longer that prince whose grace and beauty had been the talk of Christendom. But, changeable as ever, he was soon smiling again. I told him I had, at the Queen's invitation, brought my sister with me. He did not ask to see her; but still he gave no sign of anger. Maybe in his heart he acknowledged some right for her to be here at this time.

The Queen, always pale, looked tired and heavy; but for all that cheerful and untroubled. She would have liked to walk in the garden but my father thought it not seemly; he feared, besides, she might slip upon fallen leaves. Autumn had come early; in the orchard Elizabeth picked up fallen apples and plums and threw them away, mouth twisted in disgust. Another child would have bitten into the ripe fruit but she, even then, was fastidious. I noticed, too, that, when she was offered fruit or comfits in the Queen's rooms, her hand would reach out and—no picking or choosing, so it seemed—took always the best.

My father came often to visit the Queen; he would pace the room, limping a little, small mouth pouting to a whistle—a man well-pleased with himself. The Queen took pleasure in my company, as I in hers. I would read to her or play to her; and sometimes we would sit quiet, content each with the other. When she was well enough—for she easily tired—she would send for my sister. The little girl would make her deep curtsey, kiss the Queen's hand and prattle in her pretty, childish way. 'God grant the child I carry be as well-graced!' The Queen said it more than once.

On Wednesday the tenth day of October the Queen's pains began. They were, from the beginning, severe; she was paying for that narrow elegance of hers. I sat with her and my heart was wrung. She lay rigid, fists clenched, fair hair dank ribands of seaweed upon the pillows; she was colourless even to the lips, the eyes dark and sunken. She lay quiet, save for now and again a low moan, more terrible, in that quiet, than Anne Bullen's noisy cries. I knelt by her side beseeching God to give her some ease; I no longer cared whether the child be girl or boy. I feared she would never live to bring it forth nor the child see daylight.

My father came often during the long night. 'My lord King,' and the midwife knelt trembling before him, 'I fear one or the other must die. If it come to it—whom shall we save?

He stared as though she were bereft of reason; one could see his thoughts clear. *A wife is easy got; but a son.* . . .

'Save my son,' he commanded.

I think the Queen did not hear him. I pray, even now, she did not hear him. Gentle and obedient, she must have concurred; but she must have felt the pain of it!

Darkness paled into dawn; sunshine was bright in the room. All through that day the Queen's torment increased. 'She grows tired,' the midwife said, 'I fear we may lose them both! But I cannot abandon the Queen.'

Disobedience could mean her own death and she knew it; yet desire to save the Queen drove her beyond that reckoning.

That day passed and it was night again. On Friday, October the twelfth—St. Edward's Day—at two o'clock in the morning, the Queen was delivered of a son.

For the first and last time in my life I saw my father weep. When the midwife put the child into his arms, there he stood, a stout, middle-aged man, the tears pouring down his face. He tried to speak and could not speak . . . for this moment he had waited thirty years. As though he handled the child Jesus, he put the babe back in the nurse's arms and went into the bedchamber where his wife lay exhausted.

'The first! The first of many sons!' he cried out; and, tears all done, left the room as though on air.

On Sunday night the great ceremony of baptism took place. My father, according to his custom, was not present. At Elizabeth's baptism he had watched from a private chamber; this time he was sitting with the Queen who appeared restless. I was, at her request, one of the godmothers; Elizabeth, at that same request, was present. A mantle of state had been found for her; so heavy it was that she must be carried, mantle and all, in the arms of Edward Seymour, the Queen's brother. Small head proud above the great mantle, hands careful about the chrism she carried, she felt herself the centre of the ceremony. And, indeed, she took the eye from the pale babe—the red-haired, black-eyed child so quick with life. Well for her my father was not present!

Behind me stood four high peers, towels about their necks, aprons about their middles; men apter for the sword than for nursery work. At the sight I all-but smiled; yet for this honour there had been bribery, backbiting and jealousy.

I stood at the font—that same silver font that had seen my own christening and my sister's—to receive the child. First in procession came my lord earl of Wiltshire, bearing a great candle of virgin wax. Did he, I wondered, remember his dead daughter, Anne Bullen? And could he bear to look upon his dead child's child, the disinherited child? And what did he think of himself now, playing his sycophant's part? I have never loved his house; but God knows I pitied him now.

Following him, walking beneath a canopy carried by four princes of the realm, came old lady Exeter bearing the royal child. When I took him from her a rush of tenderness dissolved my very bones. I have always loved children; and this little one so tiny, so weak, so helpless, had taken from me the burden of the crown. All humiliations and dangers that might have come to me, were over and done with. I held the heir of England in my arms.

I handed the little one to Archbishop Cranmer; our eyes met in mutual dislike—dislike involuntary, but not to be denied. That one day he should burn at the stake neither of us could foresee. God in His mercy allows no look into the future.

When the water fell upon the child he cried a little; lord William Howard handed me a towel and, gently, I dried the little face. He was named Edward, for he had been born upon St. Edward's Day; then Windsor Herald cried his title. *God in His Almighty and infinite Grace grant good life and long to the right high, excellent and noble Prince Edward, duke of Cornwall, earl of Chester and most entirely beloved son of our most dread and gracious lord King Henry VIII.*

I put the child back into the arms of lady Exeter, and the ceremony being done, he was carried back to his mother. The congregation left in order of degree; I, taking precedence, led Elizabeth by the hand, while two ladies carried her train, she walking very proud—a little peacock.

And now the whole court thronged to congratulate the Queen. She had been moved from the lying-in chamber to a state couch. And there she sat, fully dressed in cloth-of-gold, my father magnificent and foursquare standing by her side. There was no colour to her— white lips set in a white face. It was as though she were drained of blood. She sat there, propped upon cushions, gracious and smiling. I remember when Elizabeth made her curtsey, the Queen laid a hand in blessing upon those bright curls . . . and I saw how weak that hand, how frail.

And still it went on and on. No end, it seemed, to those that came and went; and all the time she smiled. It was clear to me that her strength was failing; but so perfect her courtesy she smiled to the end . . . to the end, indeed! Yet, at the time, I thought little of the matter. This was the custom; and she was always pale. Her labour happily over, she would grow strong again; she would be crowned.

She grew no stronger and she was never crowned.

The first I heard of disaster was some few nights later, when into my bedchamber burst the midwife, distraught. The Queen had taken a turn for the worse. But it was worse than worse; it was the worst.

In the ante-room I found her physician. 'It is the fever,' he said, 'sometimes it follows childbirth.' So drawn his face, I had not the courage to question him.

The Queen lay tossing upon her bed, flushed and restless with fever. She did not know me and I sat down by the bed.

'They should have left her quiet to rest!' the midwife said. 'But no! They must take her from the warm bed, they must put her in full court-dress—and the womb still open. And then, all that coming and going—and she worn out with her labour and the long anxiety lest the child prove not a son. But I could do nothing. I prayed her to stay where she was but she'd not listen. *It is the custom*, she said; *the King will expect it* . . . she said that over and over again! And forbade me mention it to her physician or to the King himself! Custom it may be; but it is not good sense!' And she was bitter, seeing all her care come to nothing.

All that day I sat by the Queen and never once did she know me.

And all the time the dry lips moved, she was murmuring to herself; now and again I moistened her lips with a feather dipped in wine. Once she said, very clear, *I will speak . . . tomorrow. Speak . . . to the King . . . for . . . for. . . .* My name she had forgotten—but not her promise.

Once only my father came to the sick-room; he could never endure the sight of illness. Nor would it have helped. She lay knowing no-one nor did she speak again. Now when we would have moistened her lips she turned her head away rejecting it. She was done with life.

At eight o'clock on Wednesday morning, the twenty-fourth day of October, she died. Her courtesy had been her death.

I did not see my father until after the funeral. He was taking the Queen's death badly, they said. Certainly it had been a shock; she had been young, obedient and kind. But she had given him a son; and between wife and son he had already chosen. Immediately he heard of her death he left for Windsor, leaving the Council to deal with the funeral. Broken-hearted they said of him; I should like to believe it. But he had always been one to run from death; he feared the very mention of it. Had he truly loved Jane Seymour, he must have stayed to show the last token of that love. Some affection for her he had . . . but he loved himself best of all.

The Privy Council consulted me as to the funeral ceremony. I commanded that it be carried out with every rite of the Catholic church. It would have been her wish; her unspoken love of the old faith had been a bond between us.

The slow procession moved along the road to Windsor and everywhere crowds stood to watch it pass. Those that had black garments wore them; those that had not—men, women and children—wore a twist of black; once a woman held out a babe in swaddling-clothes and it, too, was tied with a black riband. I thought of the motherless babe and wondered if any had thought to tie him, also, with black; I hoped not. And, as the cortège passed, the people stood head bared in homage and, for the most part, in tears. She had been fair and young and kind. She had been an honourable Queen and she had given the country its heir.

Upon a black horse trapped in black weeds to the very ground, I rode all in black; behind me rode the ladies of the court, in black also, except for a white scarf about the head. I wore no white, being chief mourner; for my father had not ridden out from Windsor to lead the procession—he that should mourn her most. It was fitting I should take his place; I had cause enough to mourn. She had been a friend, true and loving, seeking only my good; she had raised me up from insult and humiliation. She had given me back some courage and pride; dying, she remembered me. Where should I find such a one again? And so riding, I could not but remember my mother's burying; how I, her only child, had not been let to take even the lowest place but had been left to cry out my heart alone. Now I mourned for them both— dear mother, dear friend; that day I was doubly bereaved.

My father remained in seclusion; he did not attend the funeral service. When I saw him again there were few marks of grief upon him. 'A King must not wear his heart upon his sleeve,' he said. True enough —if he have a heart to wear! But if not grief-stricken, he was subdued. He asked me to stay until Christmas. I had left Elizabeth at Hampton Court; I hoped he would ask for her but he never did. Once, when I mentioned her, he made an impatient gesture. He had his son. So back she went to Hunsdon with Bryan, leaving me at Windsor.

It was a quiet Christmas. There were no festivities; but my father had recovered his appetite—if, indeed he had ever lost it; he had recovered his spirits, also. He would send often for his son, finding much comfort in him. Once I found him singing to the child that lay contented in his arms. 'He listens. He *listens*!' my father cried out. 'Little as he is he loves music. He is my true son!' And he pressed the child against his great bosom until it cried out. And I knew why he would neither see Elizabeth nor hear her name. He doubted she was his.

After Christmas we removed to Richmond; and still he asked me to stay. I busied myself with my books, my music and my needle. I embroidered a cap for the baby, a box all worked in silver thread for my sister; and for my father I worked a great cushion that he might rest his lame leg.

And so the new year of 'thirty-eight came in; that February I was

214

twenty-two years old. 'We shall have you wedded soon!' my father promised. 'Wedded and bedded!' I was willing enough—so I could like the man; and so he were worthy in faith, blood and station.

My father had recovered all his buoyancy; his joy in his son was greater than his grief. Had he to choose again between wife and son, he would choose as he had chosen.

Chapter Twenty-Nine

For two years my father remained unmarried; he let it be known that his heart was within the grave. But the truth is, the earth scarce dry above Jane Seymour's grave, he itched for a wife.

And not just any wife. She must be a beauty; and she must enlarge his importance in the courts of Europe. And it did not seem to occur to him that, three wives already disposed of, and two with some unpleasantness, his value in the marriage-market was not as high as he had supposed. Nor did it help him that he still lay beneath Rome's ban; if it did not trouble him, certainly it must trouble all true believers. And more; his destruction of monasteries, his persecutions and the consequent unrest let loose upon the country was not likely to endear him to any Catholic country.

And the man himself that desired a young and beautiful wife? Older than his middle-age. It was hard for him to get about because of his weight and the corruption in his leg. He called it gout, his physicians called it a fistula—but others whispered it was something worse—punishment for evil living. And this constant and cruel pain, this frustrating difficulty with which he moved, bred in him increasing anger, increasing obstinacy, increasing inability to allow any will to cross his own. And all this led him—God forgive me for saying it, but I am bound to the truth—into increasing cruelties that, carried abroad, lost nothing in the telling.

Yet still he would marry; and upon his own terms.

France and Spain, enemies to him and to each other, were now swearing brotherhood; he must find some way to drive them apart. And what better wedge than marriage? France, he thought, the more likely; my cousin the Emperor still cherished a proper anger on my mother's account. So to France went his messenger signifying his intention to wed, with the secret request that his ambassador be shown the fairest of her noble ladies. Little secret Francis made of that! 'Our ladies are not mares to be trotted out at a fair!' he said, and his laughter shook Christendom.

My father took it ill; he was never one to suffer a rebuff. But, for all that, suffer it he must. I could not but grieve for him, knowing for myself the pain of insult and cruel laughter; I would ask myself, surprised, Do *I* pity *him*? And pitied him the more.

Slighted in France, my father turned to Spain, making little of the Emperor's anger. His fancy had lighted upon Christina, duchess of Milan and own cousin to the Emperor; a dimpled piece of sweetness she was, if her picture spoke true. He swore he'd take her naked, not a rag to her back; nor a penny in her purse. *The first is certain; the rest a man may doubt!* The witticism went about his own court to wound him further, especially when she declined the honour. *Had I six lives*—and was there a touch of ghastly prophecy there?—*I would gladly lay down one for the King of England!* she said; and that, going the round of Christendom, goaded him to desperation. A new wife he must have; *and* young *and* beautiful! He would show them all!

Since his own marriage hung fire he busied himself about a marriage for me.

It was Chapuys that knew everything, who first gave me the news. 'Wriothesley busies himself in the matter,' he said.

'Then I can look for little good!' And I was all dismayed. 'A sour man that never wishes well to my faith or to me.'

'He would persuade the King to betroth you to Bavaria.'

'A heretic. That would be Wriothesley's choice. I'd die rather.'

'Do not blame him entirely, Madam, it is good policy. Since France and Spain are not, at the moment, to be prised apart, your father would do well to ally himself with the Protestant princes. And who better than Bavaria? He leads them all; he's young and he's comely, he's honest and he's brave. Young though he is, he's honoured throughout Christendom for his courage. However we differ in worship, all Christendom calls him the *lion of Bavaria*. He's man enough to steal any lady's heart.'

'Not mine. I cannot nor I will not wed a heretic.'

'There'll be no need. Wriothesley is serious in the matter, but not your father. It is a gesture merely; a gesture to warn his enemies. So the young man is to come. Look to yourself Madam, lest before you know it, he has stolen your heart!'

'I'd pluck it from my body rather than betray my faith!'

Philip of Bavaria was more than the sum of the things they said about him. I remember our first meeting; it was in the abbot's garden at Westminster—by my father's command, very private. I had never before been alone with a young man—and I full twenty-two!

The heart melted in my breast at the first sight of him. He was handsome in his fair Bavarian way; he was gentle and he was strong. He was courtly and he was kind; he was honest and direct in speech and act.

He wasted no time. He bent, for he was tall and I was small, and kissed me full upon the mouth—a thing no man had dared. A kiss of love; even I, ignorant in such affairs, knew it for what it was. Never before had I known such a kiss; nor since, nor since. Even now my heart a little stirs, remembering.

He had no English and I no German; but in the Latin tongue he said that, seeing me, in that very moment, he loved me; that he would die to make me happy. I had come to question all fair words but this man's I believed. I did, I must confess, play with the sweet notion of wedding him and bringing him back into the true faith. But all the time the warning rang in my ears to wring my heart, *Heretic. Heretic. Heretic.*

He had brought me a gift; a great cross of diamonds upon a chain; himself he put it about my neck, bending his fair head to mine so that I trembled with his nearness.

'This man I could love, body and soul—were things different!' I told Chapuys. 'But though the Pope should grant dispensation, my own soul could give none. Marriage with a heretic is no marriage; and bearing a child to such a one is sin against the Holy Ghost.'

'Do not fret your soul to shreds!' Chapuys said. 'Your father has no intention you should wed; not this man nor any other! You are less dangerous and more valuable unwed. No! It is Cromwell you should fear. He means to marry you himself!'

Again that name linked with mine! Cromwell base in birth as in deed and spirit; worse by far than your true heretic—for the latter, at least, *believes.* But Cromwell, having no fear of God, would run with the devil if it suited him!

'It is a rumour I have heard before!' And I made my mouth to smile. 'He would not dare!'

'He *will* dare! Never ask me how I know; it is my business to know!'

'This time you are mistaken. The man is *married*!' And, in my relief, I actually laughed.

'It is easy enough to be rid of an unwanted wife!' he said, very grave.

'Marry him! The man that brought my mother to misery and death; that for all his new show of friendship, brought me heartbreak and fear to mark me the rest of my life; a man that persecutes my faith, that robs monasteries and burns martyrs. . . .'

'By his master's orders!' Chapuys reminded me. 'But have no fear.

Your father, if he meant you to wed, could get better value in any court of Christendom. Of Cromwell there's no question. Your father is heartily sick of him; he waits for the man's foot to slip!'

'God speed the day. I do pray for it!'

Of my life during the two years between my father's third and fourth marriages, what can I say? From without, it was splendid, indeed. I was the first lady in the land; and among the princesses of Christendom, I stood first. I had, thanks to Jane Seymour, been named to succeed after my brother, should my father have no more children. But look upon my life from within. I was a declared bastard still; and still my father distrusted me—not without cause yet through no fault of my own. The people were discontented and I had but to lift an eyebrow to raise revolt; or let me keep my brows never so still, revolt could still break out in my name. Since my father distrusted me, his Council must distrust me, also; for they hung upon his every mood. So it was that spies were planted in my very household; my every action watched, my every word reported. I could not give hospitality to a benighted stranger—as once I did—but my father had word of it and sent a stiff reproof.

And I was lonely. I had lost Bryan. She had been appointed lady-mistress to the baby prince—and a better could be nowhere found. She had gone and, my father allowing it, had taken Elizabeth with her. It was, I knew, good for my sister; her hard contained little heart might learn to care for something smaller, weaker than herself. I missed her; I missed her bright young presence. But Bryan I missed intolerably. So the days passed in outward security, in loneliness and inner fear.

I was twenty-three, I was twenty-four.

I should have been at court, learning the ways of men, learning to weigh up foreign policies, to take the pulse of the time. Instead I must stay at home contenting myself with the pleasurable pursuits of a gentlewoman. When I needed a change I would leave one of my houses for another, or I might be invited to visit the children at Havering or wherever they might be; baby though he was, my brother had his own princely household. Now and again I would be summoned to court, and I would go wondering what pitfall might await me. In that first year following Jane Seymour's death Elizabeth was never asked. According to Bryan she pouted and made a great pother; but she was safer at home.

I had learned to carry a quiet face above my troubles; and these days I was troubled, indeed and not only for myself. Cromwell was making short work of sacking the last of the monasteries. Hundreds of monks increased the unhappy band of the destitute and homeless, torn from the known, the contemplative life, to be thrust into a strange and savage world. And Cromwell, need I say it, was thorough, carrying away loads of treasure for my father, and for himself. And always the never-ending executions! Though the last of the Pilgrims of Grace had gone to their account, men still hanged or burned because they would not deny their God. Sometimes my father's frustrations burst out in hateful acts of blasphemy. He had the sacred bones of blessed Thomas of Canterbury dragged from the tomb and cast upon a dung-heap. And the great ruby of the Cathedral he took to wear upon his finger. I wondered whether he was not a little mad; for his soul's sake I almost wished it were so. But mad he was not; he knew very well what it was he did. These days I prayed not only for the martyrs but for my father's soul.

It was not only those that came to a fearful end for whom I must grieve; I grieved, even more, for those that, innocent of evil, rotted within our fearful prisons. My old tutor Dr. Fetherstone would visit me at times and talk of the poor prisoners. 'Those that come to their death are better off; for their pain though sharp is quickly ended. But those in prison—Madam, pray for them! I have visited many an innocent soul that lies there. They lie in the dark—and some of them blind, since for years their eyes have not looked upon daylight; and hungry so that they gnaw upon their fingers. And cold; rotting flesh with never a rag to cover their nakedness. And the filth! Madam, they lie in the slime of their own ordure. Young and old, men, women and little children, herded in such filth we would not allow our swine to make for themselves—for, Madam, we value our swine. Even the worst of men should not be so degraded. But these are, for the most part, innocent, their crime no more than yours or mine—truth to the true faith.'

'Would to God I had power to ease their lot; yes, even those that rightly lie in prison. Evil-doers must be punished; but in punishment there should be mercy and hope for a man's soul.'

'If ever you have the power, Madam, remember the prisoners. Until then pray for them.'

'I shall remember; and I shall pray.'

And soon I had even greater reason to remember those in prison, and to pray for them.

The way of it was this. My father had never forgiven Reginald Pole for refusing to admit my mother's marriage unlawful. My kinsman had fled the country and escaped beyond his reach and my father had satisfied himself, for the time being, by parting his mother lady Salisbury from me. For both of us it had been a severe blow and a punishment quite unmerited. She had left the court and, as time went by, thanking God it was no worse, I thought the matter forgotten. I should have known my father better. He waited his time and the time had come.

The hideous death of martyrs, the cruel plight of monks had so moved Pole that, though a patient man, he had not been able to restrain his anger. His pen dipped in the blood of the martyrs excoriated my father.

The King of England has never loved God nor man. More cruel than Nero he has martyrised men like More and Fisher to his own disgrace and the nation's loss. The monasteries, great and small he has destroyed and the monks horribly murdered. . . .

And of the Charterhouse monks he spoke true enough; for they had been horribly tortured before, at last, they were allowed to die.

. . . the people he has shamefully treated, making a mock of his princes, persecuting the common people, troubling the priests and destroying those men that were the country's greatest honour. He has broken faith with his people; why then should the people keep faith with him? No, let them rise against that wickedness that has torn the unity of holy church in two.

This writing he published throughout Christendom.
'Dear God!' Chapuys said, 'there'll be plenty to suffer for this!'
For the moment I did not take his meaning.
'A man must speak as conscience directs him,' I said. 'Especially if he be a priest.'
'And what of those that must bear punishment on his account? Madam, this priest speaks treason. To urge the people against their King—what is that but treason?'
'To keep silent; is that not treason against the King of Heaven? God will keep the account!'
'Your father reckons his accounts more quickly than God. Madam, prepare yourself for some grief.'
But how bitter that grief, how dire its end, I was not to guess.
On a golden summer day, Pole's brother was arrested; put to the

torture, he spoke things he should not and saved his unhappy life. Next day there went to the Tower all those of his kin my father could lay hands upon. Montague, Pole's other brother, his cousin Exeter, and Exeter's little son Courteney. But worst and most cruel was the arrest of her that had been my mother's dear friend, sole comfort of my growing years—Margaret, lady Salisbury.

'Do not break your heart for this!' old Clarencieux said, seeing my stricken look. 'She is old and she is innocent; they must soon set her free.'

'Unless death frees her first!' I said, bitter.

'Her family are with her to look to her comfort. . . .'

'Do you think her prison is the happier because she shares it with her son? And with her nephew Exeter and his wife; and above all with the little boy? She will fret her heart out for little Courteney. How shall he learn the arts of his breeding—to ride, to hunt, to hawk, to shoot? What life for a child shut within a prison?'

'It will not be like those terrible prisons the good father spoke of. In the Tower, prisoners, Madam you know it well, may receive friends, accept gifts, walk in the gardens, pursue their amusements. . . .'

'Favoured prisoners—yes!' And I could say no more, knowing my father's long anger against Pole. Yet I did not know the whole of it. How Cromwell, to thrust himself again into favour, forever worked against the poor prisoners.

When she had gone I paced my chamber. My lady Salisbury was too old for the rigours of a prison. This could be her death. I must speak for her; at whatever cost to myself, speak I must. I sent humbly beseeching the lord King to receive me.

He refused. Wriothesley, that sour, paper-thin man, brought me his answer. *Tell the lady Mary to have a care lest she join her friends in the Tower.* 'And, my lady,' Wriothesley said, 'let me add a word of my own. Do not importune the lord King further for your . . . *friends.*' And he made of the word an insult. 'You may well hasten their end.'

Upon his heels came Chapuys, all breathless with haste.

'Madam, I grieve for your friends. Let me not, I beseech you, grieve for you, also. As you hope mercy for her, send no gift nor any message to lady Salisbury; nor seek to mend her condition. Your father's wrath you cannot hope to assuage but you may well enlarge it. Any mercy he may be disposed to give, you may well cancel.'

'Mercy!' I cried out. 'Before he come to it, she will die!'

'She would rather die than harm should come to you. Any word from you in the matter not only makes her condition worse, it could bring much danger to yourself. Your grace; do you not know? *Your name appears in the charge against her!*'

I stared at him then and he nodded.

'You are in grave danger. I take it as a kindness in the King that he will not see you; for then those charges must be mentioned . . . and proceeded with.'

'Charges?' I said when I could speak at last. '*What* charges?'

'That the whole family conspired, yourself willing, to marry you to Reginald Pole. . . .'

'He is fast-wed to the church. My father knows better than to believe such a piece of nonsense.'

'The Pope was to absolve him from his vow. Then you and he were to call upon the people to rise and thereafter—Tudor and Plantagenet— share the throne together.'

'Had I wanted the people to rise I had done it long ago—as you, Monsieur Chapuys, very well know.'

'Your father, in his rage, does not stop to reason. And, Madam, he has, he says, proof.'

'Proof? Against *me*? It is not possible.'

'Those that accuse the innocent must plant their *proofs*. And, Madam, since Cromwell cannot have you, he is willing to make an end of you. These *proofs* they have found in lady Salisbury's closet; they found the Salisbury coat-of-arms quartered with the royal arms of England; the whole embellished with pansies for Pole and marybuds for you!'

'A piece of nonsense! Who would be fool enough to believe it?'

'Any man that could find advantage therein. And, forgive me, Madam! You are too ready with the word *nonsense*. This is a dangerous affair.'

'Then I must go to my father. I must go at once! I must make him understand it is a lie!'

He so far forgot himself as to catch me by the hand. 'Madam, for the love of Christ, do not go!' And when I pulled myself free, he said, 'Do not run to meet trouble. Rather give God thanks that you, also, are not in the Tower. The King's anger is so great he'd not believe the voice of God Himself!'

Wriothesley had given me that same advice. I did not trust him—a faithless man, faithless even to his master—Cromwell that had lifted him from nothing. But Chapuys; if he assured me that I should make matters worse for my old friend, him I must believe. So I kept myself from all talk of lady Salisbury. But from my heart I could not keep her.

As the summer passed, it was clear that the prisoners were being punished to the uttermost point of severity. They received no friends, were allowed neither letters nor gifts. No priest visited them, they might not walk in the air, their food was scant, nor were they allowed to add to it. In the summer months such rigours might be endured; but as winter drew on—lacking warm clothes in the prison cell, lacking firing, lacking sufficient food—they knew the despair of utter destitution. And always there hung about them the shadow of death. And yet, though I wasted my strength in useless tears, I might, save to God, speak no word for them.

In mid-December, lord Montague, lady Salisbury's eldest son, was led out to die; and with him, her nephew Exeter. Innocent, innocent, both! And now, this most bitter grief added to their miseries, two women and one little boy were left alone, in the dark cell; and, hanging above their heads, the ever-darkening shadow of death.

These days I knew not what to do. In the face of all advice speak to my father, or keep silent still, lest I hasten the prisoners' death? But was a quick death not better than leaving them to die slowly in hunger and cold and the darkness of utter misery? They were forever in my mind —the old woman, the young woman and the child; night and day I prayed for them. And since, though no word be spoken, grief will out, I again fell sick. Dr. Buttes was right: in a body undermined by ill-health, grief must, until I die, show itself in sickness. I slept little, I ate less. I had no strength to take exercise; nor would it have helped me, for my father had ordered that I be confined within the small space of the privy gardens. Chapuys, greatly troubled, wrote to his master, my cousin, that I might very well die. To me he sent in secret, asking that, given a chance—which he would endeavour to make for me— would I fly the country?

I thought long over that last. In affairs where conscience does not speak clear, I am forever in two minds. I sent him word at last. 'So long as I may hope to save my friends in the Tower, I will stay. But, if it should come to a question of my own death, then I should, if I could, fly.' And to such a question it might well come; my father had before this sought my death from an unwilling Parliament; with *proof* in his hand might he not make an end of me now?

So there I was, living in state and seeming safety and all the time in grief for my friends and fear for their lives—and my own, too. And I lived in loneliness: Clarencieux, for all her kindness, was not Bryan; Bryan I missed intolerably. I was utterly bereft.

Chapter Thirty

And still France and Spain, it seemed, were joined in loving friendship. And still my father, for all his itch to marry, remained unwed. Cromwell forever pressed him to marry into the Protestant League of princes.

'So, sir, you pleasure yourself and strengthen your position against France and Spain. And, indeed, there's but one princess in Christendom worthy of the King of England; and that is Madam the Princess of Cleves.'

Cromwell did not cease to press him.

'If the Catholic princes prove unfriendly, here, sir, is your answer!'

My father approved the notion; but still he would have a beauty. 'I'll have no hag in my bed!' And he roared with laughter at the mere thought.

'Sir, she is own sister to the lady Sybilla, wife to the Elector of Saxony; that should be enough!'

'Aye it *should*! That one's a noted beauty! Yet we speak not of the Princess of Saxony but of her sister.'

'Then, sir, let us make certain. We'll get Wotton to spy out the land; and we'll have her picture, too!'

From Cleves came our ambassador's report. 'The lady Anne outshines her sister's beauty as the sun outshines the moon!' This I suspect was an embellishment of Cromwell's own; Cromwell pressing; pressing, seeking at one and the same time to strengthen the King and to advance himself. Cromwell pursuing his own downfall.

'She is of sweet humour, gentle and obedient. She is lettered in her own tongue and in no other; but she is quick to learn.'

'The language of love, no doubt!' and my father roared with laughter. 'We, ourselves, shall be her teacher!'

'She plays no instrument nor can she sing.'

My father frowned at that; then good humour came back to his face. 'If she know her own limits, so much the better. And if she listens in silence, she'll do. We wait for the picture!'

Praise aplenty; but no picture.

'I'll not buy without I see!' my father swore it, and commissioned Master Holbein, then in Europe, to take her likeness. He was irritable until the picture came; then he was all smiles.

It was the prettiest thing; a miniature of a girl kind and fair—a flower of a girl. And—Master Holbein knew his business—the picture was contained within a frame of ivory carved in the form of a rose; and the white rose, half-open, made its own suggestion of untouched girlhood.

My father sighed like a green boy over the charming picture. The lady, he knew, had been betrothed but he made nothing of it. I wonder, now, whether he did not rather welcome the fact—a convenient loophole should he need it. My lord Blount was sent to negotiate the treaty and my father must possess his soul in patience for the arrival of his bride.

For myself, I prayed some obstacle would prevent the marriage. I had nothing against the lady but I feared a Protestant match; I feared the Protestant League. There was already persecution enough of my faith; bring the Protestant League into our affairs—and what then? I feared, I feared greatly for all poor Catholics.

But there was no obstacle. The contract was signed and sealed; my father must control his impatience as best he might, and I, my misgivings.

On the eleventh day of December in the year of grace fifteen hundred and thirty-nine, the bride arrived at Calais. And then, as though to vex my father, and to rouse in him a frenzy of longing, the bridal train could not sail; for sixteen days wind and weather opposed his will. Such a crossing of his will he did not take lightly; not even from God. It was not my father, alone, that waited so anxiously, the whole country waited, Protestants and Catholics alike; the first in hope, the second in fear.

My father had commanded my sister and me to Hampton Court that we might be present at his marriage and pay our respects to the new Queen. Margaret Bryan brought Elizabeth from Havering, and there was much joy between her and me. She was especially joyful, for her son had sailed for Calais to bring home the bride.

'God send this marriage fruitful! My little prince is not of the strongest. I'll not rest until I'm back again. They'd smother him within doors if I allowed it; but I'll not allow it; not I! I wrap him warm and take him into the air. And a sweet sight it is to see him and my little lady running and romping. He cannot bear her out of his sight; he will, I know, be fretting until he has her with him again. But, Madam, it is well the lord King has not sent for him! He has never a jewel to set in his cap. As for his best coat; it is the one your grace sent him—the one with the tinsel sleeves. A good coat; but not good enough for high occasions, and he his father's only son! As for my little lady; she has no good gown but the yellow satin you gave her two years ago. I have let down the hem and it will do—she's a thin child. Madam, speak to Mr. Secretary for my little ones.'

'It is better you write. But I can give you a guinea or two; my own purse is lean enough!' And, indeed, since Jane Seymour had sent me her last gift I'd had nothing from my father save for the running of my household; and that was not paid direct to me. He was not generous with his children; not even with the little boy that was the apple of his eye.

My sister had grown somewhat in the last year; she was tall of her age and, as Bryan said, thin. But, for all that, a handsome child with great dark eyes and red-gold curls, though the nose somewhat long. She was graceful and quick in all her ways; and already she had Greek and Latin beyond her six years. She was quick to make a joke and quick to take it—so it did not offend her dignity. A child shrewd and entertaining.

These days two words were forever on her tongue: *mother* and Queen. What she meant by *mother* I do not know. Maybe she had sweet memories of Jane Seymour; maybe she had worked out in her little mind—logical even then—that the King being her father, the Queen must be her mother. I did not ask, fearful lest I stir some half-forgotten memory. Of her own mother she never asked then or ever. *When shall I see my mother the Queen?* That question was forever on her tongue so that I, striving to play a mother's part, was pricked with jealousy. As for myself, I was more than half-reconciled to Anne of Cleves. She had never meddled in affairs nor never would, our ambassador had reported. If she made no trouble on account of her faith she would be welcome. She might, gentle as she was, speak for my lady Salisbury, for the boy Courteney and for his mother that languished still within the Tower. On such royal occasions it was not unusual to release prisoners. She might, perhaps, soften my father's heart; but would she dare?

I was a little sorry for her. She was to marry a man twice her age, older than his years and uncertain in his humours. When I told Bryan she said, 'The lady is of mature age; twenty-five or so!'

Mature age . . . the words pricked; my father's new wife was my own age, or little more. The years that had seemed so long, were suddenly gone; gone for ever. I was twenty-four, not even betrothed nor ever likely to be wed. My father meant to use me—a bright counterfeit coin until I tarnished with age; then, maybe, he would wed me where he could—he that was to wed now a fourth time. Did he think I was so different from himself? Was I not of his own hot Tudor blood?

Christmas came and went; the festival was shadowed by my father's impatience; the whole court, from Cromwell down to the smallest page, walked tip-toe. But wind and weather gave way at last. On the twenty-seventh day of December the bride embarked at Calais with a convoy of fifty ships and every ship dressed overall and hung with garlands.

A dark wet evening when she stepped ashore at Deal; there on the windswept beach a noble company waited to greet her and bring her home. Whether he would not chance his crippled leg in this bitter weather, or from pride, my father did not himself come to meet his bride.

It had been a bad crossing and she, very seasick. That night she lay at Dover Castle and thence made her slow progress to Rochester, there to rest for several days. But at Greenwich, my father could contain himself no longer. His bride, his gentle beauty, he must see. A glimpse of her *to nourish love!* he said; and his leg being, as I suppose, somewhat easier, and the winter sun shining, off he set, eight gentlemen at his heels.

He had meant to take her by surprise; but the surprise was all his! Master Holbein making too much of her better parts, and Cromwell praising her above her lovely sister, had between them done her little good.

My father's disappointment was bitter. He saw a tall woman, clumsy in a garment of outlandish cut; she was green from sickness, smudged with fatigue and pinched from riding in the bitter weather. She looked, as she told me later when she could laugh about it, like a dead fish or merrymaid.

And so he missed the beauty of her eyes and the sweetness of her mouth and the candour of her face. Nor, obstinate as he was, would he admit to any pleasing feature ever.

For her part, she saw a heavy man, the veins branching purple beneath a yellow skin; a small red, pouting mouth and eyes all-but lost in the folds of fat. A man, hair and beard grey as a badger; and old . . . old. Of the two she had more cause to complain.

'She knows very little English,' my lady Suffolk told me later. 'But some words of greeting she has learned. The court of Cleves may be unfashionable and small, but she's well-trained in etiquette.' And, indeed, however sick with disappointment she may have been, according to lady Suffolk she behaved perfectly; the reverence exactly right, head dropped in humility; and her words in answer to his greeting, low and pleasant for all her thick foreign tongue.

And, at this first meeting, whatever disappointment he too felt, he matched her in courtesy. Let it stand to his credit in this sorry affair! He gave no sign of the anger that, even then, choked him, but raising her up, kissed her upon both cheeks and spoke comfortable words.

But when he reached Greenwich again—ah then! The echoes of his fury reached Hampton Court where my sister and I waited to pay our respects to the bride. We heard, the very servants laughing and not troubling to lower their voices, how he cried out upon Cromwell that had made the match. The King of England that had been satisfied with nothing less than the foremost beauty of France, to come to this! Francis would be laughing his ass's head off. Did Cromwell truly think he'd wed a pock-marked maypole while all Christendom stood by and laughed? He could not stand the sight of her pockmarked face nor the clack of her thick foreign tongue. She must go back where she came from; he'd not bed with her!

'You have brought me a dray horse, a Flanders mare. I'll not sleep with her—she'd overlay me!' He roared out, the great, heavy man and cared not at all that he spoke of a young virgin woman, and his bride. Beyond the closed doors and along the galleries of Hampton Court, his voice thundered.

In vain Cromwell tried to excuse himself. 'Like the King's grace I heard the praises, saw the picture. No more than the King—' The flung footstool cut short his justifications.

He would not wed her; his Council must deal with the matter. Meanwhile she must stay where she was! So he waited at Greenwich, the bride waited at Rochester, at Hampton Court his daughters waited. England and all Christendom waited.

The Council could do nothing. They clutched at that straw—her earlier betrothal. It broke in their hand. It had been conditional only, and, as far as four years back, cancelled; she had brought with her written proof. To this marriage, no impediment.

'Sir,' Cromwell besought him and dared not lift his eyes, 'to send home a lady of faultless virtue, how shall that stand with your honour? It is an insult her brother will not nor cannot endure. You will set against you the whole Protestant League.'

Much my father cared for that! France and Spain were once again at their ding-dong and he no longer needed Protestant help. 'Let the Protestant League go hang itself—and you with it!' He turned his face from Cromwell and never turned it back again. He loathed the man and his clever crafty ways that had been neither clever enough nor crafty enough to save his master from this!

Nothing for it but he must wed. *Then I must needs put my head into the noose!* He said it continually, not caring that his words might reach his bride. Maybe he meant her to hear them; disappointment had a way of making him cruel.

Chapter Thirty-One

They were to be wed at Greenwich. The summons had gone forth to all whose duty required their presence at the King's wedding; and to my sister and myself came the summons, also.

From the windows at Greenwich we could see the river crowded with craft all garlanded; we could see the folk aboard and folk lining the river bank, their winter garments all gay with ribands; we could hear the music of flutes and pipes. Already there had been a great ceremonial welcome at Blackheath from the princes of church and state; and, leading them, the Lord Mayor of London and his aldermen, all in scarlet and golden chains, to bring the new Queen into the city. My father had received it all, a fixed smile upon his sullen face. Thereafter the whole procession had marched with music down to the river to embark for Greenwich.

When by the thunder of cheering we knew the royal barge was near, I took my sister by the hand and, the officers of the household, following, down we went to the river. I wore a velvet gown of green; my best, though somewhat rubbed. My sister wore the yellow satin; her red-gold curls loose beneath a netted cap of gold fell upon a small furred cloak Bryan had found for her. I daresay we went meanest clad of all; but Bryan said the gown became me; and Elizabeth was pretty as a picture.

From the foremost barge stepped my father. He was ablaze with jewels. His gown of purple velvet slashed with tissue of gold was buttoned with diamonds and rubies; about his neck glittered his great jewelled collar; and so begemmed was his bonnet I wondered any head could support so great a weight. Dressed as a bridegroom he might be, but I knew that carved smile of his, wherein the eyes played no part. Upon his arm, stiff in its jewel-sewn velvet, lay the hand of the bride.

The bride. All eyes had waited to look upon her face; yet after the first glance it was my father that drew all attention. Beside him the bride was nothing—if not a figure of fun. Her face I could not see;

I do not see clear at any distance. She was above the middle height of women—to my father a grievous error; he liked his women small. She might have looked well enough in our English dress but she wore a gown of outlandish cut; a round gown, its fullness equal at front, back and sides so that you could not tell, at a little distance, whether she was coming or going; or, like a crab, went sideways. It was cut something shorter than our fashion and she wore no train, not though this was a high ceremonial occasion, so that for all her height, she had a clumsy cut-short appearance. And this odd look she shared with her ladies that followed, so that it was hard not to smile; and, indeed, I caught something of a titter. Yet the gown's exceeding richness matched my father's. It was cloth-of-gold with great roses raised in pure gold thread; and, at the centre of each, a cluster of jewels. About her neck she, too, wore a collar of jewels as fine as my father's. Her hair I could not see, even when I stood close; for she wore a caul and upon it a jewelled cap from which hung a hood of black velvet that reached to her shoulders. It did not become her, for it gave her pale face a heavy look; and, moreover, onlookers took it for her hair and it earned for her the name of *blackamoor*. Her hair, in truth, was a light brown, fine and curling and pretty.

As they came across the sward, Elizabeth slipped from my hand and ran towards them. To my surprise, and alarm, for my father was in no good mood—she was down in her curtsey, small red-gold head bent upon the new Queen's hand. Though the child, small as she was, knew well how to please when it suited her purpose, this, I swear, was not calculated. Had she stopped to think, she must have saluted my father first. But her eyes, even this discerning character, had gone straight to the heart of the matter—the good heart of the new Queen.

It was love at first sight between those two. Anne of Cleves bent to the child and my sister clasped her about the knees—for the bride was tall and the child small—and would not let go until my father thrust her away. As for myself, when I made my own reverence, she raised and kissed me; and I knew I had found a friend—and no fair-weather friend, neither.

On the sixth day of January in the year of grace fifteen hundred and-forty, in his private closet at Greenwich, my father took to himself—if taking unto himself be the right words—his fourth wife. In spite of the invited guests he had decided upon a private ceremony and, desperate to have the matter over and done with, had appointed the early hour of eight in the morning. Long before that hour he was dressed and pacing his closet, archbishop Cranmer in anxious attendance. But for all his wretchedness, my father lacked nothing of magnificence. He wore a tunic of gold with raised flowers of silver; and over it a coat of crimson satin slashed with gold and buttoned with diamonds . . . but above his finery he showed a face of thunder.

Upon the very stroke of eight came the bride; immediately behind her I led my little sister by the hand. Eight of her own ladies followed and behind them walked Cromwell with two ambassadors from Cleves. When she came in at the door my father turned away his head. Yet one might well think her sacrificed to the corpulent, diseased old man —for not only was he twice her age he looked far more than his forty-eight years. She wore a gown of gold tissue; upon her head, rustic fashion, a little wreath of rosemary; beneath it the light curls flowed. The free-flowing curls, the hopeful rosemary, gave her a young, vulnerable look. I thought, if my father could bring himself to kindness for this young woman so full of goodness and the desire to please, he would do well for himself and for us all. But kindness was not in him.

At the door she made a deep obeisance but still his head was turned as though she were not there; she came half-way towards him and again made her obeisance but still he took no notice. Her third and humblest obeisance brought her to his very feet and now he must bend to raise her.

So in spite of himself they were married; thereafter they went hand-in-hand into the chapel to hear Mass—for my father worshipped still in the old fashion; and what his bride felt in the matter he neither knew nor cared. Then, prayers being done, they partook of cakes and wine and without a handclasp or smile even, they went each to his own apartments. But they supped together and there was music and dancing. My father did not dance; maybe his leg troubled him, maybe he had not the heart to lead out the Queen. He sat foursquare in the great chair looking ever more uncheerful; and, night drawing on, he was seen to be tapping irritably upon the arm of his chair until, heavy and slow, he rose at last and led the bride from the room.

There were none of the old bridal customs; no ceremonial putting the bride to bed, no sharing of the wine once they were abed, no throwing of the stocking nor gay, lewd jests. I could not but pity my father, that disappointed man; but the bride I pitied more—the good young woman, victim of an old man's thwarted desire.

Next day bride and groom came forth each from his own chamber; and, if my father had been gloomy the night before, anger now consumed him utterly. I doubt Cromwell had spent a better night than either of them; for my father roaring aloud for him in the grey of the morning, there Cromwell was, bowing and scraping full-dressed, even to his bonnet.

And now my father's voice came thundering all along the gallery and in and out of the ante-rooms; and all ears, be sure, were bent to listen.

'You have brought me a Flanders mare! By her breasts and belly you may tell a maid; when I felt them I was stricken to the heart, and had neither will nor courage to prove the rest. I can have no issue from her; so thick she is I cannot reach into her and do not intend to try!'

Whether she heard or not, I cannot say; I do not see how she could have escaped that voice. I think, indeed, he meant her to hear; he could be sufficiently cruel.

My father commanded me to stay with the court these first weeks of his marriage, to keep company with the Queen, to speak English with her, and to teach her our customs. She was glad of my company, talking to me at first in very broken English and soon in English not so broken, for she had a good ear, though like the most part of foreigners, her accent would always betray her; and in our customs, too she proved an apt pupil, attending first of all to the refashioning of her gowns.

Anne of Cleves was unhappy; she was scorned, held up to ridicule. She had not even the comfort of the little Elizabeth; for my sister and Bryan had been sent home, and she was not without some reason afraid; my father, she knew, had his own way with unwanted wives. Yet, save to me, whom she could trust, she spoke no word, either of resentment or of fear, but carried herself without complaint and with a most gentle dignity.

Why had my father so taken against her? He complained of her looks; yet, strangely, she just missed being the beauty upon whom his heart was set. Her forehead was noble, her skin very white and her eyes—such eyes I have never seen! They were the colour of malmsey, that same golden brown; and, as when you lift such wine to the light, flame moves in its depths, so with those eyes. Beautiful eyes; and in their expression, beautiful also—spirited, yet warm and kind. And, to add to their beauty, they were fringed with long, dark lashes, that lying upon the whiteness of her skin, gave the upper part of her face nothing less than beauty. Had her nose been a little less long, her mouth a little less wide, her chin a little less strong, she must have been perfectly a beauty. But a wise man would not have changed that face for the prettiest in Christendom; for nose and chin gave a firmness that my father, maybe, did not relish; and the mouth, quick-changing from laughter to pity, sure sign of a quick spirit and a good heart, gave interest to the whole face and held it.

She had not, I admit, good taste in dress. Like my father she loved splendour; yet while with him jewel, texture and colour combined in harmony, for her magnificence was all. Every gown she possessed, whether for the ball, for hunting or for the privacy of her closet, was stiff with embroideries and heavy with jewels—and never a thought to the general effect or to fitness for the occasion; nor, in that respect, did she ever learn better.

'Of her person the lord King has no need to complain!' Clarencieux said. 'She's as handsome as Anne Bullen and Jane Seymour, both! And if she isn't as lively as the first, she isn't as shrewish neither; and if she isn't as elegant as the second, she is not so inert, neither!'

'He complains of her as a pockmarked maypole,' I said. 'But she isn't, after all, so much taller than the usual run of women. As for the pocks; if you look close you may see one mark upon the chin and the other upon her cheek. They're fewer and fainter than those that blemish many ladies that pass for beauties. He says she has no music in her, she does not dance. But I have seen her listen with delight; and she's light on her feet.'

'The lord King, so I hear, says she has no tact, but . . .'

I knew what she meant to say and must not say; he was so angry a man these days that even an angel must have angered him. Only the Queen's good heart and good sense had saved her—and many of us also—from the flaring of his anger. And this was not because she was the fool my father, at first, pretended to find her; she could speak plain enough and quick enough in a right cause. At all other times she weighed her words. I think there was never anyone, at any time, but wished her well. The whole world was her friend—even my father when he was over his disappointment, even the little Howard girl that supplanted her and had meant to do so from the beginning.

'The lord King says she has no wit . . .'

'That, at least, is not true,' I said. 'She has a quick wit but never unkind. If Anne Bullen's tongue passed for wit—from such wit God save us! But truthful as she is, she does not care to flatter. There's an uprightness in her that reminds me of my mother; maybe . . .'

I stopped . . . *maybe because of that he cannot love her.*

But the truth is the new Queen had never a chance; already my father's eye was wandering; and where his eye wandered, be sure his body would follow.

Yet I think he would have contented himself with the little Howard as his mistress but for three things; and they lay not with the Queen but within himself—his own nature; and the shifting policies of the times.

The first was his obstinacy and pride. Disappointed in that first meeting, allowing nothing for seasickness and fatigue and for homesickness, he had spoken his dislike; he was not the man to eat his words. Secondly, he was glad to keep his anger hot—as a means of ridding himself of that encumbrance Cromwell. And the third? He was wondering about the wisdom of this marriage. Already the 'friendship' between France and Spain was stretched to breaking-point. By allying himself with the Protestant princes, did he not shut upon himself the door of France? Or Spain? Or both.

So he justified himself by proclaiming his bride ugly, stupid and tactless. But when he was no longer her husband, then he sought her company—even while the little Howard held him with her charms.

Chapter Thirty-Two

Catherine Howard, young and poor; niece to my lord duke of Nor-folk, grand-daughter to the dowager duchess—and in her blood lay her downfall. Did something perverse in himself drive my father to set his heart upon this cousin of Anne Bullen? She was small and sleek as a pet kitten; she was pink-and-white as apple-blossom; her hair, pale gold, lay in soft curls upon her childish shoulders. There were girls about the court as pretty and prettier, save for the eyes. They were truly beautiful—clear hazel green fringed with long, dark lashes. Eyes of a child, you would have thought—eager and innocent. But whatever else she was—gentle and honey-sweet—innocent she was not. Yet for all that, she wore, like a white flower, her air of innocence.

It was cruel to place this small, pretty thing as lady-in-waiting to the Queen. But Anne of Cleves had no jealousy in her; she liked young creatures, and this girl she especially liked for her charming ways. But like it or not, the Queen had no choice; the Howards had worked for it and the King desired it.

It was Gardiner, my lord bishop of Winchester, that had actually brought the girl to my father's notice. He had given a feast in honour of the King's marriage. *In honour!* He could not forgive Anne of Cleves because she was Lutheran. To this feast he invited the Howard girl; he was no fool, Gardiner! The little Howard was as different from the Queen as possible—and especially in her pretty, kittenish ways. They say my father had not taken his eyes from her.

Quite suddenly, Catherine Howard, least of ladies, had the place all ladies sought—lady-in-waiting to the Queen.

'Me, it troubles not,' the Queen said, feeling her careful way into our language, 'it is a maiden so pretty. But the aunt! Her I must also take—mistress of my ladies. And for that I am troubled . . . so much troubled. She is evil. I smell upon her the wickedness.'

'You are not alone in that, Madam. I cannot endure her, neither. She is George Bullen's widow and she swore away his life.'

She did not understand and I said, 'She accused him that he lay with Anne Bullen—his own sister!'

'Such a tale from such a woman, who could believe?'

'It could be true, Madam. They made their own laws, that brother and sister. And the wife was jealous. But true or not, she had his life—and her own reward with it. I need not tell you to beware of her! What she is you know well enough. But the little Howard—there's your danger!'

I said no more while she picked out the words in her glossary. How could I make her understand that Catherine Howard, once a humble hanger-on of her house, was now its highest hope? Once they had set that hope upon Anne Bullen. Wilful and arrogant she had proved a tool to break in their hands. Her memory, like a shadow, hung over them yet; only Norfolk's speed in casting her off had prevented that shadow engulfing them all. Now he was making another bid for favour—a simple child to do as she was bid. Sharp-witted like that other she was not, but unlike that other—obedient.

'Madam,' I said, 'her simplicity could be your undoing.'

She found the words in her book before she could answer.

'I have but one undoing. It is to be wed to a husband that likes me not; a husband I must fear.'

Poor pretty little Howard! Hope of her ambitious family, the evil Rochford, mistress of the Queen's ladies, her especial friend and guide; and favoured by the Queen. And the King? He lusted after the girl. I am a plain woman and I speak plain; and plain it was in the way he followed her with his eyes—as though he would eat her; and the way he would seek his chance to touch her, to be alone with her; and in the rich gifts he sent her. And she would lift those clear green eyes to him as though he were God Himself. She would play to him upon the virginals, sing the little songs she had learned for him. Singing and playing were commonplace, both; but he, so fastidious in music, would sit and listen spell-bound. She knew, also, how to flatter with honey-sweet words; and he, as he grew older, grew ever more enamoured of flattery.

I was on my homeward way and glad to go. My favour with my father was forever uneasy; and now, seeing my affection for his new Queen, he had, in one of his sudden fits, packed me off. It was early April and already the willows hung green hair into the river; as the barge took its way from Richmond I gave myself to my thoughts. It seemed to me that future events were casting a clear, unpleasing shadow. I thought that, in no great time, the little Howard would be sitting in the Queen's place; that I should be made to show this heedless child a daughter's obedience, pleased me not at all.

I was roused from these thoughts as the Tower came into sight. Within those walls languished my oldest, my dearest friend—lady Salisbury. Since that day they had thrust her into prison, I had never ceased to pray for her deliverance. Nor had I ever ceased to expect her death—not by the axe; even my father could not be so needless-cruel. But the rigours of her prison, dark and damp winter and summer alike; lack of fuel, of warm clothing, and the scant, poor food must surely make and end of her, old and frail as she was. Only her great spirit had kept her alive thus long. Who would help her? Who dared ask? One word from me might send her to her death; and, maybe, me to mine.

At the water-gate the horses were waiting. I am always glad to ride through London; however sad my thoughts the love of Londoners never fails to lift my spirits. But now, already saddened, my heart sank lower yet, seeing the gibbets with their hanging bodies. Some, no doubt, had offended against the law; wrongdoers must be punished and their death, in Christian charity, stand for example lest others follow in their footsteps. But so many more gibbets than I had ever seen; I guessed that the most part held not offenders against the law but those that would sooner offend the King than God. As I passed Smithfield, I caught the unmistakable stench of roasting human flesh. Riding out of the northern gate the hideous smell went with me. I was glad to be out in the sweet country air once more; to ride into my own house at Hertford, to be greeted by my household. Now I could pray as I would, read as I would; be at peace.

Negotiations for my betrothal to Philip of Bavaria had never been entirely broken off; the young man persisted still; and my father had been waiting to see which way the cat jumped. Now that he had no need of Protestant friendship he sent Bavaria about his business—and no explanation. The diamond cross was sent after him and I grieved at the whole insulting business. The young man so courteous, deserved, in his turn, courtesy; and the cross I must have treasured though it had been made of iron—for the giver had loved me. And indeed, more than once after this insult, he sued for my hand, offering to take me without dowry even when he could gain nothing at all thereby. He never married . . . and because he loved me I shall remember him all the days of my life.

And still the game went on. I was to marry the old King of France, lecherous, and diseased with ill-living; I was to marry his son. I was to marry the Emperor my cousin; I was to marry *his* son, Philip, his heir whose wife had died in childbirth within a year of marriage; Philip some twelve years younger than myself. I was to marry this one and that one . . . but never a one did my father intend for me.

My father's anger against Cromwell had been steadily increasing; and to that anger the sight of his new Queen was a continued irritant. Anne of Cleves was, indeed, the symbol of his anger. Would he turn now to Norfolk? Norfolk he had never wholly trusted—but Norfolk, too, had his symbol: the enchanting Catherine Howard.

With my father, that man of caprice, you could never tell. Cromwell, Chapuys told me, walked wary these days, affecting an ease he could not feel. My father continued sullen; and those two enemies, Cromwell and Norfolk, watched each the other's slightest movement.

Cromwell was sliding fast to his fall—men said it everywhere. But there was no accounting for my father. Suddenly the man was ennobled. Plain Mr. Cromwell was my lord earl of Essex.

And now tongues wagged indeed. *Now Norfolk must sing small . . . now Mistress Howard must leave the court. . . . Now Cromwell rides high again. . . .* And once more the old rumour. *He has been raised that he may marry the King's daughter. . . .*

'So!' I cried out to Chapuys, come himself to tell me of the news of this strange ennobling. 'Does my father intend to throw me to the dogs?' And I felt my insides cringe.

'Not to this particular dog!' and he smiled. 'It is a master-stroke. Your father is a most subtle man. This is the end of Cromwell!'

I stared at Chapuys. A strange way to make an ending of a man. Was this a cruelty in my father to raise a man higher that he might fall the lower?

'It is more than that . . . much more!' Chapuys said, softly. 'He takes from Cromwell his very name; the name before which men tremble. Now he must take the name of Essex; a name others have borne before and will bear again. But where was there ever a Cromwell? And where shall you find another? With this "honour" the King blots out the man, himself. The name *Essex* means nothing in men's mind and into nothingness it will fade. When Essex loses his head who will remember it was Cromwell that died; *Cromwell!*'

'And the man himself?'

'Is not pleased; he's no fool! He seems to me a frightened man.'

'And Norfolk!' I asked. 'It seems he gains nothing by this. I hear the little Howard has left the court.'

'She is but a step away! She is with her grandmother at Winchester House; but whether Norfolk shall lose or gain . . .' He shrugged.

And now there was fresh tongue-wagging; whispers not so low but that I might hear them. *The lord King goes to Winchester House every night. Sometimes he stays all night . . . and it is not the dowager he goes to see. . . .*

I paid a quiet visit to the Queen at Greenwich and found her distraught. She feared lest my father find no way out of their marriage but one; and she drew her hand across her throat.

I missed Elizabeth, a wilful, seven-year-old with a taste for courts, for the gaieties and the spoiling and the flatteries a King's daughter will get—if she be in favour; and especially when, like my sister, she be bright and gifted and small. She was forever asking to be with her new mother, Bryan told me; and so I found whenever I visited the children. She needed someone more immediately cherishing than I, quicker with loving words. I am one to love deeply but I have never known how to put my love into easy words. So it was she did not greatly care for me.

Love thrown back in my face, I turned to the little boy, my brother. I loved him because he was so small, and because his mother had been good to me. But most of all I loved him because I was his mother-in-God with a deep longing for the welfare of his soul.

And the child loved me, too; at the first. He would jump to come to me when I visited Havering; he would laugh and crow and chatter away in his sweet childish voice. I swear he loved me, then. And when, at five, they took him from Bryan to be tutored, to be brought up in a faith I could not share, still he loved me. Witness the small loving notes in his childish, careful hand. And for that I thank Bryan that stayed on as lady-mistress to my sister. But already Elizabeth was turning the child against me; it was a lesson he took long a-learning; and as all lessons with him, learnt thoroughly. It was an added sorrow to my life.

The two children brought up together in their enclosed world, the world of small princes, found each in the other his whole being. The boy, quiet with a reserve inherited from his mother but with passions derived from his father, fastened his lonely heart upon the other child. And she loved him with all the passion of her wayward, tempestuous heart; she, too, inherited much from her mother. Those two were forever together; they slept together, played together; together they did their lessons, each child blithe for learning—for to them learning was delight. Elizabeth, four years older, helped him as no other could. Herself a child, she understood his difficulties, explained them first in his own little-boy words, leading him on to the speech of his elders. She was the only person, I think, that in all his short life he ever perfectly loved or perfectly trusted. And in the end he turned from her, too.

And now it was June in the year of grace fifteen hundred and forty. Nothing as yet had been said about divorce and my father was still fast-wed to his Queen. Everyone knew that nothing was well between them. He scarce set eyes on her save at meals—and then he kept them, for the most part, turned away. Supper finished, he would, with dreadful mockery, bid her *Goodnight Sweetheart* and dismiss her to her lonely bed. Her fear of him grew daily; nor was she alone in fearing him. He was a sick man, never free of pain; and that pain his frustration forever exacerbated. He grew daily more angry, more unreasonable, more suspicious. He would turn suddenly upon old and faithful friends—and they would be seen never again. For they joined the sad procession of those that, dying for their faith, went to the block—if they were lucky, to the fire or to the gallows. And some, like Elizabeth Barton, died, being too simple to understand that for which they died. There was no mercy even for them.

To the traitor's dreadful death went three I held dear—my mother's chaplain, her confessor and my own tutor gentle Dr. Fetherstone; the only reason faithfulness to God and faithfulness to me. Resolute they had refused the Act of Supremacy. All that day I sat remembering the goodness of all three; and especially I remembered my tutor that, patient with an impatient child, so gently taught me my Latin; and I remembered how quick he had been to understand my hidden words when, at Hunsdon, I, myself, had stood in danger of death. The day was black for me not only for their cruel dying but with fear for my father's soul.

For it was not only Catholics that went to the fire, nor Protestants, also; but any that opposed my father in any degree; or any—and no reason given—he wished out of his way. All, all to the shameful hurdles—to the fire, the rope and the axe! There were days when I could not think about my father without horror. Yet, so curious the human heart, so binding God's commandments, so treasured my mother's teaching, that I loved him still. He was my father. And not all his cruelties could break the chain that bound me to him. Rust, it might; break—never!

These days bred in me a passion for mercy. I should never be a Queen—there was the little boy, my brother. But if Fate willed I should ever hold power over life and death—I should choose life.

My father could endure his frustrations no longer. Yet he could see no end to his thwarting. The Queen gave him no cause to complain. Never a wife so obedient, never a wife so unwilling to thrust herself upon a husband. She was speaking English quite well; but the quaint turn of her speech, the foreign accent, irritated him beyond endurance. Could he but find the faintest reason to complain, he had rid himself of her long ere this. But there was nothing. Nothing.

He turned to Wriothesley; not to Cromwell, my lord earl of Essex powerless now, for all his coronet, and shaking in his shoes. Wriothesley, sharp in the wits, and base as sharp, bade my father make no complaint but leave all to his faithfullest servant. It was Wriothesley, not my father, that, lamenting the King's hard case, opened the matter to the Council.

'The King's grace is bound to a wife he does not nor cannot love. Thus she shall never bring him issue—which is for him great sorrow, and for the country great evil.'

The Council listened and made no move. What need of further issue, the King had already three children? It was a question it did not ask knowing well the answer—the King's daughters were accounted bastards; the King's pretty boy, small and frail.

The Queen's life, never pleasant, now became unbearable. My father's ridicule grew ever more cruel. She endured it longer than one would have thought possible—and it was not for lack of spirit. And still he vexed her that her long patience might break and give him cause against her.

She had, indeed, come to that state when she could endure no more. I was with her when he came seeking her with insult. And this time he was successful—she was not a dog to be forever chastised.

'Sir,' she cried out, her great eyes aflame, 'I married with you not of my own will. For the good of our two countries I was forced. For my part I would have married with a good prince to whom I was to be promised. Would God it had so been!'

He had got what he wanted. But for all that I saw the red spark in his eye; she had wounded his vanity. He made her a mocking bow. 'Madam, I thank you for the information!' He turned his back; the door slammed behind him.

She sank down upon a stool and, for the first time, I saw tears in those dark eyes of hers. 'What have I done?' She wept and wrung her hands. 'Now I make a great trouble between your country and mine . . . and I was sacrificed to make a peace!'

I tried to comfort her, but of comfort she'd have none. She was friendless and far from home; she saw no way out of her miseries but out of life itself.

'Will the King's grace take off my head, do you think?'

I said, more cheerful than I felt, 'How? You have done no wrong! But . . .' and I remembered his jeering thanks, 'there could be, perhaps . . . divorce.'

She clasped her hands above her head. 'So hear me, my God, I do long for it! Let him make the shame upon me! Let him say what things he will. No word shall I speak in my defence; no blame upon him, no trouble between our two countries. Divorce. I do pray for it. And you, if you do love me, pray also. Your prayers and mine, they go by different roads. But you are good, so good, God will surely listen.'

My father's conscience was at work again. When he was content, then conscience slept; when he was displeased, then it awoke and pricked, and drove him along his desired path. But for all that *it was conscience*; and, sleeping or waking, it was always there. Now it drove him to the uttermost of insult; no accusation too untrue, too base, but he flung it at the Queen. Yet, after that first outburst, she answered no word. She was silent even when he insulted her chastity. Against Anne Bullen that particular insult had been a weapon; against Anne of Cleves it fell powerless, there was no woman more chaste.

'One comfort you have,' I told her once. 'My father's daughters love you.'

'That makes me courage,' she said, 'you may believe it.'

'Alas!' I said, 'I can do nothing . . .' and spread my empty hands.

'You do everything,' she said. 'You lift me up!'

But her real joy came from my sister. Parting, each had wept; and now Elizabeth was writing little love-notes to her dear, new mother. 'I had rather be mother to that little one than wife to the King of England!' she told me more than once. And once she added, 'How much I pray for this divorce the good God alone, He knows. But still I shall make me a—how do you say it?—a bargain; a little, little bargain. I shall ask that I shall see Elizabeth so often as I shall choose and not one to say me *No!*'

And she did, indeed, make that condition—and got it, too! For, the truth is, the Queen and the little girl had great need each of the other. The Queen needed the unquestioning love of the child; the child, for all she could be cold and calculating, felt great need of a mother; her own she had never known and Jane Seymour had died too soon. Against me her infant mind had been poisoned; and never, in all her life, would she love or trust me. Anne of Cleves she both loved and trusted.

Chapter Thirty-Three

A knowledgeable man, Chapuys. Within two months of his latest honour, my lord Essex that had been Cromwell went to the Tower; and Norfolk with tales of treason, meant to see that he never came out again. There had been long hatred between those two; they had shared the power—but Cromwell's had been the greater. Now Norfolk, knowing my father's caprices and fearing lest he have that able man out again, taught the little Howard her part.

'Madam,' she told the Queen—I heard her for myself, 'as long as that man lives you shall never be free!' And who can doubt that she went to the King with the same tale—but in somewhat different words. *So long as that man lives you shall never have me!*

Cromwell safe under lock and key, Norfolk and Gardiner worked for my father's freedom. These days my father was all good cheer, Norfolk all confidence, Gardiner all discretion; the little Howard all dimpled-smiling and the Queen content. The truth is that those last were hand-in-glove; Anne of Cleves had no desire to be wife to any man, least of all the King of England. As for myself, forever influenced by my father's moods, I breathed freer than for some time.

Within a few days Parliament was listening to the King's declaration that his fourth marriage was not valid. He had not known until after the ceremony that the lady had already been contracted; which, by God's Grace, learning in good time, he had not, conscience forbidding, dared consummate the marriage. 'If she brought her maidenhead with her, I never took it!'

And who could dispute that? None but the Queen; and she said nothing—she had not been asked.

Then, Parliament beseeching him to seek out the truth for the good of the realm, 'I can refuse you nothing!' my father said and commanded Cranmer to the task.

Bitter the hearts of the people might be against him; but his Parliament and his church were still dogs to eat out of his hand. By the third week in July my father was free; free to marry the pretty child that promised—if she had not already given—such delights. For there were many to whisper that those two had not waited for marriage to share one bed. Better for him and for her had he kept her for his light o' love; then he had been spared humiliation and bitter grief, and she kept her pretty, empty head—and many another kept his.

Cranmer came to Richmond with news of the divorce. I was with the Queen when she heard he was come from the King. I saw her grip upon the table lest she fall. 'Is he come to take me to the Tower?' And again she made that movement to her throat.

'Why no, Madam,' I said. 'I think he comes with comfortable news.

She was carrying herself queenly when he came into the room, this man that had divorced three Queens at my father's command; this holy man of God that played my father's game with the holy ordinance of marriage.

'Madam Princess—' and he was careful not to salute her as Queen, 'the King is free of contract of marriage with you, and you of him. That contract was never a marriage; church and parliament alike proclaim it.' He paused; then, slow and deliberate, he said, 'You are no longer Queen. If you will resign yourself cheerfully then all shall go well with you. His Grace will love and honour you as his dearest sister. He will bestow upon you incomes to the value of four thousand pounds; he will grant, also, four establishments each fitting your high condition. One house shall be this palace of Richmond if you will have it so, because he knows you love it well.'

He waited for her to speak; and, since she said nothing, continued with his careful speech so that she perfectly understood, 'Madam, you must at once release your household, highest to lowest, from their oath to serve you as Queen. Nor may you, yourself, use that title; nor may any use it to you. Madam, do you understand?'

'I understand,' she said.

'This done, you shall, in estate of the King's sister, take precedence of every lady in the land, save only that lady the King shall marry and his own daughters.' And he favoured me with not too low a bow.

She said no word but bent her head in silent obedience.

'And further, Madam; if you desire it you shall go back to your own country with all honour and dowries complete.'

At that she shook her head.

'Then there remains one condition. With your own hand you shall write to acquaint your brother with this affair; and shall assure him that all is done by your own goodwill.'

And now for the first time she spoke. 'My lord archbishop; to all this

I say *Yes*. For my part I make no condition; but one grace I do beg—
that the lord King, of his kindness, permit the little lady Elizabeth to
visit me when her good governor allow it.'

'Madam, I think there can be no difficulty.' And he permitted himself a smile.

'Then I am his majesty's most humble servant and loving sister.'

With a touching dignity she drew the wedding-ring from her hand
and the archbishop took it. 'Tell his Grace to break this ring in two for
a sign that the bond between us is broken.'

My father was as good as his word; and for her part, she kept more
than her share of the bargain. Not only did she quiet her brother's just
anger, but never, so long as she lived, did she speak one word against
my father; but rather grew in loving friendship with him. Nor did
she ever marry, being in truth a woman's woman rather than a man's;
and women valued her at her true worth. Catherine Howard, that had
known little of either, valued her goodness and truth, my sister was
constant in love and respect—which is not always her way; and to
me my father's fourth wife was a most dear friend. When the divorce
was made public, one of her women speaking for them all—and for
many another besides—said, *It is impossible for so sweet a lady to be put
down*.

But put down she was not. She was, indeed, a joyful woman. 'I am
free; and my head safe upon my shoulders. And to my own country
I will not return. Your English ways I like. Your English dress I like—'
and she smoothed the folds of a new gown—English fashion; 'and
your English food, also. And best of all your English church I like'
—and her voice sank to a whisper—'your Catholic church. In the
lights and the incense I find God!' And, indeed, later she came into
the true faith, 'for love of God—and for you!' she told me.

My father lost no time wedding his pretty child; he was crazed with
her smallness and her sweetness. They were married in secret at
Oatlands the twenty-eighth day of July—that very day Cromwell
went to the block. It was like my father to choose that day; a last
gesture of contempt—as a boy thumbs his nose.

Cromwell that, merciless, had sent so many to their death begged
most ignobly for his own life; but for all that to the block he must go!
For some little part of that day, as yet unknowing of my father's
marriage, I spent in prayer for the man whose shadow had blackened
my girlhood, whom, more than once, rumour would have it I should

marry. His death brought me, strangely, a sense of loss—one may miss the thing one has disliked and feared. A chapter had been ended in my life—a most unhappy chapter; pray God the next be happier!

'No doubt you have prayed for that man!' Clarencieux said later. 'Yet he was a millstone about your neck!'

'Yet by some miracle—for it is not in the nature of millstones—he kept me from drowning.' And that was true enough; forcing me to outward obedience he had saved my life.

'Madam, a too generous heart is a danger!'

'There is no more danger from him! The man is dead and I am alive; alive and free. I feel the sun upon me—' and I held out my hand in the sunlight, 'should I not say a little prayer for one that shall feel it no more?'

My father's marriage had been secret. But there was nothing secret in the way he brought his bride back to the court. Early in August, in cloth-of-gold and crowned—though not with the crown of the Queen consort, that she was never to wear—she took the Queen's place in chapel at Hampton Court.

I did not see her until the New Year. I had sent congratulations and a gift upon their marriage; my father, token of his pleasure, commanded me to court. I was not surprised to see the lady Anne of Cleves, resplendently gowned, in attendance.

'So kind, the little Queen, so courteous!' she said. 'You cannot think how much! I made to salute her upon my knees but she did not allow. No! Her own hands stopped me and raised me; and *sister*, she said; *sister*! so dear a child—how not to love?'

A strange couple my father and his bride. He heavy and sick and old—older than his years; she young and slight,—body and mind both—and young, younger than her years. There was about her an eagerness to live, to *enjoy*; yet it was not a greed in her. Rather she was free in her giving; as having been so poor she was glad, now, to share her good fortune.

Yet for all her joyousness I thought, at times, I saw a watching look, as though she feared—what? What could she fear, this girl strictly bred in a great household? My father she could not fear—he could find no fault in her. I saw him, the unwieldy man, bestir himself with some pain to lead her in the dance; and, indeed, she seemed to give back to him something of his lost youth. He would rise early to hunt with her or to ride with her.... but he would pay for it afterwards! This marriage will kill him, I thought; but it killed her, instead!

The old duchess, it seemed, had bred her well. The young Queen showed courtesy to all. To me, the King's daughter—but a proclaimed bastard—she showed a charming deference; to Norfolk and to Gardiner that had put her where she was, a grave respect. She had none of Anne Bullen's arrogance; there was in her a natural sweetness. I hated her house for what it had done to my mother and to me; but her I could not hate. How can one hate a kitten or a small bird?

A few days later Elizabeth was brought from Havering at the Queen's request. 'We are cousins,' she said and placed the child opposite herself at table. The place of honour for so small a creature! And my sister enjoyed it to the full. With Catherine Howard Elizabeth had always precedence over me. I did not relish it but I respected the Queen that she did not ignore her kinship with Anne Bullen. But I feared for her, too. It was unwise, this constant reminder of a hated memory and her own close kinship with a disgraced Queen.

From none but her would my father have endured it; but he doted upon her with an old man's last passion. She had neither learning nor wit and he was glad of it; they had been bitter faults in Anne Bullen. He doted upon the very look of his young Queen; he would have her always in sumptuous gowns and great jewels, relishing the piquancy of her small face amidst such splendour. For it was less her pretty face than her childlike air that whetted his appetite; that, and the desire—the jealous desire—to protect her from all but himself.

But for all her pretty ways there were plenty that waited to pull her down. There were those that trusted neither her house nor those that had set her in high place; nor, jealousy curdling, did they trust the girl herself—and certainly she had, at times, a secret, narrow look that might make one doubt her honesty. But honest or not she was a puppet in the hands of Norfolk and Gardiner; and with that we of the old, true faith must make ourselves content. If we liked not scheming Norfolk nor cunning-clever Gardiner, they were pills we must swallow; we knew that, in their secret heart, ours was the faith they favoured. It was the day of the heretic; and in those two was our only hope. But men that had cast off the Pope, prayed that Madam, the Princess Anne of Cleves be restored.

She herself would have none of it. Life was ever merry in her house, her purse and doors forever open. Free of her fears she showed herself witty, wise and shrewd; and soon enough my father himself was seeking her out—even though enamoured of his new Queen. He enjoyed her company. I have seen them, hours on end, over their cards; she was an adept and he enjoyed the battle of wits. I have heard his sudden bellow of laughter at some jest of hers; she could be broad enough to please him suiting her wit to his company. But with that same wit she never pricked him; nor did she ever quarrel with any of his children nor make dissension between us—and with the three of us born of different mothers, to make trouble had been easy enough! We loved her all three, and we honoured her. She was often my father's guest and he, hers; she and he and his Queen bound altogether in loving friendship.

Anne of Cleves. A woman of infinite tact and inner grace. A pity my father had not the patience to learn her worth; a pity for him, and for the little Howard and for those that suffered with her. But for Anne herself it was better so. She too, for some fancied slight or for none at all, might have ended on the block, that to the end of her days lived happy and free.

And for me? I think I should never have come to the crown, for there would have been children enough; she was young and healthy and knew her duty. I might have lived happier; but the true faith must have been forever lost in the land.

Who shall question the ways of God?

Chapter Thirty-Four

Surrounded by enemies it behoved the young Queen to walk wary; but wisdom was not in her gift. She had not talent nor will cunningly to influence policies, she had not wits nor memory to make a good liar. Even when, at the last, she was forced to lie she had not the wit to save her life. But all that was to come.

That first year of his marriage, my father, in spite of pain and the aging years, was a happy man. Never since his youth had his court been so gay; masquing and mumming and games—a perpetual holiday. Every man, whatever his heart might hide, there he would be with the rest, bending the knee to worship the new sun. I think she never understood until it was too late—nor could Norfolk ever din it into her head—that she had enemies and to spare. She took every man at his face's value and the handsomer his face, the higher his worth.

My father worshipped his young wife. For all his age and sickness he took part in every piece of merriment; but he worked too. He was a glutton for work, my father, sparing neither himself nor any other. He missed no meeting of his Council, he dealt thoroughly with his Parliament letting no detail escape his eye. And always that eye was watchful to punish, so that even amidst the gaieties of court men went in fear, fear of offence given unknowing; fear lest the rash word reveal the hidden faith in the heart.

And, in the world without, fear multiplied also; a fear fed by tortures and burnings and hangings that never stopped. A man could not walk in the streets without he saw the shameful sledges drawing men, both martyrs and heretics, to their death; without wondering how soon he, himself, might take his place with them. For Catholics and Protestants suffered alike; to escape such a death a man must walk, very careful, in the middle way; he must make no step towards the old, true way of Rome; nor yet towards the new way of that arch-heretic Luther. He must walk in the way my father commanded—keeping the old ways of prayer but denying God's Vicar that He has set over us. One step from that middle way—and it was the gallows or the stake.

The gallows and the stake; they ruled our lives and men took them for granted, martyr and heretic, alike, awaiting his turn. But I could never take these fearful executions for granted; there was surely another way; a more merciful way to God.

Poverty. Sickness. Corruption. Death. My heart bled for my poor country.

At Havering, save for an occasional summons to court, the children lived undisturbed. Already the little boy was wearing a delicate look that made me catch my breath in fear. Pray God he would not, like young Richmond, die in his young years. But still his tutors kept him at his lessons, and not for all Bryan's pleading was there sufficient exercise; and play there was none at all.

But the little girl was growing tall and strong. She had, like my father, a way with her to charm those she chose; like him she had a sharp tongue and an imperious way that some, like myself, found ugly in a child—though the child be a prince. And there were not a few that found it uglier because they held her to be no true prince but the bastard of an unknown father; or, worse, the child of incest—brother with sister.

'The lord prince is fortunately too young to understand such things,' Bryan said once. 'But let any address her without due deference and he will fly into a rage. Small he is and not strong; but he has all his father's great spirit.'

She was not pretty, my sister, though she had a high and handsome way with her. The little sallow face was sharp, the nose long, the black eyes watchful. But her hair! She could light up a room like a lamp! And even then her hands and feet were lovely; and even then she knew it, disposing them this way and that, to their best advantage. I, myself, had been a pretty child in a pink-and-golden way; and at twenty-five I was prettier than she would ever be. My features are neater; and my eyes—no doubt because I must look close to see—give me an attentive look which, I am told, folk find pleasing. I, too, have red-gold hair— Tudor gold; but I should never light any room like a lamp. And I was seventeen years her senior. Seventeen years. Old enough to be her mother! As she grew in looks, so I must decline. Had I been her mother I should have accepted it; but being her sister I found it—as I was always to find it—hard.

I saw little of either child. Sometimes I would catch a glimpse of them at court; or I might see Elizabeth when I visited the lady Anne of Cleves. Sometimes I would go to them at Havering but they never came to me; with their household and their tutors, it could not, I was given to understand, be arranged. So I lived my quiet life at Hunsdon or Beaulieu, obeying an occasional summons to court, or making a brief visit to the lady Anne. Now and again there would be talk of betrothal for me; but I had learned to pay no attention to such talk. For me there would be no betrothal ever, so long as my father lived.

My life was pleasant enough; but at times I longed for the comings and goings of the court; the chance to meet foreign visitors, to talk with those that could take the pulse of the times, to sharpen my home-keeping wits. I wanted to see Chapuys, to hear news of my cousin the Emperor Charles; and, above all, I longed for the gaieties of the court. If not now—when? I was turned of twenty-five; a great age it seemed to me then, and a great age it was to be yet unbetrothed.

There was no great ceremony when my father brought his young wife to London nor any crowning, neither. Marrying four wives, crowning two, burying one and buying off a fourth, had cost him more than he could easily afford. But if he could not afford a crowning, there was no gift too costly to lavish on her. There was a cloak of Italian velvet all lined with sables of Muscovy and sewn at the throat with great rubies and pearls—thirty-five of the first and seventy-two of the second. I remember that because, with childish glee, she began to count the jewels, lost count and had me count them for her. Her household was fitting to a Queen with every officer from her lord Chamberlain and her Chancellor down to the smallest page. She had her own Council, though I doubt she ever attended a meeting. She had her full court of ladies and gentlemen—and nothing to do but make merry. Nor, in this merrymaking, did she count an old husband a drawback; indeed, lacking his presence her pleasure seemed less. She showed him every tenderness, performed every wifely duty.

'It is a child so good, so kind; to the King so loving!' the lady Anne of Cleves said. 'A better wife could not be!' My father thought so too; for now he did what he had done for no other wife. He had new coins struck in her honour. One side bore the royal coat-of-arms and his own initials; the other bore between her initials a rose and beneath it the words *Rutilans rosa sine spina*.

She was indeed a rose; a golden, glowing rose. But a rose is set with thorns for a purpose; and this rose, having none, had been visited too often. Because it bore no thorn it bore its poisoned fruits; but they were not yet come to harvest. These days my father could not keep his hands from her; yet his touch was tender—as one may caress a dear child. And she, herself, had a way of putting up her hand to take his—the hand with the bracelet that never left her wrist. It bore her new device. *Non aultre volunté qhele sienne.* It was her own choice; after perilous seas her frail barque had come into harbour and she wanted no will but his.

She and the lady Anne were fast friends. Anne loved the pretty girl; and Catherine, that had known no true friend, ever, drew close to Anne's warmth as a cold child to a good fire.

That spring of 'forty-one I went again to court. My father had been ill; the open ulcer on his leg had closed and, for a whil e his physicians feared—the evil juices turning inwards to infect his ,whole body— he must die. I found him, as usual, choleric and changeable to all save his Queen. In her he delighted still; yet he was troubled that, eight months being passed, there was no sign of her pregnancy.

The Queen I found well and merry. When I came into her closet she was plucking upon a lute; she laid it aside at once and held out both hands towards me. When I would have made my curtsey she cried out, 'Not between us; not when we are alone!' She dismissed her women; then she said, 'I have some news to comfort you. There is a certain lady in the Tower; an old lady you love. Those you love, I love too!' she added sweetly.

'Madam . . . does she go free?'

'Not yet. I have not dared. But the Tower, they say, can be very cold for prisoners—' and she shivered as though someone had walked over her grave. 'I know you, yourself, must not send her comforts— the King can be an angry man; it could be the end of her. So I have sent her garments against the cold.'

'God bless you for it!' I said. 'But were you not afraid?'

'Of the lord King? Yes, very much afraid. But it was worth the risk; indeed, it was scarce a risk at all. There are those I can trust.' And she gave a little secret smile. 'I have sent a bedgown furred against the cold; a kirtle of fine virgin wool . . .' she ticked them off upon a small forefinger—she was small in every degree. 'A petticoat well-furred also and bonnets to cover her old head. Yes and four pairs of hose together with four pairs of shoes. And I did not forget the lady's high quality. For though the body be comforted, pride, also, should have its turn. I know that well; I have been poor myself. I sent her a gown befitting her rank; a grey silk gown, lutestring, lined all with fine white satin. It will set me back somewhat in my accounts,' she said a little rueful; 'but—' and she laughed a little, 'the King asks no questions. It is a secret—' and a jewelled hand went up to that rosy mouth of hers. 'We know naught of the matter!'

A secret that could mean disgrace for her and punishment! My father might love but never would he tolerate disobedience. That she had dared this for an old woman she had never seen; how could I help but love her? How could I help but disbelieve—until her own confession forced me—tales of her wickedness with men? And while I marvelled at her courage, she said, 'It is to make up to you a little for . . . my cousin; for Nann Bullen. My grandmother, the old duchess, always held your mother was true wife and Queen.'

'And you?'

'I know nothing of the rights and wrongs. I did it for you, and for the old lady that cherished your childhood; none ever cherished mine.'

'She is good and innocent!' I cried out. 'Must she rot in prison to her death?'

She made a small supplicating gesture, bringing her hands up to her breast; it was as though she prayed my patience. 'While she lives— she lives. But let anyone speak out of turn—and she may die. Should I please the King yet better, give him a son—then he might give me her life; a gift.'

I went down upon both knees and kissed her hand. I had not always shown her full courtesy as to a Queen; but she had shown me more than courtesy from a Queen.

I was home again and there was no more peace for me. In the past I had prayed long and often for my lady Salisbury. At times she haunted me and I could not keep her from my mind. Of late I had forgotten her for days on end; to my shame I say it. I make no excuse; but my own life in danger, Jane Seymour's death, my father's marriages, had all too often driven my old friend from my mind. I think one grows used to a grief, until suddenly it is pricked awake. Now it had been pricked awake and there was no more forgetting. My talk with the Queen, reminder of that rigorous imprisonment, was like a stone thrown upon glass; my peace was shattered beyond mending.

Spring wore on to summer. *Must she rot to her death?* My own question forever tormented me; and forever I heard the answer, *While she lives—she lives!* It was the one hope I had.

The hope was broken. My father had commanded my lady Salisbury to the block.

'But why? *Why?*' I asked Clarencieux and I remember wringing my hands. 'What has she done? What, in prison, *could* she do?'

'Not she; not *she*! But there's unrest everywhere.'

'I know it!' I cried out. 'And can you wonder? Monasteries cast down, taxes forever heavier, land enclosed and hunger everywhere. And punishments in the name of God—Catholics and heretics alike. The hangings and the burnings. . . .'

'Hush, Madam!' she said. 'For the love of God, hush!'

'Unrest and revolt—my father must expect it!' And I would not be hushed. 'What has it to do with my old friend in the Tower?'

'It is her son, the priest Pole. With his writings he inflamed the rising in the north—there's no denying it! And still, wherever men are discontented, those writings are tinder to spark off revolt. Madam, they are treason.'

'But *she* has done nothing. . . .'

'She is his mother. She has cluttered his prison too long, the King says; she has lived on credit, now she must pay her debt.'

'She must make way for other victims!' I said, bitter. 'And the boy Courteney? And his mother?'

'No word . . . as yet.'

'What can I do? What?'

'There's nothing you can do!'

When she was gone I walked from room to room still wringing my useless hands . . . I must see my father. I had put off the matter too long. Fear lest my old friend die for it, had restrained me—so I tried to excuse myself. I could make that excuse no longer.

My father would not see me. He guessed my mission.

There was one, one only, that might help me—if she dared.

I found the Queen closeted with a young man I had never seen. It surprised me that they two should be alone together with never a woman in attendance. I did not at that first glance—nor at any other glance—like him. Too pretty a gentleman—and only half a gentleman at that! He was older than she; he should have known the impropriety of it. And that impropriety his own manner to the Queen emphasised; he was, I thought, over-familiar.

'My secretary!' she said. 'Mr. Francis Dereham.'

I wished him gone before I opened my business but she made him no sign; clearly he was one of those she had mentioned, whom she could trust. When I begged for her help I liked him less than ever; for he stood between us saying no word while his eyes advised her to keep from this affair. But had he counselled her help I still should have found him offensive—the smooth familiarity with which he carried himself.

She stood hesitating between us. She nodded to me at last and, lest she should fail of her word, went straightway from the room.

There passed no word between the young man and me; but for all that I sensed dislike, each for the other, palpable between us.

She was back almost as soon as she had gone, and the noise of my father's anger came with her. She was greenish-pale and shaking in her shoes. The young man said no word. He took her by the hand and led her to a chair; me he stood regarding out of mocking eyes.

I did not see her again. She sent word by her offensive secretary that she could do no more in the matter. He had, it was clear, much pleasure in repeating my father's message to me. *Tell the lady Mary to beware how she interfere lest she lose her head likewise.*

On a sweet May morning my old friend went to her death. It is a thing of which I never speak; and which over the long years sickens me still. They made a ballad about it; how she would not lay her proud head upon the block.

> For traitors on the block should die,
> I am no traitor, no not I!
> My faithfulness stands fast and so,
> Towards the block I shall not go,
> Nor make one step as you shall see.
> Christ in Thy mercy save Thou me. . . .

And, since she would not, of herself, make one step, there followed what I must suppose to be the bloodiest scene that ever took place in that place of blood. For she ran this way and that not in fear but in pride—a divine madness. Let them take her if they could!

They could and they did. She fell hacked to pieces beneath the savage axe.

Chapter Thirty-Five

Prisons full, gallows hung with obscene fruit, Smithfield fires still blackening the summer sky, my father decided upon a progress to the north. What better time to turn his back upon the miseries of the south; to march with a display of power, to show these subjects that knew little of him what they might expect should they revolt again?

They set off in high summer, the King and Queen—for he could not endure to be without her—with banners and with music; with princes of church and state and courtiers splendidly accoutred; and, not least, with men-at-arms, their weapons glittering in the sunshine—warning without words.

In the late autumn they returned, my father well-pleased. He had never yet failed to win admiration and awe for his own person, and his Queen had delighted all eyes. At once he carried her off to quiet Windsor; he sent for me to join them and she sent for her favourite, the little Elizabeth.

I found my father tired and in some pain but more in love than ever. The delight of the northerners in his Queen's pretty face and gentle ways added vanity to his love. The treasure was his; in spite of the aging years he had won her—his own! Again he was showering her with gifts. All the lordships and manors he had given to Jane Seymour, he now gave to her; all the lands that had been Cromwell's were hers also, together with houses and lands of plundered abbeys. He was forever having new jewels made; there was a collar of table emeralds set with great pearls, there were bracelets of sapphire and diamonds to cover her from wrist to shoulder, there were rings to cover every finger to the tips, including the thumbs.

I found her, as ever, gentle and sweet but I fancied she had a peaked look and certainly she was quieter than I had known her. I thought she might be breeding and, for her own sake, I hoped so; it was the one flaw in the jewel. For all my father doted upon her, crown her he would not, until she bore him a child; boy or girl he cared not which, but a child he must have to satisfy his manhood. Anne Bullen's accusation of impotency rankled still.

Among the Queen's personal attendants I noted a new young man; scarce a gentleman but young and debonair. 'It is Manox,' she said, 'he makes music for me!' He played well enough and I thought no more of him . . . until what came afterwards.

I remember the day. Late October it was and we were still at Windsor. We were in chapel; my father had received the sacrament and, kneeling still, raised his hands and cried aloud, 'I give thanks to the Lord that, after so many strange adventures that have befallen my marriage, has been pleased to give me so perfect a wife!'

Such a thanksgiving while still he kneeled for the sacrament! But he was always one to do as he listed; and now he must needs add to his strange behaviour. For, rising, he requested my lord bishop of Lincoln, 'Prepare me a service of public thanksgiving to God that has blessed me with so loving and virtuous a wife.'

The next day the blow fell.

We had ridden to Hampton Court for the celebration of All Saints' Day. My father had risen from his knees when Cranmer thrust a paper into his hand.

Too many had rifled his rose without a thorn.

The tale was out; a tale that had already been whispered. It had not, until now, reached my father—for who should dare? Nor had it reached me in the country. And what of her? Had she supposed such a tale could be forever hid? Now I understood those troubled glances of hers, the pale, peaked look.

Tale of a child, ignorant, poor, and corrupted in that house where most she should be protected.

Like other girls of noble birth, rich and poor alike, she had been put into a great household to learn the formal patterns of breeding required in a lady of her high blood. The household was that of her grandmother Norfolk—step-grandmother I should say—and maybe there lay the difference; for the dowager had not troubled herself unduly with her charge. It was not wilful neglect; but the duchess was an old woman and a harassed one. Two great establishments were in her care—Horsham, where, for the most part, she lived; and Lambeth her town house. The Horsham household numbered some three hundred including the young ladies in her care. She had sufficient on her hands without troubling unduly about a child of ten. How could such a little one come to harm?

So the little Catherine shared the great dormitory with the other women; some were girls of high birth like herself—her own kins-woman Tylney among them; some were of coarser grain and some of them were married. Of them all she was the youngest . . . and the poorest. They treated her with a good-humoured bluntness; and being, for the most part, experienced in the ways of men, with scarce a thought took the bloom of her innocence.

How could such a little one come to harm? How indeed!

Every night the old duchess with her own hands locked the great dortoir; and with that safeguard was well content. So old a woman! She had forgotten her own once-hot blood; forgotten that not even bolts and bars can keep lusty young women from men; nor men from them. The child's virginity was taken before she well understood her loss.

Henry Manox had been the first. He had taught her music—and other things besides. Thirteen years old she had been when his fingers strayed from virginal to virgin. The duchess had caught them kissing under the stairs; the girl she had beaten and carried off to Lambeth. Fingered her he had; but lain with her carnally—never. He swore it and so did she; even on the rack he swore it. Well, it might be so; but he had roused her child's body and for that must take his blame.

From Horsham to Lambeth; from frying-pan into fire!

Manox was first to handle the rose; Dereham first to rifle it—Dereham the half-gentleman, the insolent young man I had disliked on sight.

He had meant no ill, he said. She was fourteen and marriage-ripe. He was a kinsman of the duchess though of a humbler breed; he had some means and they were in love. They called each other husband and wife and witnesses had heard them. 'A common-law marriage, I thought it, and I used her as a man his wife; she was as eager in that as I. I thought her family would permit the marriage and our union made regular. Why not?'

Why not, indeed? She could not look to make a great match—so he thought. He had reckoned without two things. The Howards did not lightly dispose of their women; plain or handsome, rich or poor, they were Howard blood to strengthen Howard power. Nor could he know that his particular Howard should blossom unto such prettiness and charm.

At fourteen the girl was old enough to take pleasure from her new-aroused body; but not yet old enough for true love, which is a faith-fulness in the heart. So he kept her fancy for him hot with his skilled lovemaking, and even more with his gifts—pretty things such as she had never had. There was a pansy flower all worked in silk, fashionable and costly, to enrich a poor gown; there was a quilted cap worked all with friar's knots—that some call true-love knots—all in gold. They lightened his not too-well filled pockets; but she gave him value for his money. Like a wedded pair they lay together behind the bed-curtains and made love to the sound of lewd jokes and laughter.

Of all this the old duchess, at first, knew nothing; but hearing something of their liking one for the another and, herself, catching them at their love-play, she had beaten the girl black-and-blue and packed the young man out of the house. Now, for the first time, she scrutinised her young kinswoman. Lovemaking had worked some improvement in this thin scrap of a girl. She had rounded a little; the green eyes, once deplored, were strangely attractive, they gave piquancy to the red-gold hair that curled to the narrow waist. She was a pretty thing, with pretty ways!

Now there was talk of betrothal with Tom Culpeper. I had seen him about the court—a handsome young man of doubtful virtue; but he had a good inheritance and was well on his way to fortune. Already he had risen to be gentleman of the King's Privy chamber and a great favourite with my father. He was a near kinsman of the girl—a cousin I believe—her mother having been a Culpeper. A better match than her family could ever have dreamed and one that promised to strengthen Howard's influence. And the girl was more than willing. Tom was more desirable in every way than Dereham. Why should she keep faith with her one-time lover that had gone adventuring—though pirating is the truer word—in Ireland? If she remembered him at all it was with dismay. She wanted to hear no more of him.

And then the King's eye had fallen upon her and there was no more talk of the Culpeper betrothal or any other. Now the Howards looked higher, higher . . . highest. It was not only that she was a pretty thing with pretty ways; she had, like her cousin Anne Bullen, some essence to stir the desires of men—it streamed from her like a perfume.

A pawn becomes Queen—if rightly played; a pawn to put knights, bishops and castles from their place, to put down great Cromwell himself and lift her whole family to the undisputed pinnacle of wealth and power.

It was a game Norfolk knew well how to play. The girl, if she loved anyone at all, loved Culpeper. But she knew her duty. No Howard girl had ever dared refuse her part in Howard schemes.

But what of the furtive fondlings of Dereham?

She shook them from her light head. She had said once—it had come out in her examination—*A maid may meddle with a man and no harm done*. And certainly that was a lesson she had learned well. Cunning she was in matters between man and woman; but in the world of men and women, she was not clever. How such *meddling* must blacken her honour should it become known—that she did not understand until it was too late. And besides; how should it become known? It was all so long ago.

Back came Dereham from Ireland, pockets well-lined, to find his sweetheart forever lost. To his honour be it said that he made no claim nor spoke of what had passed between them. But because the old duchess, grown somewhat soft with age, pressed the matter, and because of her own kindness, the Queen had found him a place in her own household; her secretary. Her kindness was her undoing—she had no more sense of her own preservation than a kitten. Already she had placed about her those women of other days; women that knew her secrets—Jane Bulmer and Margaret Morton, Kate Tylney and Alice Restvold. They had pressed their claims on the score of old friendship . . . and she had not known it for blackmail. They loved her and she was content to advance them.

Now she had added to their number Dereham, so ill-bred that, in good fortune, could not contain himself for arrogance; and Manox, another cheap young man but the only one of them all that, even in dire torment, did not put the blame upon the Queen. As long as their little goose supplied the golden eggs she was safe enough from her *friends;* but favourites beget envy and tongues began to whisper. It was on account of these *friends* that the blow fell at last.

It was my good gossip Nann, Edward Seymour's wife, that came down into the country to tell me how matters had fallen out.

'We have in our service, one John Lassells,' she said, 'a sour-faced piece of honesty. Men shun him and he knows it; and therefore his tongue is bitter; bitter but honest. Now it seems that his sister, Mary Hall was, before her marriage, in service both at Horsham and Lambeth with Morton and the others. So he asked her why the rest of them were now enjoying the Queen's favour and she alone had been given no place.

'This Mary Hall is just such another sour piece as her brother. She said, *I would not for all the world serve the Queen; she is a bad woman, lewd with men.*'

I said, when I could speak for shock of so vile a slander, 'Sour, indeed! But, *honest*? She should be whipped!'

'Such a tale; it were treason not to tell!' Nann said.

'On whose part? Lassells' . . . or your husband's?'

She made no answer to that.

'Do you believe it?' And I waited as though she spoke my own sentence.

She shrugged. 'The Queen is young; she lacks discretion.'

'To lack discretion is one thing—and natural in the young,' I said. 'But lewdness with men . . .'

'For that some women are never too young. The tales are true enough.'

'Dear God!' And I beat my hands together. 'What shall become of the Queen?'

'The King is just,' she said.

But not merciful. I bit back the words.

I got rid of her as soon as I might. What was the truth in the matter? Nann's husband, Seymour—my lord Hertford now—was a most ambitious man, both eyes on the future. The little Prince was his sister's son; and the King himself, worn by sickness, could not, in the nature of things, live long. No limits it would seem to a man's ambitions—save that the Prince, far from strong, might die; or the Queen bear sons. Anxious as my father—though his motives less pleasurable—he awaited news of the Queen's pregnancy. *Treason not to tell!* How honest his motive is any man's guess.

I sent for Chapuys. From that shrewd man I should get the truth—he knew everything.

'The tales are true enough . . .' he echoed Nann Seymour's words.

'Then I fear me the Queen is a dead woman!'

'Not so, Madam. She did wrong to marry the King; but what she did before her marriage is not adultery and therefore not treason. She broke no marriage-vows. The King will put her away if—' he added slowly, 'that be all.'

'*All?* Is it not enough?'

He gave me a long, troubled look. 'If there be more,' he said, 'be sure Hertford and Cranmer will smell it out!'

'Hertford's reasons we know,' I said. 'But Cranmer's?'

'He fears her influence with the King. When they were in the north they stayed with one of her friends—a good Catholic gentleman. Cranmer regards it as a pointer—a pointer only, of which an archbishop must take count.'

'Cranmer will work for her death,' I said.

'If she be innocent as to adultery, she will fall; but not to her death.'

'If . . . !' I cried out. '*If . . . !*'

My father refused to believe the writing upon Cranmer's paper; he thrust it back again. 'She is the purest soul alive and those that have spoken to her dishonour shall be punished! Search out the matter, but be secret; thrown mud sticks. I'll have no filth upon my Queen! But you'll find nothing to her dishonour, nothing! It is all in the sick mind of the fellow Lassells and his thrice-damned sister. Let Wriothesley question them close; spare them no torment. They'll not, I warrant, stick long to their tale!'

But they did stick to their tale. 'You may rack me but I'll say no other!' Lassells told them. 'I had rather suffer for the truth than the truth should suffer for me!' And though rack him they did, not a word would he retract. Mary Hall, too, stood by her words; and her, also, there was no doubting. Her very unwillingness to speak damned the Queen.

Manox had been arrested but the Queen knew nothing of it. The King had been somewhat low in spirit, but that was nothing new. So she played upon her virginals and sang her little songs, and with gentle words tried to cheer him.

Dereham had been arrested; but she did not know that, neither. Nor would it have troubled her overmuch—for the charge was piracy. Now they had him under their hand; soon he was telling all they wanted to hear.

'Yes, it is all true. I lay with her as a man with his wife; we were promised to each other and we regarded it, both of us, as a marriage. When I went into Ireland I left money with her as a man does with his wife. But it is all years ago. Since I came back from Ireland I never, as God hears me, touched her; she belongs to the King. You may tear me limb from limb but I'll say no other!'

By now the tale was being spoken louder; but still the Queen heard nothing.

My father summoned me to court. Yet he scarce saw me nor, save to command to silence in any matter concerning the Queen, did he speak of his trouble. He was a sick, sad man; he was a shamed man; he was a battered and bewildered man. I grieved for him; and for the Queen I feared. For now, it seemed, he could no longer endure any place where she might be. He said no word of Farewell to anyone; from the window, I saw him, slow and heavy, ride away.

The Queen came upon me as I stood watching. 'He rides away upon some business,' she said. 'Pressing business; for he did not stay to say Goodbye. And I have a new song for him! Manox made it for me. I shall not sing it until my lord return!'

The song was never sung . . . it died with her.

Chapter Thirty-Six

Next morning the Council waited upon the Queen. In silence they came but in silence did not depart. Room after room rang with the cries of her terror, as she ran wildly to seek the King—the King that was no longer there; running and screaming until they caught her and brought her back again. They say her poor distracted ghost haunts the long gallery but I have never seen it. Perhaps she does not forgive me that I did not go to her then. I did, indeed, reach her door; but there stood men-at-arms, halberds crossed. She was already a prisoner.

A bare twenty-four hours later Norfolk and Cranmer appeared in the Queen's rooms. From neither could she expect kindness and she knew it. Her uncle she feared more, remembering his unkindness to Anne Bullen in just such a case. They questioned, they accused, they suggested; they repeated such part of the confessions of Manox and Dereham as pleased them. They had the whole story they said; useless for her to deny anything. *Confess. Confess. Confess.*

But still she went on denying, denying, denying. They left taking with them her jewels. At that she wept bitterly. Not for the jewels themselves, she was beyond that. It was a bad sign and she knew it.

Neither of them was to be softened by a woman's tears. Norfolk, for the second time, stood to lose his head; it was just possible to save it by the loss of the Queen's. And Cranmer? He feared her influence over a love-besotted King, in her secret heart she was a Catholic; for his church's sake he would stop at nothing to be rid of her. Three Queens he had already divorced and one of them would have made ready to meet her God—but that she had refused him. He was prepared to do both for this fifth Queen. He hounded the frightened little creature now with threat of death, now with promise of mercy until he got what he wanted . . . but not, as yet, as much as he needed. There are some to say that I am blinded with my own wrongs against him and can allow him no good. It could be so. As we are—we are.

Yes, she confessed, she had allowed Manox to finger her—that and no more. Hearing this, my father, they said, broke into a passion of weeping; for Manox had been the first to desecrate her sweet body—Manox that half-gentleman. It was the first time my father had been seen to weep for sorrow, even the death of his first born, the infant son, had not drawn tears.

Yes, she had lain with Dereham; he had forced her. And then, having confessed so much, down she sat, tears streaming down her face, to implore the King's pardon.

. . . most humbly upon my hands and knees although, of all creatures I am unworthy either to be called your wife or subject . . . I was so desirous of your Grace's favour I could not conceal how great a fault it was to conceal my former faults. My sorrow I can by no means express.

She asks his grace and pity because of

my youth, my ignorance, my frailness and my humble confession of my faults. . . .

There it stands, her confession for all Christendom now and here-after to read; in her unformed, childish hand too pitiful to read without tears for a young life wasted and corrupt.

So far, so good. But it was not enough. Had lewd behaviour *before* her marriage with the King been all, she must, though fallen from her Queen's estate, escape with her life. If Dereham had spoken truth, if she were, indeed, his common-law wife, then she had wronged no man but him; if she had committed adultery it was not with Dereham; it was with the King. But there were other rumours and Cranmer meant to prick them out.

That same day my father commanded my sister and me to Syon House; we were expressly forbidden to attempt any Farewell to the Queen. I never saw her again; but always I shall remember the way she had turned to me saying, childlike, *I have a new song. I shall not sing it until my lord return. . . .*

Day by day Cranmer thrust himself into the Queen's rooms; day by day he tormented her with his questions. And all the time, in the Tower, Manox and Dereham lay in anguish of mind and body both. *Time and torture will disclose further information* Norfolk, in the name of Council, wrote to the King.

Torture did not wait upon time; and it did disclose all. Dereham, being racked, cried out those things his tormentors needed to hear.

Adultery against the King.

'But not with me; never with me! I had nothing further to do with the Queen's person. It was Culpeper she favoured, yes, even in the King's bed! Ask those ladies she favours, they will speak.'

And Culpeper, all unaware of his danger, hawking with his friends!

Now Cranmer was indeed a dog on the scent. Rochford, Tylney and Morton were arrested, Culpeper brought from his sport and all four cast into prison.

At last Cranmer had what he wanted. He went direct to Hampton Court where that other prisoner lived behind locked doors. What happened then all Christendom knows; we have his own words.

'Madam, your sins have been examined and found true. You have committed adultery; and, so doing, you have committed high treason. And there are other charges of treason, also. You have conspired against the lord King to take away his life.'

And 'No!' she cried out. 'No! No! No!'

'Yes, Madam, yes! Dereham has confessed it. He told us how, yourself present, he had often said, *Were the King dead I know I should have her!* To look forward to the King's death—that is treason, Madam! And, in such a context—double treason.' He let that sink in. Then, deceitful as was his way, 'Confess your sins and the King will show you mercy.'

And she, poor wretch, all undone with fear and shame, unable to speak, nodded and held up her clasped hands to thank my father for his goodness. So little she knew of her husband; or of this same holy priest that would stop at nothing to bring about her downfall.

Cranmer was not one to let his hot iron cool. Now, without mercy, he pressed her, nor gave her any rest until he had her full confession. So she, all helpless, with no friend to advise, and assured of the King's mercy, threw away her life.

One thing, only, she would not confess—any contract or common-law marriage with Dereham. Confess she had never been the King's wife and Queen of England, that she had been the King's mistress only! Howard pride forbade it. Cranmer, do him justice, pressed her for her own sake. 'You have committed carnal sins but you have not betrayed the King—he was never your husband. If you were wed or contracted before ever he set eyes on you you have betrayed no-one but Dereham your true husband. You have behaved very ill; but there is no treason in it!'

Why did she not confess? I cannot think Howard pride is the only answer though it played its part. I think that, ignorant and young, she had not understood that contract is binding as marriage; or even that she had bound herself all. Or maybe she spoke the truth and it was Dereham that lied—Dereham stretched upon the rack and able to endure his torment no longer; Dereham lying, hoping to save his own skin and hers, also. I believe her in the matter rather than him—for she had little wit to lie. Certain it is that, still denying, she went to her death.

Early in October the Council commanded the Queen to Syon House—a prisoner still. I knew nothing of it until my sister, white and scared, burst into my closet. 'We are commanded to leave at once! Wriothesley has brought the order. Already they are taking down the hangings, they are carrying away the best of the furnishings.'

And while I stood, not believing such orders be given and I know nothing, she burst out, 'They are bringing the Queen here! They are preparing her rooms. Three. Three only for her and her women; the smallest and the meanest—I've been to see them. The servants are putting up mean hangings, bringing in pallets and stools. Such poor pieces you never saw! She stopped; she cried out, 'No canopy of estate! It means . . . it means . . .' Her face was twisted in horror. 'They will cut off her head as they did . . .' Even then she could not bring herself to mention Anne Bullen's name—nor did she ever. 'But you'll not grieve!'

She looked at me, eyes black as onyx and as hard. There was, I swear, hatred in them. That she did not like me, I had long known; but that she should *hate* me . . . !

'Not grieve; how so?'

'To take a Queen's head pleased you once well enough!'

'I prayed for her soul,' I said. 'And it was all long ago!' I laid a hand upon her shoulder and felt her shrink.

I sent to Wriothesley to see the orders. They were written in the name of the Council.

. . . The furnishing of three chambers is to be hanged with mean stuff without any cloth of Estate. No man would consider it reasonable that the King's Highness should entertain her in the high degree and estate of a Queen for whose demerits she is so unworthy the name. . . .

No trial. But already she had been judged.

Nor was she to bear the name of Queen; she was nothing now but plain Catherine Howard. All her courtgowns were taken—her jewels they already had; she was to have only the plainest dress of the humblest gentlewoman; six hoods, six gowns, and six kirtles of sober material, colour and cut; an edging of gold there might be but no embroidery nor any precious stone.

It was clever; clever as cruel. To deprive her of every show of Queenship—fair chambers, cloth-of-estate, her gowns even; it was designed to take down her courage. But six hoods, six gowns, six kirtles! It did not look like immediate death; for then one or at the most two had sufficed. Was there in the very number the repeated promise of mercy should she confess?

The orders commanded my sister and me to Havering and the best part of the Syon household to be dispersed. The Queen's own women were taken from her, save four that wished themselves elsewhere. None might come within the house or leave it, save by the King's signed consent. So there she was, a prisoner in such mean estate as made nonsense of Cranmer's repeated promise of mercy.

There was great rejoicing between the two children at their reunion. Away from the Queen's unhappiness Elizabeth was herself again; a child of eight cannot forever grieve. But this was a child that understood more than most. I had expected some tears; but even then she knew how to shut away grief beneath a smiling face.

If in looks she more and more favoured her mother, so did the four-year-old favour his own. I found him lovable and loving but my heart ached seeing his pale and delicate air.

At Havering the thought of Catherine Howard was forever with me. Elizabeth's words—by her seemingly forgotten—I could not forget. *They will cut off her head like . . .* Simple words spoken from a child's heart they carried a sense of prophecy. Whether the unhappy Queen was innocent or guilty, she'd find little justice in a court ruled by Norfolk or Cranmer. Yet I thought, whatever she deserved, my father would stop short of death—if she were innocent with Culpeper; only then. I prayed unceasing that, innocent or guilty, the court—if it could not give justice—might be moved to the miracle of mercy.

I was scarce settled at Havering when my father sent for me to Oatlands where in solitude he waited the outcome of the examination that should decide whether or no there was a case against the Queen. If they decided there was, then trial or no trial she was a dead woman. I wondered that he had chosen this where he had wedded his young bride. It was as though he himself must press the sword upon his heart.

In spite of his great bulk he looked shrunken, his face hanging like the dewlaps of a dog. He no longer attempted to hunt or even to ride;

it was as though some mainspring in him were broken, destroying the last vestige of middle-age. He had won his golden rose; he had not been able to keep her. Younger men had rifled his sweet flower, bespattered it with dirt. He had never faced the fact that he was old; now he was forced to face it. Heart and pride, alike, had suffered a mortal wound.

For long hours he would sit silent; then suddenly he would cry out, *She has betrayed me, cuckolded me, shamed me in the eyes of Christendom. Naught but her blood can wash away my shame!* Or, remembering her pretty ways, he would weep and say very pitiful, *Must so sweet a thing be destroyed?* And then, remembering that all Christendom laughed— and especially his enemies, France and Spain—he would cry out all passionate, *Sweet to the eye but rotten at the heart.* He knew well his own caprices and feared to attend the examining court lest he halt the whole affair and spare her. With the matter he would have nothing to do; he left it all to Cranmer, to Norfolk and to Wriothesley.

Not one of those three knew the meaning of caprice. And the Council, too, understood very well it had been summoned to make an end of the Queen.

What she had already confessed to Cranmer concerning Manox and Dereham she again admitted. That she had ever promised Dereham or made any sort of contract with him she most vehemently denied. Cranmer had once explained to her the importance of such a contract but now no-one raised the matter. It had been forbidden. Since Culpeper had come into the matter and was being questioned, the King's heart had hardened into bitterness. His friend and his wife together betraying him! There was no more softness in him. She should not go free of death. For now it was my father wrote to the Council

> . . . It is the King's intention to lay before Parliament and judges the abominable behaviour of the Queen, but without any mention of precontract with Dereham that might stand to her defence.

Without any mention of precontract with Dereham . . . without any mention of that which must have saved her life. And she, too feather-brained, too distraught and too ignorant to understand Cranmer's advice, or even to remember it, persisted in her denial. There had been no contract with Dereham.

I remember talking to Chapuys on the matter.

'Will she, death at her very throat, go on denying?'

'I think she will,' he said. 'She doesn't understand the importance of it and no-one dare tell her. If she admits to a precontract with Dereham, she must go free. Even if she and Culpeper admit to misconduct,

she has done the King no wrong; all wrong-doing is against Dereham
—her true husband!'

The truth about Culpeper we shall never know. Childhood friends
and kinsmen—was it strange she should grant him freedom of the
Queen's rooms? But did she grant him the freedom of her bed also?

He denied it. She denied it. Her women denied it.

There is an unfailing method of making folk speak, but whether
they speak truth or what their tormentors wish them to say, is another
matter. Culpeper and the Queen's most familiar women were put to
the torture—all save my lady Rochford. She waited not for torment
to say the things they wanted.

'Her mind ran forever upon Culpeper,' the woman said. 'She told
me—and more than once—*were I in the maidens' chamber I would have
him!*'

Were I in the maidens' chamber she had said. Were I . . . But she
was not in the maidens' chamber, she was in the King's chamber.
Those words—if indeed she had said them—smacked to me of lewdness but denied adultery.

'She forever pressed me to let her have the thing she said I'd promised.
The thing was Culpeper. But I never promised; by Christ I swear it!'

As for the women under torture, out the story came bit by bit.

. . . Yes, he came often to the Queen by night; and my lady Rochford
let him in. Sometimes he would stay so long that my lady, set to watch
against surprise, would fall asleep in her chair. . . . Sometimes he would
stay all night. On the journey north it was arranged where and how he
should come at her. It was my lady Rochford that arranged all. . . .

And Culpeper, himself? He denied everything—until the rack loosen-
ed his tongue. *Yes, yes. I intended to do ill with the Queen and she with
me.*

And to crown all they had found a letter written to him in her own
hand. Hearing he had been sick she wrote,

. . . I never longed so much for a thing as I do to see you and to speak
with you. When I think that you shall depart again from me again
it makes my heart die to think what fortune I have that I cannot
always be in your company. . . .

She signs herself, Yours as long as life endures.

I have pricked out everything that is like to serve our business, wrote Mr.
Secretary Wriothesley in charge of the examinations and not above
lending a hand himself to the instrument of torture, *The woman Tylney
has done us worthy service.*

Worthy service. Poor racked creatures saying whatever their tor
mentors put into their mouths, and weeping afterwards for thei
share in the Queen's death. Well, I cannot blame them; how much
in such torment, could my own flesh endure?

Everything against her. The confessions of Manox and Derehan
and their appointments in the Queen's own household; Dereham'
boast *If the King were dead I know I should have her*—in such a contex
undoubted treason; the confessions of her women—Tylney, Mortor
and the rest, above all the poison-tongued Rochford. And finally
Culpeper's confession and her own letter to him . . . a love-letter i
ever I saw one!

At Syon the Queen had stopped weeping; like the ill-fated cousin
before her, she laughed long and shrill and could not stay her laughter
so that fools put it about that she waxed merry. From such a merriment God save us all!

My father could endure Oatlands no longer; he was back at Whitehall
and I at Beaulieu. And there I found Bryan's letter. My sister, she wrote,
spoke little yet suffered much on the Queen's account. She looked
far from well; all the spirit out of her. A change of air, Bryan thought,
would be of some benefit.

I sent for Elizabeth hoping to comfort her and myself. She came looking thinner, sharper, more distrustful than ever. Never was there so
unchildlike a child! I had done her wrong; distance had not lessened
her fears for the Queen.

'What the Queen has been accused of she does not understand, God
be thanked; she is too young!' Bryan said. 'But that the Queen has
been accused of some wickedness, disgraced, kept close and not allowed
to speak in her own defence—that, my little lady knows.'

'My sister's heart is hard to win, but the Queen won it; she made
much of the child, calling her little kinswoman, giving her precedence
over me—ointment to bruised pride.'

We were silent both of us remembering how at one stroke the child
had lost both her mother and her consequence; like myself, degraded
from royal heir to bastard. Infant though she had been, knowing
nothing, here and there she must have picked up a word not understood yet building into a horror so dark, it had locked up her tongue.
Now, fear for another had unlocked it; unknowing and in sleep she
had cried out her fears.

'Of her own mother she still never speaks,' Bryan said, 'but of the

Queen speak she must; not to me nor to anyone, but in her sleep. *They will chop off her head* she cries out over and over again. And sometimes she cries out *It is wicked, wicked, wicked.* . . . I wonder, at times, whether it is for her mother she cries out, or for the Queen, or whether in her mind they are somehow one!'

Once I heard her for myself, crying out wildly, and went quickly to her bedchamber lest some listener carry her words to my father. He had at this moment no love for her. She was only eight years old— but she was Anne Bullen's child, and of that same blood as Catherine Howard. My hand upon the door I heard Bryan say, 'Hush, hush . . . and remember your father suffers, too!'

'His sufferings will end with her life!' my sister cried out in a hard unchildlike voice and then, like any child, burst into tears.

Chapter Thirty-Seven

The mockery of the Queen's examination all Christendom knows. Never once was she called to hear the evidence against her nor allowed to speak in her own defence. Dereham's statement concerning a contract and common-law marriage was struck out; and with it every word that might help her.

To the Tower went the old duchess of Norfolk, the charge against her, trumpery; she had destroyed some papers Dereham had left with her. Of no further use she said, and she needed space. Her real offence was that she had known about Manox and Dereham and had said nothing; and, even greater offence, she refused to testify against the Queen. Condemned to die, she was offered life and freedom to speak against the Queen.

She had played her part in the sorry affair so let her answer stand to her credit. 'I am an old woman. Soon I must answer to my Maker. Let me die a little sooner—it is all one!' And would say no more. So she tried to make amends for neglect of the little Catherine. But it was too late . . . too late.

To the Tower, also, went her son and his wife, innocent in the business but for all that attainted and their property confiscate; Norfolk, treading delicately and very zealous that the Queen should be punished, kept himself safe. And still in the Tower awaiting trial lay Manox, Dereham and Culpeper—and not one of them debonair now; twisted limbs and faces marked from the torment, all three cursed the day they had set eyes on the little Howard's pretty face.

And now the evidence was in; the law must take its course.

In the first week of November, Culpeper and Dereham came to their trial, charged with defiling the Queen—and both were found guilty. For judgment against Culpeper there was some justification; for that against Dereham—none. He must die because of that long-ago love-making with a girl that was not a Queen nor ever thought to be one; a girl that he looked upon as his wife. But both alike must die. My father had signified his will to the judges and with them sat my lord Chancellor, my lord Privy Seal and Norfolk, himself, to see that they obeyed. So the two men, alike, were condemned to the fearful death of traitors; but they did not die alike. Culpeper, being of noble blood, lost his head to the axe; but Dereham, being but half-gentleman, suffered the full, ugly sentence. Manox, that pretty piece of trash, was spared; even the child Catherine had known better than to allow him more than a pawing or a tickling. He left prison a broken man; broken body housing a broken spirit.

It was about this time that the strange rumour arose that my father had consoled himself with the lady Anne of Cleves and that she was pregnant by him. Certainly she had grown plumper and certainly there had been opportunities. And certainly it was a lie. She was the chastest of women, and he, though he relished her company, did not relish her body; and besides, at the relevant time, he was deep in love with his Queen. A few careless words—and there was the lady Anne accused. Might not the little Howard be innocent of everything but indecorum both before her marriage and after? And what of Anne Bullen? If so chaste a woman as Anne of Cleves be scandalised—then who should escape?

The year of fifteen hundred and forty-two came sadly in. There were no festivities. The Queen had spent some two months in Syon House, a close prisoner. My father was morose and withdrawn. He suffered much from the ulcer eating ever deeper into his leg; and this, aggravated by his increasing weight, made it an agony for him to move. But more cruel than the ulcer eating into his flesh was bitterness that his rose without a thorn had proved dishonest; shame that his old man's impotence had driven her to other men. That he could not forgive.

The sad weeks moved on. Elizabeth was not happy with me and I sent her home where clearly she longed to be. I went, several times, to comfort myself with the sight of the children but there was no comfort in it. The little boy, also, had shut himself from me. He had been sweet and loving, running to meet me; now he would scarce look at me; the little girl stood commanding him with hard, compelling eyes.

In the middle of January, my father, that sad and bitter man, met his Parliament. My lord Chancellor addressed the House. 'We thank God,' he said, 'in having so wise and noble a King that puts the law and the good of the state before all things.' And, at that, every man stood up and with bowed head saluted the King. Did it comfort his sad heart? I pray it did. Consolation he needed then; consolation and comfort in his shame—he needed it as he needed the breath of life.

Parliament's first business was to deal with the Queen. Her guilt had been found and early in February a true bill was drawn against her; it spared her nothing.

> ... that the Queen of England, formerly called Catherine Howard, before the marriage between the King and her, led an abominable, base, carnal and voluptuous life like a common harlot. ...

There was a great deal more of it, too shameful for me to set down. It was followed, immediately, by an act of attainder that must bring her to her death.

'What of the holy archbishop's promises now?' I cried out to Clarencieux. 'As with Anne Bullen so with Catherine Howard! Again Norfolk plays his coward's part! He should have demanded a trial—can even now demand it. He cannot be refused. He should demand, at the least, that the Queen be allowed to speak on her own behalf. But not he! She was put into the King's bed to raise her uncle to the highest point of power, not to bring him, maybe, to his death!'

'He cannot hurry her fast enough to her own!' Clarencieux said and sighed. 'It is his only safety!'

It was my lord Chancellor that pressed she be given a chance to clear herself; but, fearing my father, the Privy Council refused, led by Norfolk crying out, *Let her burn! Not the merciful axe for such a one but the tormenting fire!*

So she must die; and with her the adder-tongued Rochford that had aided and abetted. They must die, both of them on the block. It was with difficulty, Gardiner and others advising,—for still Norfolk spoke not a word—that the old duchess was spared. In her own fear and shame Catherine could still thank God for that. To the end there was a sweetness in her.

My father steeled himself to her death and to the block she must go; but for all that he could not bring himself with his own hand to sign her death-warrant. The bill shows royal assent by the Great Seal—the seal alone.

How did she look when they came to take her to the Tower? Had she always known, deep in her heart, that Cranmer had lied, and that she was betrayed? Did her small mean rooms suddenly become a safe haven? Did she remember how once she had said in pity for another, *It is cold in the Tower . . .?* I prayed for her continually these days—the unhappy child. For childlike she was; and, for all her wantonness, wore still the look of innocence.

On the tenth day of February she was taken by water to the Tower. She went obedient; but, as she stepped into the barge all hung and curtained with black, full understanding of that journey fell upon her. She made a movement to run, struggling like a wild bird beneath the hands that held her fast; but lifted within, she sat very still. From that moment to her death she bore herself queenly. At the water-gate, that some call Traitor's Gate, guns fired a full salute. Last honours to a dying Queen.

On Sunday evening, the twelfth day of February, she was told that on the morrow she must die. And she that like a sloughed skin had cast off the lightness of her nature, stood there—Queen of England; no less. One thing only she asked; the block to be brought that she might learn how to dispose herself seemly. And that being granted she laid her bright head upon the black-cushioned thing and prayed, making her peace with God.

Seven o'clock on a bitter winter morning, Catherine Howard that had been the King's delight came forth to die. A small, slight figure all in black, her face white but calm. She had prayed the night through wasting no time in sleep, and as she went up to the scaffold, stumbled a little from weariness so that her confessor who walked with her must put an arm about her. Being ascended, the masked man at her back, she faced those that had come to see her die—my lord mayor, as was his duty, a handful of privy councillors and some few ambassadors. Norfolk was not there, nor the archbishop that had so shamefully betrayed her.

It was to the common people she turned . . . and the masked man waited.

'Good people,' she said, her light voice faltering yet gathering strength, 'I am come here to die, justly condemned by the law and by Parliament. But, for the act on which I stand condemned, I take God to witness and as I hope for salvation, I die guiltless. Never did I abuse my sovereign's bed. Other sins and follies I have committed. I have broken God's commandments; greed and grandeur have blinded my eyes. It is for these God has brought me to this just punishment; and in His Mercy may He remit my sins.

'I beseech all those that lead ungodly lives to take example by me. And I beseech you, also, gladly to obey the King in all things, for whose preservation I do, with all my heart, pray. And now, I beseech you all—and you reverend sir—pray with me unto God and unto His Son our Saviour Jesus Christ.'

She knelt to pray; and praying took the quick stroke and died.

There followed her to the block the woman Rochford that should have kept the young Queen from evil but instead had carried messages and made chances; without her the Queen had not dared. With that death an evil thing had been removed from the world.

They say that dying the Queen proclaimed *I had rather been wife to Tom Culpeper than Queen of England.* They say that Rochford, the fear of death upon her, cried out *I am punished for my part in my husband's death. The evil I spoke against him and his sister are lies.*

But no man heard either the one or the other; for I sent for the chaplain that stood by the block. Of the Queen he said, 'It is a lie.' And of Rochford, 'She cried out like a madwoman and no man could make sense of her words; it was as though she spoke in an unknown tongue.' For the sake of my sister Elizabeth I do pray that those who spoke of Rochford's confession spoke true.

My father spoke but once of his rose without a thorn.

'I saw that she was fair and I thought she was honest. So many griefs in my marriages, so many disappointments; I thought in my old age to take comfort in her youth and kindness. She was to me the very jewel, the very flower of women. I thought her perfect towards me. I honoured her, I loved her. I thought to raise up sons to me. Well, it was not to be!'

It was not to be. Her death had made an old man of him.

After this he spoke of her no more. But we spoke of her, the lady Anne and I.

'Culpeper? Was she his mistress?' I asked.

She shrugged. 'She loved him. I have watched her face, let me but mention his name . . . and she was child enough to deny herself no sweet thing she fancied.'

'Dying she swore to her innocence. Foolish she was; but not so foolish as to lie in the name of God at the moment of her death!'

'Then we must leave it to God,' she said.

I was silent remembering how the dead girl had sent warm clothes to an old woman in the Tower whose name alone she knew, and with them a gown fitting the prisoner's dignity. And I remembered she had braved the King's anger on that same account because I had asked her.

'Foul accusations,' I cried out. 'And maybe, some of them true. Yet for all that a most sweet soul . . . a sort of innocence to the end.'

'Then let us pray for her together,' she said; for in her secret heart, the lady Anne had turned to the true faith. 'Now our prayers reach God the same way.'

Chapter Thirty-Eight

My father was a broken man. A swollen, heavy, irritable old man moving very slow upon two sticks. And move he must, not able to sit long for cramp. When he would rise to ease himself of pain, several men must help lift him, which aggravated his misery, until he bethought himself of a sort of engine to lift him more steady and then things went easier. But always there was discomfort, always there was pain. The fistula upon his leg was not allowed to heal lest the poison drain inwards and so make an end of him. I have seen him bite upon his lips until blood bespangled his grey beard.

For over a year since Catherine Howard had come to her death sunk in gloom he cast no eye upon any woman. But he was a man that needed a woman; not now for desire—Catherine Howard had made an end of that—but for his comfort. He needed a never-failing kindness and the heart forever willing to his service.

And such a wife he found in Catherine Parr. Had God made her to my father's commands there could be found none better. She was of great birth, in her veins royal Plantagenet blood; and being but thirty years of age, old enough for steadiness and young enough to please him. She was small-made—my father's fancy ran to small, neat-made women; she was good to look at—the features fine, the eyes thoughtful and sweet, the hair of that bright gold my father had made fashionable. Her taste in dress was elegant; her gowns rich but simple, her ornaments few. She would wear a jewelled girdle, with perhaps a collar to match, and no other ornament. She did not, like many ladies, bedeck herself with ribands and rosettes and other gewgaws. In court etiquette she was well-versed, having been lady-in-waiting to Jane Seymour. She was amiable and quick-witted; she was an accomplished scholar and one that bore scholarship lightly, for she was both clever and gay. What more endeared her to me was that she had been brought up in the true faith. But most I welcomed her as my father's wife because she was used to the ways of irritable old men—understanding, gentle and patient. Her father dying, and leaving little for his wife and children, she had been married, very young, to one rich widower and then to another; and they, being old, had died leaving her a rich woman—which was not without its appeal to my father.

The first I heard about my father's proposed marriage came from the lady herself. In February, about a year after Catherine Howard's death, I was summoned to court; and there I found Elizabeth also, come from Havering. My father seemed more cheerful than I had seen him for some time; there were games and merrymaking, and, when he drew Catherine Parr for his valentine, I suspected no juggling. It was later, the games ending early, since my father tired easily and would allow no festivity in which he could not share, that Catherine sought me in my closet.

'Madam,' she said, 'Madam!' Suddenly she flung herself on her knees by my side. 'Oh!' she cried out, 'I'll not beat about the bush. The lord King . . . he offers me marriage!'

So the valentines had been juggled! That he meant to marry was no great surprise; but she, I thought, did not look happy.

'And you?' I asked.

She said, and she was pale indeed, 'The King's offer is the King's command.' And then she cried out, 'Twice I did my duty; twice I married an old widowed man. I would not—save I must—do it a third time, not though the man were King!'

I looked at her. 'That is not the whole reason!' I said.

The quick colour stained her whiteness. 'I have found a man after my own heart. It is Tom Seymour!'

Thomas Seymour, brother to Queen Jane. As handsome a man as you'd hope to set eyes upon; debonair and dashing, laughing and lively, forever jesting and skilled in every manner of sport. Tom Seymour envied by men and loved by women!

That she loved him was no wonder; she had yet to learn he lacked discretion—a man of straw.

'And he?' It was scarce a question; so fair, so well-endowed, so desirable she was.

'He's been at me to wed these past months. But I judged it lacking in respect to my late lord that was, of husbands the kindest. I said we must wait.'

'You are betrothed?'

She shook her head. 'We could not, without the King's permission—Seymour stands too close to him in kinship. Now I fear Tom is forever lost to me!' And she fetched up a deep sigh.

I could not blame her for that sigh. What had my father to offer but his aging, unhealthy body, his unequal humours, and his consort's uneasy crown? How should she forget that upon all his wives he had visited his anger, save for the one that, by good luck, had died in childbirth; and two of them come to a bloody end?

But a King's offer is a King's command—she was right there! It would go ill with Tom Seymour did she not obey. She had waited long for her happiness; now she must put it by.

'Pray for your happiness!' I said. 'Beseech the blessed Virgin to intercede; and I will pray with you!'

If she had been pale before she was dead-white now.

'Madam,' she said, low and slow, 'I have a perfect faith in you and so I tell you what I dare tell no other.' She stopped; she took in her breath. 'I hold no longer by the old faith. I cannot acknowledge the bishop of Rome to direct my conscience.'

I felt the sharp shock of disappointment. I wanted her for my friend and I wanted her heart-whole in my faith.

'To cast off the Pope and acknowledge the King head of the church—it is the law. You are safe enough!' It was a speech not over-sweet.

'Madam, you do not understand. I am not of the King's middle way. I cannot use that form of prayer. I am a Protestant!'

It was as though she had slapped me full in the face. For myself I knew bitter disappointment; for her, deep fear. She had spoken words that could take her straight to the fire.

'I was born in the old faith,' she said, 'and my husbands were of the old faith—both of them. I was young and burdened with the cares of a great household; there was no time to think. And, moreover, a wife must not make dissension in her husband's house. Now I have time to think. I listen to good, learned men that profess the new faith; I read what they write. They tell it is by faith alone, not by saints and cere-monies that we can speak direct to God!'

'What they tell you is best kept to yourself! Marry whom you must, worship as you will; but for the love of God keep a still tongue!'

She took my hand and kissed it. I bent forward and kissed her upon both cheeks. For all her heresies she was good; I loved her and might win her back for God.

All that night I could not sleep for thinking of her. Unless she kept a guard upon her tongue she stood in peril; though she wore the crown itself, it could not save her. But she knew the risks and must take her way.

If I feared for her, I envied her, too. Three years older than myself, and not a great deal handsomer, she had been twice married and thereafter sought in marriage twice more. She knew the mysterious bond between man and woman; she had knowledge of a life closed to me now and, very like, for ever.

For still it went on, the senseless playacting concerning my marriage; for still my father had no intention I should wed. I was still his most useful piece on the board . . . but youth doesn't last forever. I was twenty-seven; my sister was already ten years old—a tall girl that looked and behaved older. I was doomed to virginity.

How much Tom Seymour loved his love I cannot say; but certainly he loved his life more. He left the court and where he was no man knew—nor woman, neither.

For Catherine Parr destiny had spoken. For a third time she must wed an old widowed man—and this time a man to fear.

In the summer of fifteen hundred and forty-three they were wed at Hampton Court, in the Queen's lodgings, very private. By the bride's own wish my sister and I were present, and Gardiner, lord bishop of Winchester, performed the ceremony. Since the Howard affair his star had been somewhat clouded; was it to shine bright once more? I had no liking for him—he had worked against my mother; yet it would not displease me to see him in favour again; to the true faith he was a staunch if secret friend. But what of the new Queen? *What?*

I watched her throughout the service. A willing bride, you might have thought; and, maybe, she was. 'Since I cannot marry Tom Seymour,' she had told me, 'I can, at the least, make an old man happy!'

But, this old man? Could she? And for how long?

'A better chance than any of us, she has!' Anne of Cleves said. 'The ways of old men she knows; even the King she will manage. As for him, into this marriage he comes with a mind different from any of the others. That he is an old man, for the first time, he truly understands.'

Yes, that was true. He had learned his bitter lesson well!

'The little Howard was his love, his cherished child,' I said. 'She leaned upon his strength. With her he felt young; and for all his sickness strong—a full man. It was her gift to him. When she took back her gift she broke his heart. It was that, I think, turned love to hatred.'

She nodded. 'Now once more a young wife he takes; but this time upon *her* strength, *her* care he must lean.'

A good marriage for him; and for us, his children. She was the perfect wife—gentle, kindly, watchful in her care of him. If she could not take away his pain she could, at times, divert his mind from it. I have seen him, his face crumpled with the agony of his ulcered leg, look to her, helpless as a child. And I have seen her drop to her knees and take the swollen leg in its stained bandages upon her lap, regardless of the fine gown—she was that so fastidious in her person. And there she would kneel, patient, unmoving, until his eyes closed. He fell asleep often these days; but for all that, when he was awake, however bad the pain, there was no man shrewder.

She made much of my sister and me. We had our place next to the Queen herself, not by right, but by her courtesy—we were bastards still. It was an injustice her upright nature could not endure; nor her courage allow her to endure. 'The King's daughters have their rights; to be named in the succession is one. I shall look to it!' she told me.

And look to it she did, very quiet, very tactful, hardly to be noticed in the matter. She began by giving us valuable gifts to show how much she esteemed us. To me she gave a pair of gold bracelets set with rubies, but, more useful, she kept my lean purse filled; had it been left to my father I had fared ill indeed. He was no more generous with his idolised son; even now his governor must write to Mr. Secretary—as once Bryan had done—for money to clothe him as befitted a prince, though a small one. My household expenses were paid, the exact amount and not direct to me; for my personal needs I was always short. And there were my duties, also—masses for my mother, for my lady Salisbury and for Catherine Howard. There were alms also to be given, and especially for those that lay in prison—some for their faithfulness to God; some for their crimes—and those, perhaps, we should pity more. But guilty or innocent their cruel condition troubled me.

So good a step-mother as Catherine Parr there never was—nor many a true mother, neither. She was not only good, she was easy, never thrusting her greatness upon us nor forgetful of our own. My brother and sister she made her especial care, she directed their studies as she was well able; she had so directed our cousin the little Jane Grey already known, at the tender age of six, for her scholarship. . . . She wrote often to Master Roger Ascham at Cambridge for guidance of her two small princes and gently directed their tutors to follow that advice. My little brother loved her tenderly and obeyed her with joy—

285

and he was a child whose heart and obedience were not easy to win. I saw him once when he had received a letter from her. Small pale face lit with joy he set himself at once to answer it; and I saw the anxious care with which he copied her every stroke and loop. His childish hand was as faithful a copy as he could make it. It was touching to see.

So with her kindness she kept us all three—herself the link—in friendship with our father. She was a light and a blessing upon my life.

Chapter Thirty-Nine

She was a blessing and a light upon a life lived in fear and the shadow of death. She called me by my baptismal name and I loved her for it. To all others I was *Madam*, or *daughter* or *sister* or *cousin*; the name *Mary*, unused since my mother's death, fell sweet upon my ear. In taste and scholarship we were alike, in faith we differed; that, we agreed, must not divide us.

Though better in health I was still not strong. One cannot suffer years of grief and fear and expect them to leave no mark. Without warning, migraine would fall upon me to be endured while it grew to an agony and then diminished leaving me weak and useless for days. I remember once, when journeying to Woodstock, I was taken by such a migraine; and she, hearing of my sickness, came herself to carry me in her own litter to Ampthill where she nursed me like an angel.

She was forever watchful for my good. Once she said, 'You are so *pretty* . . . but you do not do yourself justice. You dress fine enough but . . .' and bade her woman, 'Bring the gown I have chosen for the lady Mary's grace!'

So lovely a gown. Stiff green silk with raised roses of gold and sleeves lined all of gold. It was cut somewhat lower than I would have chosen for I was—and am—somewhat meagre about the bosom. I must have looked my doubt for she laughed. 'Here is something to cover your modesty!' And she put a collar of sapphires about my neck. It was truly perfect. The green brought out the clear colour of my skin, the gold, my hair, the jewel gave depth to the pale grey of my eyes. My father, coming upon us at that moment, said, 'You are gay as a paroquet and pretty as a flower. We must find you a handsome husband!' But that I took at its true worth. While he lived there would be no husband for me!

These days my life went peaceful enough. I lived, for the most part, in the country, moving now to one of my houses, now to another. I read, I studied, I practised upon my instruments; there was music aplenty and dancing, too. I made my visits; now to the children at

Havering, now to my lady Anne of Cleves, growing fat with content, now to the court at my father's command, where he was gracious, or not, according to his mood.

That my position had altered for the better was clear in the respect shown me, even by Gardiner, that, heretofore, had not been over-sweet. The reason for this respect I knew well. Through the Queen's favour I had been named—failing children of this new marriage—next in succession. To be so named was for me a very great thing; and only the Queen's kindness and courage had brought it about. In that act I had been named as my father's daughter, only; I grieved at this slighting of my mother's memory and because I was a bastard still.

To my sister the Queen was better than best. She had persuaded my father to name Elizabeth after me in the succession. She admired my sister's learning beyond anything she had seen; Elizabeth has my father's ease with languages, mine is a scholar's Latin but hers comes clear and direct as her native tongue; with French, Italian and Latin she has an equal grace.

Nothing would please the Queen but that Elizabeth should live beneath her own care. She gave my sister apartments next to her own; she saw to it that the girl wore gowns fitting to her age; left to herself Elizabeth would have dressed beyond her years. She saw to it that the girl applied herself to her lessons, and that she practised upon lute and virginals; for music my sister had aptitude but little taste. No need to teach her to dance or to carry herself with grace; those were her natural gifts. No need, either, to teach her the art of discretion—that matter was already in her.

But all her discretion could not hide from me her ambition; her burning desire for the crown. She was not yet ten and already, silently, she was fitting herself for the part. Wherever men spoke of affairs she would listen, all ears; she would have crept into the Council chamber had she been let. It was my chance of the throne she coveted, not our brother's; unloving as she was, him she truly loved. For our father she had a deep pride but no love. For me, too, she had little affection; but she did show obedience and some humility—I might, one day, come to the throne.

She that could be sharp with her tongue had a way of winning hearts—when she chose. Always the right word, the right gift. She knew when to come and when to go; her coming was always welcomed, her going regretted. I have seen the eyes of the Queen follow as if they could not bear to lose her; and so it was with the lady Anne. This was the daughter each would have loved to have.

Yet that my sister lied with an ease, an assurance, a pleasure, even, the Queen knew as well as I. 'She is young; she will grow from it!' she said. But there's no escaping what's born in bone and flesh; my sister was Anne Bullen's daughter—as Catherine Parr was to find one day to her cost. Meanwhile the girl was bright as a humming-bird and as charming; whenever she was present, I must take second place. I did not relish it.

So here was my father in the winter of his life as contented in his family as a sick and aging man may be. He had an amiable wife, the son for whom he had yearned, a daughter in budding girlhood, and another, comely still but passing, regretful—according to his plans—into spinsterhood. Simple chronicles—on the face of it! But look beyond the face. A court where each man distrusted the other and all men, the King. Look further still; a country wretched beneath its taxes and debts, overrun with thieves and beggars; and above all, a country most wretched in the name of God. I could never forget in the stench of the fire and the gallows that my father, alone, in every Christian country in every Christian age, was the only man, ever, to destroy Protestant and Catholic alike. Protestants are heretics and know their terrible punishment; a Christian King can do no other. But Catholics! His *church of England* was our own true church; in its beliefs, its rites, its services, exactly our own—save for that one thing. To obey the Pope before the King—it has been from time immemorial a Catholic duty. And, for continuing in that duty must a man hatefully die? It was a question I must ask myself again and again; and always the same cruel answer. Such obedience must hold me true-born and inheritable to the crown. For that, for that alone, a man must die.

More than once the Queen had spoken with me, trying to win me for her faith. I listened, courteous but unwilling; I'd have none of it. 'It sweeps away the rituals of holy church,' I cried out. 'It believes no more in the holy miracle of bread and wine.'

'It offers a holier miracle. When we take the bread and wine we take into ourselves not the very flesh and blood of Christ but that which is still greater—the spirit of God.'

At such a travesty of the Mass, such blasphemy, I had nothing to say and she went on, 'This new faith offers the greatest miracle of all—the way clear and unimpeded direct to God.'

'We need the intercession of the saints. Man himself is not worthy to speak to God, he is too ignorant, too undeserving.'

'We cannot ever *deserve* God. It was for sinners, ignorant and un-worthy, that our Saviour died.'

'Dare a man stand naked before his God? And, without intercession, shall God listen?'

'Our Saviour covers our nakedness. When a man speaks the truth of his heart in our Saviour's name God will listen.'

Useless to talk more of the matter; useless and dangerous to us both.

'We should speak no more of this!' I told her. 'It helps nothing and may harm much—a danger to the one that listens and the one that speaks. And to you, Madam, it could be the greatest danger of all. Beware of Gardiner. He guesses how religion stands with you; let him have proof—and he has spies enough—and he'll have your life. Never laugh, Madam, I beseech you! To make example of the Queen—what greater victory to his cause?'

I knew the man and I knew his cause. He meant in his secret heart to bring the country back to her true obedience, Rome. My own heart was in it . . . but I had no mind that this good Queen should come to her death.

'He fears you, Madam. He fears lest you nudge the King over the middle line to heresy.'

'He need not fear. Not for anything would the King turn his back upon his beloved rituals; he is growing old—fear alone would keep him true.'

Gardiner watched his chances. He spoke no word against the Queen; rather he praised her. He smiled, he bowed, he showed her deep respect; he was, as far as so proud a man could be, all humility.

But he wasted no time. Already he was rounding up all Protestant suspects in Windsor; he started with the town, leaving the castle . . . for the present. And he played safe by starting with the poorest.

The Queen went about outwardly calm; but to me she spoke her heart. 'They have dragged from their homes poor, good men innocent of any fault; men that worship in their own quiet way; that speak no word to spread their faith nor testify against the faith of others. They have taken Persons, a poor young scholar. They have naught against him but that he reads to the poor from Master Coverdale's Bible. . . .'

'It is forbidden for any man to read from the Bible unless he be licensed priest or head of a family. And, indeed, such matters are best left to priests. My father says too many take upon their tongues the name of God to bawl it in the market-place or tavern.'

'Persons translated for his pleasure passages from the Bible; he thinks some passages in the translation of Master Coverdale not faithfully rendered. You and I have done as much—and shall we die for it?'

My heart stood still. I had, indeed, translated from the Latin a paraphrase of the Gospel of St. John according to Master Erasmus. I had not known that, once honoured by the Pope and dying in the true faith, he was now blamed that in his writings lay the seed from which Luther had raised his monstrous tree. I had done it to please the Queen. I had allowed it to be printed because she had asked me; I had not allowed—for all her asking—to let it go forth in my name, for which piece of modesty I now thanked God.

'We'll not die, nor he, neither. He'll not come to much harm. A fine; a few weeks in gaol, maybe. A man burns only for obstinate heresy—the chief being denial that bread and wine shall be made into flesh and blood.'

'If they question him he will deny it, poor honest young scholar.'

'Then get him from Windsor as soon as you may! And, Madam, forgive me that I say this thing again, I beseech you, yourself, to have a care. Watch yourself. I have heard you argue with the King on points of faith; with him, of all people!'

'Not faith!' she said. 'Points of theology; no more. He likes a brisk argument, it helps him to forget his pain!'

'Pain is not so easy forgot. Nor does my father relish an argument; he never did. He's not a patient man. Pain and argument move him to anger; and anger can move him in strange ways.'

'Not against me. I seek only his good and he knows it. He's a sick man and should look to his soul! I would give much to bring him into my own faith.'

'Your life?' I asked, very blunt.

'God forbid!' She all-but crossed herself, staying her hand at the forehead.

'There are laws against those that do not conform; and even the Queen may suffer its penalties . . . unless she walk with care.'

'And you? What of you?'

'I have walked in the shadow of death and may walk again,' I said. 'Meanwhile I am content to hold my tongue—so long as I am let to hold the true faith in peace.'

'How long may that be?'

'Who knows?'

She gave me a long, steady look. 'One of these days,' she said, 'you may wear the crown yourself. What should you do then to those you call heretics?'

'What my church tells me. But I am better without the crown. It is too heavy for a woman, its duties too hard; and especially the duty to punish. But why talk of it? It is not likely. . . .'

'It could be only too likely. For the King there'll be no more children. And the little prince? I am troubled. He grows tall but not strong. A pale child, listless. . . .'

'They keep him overlong at his books.'

She shook her head. 'It is a child that delights to learn. He drinks knowledge as sand drinks water. I fear . . . I fear it is something quite other.'

And when I pressed her further, she said, 'Tudor boys die young. They begin well enough but in their growing years they fade . . . so it was with your father's elder brother, so it was with his son young Richmond. How if the pattern be set? I pray God it may not be but . . .'

'There is no pattern!' I cried out. 'There must not be such a pattern! 'Speak to my father, Madam; he must send his own physician. The child seems well enough, but we must set our minds at rest.'

'Yes we must do that!' But for all that she sighed.

Three humble scholars of Windsor, men of the new faith, went to the fire—one of them the poor young man of whom the Queen had spoken; he had not understood his danger. What he had done seemed so little. The day of their burning the Queen walked with me in her privy garden and she looked sick. But still, I thought, she did not understand that Gardiner had taken the first step towards her own death.

'Persons was so young; a boy!' she said. 'When they chained him to the stake he cried for his mother! I tried for him with the King but it was no good; no good at all! I did but anger him. His mind in this is Gardiner's. All this burning!' and she wrung her hands. 'Sweet Christ why must such things be? Should we not leave God to look to His own?'

'Maybe this is His way of looking to His own!'

She sent me another long look. 'Is God so cruel?'

'God is kind. The stake looks cruel to our mortal eyes. Yet it is, I am told, the last, sure way to save souls. A Catholic testifies for his faith; his body burns but his soul, purged of its sins, is accepted of God. A heretic comes to the stake; the agony of the fire burns away his heresy and the soul, crying out for mercy, is accepted of God, also!'

'And what of the heretic that, in the fire, stands firm to the end?'

'I do not know. How shall I set my ignorance against the wisdom of my church? If I have doubts in my heart, it is not for me to speak. But should I come to the throne—which God forbid—that's another story! Then I must speak; then I must condemn; then I must, if need be, burn. I must obey my church, though I sicken at the stink of burning flesh and the agony of men. For freedom in worship is no freedom at all; it weighs nothing against the salvation of the soul. So you see why I am better without the crown.'

'And if it should come to you?'

'Then it is God's will. I shall take it and do what my church commands me.'

'God grant you never come to it!'

'God grant it!'

Chapter Forty

Gardiner must wait to destroy the Queen. There were matters of greater concern afoot. My father was preparing for war with France. Francis, hostile and greedy, had made common cause with the Protestant princes—an alliance as unlikely as sinister. My father and my cousin the Emperor, looked on with alarm. Each had his quarrel with Francis; my father on account of interference in Scotland where even now his forces were putting down trouble of French making. My cousin had equal cause for anger; Francis was stretching out greedy hands to Milan, the Emperor's prized possession. They swore a solemn covenant to attack France; my father to take Boulogne, my cousin to invade from the north-east. Boulogne taken, their joint forces were to march on Paris. An excellent plan—if they could trust one another!

On a fine summer day my father sailed; like a King in an old tale his flag-ship had sails of cloth-of-gold; his fleet was glorious to behold. As for himself; difficult to believe that these great, glittering garments housed a sick old man. He had left his affairs in order; he had chosen his Council with care. It pricked me that I had not been named; at twenty-eight I was full old enough. The Queen he left as regent—and no better could have been found. She was discreet, she was wise; she was just, leaning always towards mercy. She was firm; yet so gentle her manner that even Wriothesley, my lord Chancellor now, and Gardiner that meant to destroy her must hold their peace. But sour Chancellor and sour bishop forever watched her.

News from France was good. Calais, English Calais, had welcomed their King with joy. They had flocked to his standard; they were marching with him for Boulogne. To celebrate the glad occasion the Queen sent for my brother to join us—my sister already being of her household. For the first time since I was small, I knew the joy of living within a family—a happy family.

My sister had grown into a tall girl, striking rather than handsome, carrying herself with a dignity beyond her eleven years. But for all her dignity she had not learned perfectly to control her high spirit—though for her years she did well enough. If she had grown in height she had grown in vanity too. She could not wear a new gown nor take a step in the dance without glancing sideways to see whether eyes watched. And watch they did! The young pages could not take their eyes from her; gentlemen that should have better sense flattered her as though she were a woman grown—and a beauty at that! She was a lodestone to draw all eyes.

For the Queen's concern about my brother I could see no cause; and told her so. 'Certainly he is pale; but he is tall of his age. And listless he is not. He rides and hunts with the best of the palace boys....'

'Yes,' she said, 'but afterwards? Have you seen him then? He is so breathless, it alarms me; and so weary! In a young child it is pitiful to see!'

'He will grow from it. But I still think he is kept overlong at his books.'

'Kings must learn!' she said. 'But, indeed, lessons come to him merry as a jest.'

I found him courteous as ever but no more. 'Once he could not run fast enough to come to me,' I told the Queen.

'He is a *boy*!' she said. 'And one that from his birth has known his destiny. All his breeding has worked towards that one thing.'

'I think, rather, it is his nature. He is Jane Seymour's son; she was always discreet.'

'You mean ... devious?'

'I'd not use such a word. She loved my mother and she was good to me.'

'Yet she played her Queen false.'

'I cannot judge. Hatred of Anne Bullen clouds my judgment. If Jane Seymour betrayed her mistress, that mistress showed her the way!'

'Do you make that an excuse? I judge it rather a fault in character. And the little boy is his mother's son rather than his father's. And more ways than one! He has no love of music. He actually asked me—' and she laughed a little, 'to warn you that it is better to care for your soul than for music!'

I laughed too; but, for all that, I was nettled. I was his godmother; it was for me to look to his soul not he to mine!

'So quiet a child,' she said. 'Save for his sister, lonely.'

'The palace boys?' Ever since my sister had come into the Queen's care, these sprigs of nobility had joined my brother's household to share his lessons and his sports.

'He moves among them like a spirit apart. Oh he's courteous enough; but never must any one of them fail in a hair's-breadth of etiquette due to their prince. And yet there's a little girl for whom he shows real affection. Jane Dormer—'

'The tutor's daughter?'

She nodded. 'She's some months younger than himself. He's gentle with her. *My Jane* he calls her; it drives his sister wild with jealousy. Once when the two little ones were playing at cards, Jane lost her King and I heard him cry out with glee, "Why, Jane, your King is gone; now I shall have to be good enough for you!"'

'It is good to know he can be merry,' I said. 'It is a child that speaks little and laughs less. And let even the cherished Jane step across the line he sets—and she'll feel the cold winds blow!'

I have said that the Queen was a light and blessing upon our lives. It did not seem possible that she was to prove a darkness and a curse upon my faith; that even now she was setting her mark upon my brother and sister, turning them towards her own Protestant worship. They were young and they took her impress like wax. To herself it was a danger, for Gardiner forever watched. But to true Catholics it was a disaster beyond imagining . . . one day the little boy would be King.

But that was hid in the future. Now we were all happy together. The Queen was gay and so easy of her manner that neither the proud girl nor the imperious little boy ever thought to question her will. As for myself—my father's obedient daughter I might be; but freedom from his caprices, his sudden rages and that great looming figure let in the sun to shine upon me.

My father had taken Boulogne. He had done his part and done it well. But for all that he must make his peace with France. Behind his back my cousin the Emperor had made his separate peace; nothing for it but that my father must make his own and return home.

And home he came, an angry man; yet I suspect the most part of that anger to be assumed. He had acquitted himself with honour; and the strength was not in him to fight more. He was old and full of pain and he needed the comfort of a wife; he needed to grasp once more the reins of government. And above all he needed England, his England, his own place, and the voice of his people cheering as he rode by. He had never shown himself—save when he had ridden with Anne Bullen—but the people, whatever their discontent, had cried out their loving greetings. How much more then must all discontent melt now beneath the sun of his success?

On the first day of October he was home again to carry us all to Hampton Court for a holiday. It was now that he commissioned the painting of us in a family group. The picture is less than life-size. My father is seated in the middle; the painting shows him a much younger man. There is no hint of sickness nor age; those poor swollen legs are strong and shapely. It is the father of my childhood grown a little broader. He wears one of the gold-embossed tunics he loved, his feathered bonnet and gold chain. His arm lies, very loving, upon the shoulder of the small, grave child, his son. By his side sits his Queen. She wears, at my father's request, the old-fashioned head-dress that allows little hair to be seen; ten years out of date and difficult to wear. But she was handsome enough to carry it well. 'An old man's whim,' she said, 'I am used to them!' They are sitting, all three, beneath the cloth of estate.

My sister and I wear the round cap that sits snug at the back of the head and allows the hair softly to frame the face. We are dressed exactly alike, also by my father's command; a command that came hard upon me that was so much older than she in her pretty youth. We take our position, meek hands folded; I to the left, she to the right, facing inwards towards those three. We stand some paces from the throne; for us there is no cloth of estate. Symbolic. Bastards both.

We were not allowed to see the picture until it was finished; and then we understood my father's whim.

The Queen that looked out of the painting was Jane Seymour.

The painter had been given a miniature and his instructions.

We stood staring at the picture—all of us save my father, he was not there; maybe he judged it wiser to stay away. I looked at the Queen. Hot words were on my tongue; but, pale and smiling, she shook her head. The little boy was staring in rapt adoration. Although a medallion of his mother never left his neck, he was for the first time seeing her head-to-foot, a whole person; and in the full context—as it might have been—father and mother and son.

It was a deadly slight to the Queen; but she was too wise to show the hurt, too good to spoil the child's pleasure. 'It is very beautiful,' she told him. Afterwards she said, 'It gives the child pleasure; and it gives an old man pleasure. . . .'

'And you?'

'I am used to the ways of old men!' and she sighed.

A Christmas gay with gifts. I sold a pair of silver-gilt bowls and a tippet of muscovy fur that I might give as well as receive. I took much thought for the gift to my sister, hoping to win that formidable girl, and with her the little boy, my brother. I gave her fine silk hose from France all stitched with arrows of gold. Very proud of them she was, walking with her gown lifted higher than need, so that all might admire pretty ankles and pretty hose. But for all her pleasure it was little good I got from it; the children continued cold as ever.

A merry Christmas, that year of 'forty-four—so it seemed; yet beneath it all, a current of unease, of distrust, of stirring anger. It had nothing to do with the discontent of the people; it was a private thing, reaching out from my father towards the Queen.

To begin with, Tom Seymour was back. Never a discreet man, he forever languished after the Queen. She was cold to him; yet it was clear his presence troubled her. How could she help but compare the laughing, handsome man she had all-but married, with the obese, disease-riddled man she had married? Yet she was even kinder to my father than before. She gave him everything devotion could give; she shrank from no duty—not even from the great tumbled bed in the close, stale room. His ulcerous leg was mortifying now and none but she might touch it. With careful hands she would unwind the wrapping, giving no sign of disgust at stain and smell. She would sponge, anoint and rebandage; then, since it seemed to give him ease, she would take the thing on her lap. I have seen her kneel hour upon hour until my own knees ached at the sight. I think no man ever had such a wife.

Yet I cannot remember that he ever thanked her. And always I sensed it—the current of unease. If he should turn against her, nothing could save her.

I tried to warn her as I had done before. 'You are too open in your faith. You read books that are forbidden, seditious books—and that is accounted treason. You utter words for which lesser folk come to the stake. And your women follow your example; your own young sister for one, Anne Askew for another, and I could name others! I beseech you, Madam, be warned!'

'Do you hide your faith!' she asked.

'I did once; I was promised absolution.'

'No-one can absolve me save myself!' she said.

Spring came in, the spring of 'forty-five; and always the feeling of unrest, of distrust! In May I lost my dear, my wisest friend; Eustace Chapuys, Imperial ambassador, was going home. For sixteen long years he had watched my interests, given me wise advice and unstinted devotion; his love too—which is something quite other. I was walking in the maytime garden when they carried him through in his chair, to make Farewell to my father; so ill he was, my poor Chapuys, so crippled with gout, he could not set foot to ground. The chair stopped while he made his Farewell to the Queen and she spoke some gracious words. But I standing there, remembering my sad girlhood and the memories we two shared, and how he had forever stood my friend, could speak no word. I gave him my hand and he kissed it; and, turning away, my eyes were blind with tears. There are some that censure me for a cold heart that I spoke no thanks; but he knew my heart and was content.

Slow, silent, Gardiner and Wriothesley were moving in towards the Queen. They took their time; they meant to make certain of their quarry. Now their victims were no longer humble. One by one the Queen's friends were taken—gentlemen of high rank and dignity, ladies actually in attendance upon the Queen; and with them the Queen's own chaplain. There followed other members of her household. If no fault could be found on the score of worship they were indicted for sedition and judged all worthy of death.

'Woe unto the country when her princes turn traitor to the truth!' the Queen said; these days she was grown pale, indeed.

Gardiner took his last step-but-one towards the Queen; for this step he had waited a whole year. He arrested Anne Askew. She was of the Queen's bedchamber, a gentle girl, much cherished by her mistress. From her they would get all they wanted—of that they were certain. So young she was, so guileless, so delicately made—it could not be long before she said enough to strike down the Queen!

She was a heretic, this Anne Askew; yet no martyr ever stood more steadfast. Bribes and threats alike proving useless, they tortured her to the uttermost point of cruelty. For when, being racked, she still would utter no word against the Queen, Wriothesley, that fine gentleman, flung off his coat crying, *You do not pull hard enough!* and seized upon the handles with such ferocity that he all-but pulled her limb from limb. She was a heretic and he in his secret heart of the true faith; yet I pray God accept her into His loving arms and spew out the other.

We knew nothing of this brutality until Sir Antony Knevet, Lieutenant of the Tower, arrived to complain in the matter. I saw him as he went into the King's lodgings; he was yellow, he looked sick. I watched for him that I might bring him to the Queen.

She listened, her face sick as his. 'I must speak with the King!' and her voice was steady, 'the child is under my protection.'

'Madam!' And he was kneeling not like a courtier upon one knee but as a suppliant that begs for life—and the life he begged was not his but her own. 'Madam, you can do no good but much harm. The lord King has sent to stop the racking; but the trial, in the name of justice, he cannot stop. What the outcome must be—alas, we can guess. But what it may bring in its train if Madam the Queen speaks—I dare not think!'

She seemed not to hear; she stood there white and wild, poised upon one foot to fly to the King. I caught her by the shoulder. 'Your own life you may throw away, but not the lives of others. Keep silent lest your family and friends suffer also. And, Madam, consider! Whatever you may say, the judges will not be moved. As you love God, keep silent!'

I think she did not hear me. She had fallen back against her chair. Watching her women loosen her gown and bathe her temples, I wondered how long she herself would last in the hands of her tormentors, and how many she might bring to the fire. We put a sleeping-draught into a cup of wine and when she awoke it was too late. Anne Askew had gone to the fire.

Anne Askew had gone to the fire; they had to carry her to the stake because her bones were broken. Nor did she go alone; too many went with her. Yet of all that suffered that day not one said a word to injure the Queen. They were heretics; but God, I think, will forgive them. But their judges? If a man must die, in God's Name let him die. But let those that condemn, judge without malice; let them behave like men and not like wild beasts. For such men—be they Catholic or Protestant—God will not forgive, not though they carry out His law to the last letter. It is they that shall lose their souls.

Now that they had brought treason into the Queen's own chamber they might safely accuse the Queen herself. With half-lies and flattery they sent my father's anger flaming. Once I heard Wriothesley for myself. 'You excel all doctors of divinity, all priests and bishops. If any man . . . or woman, seek to put his own opinion before that of the King, it is blasphemy—for God made the King supreme head of the Church.'

I noted how slyly he brought in the word *woman*, dwelling upon it without ever mentioning the Queen. And my father noted it too. He forgot her loving-kindness; he remembered only that she had dared to set her opinions against his. She had pretended it was all a game; but she had made of it a duel to fool an old sick man. Always he had loved flattery; but once he'd had the wits to assess its worth. Now anger had stolen those wits. 'A good thing,' he cried out, bitter, 'when women become scholars to instruct their husbands!'

But still no blow fell. The Queen went her gracious way; she was perhaps a little graver. The King allowed her to dress his gangrenous leg and gave her no thanks. She was a little troubled; never had his humours been so dark. But there was little wonder in that, she thought; he was a sick man and heavy with his pain.

Chapter Forty-One

They had drawn articles against the Queen. Now they waited to catch my father in the extremity of pain.

They had not long to wait. Goaded by their suspicions, at the end of his endurance, my father signed the warrant for the arrest of the Queen. Without warning she was to be carried to the Tower. With her were to go such of her household as might do good service to her accusers. All, all to the Tower, all to be questioned by whatever means should prove useful; not one to be spared; not even my cousin Jane Grey—and she but eight years old. And, having incriminated themselves as well as the Queen, to their death the most part of them should go.

And still, so secret the matter, the Queen knew nothing.

And then God moved. Wriothesley carrying the warrant all signed and sealed, God gave him a nudge. It fell from his papers and he, all unknowing, strode on. And, since God does not do things by halves, who should pick it up but Sir George Blagge, the Queen's good friend? He took it straight to the Queen.

I was with her when she unrolled the thing. I saw the eyes darken in her head. I saw how she tried to speak but could not speak. She sat there rigid as the dead.

I picked up the paper.

It was all there. If half the accusations were true, then one time or another she had said as much as any heretic that had gone to the fire.

The rigid face began to work; at last the voice came forth. Cry after cry of desolation, of mortal terror. Cry after cry that could not be stilled.

Her physician came hurrying. So distraught she was, he would have quieted her with a sleeping draft, but I took it from his hand. Let her go on wailing—she had cause enough! Let it reach my father's ears! Unless she could move him to pity she was a dead woman. She would not be his first wife, nor his second, to come to her death!

To my father, nursing his sick leg in his closet, came the cries of her anguish. He endured it, I must suppose, as best he might; until unable to endure it longer he had himself carried to her apartments.

There she lay, his kind wife, his good Queen, pale as ash, eyes closed, lashes lying wet upon her cheeks. At the stir of his coming she opened her eyes. She made a movement to rise, then, for very weakness fell back, holding up her clasped hands as though for mercy.

And, since still she could not speak, her physician spoke for her. 'Sir, the Queen has bad news—I know not what! It has thrown her into a despair from which I think she may die!'

'Why, Madam!' my father said and, I think, pity stirred, for she was a piteous sight, and a pretty one. Or maybe a stab from his ulcerous leg reminded him of what—she being gone—he must miss, for I saw him wince; but whether from pain or pity I could not know.

'Be easy, Kate,' he said. 'Your bad news shall be turned to good—if I may do it!'

She made another effort to rise but fell back into her chair.

'Have no fear, Sweetheart,' he told her. 'Rest now; and tonight you shall sup with me and tell me your trouble.'

All that day she lay upon her bed; in the evening she rose and bade her women dress her. She wore that night a gown of white and never a jewel; young she looked and good—and pale as her gown. I attended her to my father's closet for they were to sup in private; he bade me stay to stand behind her chair.

While they supped he paid her every kind attention, chatting of this and that—idly it would seem and merry. Then came words careless-spoken, it would seem, that might well prove her undoing.

'I have been sent a book that supports the Protestant worship. It makes, I think, some fair points. Now listen and tell me what you think!'

But she was as clever as he!

'Sir, I am only a woman; and, like all women, I am glad to learn from my husband. How much more so when God has appointed him to be supreme head of the church in this country and lord of all—including his most humble and obedient wife!'

'Oh Kate, such modesty! You have learning enough to instruct us all—including your humble and obedient husband!' He smiled gracious and encouraging. She knew that smile!

'Sir,' she said, 'if the King's grace has misconstrued me, I am sorry indeed! For I hold it monstrous that a woman should presume to instruct her lord.'

'Yet you have argued many a point!' The smile was gone; the cold eyes waited.

'Sir—' Her hands went outwards, palms upward. 'If ever I ventured to argue it was that I, myself, might learn from you. But even more it was because I saw that when your mind was engaged in argument, you were able a little to forget your pain. As God hears me, it is the truth!'

'Is that so, Sweetheart?' And now he was merry again. 'Why then we are perfect friends!' And he gave me the nod to leave them together.

I was looking from my chamber window next morning, watching those two as they walked together in the garden, she taking his weight upon her arm and suiting her light step to his painful limp, when Gardiner and Wriothesley appeared together—armed men at their back. I saw her hand fly to her heart; my father, capricious and passionate, was not to be relied on.

Wriothesley took a step towards her.

I saw my father lift the stick in his hand; he roared out so that the words came up clear to me. 'Fools! Knaves! *Beasts!* Get from my sight. By God, I'll be the death of you both.'

I saw her kneel in the bright grass; she that had stood on the very edge of death, asking, I must suppose, some mercy for them; it would be her kind way. I saw my father shake his head. Yet for all that Wriothesley he kept by him—the man was useful; but Gardiner he forbade the Council.

The incident aggravated my father's illness. Though he feared nothing so much as death he knew himself a very sick man; his will was made and his instructions set out—though what they might be we none of us knew. Nor was it too soon. For now it was not the mortifying leg alone but a dropsy swelling his great bulk and adding yet more to his pain. Now his swollen hand could no longer hold the pen and he must content himself with a seal cut with his signature.

Yet still from pride and fear he defied death. How should he believe that great Harry should ever be no more; or the day come when no man should tremble at his name?

Sick he might be and near to death but while he lived—he lived; he lived and held the power. At court, and beyond, men must walk as on a tight-rope; and the Queen, especially, must walk wary. For Gardiner was back. He was too shrewd, too able a man for my father to go lacking him—but for all that my father never forgave him, as will afterwards appear.

Chancellor and bishop meant to make an end of the Queen before the King died—lest afterwards she and her Protestant friends make an end of *them!* They knew her influence upon the little prince. If she were let to live until he came to the throne the Protestant faith would become the King's faith, the nation's faith. New gallows must rise, new blood stain the block; and to gallows and block themselves must go.

I thought they were running to meet trouble. The Queen could have no power save through her influence upon the King; and so little a child could not do as he chose. Even were she left as Regent—there was still the Council. The Council must rule for the King. It was the Council those two should fear rather than the Queen . . . and upon the Council they had many enemies.

As my father drew nearer his death his mind ran much upon the country's division in faith; for upon unity the peace of the whole nation depended. He would speak to me on the matter.

'My girl, the middle way is best and that's the way I'll have when I am gone. I'll have no anarchies nor yet a putting aside of laws I have made; they are good laws. My son being little, I have appointed for him a Council, well-balanced in policies to hold the ship steady. I'll have no firebrands for her destruction nor fools to drive her upon the rocks. Each councillor I have named by name. There's some will be surprised, finding themselves with no place!' And he gave a grim chuckle. 'There's none shall have greater power than another. And so I save the realm from tyranny and leave the land in peace.'

'God grant it!' I said.

'I have spoken with Him. He will grant it!'

Chancellor and bishop must work quickly; but their work grew easier every day. Because my father feared death he was forever casting black looks upon the Queen. It was as though, being sick, he could not endure she should be well; and since he must die, could not endure that she should live. He was sick now in mind as well as body.

And those two were forever at him, stinging, stinging.

'They tell me the Queen is a traitor,' my father told me fretful. 'They are forever at me, those two, like hornets. *Sir, the Queen is disloyal. Once already she was attainted but of your great mercy you spared her—to the great danger of yourself and the state.* Thus Gardiner. And Wriothesley, *I beseech you, sir, sign a warrant with your own especial seal. I have it here, already drawn.* Then Gardiner once more, *She is a traitor to God and to you and to the lord Prince whose soul she corrupts with her abominable faith.* And by Christ they are right and sign it I will and at once!'

'Sir,' I told him, 'the Queen is no traitor. Upon that I stake my life. But your grace should need no stake, seeing her loving-kindness towards you!'

'Are you and she in league together!' He bent his black brow upon me and cried aloud for his seal.

The seal, God be thanked, could not be found. I think the Queen knew more than somewhat of that loss; for it turned up, very innocent, after my father's death within a drawer that had been searched and searched again.

Certainly the Queen was no traitor. I abominated her worship and the cruelties practised upon poor Catholics. But the cruelties were none of her making; Protestants and Catholics suffered alike. Making an end of her could help neither Wriothesley nor Gardiner. My father had settled the matter of faith in his will and appointed a Council strong enough to enforce it. I foresaw little change. But who—even so far-seeing a man as my father—can see into the future; much less command it?

For the moment the Queen was safe; but, with their other enemies, bishop and chancellor had better luck. Already Norfolk and his son Surrey were in the Tower—and treason the charge.

'It's a charge easy to press!' the Queen said. 'For both are quarrelsome and both are arrogant and neither over-blessed with wisdom. And both are loud in their scorn for *jumped-up* men—especially of Wriothesley.'

'Surrey, so I hear, has quartered the royal arms with his own!' I told her. 'He'd not dare; he's not such a fool!'

'He might well be! But there's no proof. Well, true or not, they'll suffer for it!'

There was no proof and they did suffer. In mid-January Surrey went to his death. Norfolk's death-sentence waited but for my father's private seal.

If they meant to make an end of the Queen they must lose no time—for Wriothesley had been heard to say *the King rots to his death.*

There was no personal enmity in the matter; she, herself, had made no enemies. But she was shaping the little heir of England into the most bigoted of Protestants. She and Edward Seymour, uncle to the prince, together with Cranmer—the one man my father truly trusted—were hand-in-glove together. They meant to seize the power and force the Protestant faith upon the people.

To so ardent a Catholic as Gardiner the prospect was terrifying. Ardent he was; yet content with Wriothesley to walk my father's middle way, fearing—as my father feared—a sudden turnabout must bring misery and death to a bewildered people. And more; the country, torn in two, must be an easy prey to the enemy without. France, for instance, hiding her long enmity under the banner of God, would not be slow in the matter.

I see it all now—the pattern set out clear. But then I knew nothing, saw nothing but those two about the business of making an end of the Queen.

Wriothesley's ugly words were true. My poor father was, indeed, rotting to his grave. Yet still he would not admit that Death, which comes for all, must soon come for him. And none dared tell him save the Queen—the Queen alone. And that, even without considering the disfavour into which she had fallen, required true courage. Mention his death! He could make a treason of the matter.

She went to it roundabout.

'Sir, would it not be pleasant to send for the Prince?'

'Why so?' And the once-great voice was cracked and broken with sickness.

'We have not seen him this long while.'

'Have we not? Why then—' and he had forgotten his rancour against her, 'we shall go together!'

She had not the heart to press him further.

It was Sir Anthony Denny that, all compassion, told him the truth.

The words of doom had been spoken. My father took to his bed; he would fight no more. The Queen came once but he did not know her —or perhaps he did; for he peered at her, eyes slits of suspicion. She would not go again unless he sent. He never did.

He sent for me instead. He seemed to like me near him. At times his mind was clear and he would speak of this one and that—but never of my mother. Once he said, 'Forgive me, child, my unkindness that I did not find you a husband! But kings, more than other men, are driven by circumstances. I could do no other.' All other unkindnesses he had forgotten. And, maybe, my age, too, he had forgotten; for he called me *child* and I was nigh on thirty-one. And once he said, 'I pray you, by Christ Jesus, look to your brother and sister. But especially look to my son. He is a little child. Keep faith with me and with him; so you keep faith with God.'

'I swear it!' I bent over and kissed his cheek and it was wet but whether with his tears or my own I did not know.

I would I might say this was the end; but it was not. His failing mind was wandering back to his youth, seeking the shade of Anne Bullen. Dying he believed her innocent and grieved for her death. *Anne . . . Anne . . .* he would lie whispering her name. And sometimes it was *Sweetheart*; and always it was *Forgive*. My heart was grieved at his dying, yet there was, God forgive me, anger, too, that, dying, he grieved for the wrong done to his harlot; but of the true wife he had so bitterly wronged—neither word nor memory.

The last time I was let to see him he did not know me but sat upright in his bed crying out that Anne Bullen stood by his side, no jewel upon her naked neck but only the bloody line where the sword severed her head. After that the horrors fell upon him and none but his physicians were allowed into his room. At the sight of his confessor he reared himself up in terror crying out that priests and monks were crawling from their holes, dead men rising from their ashes to do vengeance upon him.

All that night he lay whispering and muttering and weeping. But God that rejects no true penitence, even though it be at the last moment, remembered him. For the sick, confused mind clearing, he said very weak yet clear, *The mercy of Christ is able to pardon all sins.* He lay silent a little, and then his mouth shaped a word, *Cranmer.* Thereafter he slept and waking at midnight, found the archbishop kneeling by his bed. My father could no longer speak and the archbishop took the hand of the man he had served before his God, and, holding it, my father died, comforted and unafraid.

At two o'clock in the morning of January the twenty-eighth, in the year of grace fifteen hundred and forty-seven, my father rendered up the ghost. He was fifty-five years old, and old beyond those years.

Christ receive his soul!

Chapter Forty-Two

My father was dead. My first feeling, God forgive me, was of release. I could breathe free. The Queen was safe and I was safe. For though of late he had been kind to me, I never knew when there might not be a turnabout and I, without warning, cast into the Tower. But soon I began to miss him—his great presence, his sudden kindnesses, even his sudden rages. The long years fell away; I saw him as in my childhood, golden and strong and heavenly kind. And not even the sight of the huge coffin, beneath whose weight sixteen men staggered, could wipe away that picture.

The children had been sent for; they arrived looking pitiful; small faces pale against the dark of their hurried, ill-fitting mourning. Elizabeth was over the first of her shock; she was miserable, not so much for the death itself, as at the trappings of death. Like my father she could not endure, even as a child, the thought of dying; she knew that even the very young may stand within that shadow. My brother was not so much pale—for that he always was—as white, white to the very lips; and those lips he held firm-pressed lest he disgrace himself with tears. He was King of England. But for all that he was a child of nine to know he had lost a father that had loved him above all earthly things. A child desolate and small; my heart ached for him. But there was nothing I could do. He kept me at a distance, allowing only the strict etiquette observed to a King; already he carried himself with something of the isolation of majesty.

My father was buried, as he would have wished, with every rite of the old faith; he could, indeed, have thought of no other way—for his personal worship differed from it in nothing. Five days his body lay within the circle of eighty tall candles that forever burned; gentlemen of the Privy chamber never ceased their vigil nor priests to pray. The candles, the incense, the breath of folk coming and going within the black-hung chamber, the smell of corruption, faint at first but steadily growing, made the air within the room insufferable. I would make a short prayer for his soul and be gone; but in the quiet of my own closet I did not cease to pray.

On the sixth day the coffin was covered with cloth-of-gold and carried into the chapel. For six days Norroy King-at-arms stood by the door exhorting all folk of their charity, *Pray for the soul of the high and mighty Prince our late lord and sovereign King Henry the Eighth*. On the twelfth day they carried the coffin in high procession to Windsor; and, on that journey, a fearful thing happened—a thing so horrible, so appalling that even now, thinking upon it, the blood runs cold. I had heard some dreadful rumour; I am not one to be satisfied with rumour when I may have the truth. I sent for the two yeomen that had started the tale.

'It's true, my lady, as God hears me!' And the man turned to his fellow that nodded confirmation. 'It was at Syon House. . . .'

Syon House. That house from which my sister and I had been sent to make room for the pitiful prisoner Catherine Howard; the house from which she had gone to her death. Had ghost met ghost that night?

'It was the first night of the procession and we was pretty done for— what with the weight of the coffin though there was a score of us to carry it; and then all that walking—walking slow, it's hard on the feet! Your grace will understand we was fair ready to drop. So we put the coffin down in the chapel at Syon and me and my mate was told off to watch. We must 'a' fell asleep, God forgive us! Because the next thing we knew was the sun coming in through the windows. And Madam . . .'

He stopped and the other took up the tale.

'Underneath the coffin the ground was red. We thought, at first, it was the light coming in through the coloured window. But it wasn't. It was thicker than light. Madam—it was blood. The King's blood. There must 'a' been a leak in the lead. And then, Madam . . .' He put his hand up to his mouth as though he were going to vomit and the first man took up the tale again.

'. . . and then we saw it. A dog. A little black dog . . . creeping from beneath the trestle . . . and its mouth was red with blood.'

The King's sacred blood. I shivered; and not with the cold of the winter morning. Years ago—and I but eighteen—a priest had cried out against my father, *The dogs shall lick his blood!* And I remembered Anne Bullen that I had held to be a witch. Had her unquiet spirit from her nameless grave sent out her familiar to wreak vengeance for blood spilt; her own and her cousin's blood?

The funeral procession took its slow way to Windsor; and there it was met with priests and prayers enough to exorcise all evil.

It was a very great gathering that saw my father laid to rest. But even as I prayed for his soul I was pricked with anger that the banners of Jane Seymour and Catherine Parr hung each in its place—but not my mother's; not hers! I was angered against him for whom I mourned; I was angered against myself that I could not reject his memory as he had rejected hers. I turned my face from the banners to where my brother sat—a small, stone image, taking no part in the service. It was clear that the prayers my father had cherished and ordained, the old prayers of the true faith, were unknown to him. I was his godmother and greatly troubled.

That same day I spoke with the Queen on the matter.

'He is being brought up in the Protestant faith!' she said, calm and assured. No need now to hide her beliefs.

'It is a faith my father detested. He desired his son to be brought up in the worship he himself practised.'

'The tide runs the other way. Recognise it. You have suffered enough for your faith. Do not let yourself suffer more!'

'I am his godmother. I must look to his soul.'

'The tide runs against you. You can do nothing!'

'Must there be more deaths, more martyrs?'

'For the love of God do not add to them!' she said.

At that, memories of my girlhood swept over me in a bitter tide. Must I taste that bitterness again? And would it now be worse, worse still? All this time I had been let—so I submitted to my father's will—to worship in the way of my childhood. Was I now to be persecuted afresh, hounded to accept an alien worship; must I never be free to worship God in the way of my childhood?

'You are to blame in this!' I cried out. '*You!* None but you! I see it now! From the beginning you marked the child for your faith!'

'God's faith. And God, not I, marked him. It is God's will that carries him. Let it carry you, also. Do not fight against its might; do not drown!'

'Would to God my father were alive!' I cried out. 'I am alone in the perilous sea—and there is no hand held out to help me!'

My father was dead and the strange little boy, my brother, sat on the throne. A cold, pale child, more than ever drawn within himself. He perfectly understood the greatness of his position; a position as fearful as it was great. And he knew that, too; knew his lack of years and his little strength. He was also, I think, hiding the shock of our father's death. To the child he had been as enduring as God Himself. His fears and his loss he hid beneath a cold and watchful courtesy.

I loved him with all my heart, the little boy to whom I owed a three-fold loyalty—the loyalty of subject to King; the loyalty of that oath sworn to our dying father; and most of all loyalty to his salvation—I was his mother in God. But the little boy that had once written so sweetly to me in his careful Latin, kept me more than ever at a distance. And now it was more than the influence of my sister. It was the faith in which he and she had been reared, the faith he shared with the Queen he loved, and the sister he loved; a faith he did not share with me. And so rigid his rearing in this Protestant faith, he could not forgive me my own. The triple bond that bound him to me he found increasingly irksome. He could not like me; nor would he ever.

Always I had grieved that he had little of the natural merriment of a child; now I must grieve more—for he showed none at all. He spoke little, he smiled less and he laughed not at all. What he felt he kept within himself. He had wept bitterly when they told him of his father's death but that was the only time. Thereafter he was *the King*. Not a doubt of it. Every least homage paid to my father must now be paid to him. As with my father one must address him kneeling; and not the oldest nor the wisest nor the dearest—not Elizabeth nor the Queen's self—spared. He would sit in the great chair, the pale child, stiff as an idol in his jewelled clothes. You never knew what he might be thinking; more than one was to find that to his cost.

My father had chosen the Council of Regency so that no man might hold more power than the next; he meant no Protector to act the tyrant. But in such a gathering one man stands out as leader to force or to persuade the rest and to get his own way. Gardiner might have held the balance steady; but Gardiner had not been named. Nor had William Parr a place nor any Howard. *There's some will be surprised finding themselves with no place!* my father had promised me; a promise he had kept. But Cranmer was named and Wriothesley; and Edward Seymour—my lord Hertford, the King's uncle—that same of whom Gardiner and Wriothesley had sought to make an end. And would to God they had! For it was this very man that stepped forward to lead the Council, his chief adviser, Cranmer. No longer fearful, either of them, of proclaiming themselves Protestant, but busy, indeed, about that business; enemies to my faith and to me.

Once I had thought my father over-suspicious of Catherine Parr;

now I thought he had been over-trustful. He had left my sister in her care, never considering it possible that his daughter should be moulded into the faith he detested and whose adherents he had burned. And yet, in a way, it was natural enough. Catherine had always shown herself amiable, wise, decorous and learned; she had assured my father that she held no opinions in any matter other than his own. Her household was the admired school of fine manners and accomplishments. Who then so fit to take charge of my father's daughter?

Now the Council gave her responsibility for the King, too. He was to continue in his own household but she was to decide upon his personal affairs, to have the last word in appointing his tutors and his priests. She appeared to interfere little, but from a distance she kept a watchful eye; her influence rained upon him. I said once that he was his mother's child; but if he were anyone's at all he was Catherine Parr's. So my brother as well as my sister were to be bred in the Protestant faith against my father's expressed commands.

And now I understood what the Queen had meant when she spoke of the rising tide of the new faith. The careful balance my father had designed for the Council was destroyed—and with it his desire that no one man should hold power. For now it was led by Edward Seymour—led by the nose, or else whipped upon the rump to follow him; and it was now, for the most part, Protestant. Within a few weeks of my father's death, Wriothesley was relieved of his high office—to speak plain English, kicked out; chancellor no more. A little later Gardiner was cast into prison for no offence save that he would not embrace the new faith; other bishops followed him and there they remained all the years of my brother's reign.

A Protestant country; and one man, Edward Seymour, to rule all. I wondered my father could rest in his grave.

If my brother was to prove no problem to his step-mother, my sister was to prove a thorn in the flesh—and not on the score of faith, neither! The Queen had retired to her dower-house at Chelsea; a beautiful house, commodious in the modern style with large windows that looked out upon pleasant gardens and the gentle countryside beyond. Here one could watch the traffic upon the river and, on summer evenings, listen to the singing from the boats, the river running in ribands of coloured light from lanterns reflected in the dark water. Life went leisurely in this sweet place; and there's an old saying about the devil and idle hands.

Here my sister went to live. She took up residence with her tutors and her servants. Among the latter were Catherine Ashley and Thomas

Parry. Ashley her lady-mistress was a foolish woman all unfit for the charge of a clever, high-spirited, devious girl. Parry acted as cofferer; he was as foolish as Ashley and each as untrustworthy as the other. Yet these two my sister loved with a deep and abiding loyalty. For here is a strange thing! Though she never mentioned her mother, keeping all thoughts of Anne Bullen in her own heart, and faithless though she could be, she never failed in love and loyalty to these two that were Anne Bullen's humble kinsfolk. I was not happy that she kept them close by her; but she was not in my charge; and with the mistress of the house so wise, so discreet, I did not think she could come to harm.

But soon I began to doubt that wisdom, that discretion. Scarce a month had passed since my father's death—and there were signs that, grief somewhat lessened, the Queen was allowing herself some consolation. I could not, at first, find it in my heart to blame her. Childhood and young womanhood spent in the service of old men, she might well be forgiven a little harmless enjoyment. But the lady Anne of Cleves, come upon a visit, brought with her fresh tales—not so harmless.

'If they are true,' I said as we sat over our needlework, 'the Queen is changing. . . .'

'They are true enough! And no—she is not changing. Rather something in her true self is set free. . . .'

'. . . as though a great thumb has been lifted.'

Anne nodded. 'Now she unfolds, she flowers. She looks young as I have never seen; a young woman to enjoy life a little—the life she never had. Can you blame her?'

'For enjoying life—no! But if she has truly taken a lover then I should blame her, indeed! It is too soon after my father's death; it would lack in respect!'

And if it is true, what sort of guardian will she make for Elizabeth? It was a question instant to my mind. My sister had always been one eager for pleasure, between the Queen diverting herself and the foolish Ashley, who would restrain that headstrong girl?

The twentieth day of February, in the year of grace fifteen hundred and forty-seven, my brother went to his crowning. The child, white as his white suit, rode the great horse all trapped with crimson. He rode upright as beseems a King; but for all that, so frail he looked that, from my place in the coach where I sat between my sister and the lady

Anne, I wondered with pity how that thin neck could carry the weight of his head—let alone a crown. I need not have feared. He was my father's son.

From the Tower, through the streets went the great procession. Huddled within their warm clothes the people waited to see him pass—the child so pale, so small, so good; on the great horse so exposed to the bitter weather. London had gone gay with riband-flowers and evergreen garlands, with fine carpets hung from windows, with pennons and flags and fountains of wine; and everywhere bells, bells, bells! Now and again the procession would halt so that he might see the fine sights prepared for his pleasure. At St. Paul's a tight-rope dancer slid from the high steeple upon a thin rope not clear to his weak eyes so that he took it for a marvel. As we came into Westminster, there stepped from an archway painted blue as a summer sky and all bright with stars, an angel to present him with a purse containing a thousand gold pieces. He touched the great purse upon the velvet cushion, smiling in wonder to think of so much money together in one place—and all of it for himself! A king he might be—but he was a little boy, too!

The great ceremony of crowning had been shortened; and that is the one thing I put to Cranmer's credit. For the full service is arduous and the child was tender in years and frail in body. In that sacred moment when the archbishop presented the King to the people and the great titles of majesty went resounding through the Abbey and the congregation with one voice cried out *Yes, yes, King Edward, King Edward, King Edward!* my heart swelled with pity for so great a burden upon so young a child. When they put the crown upon his head—the small, light crown—I saw his head bend a little like a flower too heavy upon its stalk. And then I saw his whole body tremble and could not wonder. The most kingly man in Christendom, my father himself, had surely trembled at the first touch of the crown. And, at the sight of that small, trembling body, I renewed the oath I had made to be his faithful friend and subject as long as he should live.

Edward Seymour, my lord Hertford that led the Council, had made himself Protector of the Realm to govern the King and to rule the country. He had a greater title now—my lord duke of Somerset; his brother, the admired Thomas, he had made my lord Sudely and High Admiral of England. William Parr, the Queen's brother, he bound to him with the high title of earl of Northampton; and Wriothesley he sweetened for loss of his high office by raising him to the earldom of Southampton. The rest of the Council he kept quiet with lesser new-gilt titles, and with promise of reward—or punishment—to come.

I went to Chelsea at the Queen's invitation. She had, indeed, as Anne said, flowered. She looked young, happy; there was a brightness about her, a light glowing from within illuminating her eyes, her mouth, her every movement. A woman in love if ever I saw one! It was neither in my heart nor in my situation to question her movements. Elizabeth was clearly on the best of terms with the Queen, there was a gaiety about her that softened her usual coldness, she seemed less guarded, also, but not to me; to me she behaved as always; with respect—and nothing more. I might look in vain for one word of affection from her.

If I might not talk with the Queen of her own affairs, I might and did discuss Somerset with her; for still I valued her wisdom and her commonsense.

'Somerset holds the King in his hand and the country beneath his heel!' I told her.

'It cannot be for long. He's not the man. Ambitious, of course, like all his family, but . . .' She shrugged.

'A handsome presence, a commanding manner,' I said.

'It covers a weak character. I know him.'

'A fine soldier,' I reminded her. 'A leader of men.'

'In the field yes. But no statesman—nor ever will be. Watch him! He's one to hold back when he should go boldly forward; and to rush forward where he should hold back. A leader of men he may *seem* but he lacks discretion. And more; it is not in him to be sufficiently ruthless. If necessity drive, he'll put a man out of his way—friend or enemy. But he's a kindly creature on the whole; he'll do a good turn if, without injury to himself, he may. He'll not last. While he does, you need have no fear of him.'

'For myself I am not afraid. His wife Nann's my good gossip; and his sister was a good friend to me. As for himself—he has always shown himself friendly. I like him; but I deplore his disobedience to my father's expressed will. My father determined no one man should govern; yet Somerset rules all. My father forbade the Protestant worship; and in this worship his son and daughter are being reared and the whole nation coerced. I am your true friend, Madam, but I should be a fool if I did not see your hand in this!'

She shrugged. 'We must be true to our faith; *you* know that!'

'Those that would obey my father must suffer.'

'*You* have never been obedient in the matter and suffering with you is no new thing. But—' and she smiled, 'you need have no fear. Somerset, I promise, will never force you.'

'Maybe. But what of the wrong done to my father in the rearing of his children? And what of the wrong offered to the country? What of those that cannot turn their coats at Parliament's commands? Already Parliament seeks to bind us with new laws in this matter; already it has swept away the good old laws against heretics.'

She nodded smiling.

'What will the next step be? More deaths? More martyrs?'

She did not answer; it was a thought she liked no more than I. That she did not answer was answer enough.

That autumn of my brother's crowning I wrote to Somerset imploring him to respect my father's commands with regard to my brother at the least. I had no fear of drawing attention to myself. For years now I had been left to pray as I chose. I did not think any man would forbid me ever. Yet had I feared for myself I must have spoken; there was that promise to my father. Nor did I fear Somerset himself . . . then I took him at his face-value—a kindly, honest man.

Somerset's answer, full of friendly protestation, full of evasion, opened my eyes to something of his true character. But even then I had no fear for myself. I stood next to the throne. And I forgot that standing next to the throne had not saved me before from the shadow of death.

Chapter Forty-Three

Catherine Parr was married—and my father scarce cold in his grave. She had married her old love, the debonair Tom Seymour, lord High Admiral of England. The man had been ambitious enough and bold enough to ask for me, myself; Parliament refusing, he had asked then for my sister—and, judging by events—not without her goodwill. She, also, being refused, he took the next best; if not my father's daughter, then my father's wife.

They had meant, those two, to keep the marriage secret, until time should lend them some appearance of decorum; but discretion had no part in Seymour. He was one to take what he wanted when he wanted. He would steal under cover of darkness into the gardens at Chelsea and into the Queen's bedchamber. In so great a household, and to so high a person, such visits could not go unknown. Tongues began to wag; and, fearful lest the matter reach the Council and they make a treason of it, Seymour wrote asking their leave to do the thing already done.

To me he wrote also. I was not sweet in my reply knowing those two already wed; but of that I made no mention. It was strange news, I wrote; and considering *whose* wife her grace had lately been I could not, with honour, meddle in the matter. Nor could it help. If she were minded to marry him, then he needed no goodwill of mine. If on the other hand memory of the late King's majesty would not allow her to become his wife, I was not able to persuade her for the loss of one that was still rife in my own memory.

> . . . Therefore I most earnestly require you to think it no unkindness in me that I refuse to be a meddler in the matter, wherein, being but a maid, I am nothing cunning. . . .

This letter was written in the first week of June—a bare three months after my father's funeral. I might have written more kindly but that I thought their haste a slight upon his memory. Now, as I copy it, I see some bitterness in those last words, though at the time I had not been aware of it; for I was a full year above thirty and unwed; and like to remain so. And she, already thrice wed, was wed again—and this time to a young and virile man.

My sister wrote me a letter full of anger against them both—a righteous anger, as I thought; but she had, indeed, a deeper reason that I did not know until later. Like many an older and wiser woman, my sister had been taken by Tom Seymour's handsome looks. That he had asked for her hand she knew; she had, indeed, consulted the Queen on the matter; It was the Queen herself told me of their conversation.

'I told her it was not to be thought of; she would shame her station —she was her father's daughter. And, besides, I said, it is full early. Your father is but ten days in his grave.'

'You said well, Madam. She is fortunate in so wise a counsellor!' But like my sister I did not know then what was in the Queen's mind.

So it was that Elizabeth, knowing herself cozened, also made no sweet answer. To meddle in the matter, she wrote, was not her business; she had neither the years nor the inclination.

I thought she answered well, not knowing what lay behind all this. I asked her to leave Chelsea and to come to me. She should bring with her all her household, keeping the state that became her rank. To my surprise and hurt, she refused. Her refusal was reasonable—with never a hint of the true reason.

She could not, she wrote, publicly insult one into whose care she had been given by our father; and, since neither she nor I was in a position to object to the marriage, we were wise to submit in patience. We must therefore hide our pain at this slight to our father's memory. And then, since she could never lose sight of the fact that I stood next to the throne, and it were wise not to offend me, she added,

I shall always pay the greatest deference to the instructions you shall give me and submit myself to whatever your Highness shall be pleased to ordain.

But her real reason she was too clever to give, knowing that had I so much as guessed at it, I should, in spite of her protestations, dragged her hence by the red-gold hair.

Useless to withhold permission for a deed already done. Somerset had no wish to make a treason of the matter; and the Council gave its consent. But a letter written to Seymour, sharp and ungracious, shows its feeling in the matter.

. . . You married the Queen so soon after the late King's death that, if she had conceived strait after it, there should have been great doubt whether the child born should have been accounted the late King's child or yours; whereupon a marvellous danger and peril was like to have ensured to the King's Majesty's successor and to the quiet of the realm. . . .

Written in my brother's hand and copied by him into his private journal, it was I make no doubt dictated by Somerset, anxious to dissociate himself from the business, unwilling to take off his brother's head but not at all sorry to take down his pride. And fortunate Seymour was, indeed; for this was truly treason! He had not only married the Queen without the Council's consent but he might very well confuse the succession. That this marriage could possibly strike at my rights or my sister's had not yet entered my thoughts. But now it was only too clear. For we were named in the succession only *after* any child my father might have by Catherine Parr.

You may imagine how anxiously we watched the Queen for signs of pregnancy, but the months going by relieved our fears; any child she might now bear could not be my father's. So, seeing all safe, my brother forgot his anger—at ten one cannot be angry forever—and Christmas is the season of goodwill. That first Christmas after my father's death, we kept all together at St. James's—a house favoured by my brother as being smaller and warmer than Westminster and Whitehall.

Elizabeth I found courteous but, as ever, guarded; my brother I found even more withdrawn from me. He did not approve of me or my faith. He did not approve of my dancing, though I danced little enough and danced well; nor did he approve of my music—both things strange in my father's son. It was still on his mind; for he sent to the Queen again desiring me to make no music nor to dance, since neither could advantage my soul. I was nigh on thirty-two and he ten!

'I know not whether to laugh at such a piece of nonsense—I am his godmother to look to his soul; or to cry at so joyless a child!'

'Laugh or cry it's all one!' she said. 'He is the King!'

'And well we know it!' Laughing Tom Seymour had come upon us. 'Well, Madam, you must wait till you are home again! Then I will send you, if I may, my best musician—and there's none in England finer—that you may make music and dance to your heart's content!'

Kind Tom Seymour. It is easy to see why folk—and especially women—had a fondness for him.

The months went by. My sister remained with the Queen. Now and again she would pay me a visit; but always she was wild to be home again. Catherine, I must admit, had done well by her. Her manners were perfect, her scholarship increasing, her looks ripening. I could find no fault in her; but always I was aware of those watchful eyes, that quick brain, that clever, cautious tongue. She never came but in Ashley's company and that woman I distrusted completely—a flatterer, a fawner and a fool. I was more then ever certain that this was no governor for so wilful, so clever, so attractive, so important a young woman; and so very young a young woman!

Scandal was beginning to spread from the Chelsea household. It reached me in the quiet country; there were whispers at first and then voices not so quiet.

I sent for Elizabeth. It had been nothing but a piece of fun; a romp; no more—if I were to believe her. And innocent; innocent!

'At best it was unseemly,' I told her, 'but . . . at worst?'

'No wrong in it!' She was obstinate, sallow cheeks crimson, black eyes aglitter. 'Madam the Queen knew of it; she made no objection!'

'Then she was wrong and you were wrong; wrong from the beginning. You should have come to me when she was first wed!'

She made a mutinous mouth.

'It is quiet down here. By God it is quiet!' she cried out. And she might as well have cried *You are old and I am young.* 'At Chelsea there's music and dancing and games . . .'

'Too many games!' I interrupted. And even then I did not understand that it was not the gaieties that kept my sister at Chelsea; it was Seymour. Seymour himself was the attraction.

But soon enough all was made clear. Ashley, her husband and Parry summoned before the Privy Council, could not answer fast enough, so eager they were to save their own skins.

From the first day of his marriage, Ashley told them, Seymour had made a practice of going into my sister's bedchamber. 'He would be in his bedgown and she not dressed, or, it might be, still in her bed. He would bid her Good morning and ask her how she did.'

'And then?'

'He would strike her upon the back . . . upon the buttocks.'

'And she?'

'She took it in good part. Sirs, she is but a child!'

A child! And she but six months from her fifteenth birthday. I doubt she had been a child this long while—Anne Bullen's daughter.

'And if your lady were still in bed?'

And Ashley with answer pat, 'He would pull the bedcurtains and make to come at her; and she would go further into the bed so that he could not come to her!'

She did not, it seemed, go far enough! For Ashley's husband made no bones about telling them all, the grave gentlemen of the Council, that the Admiral had sent my sister a message enquiring, among other things, whether her great buttocks were grown less or no!

'Your lady was in your charge, mistress, yet all this unseemly behaviour you allowed!'

'Sirs, it was innocent. . . .'

'There's no innocence when it besmirches the lord King's sister.'

'Sir, Madam the Queen knew and she made nothing of it; and it is she rules all. Indeed, my lords, it is easy to make too much of the matter!'

'Or too little, as you may find!'

'My lords,' the woman was a little frightened now. 'I did speak to my lord Admiral; but I had done better to hold my tongue. His anger was very great. He swore he should complain of me to his brother that I spoke scandal of my lady Elizabeth. And how should I, or any other, stand against the lord Protector?' And now she was down on her knees, both hands out to Somerset that did not deign to glance at her. 'So then, my lords, I spoke to Madam Queen Catherine herself. She laughed the matter off, but, sirs, she took care to be with him when he played his morning games.'

'And then?'

'My lords, matters went no better; indeed you might say they went worse. For Madam his wife would laugh louder than he, to show she thought nothing of it. And they would set upon my lady Elizabeth, he and she together, to tickle her; and more than once he kissed her in her bed. . . .'

On, and on, the woman babbling; and now, it seemed, she could not stop.

'Once, when they were in the garden, my lady Elizabeth wearing her black gown, Madam the Queen cried out upon her that she went so sober-suited; and having shears in her hand, the Queen snipped at my lady's gown in play; and he set to with his hands and soon they had her gown in ribands, she standing there in her petticoats.'

They had cut her gown to pieces; the mourning gown she wore for my father! They had no respect for his memory; nor for his daughter, neither, that they laid wanton hands upon her. And it was the Queen that had done this thing, Catherine Parr, the very pattern of discretion, behaving like a gutter-wench. And still I found excuses for her. Such light behaviour was natural; she had been held down too long. Or maybe she was breeding. I hoped it might be so; for all her marriages with old men had left her childless, and her being with child could make no mischief now. Soon all would settle and she be her admirable self again.

But things did not settle; rather they grew less innocent. I believe my sister did not lose her virginity; neither he nor she had dared. But he had pricked her young flesh with desire. And the woman Ashley—as witnesses confirmed, chief among them Parry—never left off talking of the man. *It was you he wanted, my lady, and always did! And your father would have given you to him—a gentleman fit for any princess in Christendom.* She was forever at my sister so that it wanted but the mention of his name for the girl to flush and flare and burn like a fire. And if Parry spoke true, my sister, so watchful of her words, had told him, 'I do feel that the Admiral loves me too well and that the Queen is jealous.'

Catherine was indeed jealous. And who could wonder! My sister so young, so handsome; so quick, so light—more ways than one! And she, herself, breeding now, heavy and sickly with pregnancy. But it was more than jealousy led to their parting. My sister was in her step-mother's care. If she came to harm while within that care, it could be death for my lady Sudely, Queen dowager.

The end was easy to foresee. There was a quarrel. What was said can never be told; my sister would not speak of it. I gather that the Queen spoke her mind and that my sister took the reproof in silence. But whichever way it was, Elizabeth left for her own house at Cheshunt; left with all her household, never to return. I hoped she would come to me—if only to stop the tongue of scandal. But she didn't like me and I didn't trust her; so there she stayed in Cheshunt—a girl not yet fifteen, mistress of a great household and doing exactly as she pleased.

Elizabeth wrote a pretty letter of thanks to the Queen; and the Queen answered in like style . . . but they never met again. For in September Catherine died in childbirth, crying out that those who should love her worked only to her hurt. And it was true. Her old husbands had cherished her, returning good for good—even my father when pain and anger did not drive him. It was left to the young beloved one to give her *many shrewd taunts*—her own words—to bring her to sorrow and to death. So short that married life—eighteen months; and in that time so little of happiness, so much of sorrow.

I mourned for her. She had been good to my father and if her hasty marriage had slighted his memory I could no longer blame her, her time had been so short. And if she had been over-complaisant with my sister it had been the defect of her virtues—an amiable heart. She had, indeed, died forgiving Elizabeth; for she left my sister all her jewels. I wanted nothing from her; nothing but some small token of friendship; but for me, never a word. For Elizabeth that had so grieved her that, dying, she had cried out none loved her, she had left not jewels alone but her love.

I went to London thinking to comfort my brother. He was, as usual, self-contained. He must have wept for her he had loved, but I never saw it; my sister was with him, she looking subdued, and no doubt they comforted each other.

Van der Delft, the Emperor's ambassador, in place of my dear Chapuys, and whom as yet I scarce knew, came to pay his respects. He found me weeping.

'Highness, why do you weep?' he asked, giving me that title England denied.

'Should I not? Her grace, the late Queen, was good to my father and to my father's children.'

'How good, Highness? How good to the late King whose memory she slighted in a so-hasty marriage? How good to Madam Elizabeth whose fair name she allowed to be tarnished? To the little lord King whose soul she has imperilled with false doctrine—how good? And how good to you and to this poor country that through her is rotten with heresies? Highness, you have cause to weep—but not for her! Weep rather for your country and your faith and for those that now stand in danger of the fire.'

'She was my friend,' I said, the more stubborn that what he said was true.

'From such friends, Christ save us!' he said.

Now the handsome Admiral was free to marry; and once more that fool Ashley was up to her tricks. *Now you may have him if you will! Where shall you match him, the handsome, highborn, loving gentleman? Your father would have given you to him and that the Council know well— for where in Christendom shall you find his equal?*

My sister admitted nothing, ever; but we may read her mind in the

324

matter. Actions, they say, speak louder than words; and the trusted Parry was forever in London closeted with the Admiral. The Admiral —as Parry testified later—was forever enquiring of my sister's incomes and the disposition of her estates. There was more than one suggestion that she should dispose of some lands and acquire others that marched with his own. He meant to have her this time!

And now it was Christmas once more. My father had been dead close on two years and the Queen some three months. In every place I missed his great presence—a man to be feared, yet genial above all men; he had given the court glory. The Queen's rooms, which my sister had taken, were empty for me; empty of the friendship, of the shared reading, of the pleasant gossip. Yet gossip there was and it was not pleasant. Tongues were busier than ever about my sister and Tom Seymour; scandal was loud not only at the court but in the market-place, at every booth and stall. Nor was that any wonder! She stood, after to myself, next to the throne; and he was the handsomest man in England, of great position, standing full in the public eye.

The rumours grew ever more scandalous. . . . *The lady Elizabeth has wed the Admiral. They mean to put the King from the throne to take it for themselves.* And some did not even wait for marriage. *The lady Elizabeth is with child by the Admiral.*

If he were the handsomest man, certainly he was the most foolish. For he went his careless, debonair way and did not seem to know that, once again, the Privy Council were deeply concerned with his behaviour. They were building up a charge of treason on more than one count —and that charge they meant to press home.

Chapter Forty-Four

Seymour was in the Tower. It was January and bitter-cold. In February elm flowers are red aganst the sky; that February of 'forty-nine I remember because trees were black and bare . . . and because I was thirty-three. I thought of Seymour often those days, wondering how he that loved fine living fared in the rigours of the Tower. Maybe not too ill. He had a debonair way with him and a purse to buy comforts; those comforts I hoped with all my heart he had, for there he was like to remain—if nothing worse befell.

He lay in prison not because of the scandal; the Council had no wish further to tarnish my sister's name. There were charges of piracy; piracy against the lord High Admiral of England! And there were charges of forged money; even his great wealth would not match his wild extravagance. And in the Tower he should stay while the Council examined the gravest charge of all.

High treason.

He had, according to information laid, suborned men from their loyalty, held armies in readiness for rebellion against the King, planned to marry my sister and with her share the throne. But though against her chastity the Council breathed no word, scandal pointing at their too-close intimacy, she herself might stand in danger of sharing the charge.

The Council wasted no time. All Seymour's servants were arrested; from my sister's household Ashley and her husband, Parry and any other that might know aught of her private affairs were carried to Westminster. As for herself she was commanded to Hatfield under charge of the Tyrwhitts, my lady to keep close guard, her husband to conduct an enquiry. These two had shared charge of Anne Bullen in the Tower, and neither was friend to Anne Bullen's daughter.

No word spoken; but, none the less, my sister was a prisoner—and naught but her own wits for her defence. Innocent or not, she was young and forlorn, without help or comfort. For no-one was allowed to come to her save the Tyrwhitts, ears wide for every unguarded word the prisoner might drop. I could not sleep thinking of Elizabeth alone and frightened. Let Ashley or Parry or any other drop but one foolish word—and it was the Tower for my sister also; the Tower, the charge . . . and the punishment.

Now she must watch her every word, her every look; must try, in her fearful mind, to guess what things had been witnessed against her. She must, with cunning, inveigle her gaolers to talk on the matter; and then weigh up in her mind whether they had spoken truth or lies. All this; and her heart shaking and breaking for Seymour.

She was equal to it. Every question, outright or sly, she met with silence. The Tyrhwitts, eager in their work and not unskilled, found themselves outwitted. Not one word did she say to incriminate herself; not one word they uttered—and some were scandalous enough— appeared to trouble her. It was Tyrwhitt that was troubled, for he wrote to the Council, *She has great wit and nothing is to be gained from her but by great policy.* No! But she carried the war into the enemy's country. She wrote to Somerset, to my lord Protector himself, and did not mince her words. She requested that she should, herself, appear before the Council, to refute the calumnies—and especially the dishonouring lie that she was with child.

> . . . There go rumours abroad which be greatly against my honour and honesty which above all other things I esteem. The rumours be these—that I am with child by my lord Admiral. My lord, these be shameful slanders for the which I shall most heartily desire your lordship that I may come to court that I may show myself there as I am. . . .

A plain letter and a plain request; and great wisdom therein. Yet a letter an older woman might well hesitate to write; penning those words I think I, myself, must have died of shame. Such a letter—and from a girl of fifteen! She was formidable even them.

The Council refused her request. It was not seemly, they wrote, she should regard such slander nor show herself for such a purpose; they offered instead to punish anyone she named as slanderer, high or low. But even then she had a matchless prudence. She had no mind to let the dirty story spread. She did not say so; she said, instead, she would have no hand in such punishment; for, did she appear glad to punish, she must lose some of the country's goodwill. As well as the value of prudence she knew the value of such goodwill; she sought and cherished it.

The Tyrwhitts continued unresting in their work. Sir Robert

browbeating my sister and all her household; his lady all friendship above her malice. But, for all their pains, nothing did they get. The servants were loyal; or perhaps there was little to tell. And though those two were forever at her, not one word would she utter against Ashley or Parry. She had a passionate loyalty to the worthless pair that knew no loyalty to her, nor prudence.

Seymour came to his trial and the deadliest witness against him was the King. Calmly and with complete understanding, he sent Seymour to his death. Ever since my brother had come to the throne the Admiral, it seemed, had been playing the King as he might a fish . . . or so he thought. He had not the wit to know that the child's wits were keener, his mind more calculating than his own. He played the most dangerous of all games; he had tried to turn the boy against the Protector himself. He had forever spoken against his brother Somerset as the King himself testified.

. . . *You are the King. You and not any Protector! Your father never meant any one man to bear rule—save it be yourself. The country groans beneath this Protector. We want no Protector; we want the King. Choose your own Council. You are the King. . . .*

You are the King. Over and over again; nor had Seymour been ashamed to bribe the boy with money. Somerset kept the King with a lean purse. He had everything a boy could wish—horses, hounds, clothes and jewels—but money to make a gift or to reward a service, he had little. So Seymour would put his hand into his pocket and bring out a handful of gold. *It is disgraceful to keep a King so short. Say nothing to my brother. There's plenty where this comes from. You have but to ask. I'll not see you go short!*

And *Yes,* the boy would say, *Yes, you are my dearest uncle!* And never a sign on that pale face of the anger that consumed him; anger that this fool should not only try to fool the King but dare aspire to the King's own sister.

But more, beyond everything more! This same *dearest uncle* had dared plan the King's marriage—the King who had been meant for the little Queen of Scots! The bride Seymour chose was the lady Jane Grey—no princess at all. That the boy knew anything of these machinations never entered the man's handsome foolish head. Already the girl was in Seymour's household bought from her father at a high price. The Admiral meant to have them both in his hands—boy and girl; King and Queen together.

So Seymour had gone on with his honey-sweet words and his handsful of gold, all unaware of the boy's deadly anger that the man should dare plan to marry his King to anyone less than a royal princess. He said nothing; but he wrote of it in his journal, adding: *I mean to marry a foreign princess bejewelled and well-stuffed.* I think he meant by that last a great wardrobe; and maybe he hoped still for the little Queen of Scots.

So while Seymour spoke the boy made no answer; but he remembered it; he remembered it all against his *dearest uncle*.

If Seymour was a fool to think he could cozen the King, he was even more of a fool to think he could keep anything at all from the Protector. Somerset knew very well that his brother plotted against him; knew all about the proposed marriage and his fury at that last exceeded his nephew's own. The King was meant for the Protector's own daughter. Boy and girl in his own hands, his and no other; King and Queen together.

Seymour was found guilty of high treason; and now my sister might well fear for her own life. Even if the Council believed there had been no guilt in their intimacy—intimacy was undeniable; she might well find herself charged with treason also. It could mean her death. Would the King lift a finger to save his *dearest sister* any more than he had lifted it to save his *dearest uncle*?

That Seymour meant to marry my sister is beyond dispute. And that alone was sufficient to make an enemy of my brother; not even my father had greater notions of kingship than this young child. Seymour had kept his dead wife's personal household together, in readiness for a new mistress—and that mistress the Princess Elizabeth; he made no bones about it. But she? With her usual prudence she had sent him about his business. Yet truly, I think, she loved the man—her first and, I believe, her only love.

On a spring day towards the end of March, the whole world eager with new life, Seymour knew he must prepare himself for death. My sister knew it, too. Yet, still, the Tyrwhitts forever watching, she must show no sign of grief. If she wept at all, it was into her pillow at night, without a sound, so that the Tyrwhitt woman that shared her chamber heard nothing.

On the twentieth day of March, Thomas Seymour, my lord Sudely, lord High Admiral of England, laid his handsome head upon the block. Even throughout that day my sister gave no sign of grief; no with-

drawal, even, into her own chamber. Tyrwhitt—she told me so herself
—watching my sister very close, said, 'There goes one traitor the less!'
And my sister, 'He was a man of much wit and little wisdom!'

'A hard heart,' the Tyrwhitt woman said. Well, hard she could be.
But in this case? She was so young, so deep in love; in such danger
and such fear . . . and alone.

What my sister suffered that day I can guess; for even I, that liked
him a little and disapproved of him much, was moved to the heart.
The lady Anne came from Richmond to keep the day with me and I
remember how we talked of him.

'A man so handsome, so gay!' she said, 'and kind. Dear God, how
kind!'

'Beyond the run of men, kind.' And I remembered his kindness when
my brother forbade me to make music in his house. 'I grieve; I grieve
with all my heart. For his last words were not only to my sister but to
me; to me, also!'

She looked her question and I said, What they were we shall never
know. To me a cry for help? To her for forgiveness? They'd allowed
him neither pen nor ink; but he plucked a tag from his hose; and the
ink? Maybe soot from the walls of his cell mixed with water . . . maybe
his own blood. Who knows that, either? For his man was caught and
the letters taken. . . .'

'For this your heart must not break. Nothing could you do. Not
she; not you!'

'But still it grieves me that he should go to his death hoping against
hope . . . and never a word.'

'A brave man!' she said. 'How to die he knew well!'

One other took Tom Seymour's death with a young, untroubled
face; but that face reflected the heart. My brother felt no grief; and
when, later, the Protector himself came to the block, Somerset, uncle,
guide and true friend, the royal hand signed the decree with never a
tremor; nor was there a sigh upon the breath of the child that wrote
it.

A hard heart, the Tyrwhitt woman had said of my sister; and it was
true enough. Yet for Ashley and Parry that had betrayed her, she that
had stood so near to her own death, being new-cleared, must needs
again court danger. Whatever they had done she loved them. They
lay in the Tower, there to rot to their death—if they were lucky;
or to come forth to meet the traitor's fearful end. Yet, knowing well

her own danger, she wrote to Somerset pleading for mercy on account of their long and loving service; and especially she pleaded for Ashley.

> . . . because she has been with me this long time and has taken great labour in bringing me up in learning and honesty. And therefore I ought, of very duty, to speak for her. St. Gregory says that we are more bound to those that bring us up well than to our parents. For our parents do that which is natural to them that bring us into the world; but our bringers-up are a cause to make us live well in it.

It could be argued whether Ashley had, indeed, brought her up well; but fortunately my sister had, even then, an eye to her own interests, for she adds that, the Ashleys being kept in prison,

> . . . it shall make men think I am not clear of the deed myself; that it is pardoned me because of my youth while she I love is in such a place.

I think that last piece of commonsense carried more weight with the Council than her plea for mercy; for those two fools were returned to continue their foolishness. A fool is never turned from his folly.

My sister had learned her lesson with regard to levity. She was not one to need the same lesson twice. A natural levity she had inherited from her mother; that levity she now learned to hide. She that had loved to go gay as a paroquet, affected a modesty of dress, wearing white or grey—and never a jewel. Of jewels she had great quantity; my father had left her some handsome ornaments and the late Queen had added to them. But for long years she wore nothing save a cross upon a chain. But in her private closet it was another matter. She could not deny herself her passion for rich clothes and great jewels. The lady Anne told me how once she had gone seeking my sister in her closet. 'There she was in a gown of silver with raised roses all of gold. And she was hung with jewels head, neck and waist; as for her fingers, you could not see them so covered they were with rings!'

So in secret she indulged her passion, showing herself to the world the pattern of young simplicity—she that for so little a time was young and never simple.

Never a maiden so modest, so scholarly; never such a pattern for all well-bred young ladies. Roger Ascham was her tutor now and she gave herself to her studies with a quick, clear mind. She would make translation from the prayer-book in her fine Italianate hand; and in hopes of coming again into my brother's good graces, would send him the writings stitched into a cover with her own fine needlework. Ascham that had been tutor to Jane Grey, that twelve-year-old nonpareil of learning, said of my sister, *She shines like a star more by her virtues than by the glory of her birth*. Splendour of her virtues! She with her hole-and-corner flirtation with Seymour! And *glory of her birth*! When I remember Anne Bullen and that no man can say for certain who fathered her daughter, I give as little for her birth as for her virtue!

But in learning she outdid me in everything save music, though myself I am reckoned no mean scholar. French and Italian, Latin and Greek, Mathematics and Astronomy—in all alike she excelled.

So she lived, effacing the scandal and forever writing to my brother with honeyed words until she had made herself once more his *sweet sister*, his *sweet sister Temperance*.

Chapter Forty-Five

When I look back I see very clear that my brother's short years as King were full of trouble. The country, unhappy enough during those last years of my father's reign, was wretched as never before. The Protestant faith thrust upon the country did indeed split it in two; and even then the split was not clear-cut. Some heretics believed in their new faith; but others—bishops among them that should lead their flock—seduced by fear, made a show of belief. And many a rich man fattened on wealth stolen from the church and fearing lest, should the old faith return, they be forced to give back their treasures, extolled the new faith. But many stood fast by the old true faith; and some languished in the prison-cell all the years of my brother's reign but many more went to the rope.

So the country by and large was troubled and full of fear; and, at the same time, blasphemy and bawdiness sickened the very air. Maybe it was to hide that fear, or maybe a man released from his old beliefs fears nor God nor devil; maybe both. In the alehouses they spewed forth blasphemies with their vomit; you could not walk in the streets without lewd songs bawled from drunken mouths to offend your ears, lewd antics offend your eyes. Men spat in the face of Christ—and those are not mere words; for standing before images and pictures, they spat into His very face. They had lost all respect for their own priests that, encouraged in the lusts of the flesh by this new 'free' faith, were allowed to marry and beget children—a thing impossible to a true priest. For those that serve God put God first; and how shall a man do that, seduced by the snares of the flesh? Is it any wonder that I looked back to the days of my childhood with longing when right and wrong were made clear to all; when the church set her loving penances and gave forgiveness; when law and obedience reigned?

The very look of churches was changed—altered and strange. Into such a church I never in my life went; but I heard . . . I heard.

'Madam, walls and windows are thick-coated with white,' my chaplain Hopton told me. 'Statues and pictures that tell of the Passion of our Lord carried away.'

'All the things that speak to them that cannot read and move the heart to worship.'

'That is why, Madam.'

'What will poor good folk do now?'

'What they can, Madam. Meet, maybe, in secret to hear the word of God.'

'It takes too much of courage. I know it, I! Too much! Too much!'

'God gives courage....'

'Aye, He *gives*; but it needs courage to take!'

'They are carrying away everything of value. Every piece of plate large and small, every tapestry, every cope so it has but one gold thread. To make themselves richer, the Protector and his friends stripping God!'

'You cannot steal from God. All will return to Him one day—I know it!' And it was as though it was not my voice but the voice of prophecy that spoke.

But now the poor were to be deprived of every chance to hear the true word of God; and those boys, brighter than the common run, that once had been taught to read and write would learn no more. For the chantry schools were being pulled down and the money diverted to the King . . . so they said. But the best part of it went to those that ruled him. I have heard it said that my brother built schools to the glory of God, but, I fear, the only schools he 'built' were those he did not destroy.

And, adding to all the misery, the fear, the destruction—the taxes; always the taxes, the crippling, cruel taxes. My father had left the country all-but bankrupt; but now, it seemed, one could always make things good out of the misery of the poor. All through the years of my brother's reign things grew steadily worse—the rich grew richer, the poor, poorer. Whatever my father's faults—and he was a man of iron will that made no scruple to take the things he wanted—he was yet a man that understood his people and could win even the bitter heart with that charm of his. I, that had suffered his cruelties, could yet weep when he was gone and wish him back. But my brother, so young, so little-wise, how could he know the answer to all these troubles; how in his weakness could he withstand those that, for their own ends, commanded him? It is truly said *Woe to the country whose ruler is a child.*

To this new worship, thrust upon the country by Somerset, by my lord archbishop turncoat Cranmer and their party all eager for their own advantage, my brother was selfless and devoted. From his earliest days Catherine Parr's influence had been paramount; at my father's death she had been left to supervise his upbringing, Now, herself dead, the imprint she had sealed into his tender flesh remained fixed. With his whole soul he believed in the rightness of this new faith and the wrongness of the old.

A young child and a bigot. A young child in hands that worked him like a puppet, and that allowed himself to be worked because he believed the new faith to be God's faith and the old a device of the devil. The most terrifying of adversaries.

One of the first acts of Parliament had been to repeal all laws against heretics: and at first, save for loose behaviour in street and alehouse, and the sight of priests walking with their wives and the changing face of the churches, things seemed little worse. Not that this was not bad enough but it need not touch one's inner self; there seemed no pressure from above. But all the time we felt the terrifying, increasing pressure. The hand of persecution reached out to take the faithful to the torture-chamber, and the final torture of the gallows. How many true hearts died in that torment?

I have said that Gardiner was in the Tower; but I did not say who thrust him there. It was Cranmer that had no right in law to cast men into prison; nor, as a priest, to dip his hand in blood. Yet that same hand signed many a man's death-warrant; Cranmer defying alike the laws of his country and the laws of his God.

As for Gardiner, no threat could move him. *I shall think the tragedy of my life well-passed over so I offend not God's law but the King's. I am by nature condemned to die, which sentence no man can pardon.*

Brave words of a brave man. I had disliked him because of the part he had played in my mother's tragedy. Now I understood he had done it because he had thought it right. He and Cranmer alike had helped my mother to an early grave; but the one was a man of rock, the other a man of straw. I could not like Gardiner but he was a man to respect. Now he lay in prison for his faith, I treasured his words as strength to my weakness should my own turn come.

It was not to come just yet. For those first two years of my brother's reign, the Council, its hands full, let me to stay quiet in the country and I prayed I might remain so. In my faith I could find some comfort for my griefs; for the pitiful death of Catherine Parr; the scandals concerning my sister and the dangers to which she exposed herself; for my brother's frail looks and his coldness, an inviolate coldness that would not save the sister he did love, nor the sister he did not. But greater clouds were gathering; dark storms to overthrow God's faith —and myself with it.

Cranmer had been at work translating the prayer book into an Englished form. In the new year of fifteen forty-nine, two years, almost, to the day of my father's death, Parliament passed a law commanding all men to use this prayer book of Cranmer's.

This Englished prayer book filled me with desolation.

'Yet you yourself, made part of the Bible into English,' said Anne of Cleves come to comfort me.

'It was for my own pleasure; not to force upon others. And besides, bible and prayer book are two different things. One is for contemplation, the other for *praying*.'

'Do they matter the words we use, if we pray from our hearts?'

'We must always pray from our hearts; but there are two sorts of prayer. There is the prayer we make in the secret heart using our own words and God is good enough to listen. But the prayer book is for the great prayers we have always used. Such prayers are not for the vulgar tongue. We must give ourselves pains to learn the sacred words. And if we be too unlearned, too simple, then the priest shall speak for us. So it has always been. Now in the place of the great Latin tongue we are to have our prayers Englished, scant and poor. And what is worse, these prayers betray the Faith.'

'Have you seen them?'

'Not I. Nor never will!' And I crossed myself.

'What shall you do? The law commands. In every church, every man, whatever be his faith, those words and none other must hear; and those words and none other speak.'

'And if he will not?' I asked.

'You know!' And she threw out her hands as if she entreated.

'I know. Punishment by law follows disobedience to the law,' I said, and I kept my voice steady.

She nodded. 'For priests and congregation alike.'

I remembered Gardiner's words in prison. Should I have the courage to follow them?

Not only were the words of our prayers forbidden but the rites hallowed throughout the centuries and bred within our very bones were forbidden . . . no sprinkling of holy water nor of ashes in Lent; no candles for our Lady nor creeping to the cross. Even the sacred mystery of holy Mass purposely left unclear, corrupted, degraded.

'He translates, as it were, sitting upon a fence,' my chaplain Hopton said. 'He does not say God's body *is made* flesh; only that the Bread may be to us *as* the Body of our Lord. And that is something quite other!'

'I remember Queen Catherine Parr saying the bread and wine were symbols; symbols only. It was a notion, God be praised, she must keep to herself. How shall it be when every Tom, Dick and Harry believe the same?'

'It was wrong for the Queen; it will be wrong for them!'

'And wrong for me, also! I'll not pray in Cranmer's words nor behave in my own chapel as he directs. I will not, because I cannot.'

'God give us all strength!' he said.

You cannot interfere between a man and his God. North, south, east and west, revolt flared. In Cornwall men spoke out clear.

... We will not receive the new service. We will have our old service of matins, mass and evensong. And we, the Cornishmen, whereof certain of us understand no English, utterly refuse the new English service....

And everything else apart, surely that is reason enough. For until this time, let a man go where he would in his own country or beyond the sea, still he might hear and understand the word of God.

And the document went further.

We think it meet, because the lord Cardinal Pole is of the King's blood, he should not only have his pardon but also be sent for from Rome and promoted to be one of the King's Council. ...

You may imagine how my heart leaped at that; how I prayed for it! It was this kinsman of mine, son to my dear lady Salisbury, that had spoken against my father's union with Anne Bullen—*marriage* I'll not call it. If he came home again, if he sat upon the Council, he would not allow persecution of my faith—his faith; and surely he would lift the slur of my bastardy. *Sweet Christ let him come. Let him stand by my side and I shall have courage to speak out for God!* But for all my praying he did not come; God chooses His own time.

Revolt and petitions ended in one thing—blood. Again the prison-cell and the rope. And now they were hanging priests from their own steeples; priests of God hanging high, fluttering with every wind like bundles of black rags; a sight loathsome alike to God and man.

Such a thing had never been seen before. Bitterness ran underground like a poisonous plant. I, myself, might have lifted the banner of revolt; to my quiet house in the country came messengers with urgent words. *Bring back the true faith. Proclaim yourself Regent, Queen, what you will. These are cruel times and good men of whatever faith look to you in the name of God.* With rebels I'd have naught to do; God would find a better way!

But for all that, the King—the Council forever at his ear—began to look upon me not only with dislike but with suspicion, too. And now I must walk as upon a tight-rope in the eyes of men. But in my own house I should worship as I chose, and my own chapel must be open to any that would share my worship. It was dangerous but I could do no other; yet I craved nothing but to be left in peace. I was unwell—as always when I am troubled. I was troubled not only for myself and for those that shared my faith; I was troubled for my sister. Seymour's blood was still fresh on the block and times were uneasy. She was still close-watched by the Tyrwhitts and might, at any moment, be taken for treason. And for myself; how if I were not left in peace? Could I stand fast by God?

Courage comes hard to me, save when I am driven by anger; nor was I helped by blinding migraines, by vomiting and the pains of my uncertain rhythms. These days I would weep for very weakness. From the time of my wretched girlhood, separated from my mother, persecuted in the house of my enemies, I had fallen into the habit of weeping. It had been a solace because I dared not speak my miseries. Now again the old habit fastened upon me. I was thirty-three. I had fought for my faith and betrayed my faith; I had been young then. I swore never to betray it again. But was I strong enough? The new prayer book was to become binding by Whitsun; and through the slow procession of weeks I did not know what it was close to my eyes in peace; nor in peace to open them.

I wandered from one of my houses to another—from Wanstead, north to Kenninghall and then south again to Beaulieu, hoping to escape a summons to court. But it came, it came. I dared not go. I knew well what it must mean. Pressure upon me publicly to forswear my faith. At the very thought sickness came upon me. Let me leave my quiet place and I should never return. I sent my message; I prayed the lord King's forgiveness but I was sick. And that was true enough. Migraine, that old enemy, now fell upon me in the guise of a friend, and chained me not to my bed. My brother took my refusal ill. *The lady Mary refuses to come*, he wrote in his journal.

The King angered, the Council adamant, myself sick with fear, and with fear, sick, knew not which way to turn. I wrote to the Emperor and he instructed his ambassador in the matter. I have said little about Van der Delft, the good Dutchman. After Chapuys, that subtle aristocrat, the blunt Dutchman was a change, indeed. But not for the worse. He was to prove as devoted a friend as Chapuys; and so honest that his plain speaking caused less honest men to deem him subtle. Now he was to inform King and Council that my cousin would allow no force put upon me. Should I be constrained he would let loose the dogs of war.

The Council denied his right to interfere; but Somerset—that himself, not pressed, could be a kindly man—sent me private word, *The lady Mary shall do as she pleases until the King comes of age. Meanwhile she shall find me as I have always been, her very good servant.*

It was Van der Delft brought me this comfortable message.

'Can you trust him?' he asked.

'Why not? He need have said nothing. He'll keep his word.'

'If he is able. . . .'

'Then I am safe enough. Somerset rules all.'

'The lady Mary's grace is not often at court. Somerset's power grows daily less. Not only with the King and Council but with the people also. They do not forgive him Seymour's death—the Admiral won all hearts with his pleasant ways. Now all turn to the rising sun.'

And in answer to my question unasked, 'My lord earl of Warwick. Already he casts his shadow. He works against Somerset.'

'Somerset is the King's uncle. . . .'

'So was my lord Admiral; but it availed him nothing. You are the King's sister; yet it shall avail you nothing, neither—unless my master move; and then it could mean war!'

'God forbid!' And I crossed myself.

Whitsun drew near. The Council worked upon by Dudley, that same Warwick, sent spies into my very house. Also he sent me a plain message. I heard it with a quiet face, the heart within me desperate as a bird that throws itself against its cage.

'Sirs,' I told them, 'the Council forgets the oath sworn to my father. I pray you, remind them how, kneeling at his death-bed, they swore to uphold the faith as he ordained it, throughout the land. To his dying wish they must be faithful.'

'Madam, do not put it upon the Council. It is the King's own wish.'

'The King is still a child; when he is older he will wish to consider the matter again.'

'Brave words, Madam!' They bowed and left me.

Brave words, indeed! And I am not brave unless God give me

courage to forget the pains of this earthly journey—the rope or the axe that could so terribly end it; to remember only our eternal life.

Somerset, Protector now in name only, ruled by that Council himself had ruled, sent commanding me to deliver up my Comptroller Rochester, and Hopton my chaplain.

I refused. I wrapped it up very courteous for Somerset's sake as well as my own. My chaplain, I wrote, was so sick a man he must surely die on the way—and of what use a dead man? As for my Comptroller, I could not spare him. He ordered my affairs with such skill that, lacking him, my small incomes could not be stretched to cover my needs—a neat reminder of their meanness. And since he was innocent of all disobedience, he also could be of no use.

Reasonable. But for all that, defiance. It took toll of me in the sickness that always follows panic-fear.

Whitsun came and went. In my house the Englished prayer book had no place. I went my accustomed way—forgotten you might think. Summer wore on to autumn; still the Council made no move. No doubt it would have dealt with me sooner but its attention was elsewhere; it was upon Somerset fighting his last battle. My Comptroller brought me news of the man's desperate state. It was, I remember, a clear autumn day, leaves wet underfoot as I walked in the garden, spiders busy so that bushes glittered like jewels in a crown.

'Madam,' he said, 'the uproar against the lord Somerset is so fierce he cannot withstand it. It is not only the Council; all London calls for his blood!'

By the end of October Somerset lay in the Tower and Dudley, my lord of Warwick sat in his place.

Now I had more cause than ever for fear. This was a man of a different stamp; harder, warier, cleverer; a man in whom few, if any, caught a hint of softness. He was not a man; he was an engine of war to cast down and crush all that stood in his way.

The new year of fifteen hundred and fifty came in. Somerset, come to trial, pleaded guilty to every charge—he could do no other. He was no longer a menace to any man, so they fined him heavily and they let him go free. I think he had rather died; when pride is broken, a man is broken. He left the Tower a broken man.

That February I was thirty-four; time to give up counting birthdays. All the long summer, waiting for Warwick to move, fear gnawed at me like a rat. Migraines worse than I had ever known sent spears of pain driving through eyes, ears and teeth to the very bone so that I could never forget the grinning skull beneath.

My little strength run all to waste, my physicians thought I must die. Day by day I lay, not daring to open my eyes upon a world that forever swung in dizzy arcs of light and praying it might be God's will for me to die now in my weakness, in my own house among my friends. Sometimes, wits wandering, I thought my mother stood by and spoke to me. *You must live. You are to bring back the true faith to this poor country.* And *Yes,* I would answer, *Yes.* And all the time the tears running down my face from the pain and the fear. And the fear was not of death but of the crown.

I did not want the crown. I did not want the burden. I did not want to punish heretics in God's Name. Let some other do it; someone wiser, stronger for the work.

'*There's none but yourself.*' And did my mother whisper; or the anguish of my own heart? How much easier to die then than to live! I should never be well, Dr. Buttes said, until I were a wedded wife. That I was not like to be; but not for want of offers. Since my father's death offers had been made for me time and time again. I was the greatest match in Christendom; and, for all my sickness, was not ill-looking—a handsome lady still, they said. Ambassadors came and went; a Protestant prince I would not wed, a Catholic prince I must not wed. And so every offer came to nothing.

Myself, I was in two minds in the matter. Those that had been children when I myself was full grown, I saw now, happy wives and mothers. Fearful and lonely I longed for a husband's strength to shelter me; I longed, above all things, to have a child of my own—I that was godmother to so many—to love and to guide as my mother had guided me. But it was all a useless wishing. Let the match be never so perfect the Council would not countenance it. The country was in such a state of unrest, it would take little for any husband of mine—Catholic or Protestant, English or foreign—were he so minded, to stir unrest into open revolt and put me in my brother's place. And for that same reason the Council would never let me—wed or unwed—leave the country.

Against the true faith laws became ever more cruel. Every least rite was forbidden. It was dangerous to cross one's self; it was openly said that we did not, nor could not, partake of Christ's body in flesh and blood; no longer might we hear the small, sweet bell as the priest lifts high the sacred Host. Nothing but the stark ceremony in the vulgar tongue as sanctioned by the law, the very altar cast to the ground;

and everywhere the spying and the fear; and everywhere the torment, the hangings. As for myself, the Council, led by Warwick, did not cease from bullying and threats.

'That I am a sick woman they care not at all,' I cried out to Mynheer Van der Delft. 'What better time to beat me into submission. And if I die under it—what also could be better?'

'God will not let you die, Highness!' he said. 'He has work for you to do!'

'I am afraid; forever afraid! Not so much of death in the body, as death in the soul; fear lest I give way, at the last, to betray my God!'

'He will give you strength.'

Yet let me confess it. *It was fear of the body also. It was fear of the body.*

Once more my cousin demanded freedom for my worship; again he threatened war. We were at odds with France and in no state for war; the promise was made. I rejoiced too soon. It was couched in terms meant to deceive; words that a crooked man like Warwick could discount and a true one like Van der Delft take as honest. So for a little time I was left in peace. And then again—the bullying, the threats. I wrote to my brother, I reminded him of the promise made.

Van der Delft brought me the answer.

'There was no promise ever—the lord King says. There was permission only; permission to last a short while; such permission to apply, Highness, to you alone. You were not meant, the King says, to extend it to friends and servants. You keep your chapel open; and that is enough to cancel all permission.'

'How might I refuse it? May one refuse water in the desert to men that die of thirst? How much more then to those whose souls thirst for God? And if I look to my own soul, alone, shall I not most certainly lose it?'

He spread his hopeless hands. 'God will look to your soul.'

'You put too much upon God!' I said. 'We must look to our own souls!'

And so it continued; from the Council never-ending messages, never-ending procession of their priests—priests that had so little care of God's work that they had married, some of them, and begotten children. And all these months of coming and going, my heart never kept its proper rhythm. When I received the messengers it beat faster, faster; when I sat down wretchedly to write my refusal, it beat slow . . . slower, until it would seem to stop altogether.

The Council could afford to break its promise; it no longer feared the Emperor. Once more affairs had shifted in Europe; we had made peace with France and his help was no longer needed. It was a peace we should never have made; and we paid for it with Boulogne. Now we had nothing of France left, France that belonged to us, save Calais and the Calais Pale.

In vain my cousin quoted the Council's own letter to him,

The lady Mary shall retain the ancient religion in such sort as her father left in this realm according to the promise made to the Emperor until the King should be of more years. . . .

The same lying excuses were made. The Emperor was feared no longer.

Chapter Forty-Six

I could endure my life no longer—the fear, the constant threats not to myself, alone, but to those that loved and served me. I sent for Van der Delft.

'I must fly the country.' I told him, 'lest body and soul perish together.'

He said nothing; but a movement of his hand, empty, helpless, betrayed him.

'If the Emperor will not help me, I must help myself. Before God I'd rather be a serving-wench in Holland if I might freely practise my faith.'

'Highness, this is no easy matter for my master. Times have changed. Your country's new friendship with France . . .' and he shrugged.

'It is easy enough!' I said, stubborn. 'We are near the sea. I can get there without help. I can, if I must, walk. Let my cousin send a ship; one ship only!'

'Highness, I will write to my master; I will write at once. But you'll not find it as easy as you think. You are close-watched. How near this house stands to the sea, the Council know as well as you!'

And that last was certainly true. The Council, of late, had been sending with the request that, for my health's sake, I should leave Beaulieu. It was flat and damp and I, myself, unwell. *Too near the sea.* Beneath their thoughtful solicitude the meaning was plain. My replies were courteous, were full of gratitude for their concern. I stayed where I was.

Now I had sent to my cousin I found myself rent by my doubts. For I am one—unless conscience speak clear—to be swayed this way and that by the voice of reason.

Escape while you can. Keep your soul alive—and your body also. For if your body die, who shall bring this country back to God?

But, *Run away! Leave the succession to Elizabeth that uses the new faith to hoist herself into favour?*

I prayed, with a true heart, that my brother might live to beget his

344

heirs; but yet my heart knew the truth. He was a weakling child. It was my duty to stay, to take the crown at need, to bring back the true faith . . . if I were let to live so long.

Had my cousin sent with promise of help, my answer had depended upon the mood of the moment.

The matter was taken out of my hands. In November I lay once more upon a sick bed and all that winter continued sick. And all that winter the Council, unmerciful, troubled me still. Even in my sickness they did not spare me, but rather grew more cruel in their demands. In my private chapel my priests still celebrated the Mass; now I was commanded to give them up to the King's officers for punishment.

Letter after letter I received; letter after letter I wrote, in my aching head fumbling for the words. Now I would write to the Council, now to the King himself. How humbly I wrote beseeching this young child—my godson—that I might have freedom for my faith. How many times did I write, using different words, different forms, but forever pressing home the same point!

In February I wrote to my brother from Beaulieu a long and humble letter.

. . . Albeit your Majesty, God be praised, has at these years as much understanding and more, than is commonly seen at your age, yet considering you do hear but one party (your Highness not offended) I would be a suitor that, till you are grown to more perfect years, it might stand with your pleasure to stay in matters concerning the soul. So undoubtedly should your Majesty know more and hear others, and nevertheless be at liberty to do your will and pleasure . . .

I might have reminded him that, as his mother in God, it was for me to look to his soul; not he to mine; I told him, instead, that the Council's commands were worse to me than death; and death I would suffer rather than obey them. I would, I said, obey the King's will in all things but the voice of my own conscience.

Rather than offend my conscience I would desire of God to lose all I have and also my life; and nevertheless live and die your humble sister and true subject.

To have reminded him that he was young and would grow to wisdom! I see now it was a stupid thing to have done. He was a child surrounded by flattery. Whatever his rulers thought in their heart, their voices hailed him the miracle of wisdom, of goodness. Little god without a fault.

All winter I had been a sick woman. Springtime that brings fresh hope could bring none to me. For now my case was worse than before. If the Council could neither coax nor whip me into obedience, they could certainly starve me of God's word. They forbade my priests to say the Mass under pain of death. And for myself there were threats I dared disregard no longer.

The need to escape fell upon me more urgent than before. And now there was no hesitation while I balanced argument. I was like a wild thing that, without freedom, must die.

I sent for Van der Delft. 'I must get away, away!' I was frantic, wringing my hands. 'Let my priests continue and they stand in danger of the fire. Without the Mass I cannot live; and with the Mass I'll not be let to live. We deal no longer with Somerset that had, at times, a gentle heart. We deal with Warwick that boasts he fears no man; nor God, neither!'

He nodded. Everyone knew that Warwick had so boasted, taking his wine at table from a chalice that had once held the blessed miracle of the precious blood. One that could so spit in the face of Christ would stop at nothing to pull me down.

'Mynheer, you do not altogether trust me. You think me too full of fears and doubts. Well, I cannot blame you! Life has made me so; nor has this long winter of sickness helped me. Since girlhood I have stood upon a quicksand. Yet as a child I was quick and proud and brave. You may find that hard to believe, yet Monsieur Chapuys will tell you! But then it was all bright morning with me!'

'You have walked in darkness too long. Who does not fear the dark cell and the bloody end?'

'Yet I fear God more. Once, long ago, I denied my faith and God forgave me. I cannot think He will forgive me twice.

'God knows the inmost heart and will forever pardon. Madam, I will write to my master . . .'

'You will write! Write while I perish body and soul! Chapuys would not have waited. Oh, you will do what you can for me, for the sake of your master and the faith we share. But not for me; not for me, myself. . . .'

And I longed for Chapuys that had loved me, a little, as a man loves a woman.

'I need help!' I cried out. 'Now! Before it is too late! With your master's help or without I must escape.'

He looked at me out of bright blue eyes. He was moved, I think, less by my words than by my looks—thin, bloodless, desperate.

'For a princess of England to fly the land is a hard matter; yet it shall be done, I swear it!'

I looked at him; kindly, honest, a man to be trusted.

'I will wait,' I said. 'But for the love of God do not make me wait too long.'

I moved to my house at Woodham Walter; it is even nearer the coast than Beaulieu; it stands close to the salt marshes where the Blackwater river runs to the sea. And there, in less time than I had thought possible, Van der Delft brought me my answer.

'My master will send help!'

It was as though God Himself had reached out from heaven.

'Already steps are being taken,' Van der Delft said.

But I am not one to throw everything upon God.

'All I need is my cousin's goodwill and that he will receive me in friendship. My own part is planned and ready,' I told him. 'My Comptroller, here, has a friend with a boat; a man that brings corn for my household up the river from Maldon. He shall take me in his boat to Holland. There's none to question him; he is well-known hereabouts.'

He shook his head. 'Highness, it will not do. It is too dangerous a thing for one man—and one you scarce know!'

'*I* know him!' my Comptroller said, pricked. 'I can vouch for him. He'll not fail!'

'Who can swear to that? Sickness; an accident—' Van der Delft spread his hands. 'But let us leave him for the moment. First, Highness, search your mind. Are you firm in this matter? Once before . . .'

'I was sick; nor was help firmly promised. And, indeed, the matter, though grave enough, did not press as it does now. It is no longer a question of whether I will or will not. It is a matter of *must*!'

'My master, the Emperor, bids me remind you that the King is frail in body; have you allowed that in your reckoning? Suppose he should die—and you across the sea? What danger to your succession! And if, for your sake own, you are willing to forgo the crown—what of our faith? How shall it fare in the hands of the lady Elizabeth?'

'Do you think I have not lain sleepless over this matter? If the King die—which sweet Christ forfend—then in that same hour I die too . . . if I am let to live so long. Warwick knows my right to succeed; he'll not dare to let me live knowing the evil he has done me and my faith. The marvel is I am not yet in my grave. No! If I stay here I am lost; and our faith is lost. But If I am safe across the sea I shall come home again. The people love me—and not only those of our faith; there are

347

very many that, accepting the new worship, still hate these wicked times and long for the old, good days.'

He bent upon me his grave and troubled eyes; and all the arguments I had thought so strong broke into pieces. I cried out, 'For the love of God advise me. I am a woman old enough to know her mind; yet I am like a child that is lost and seeks comfort and direction from one wiser than itself. But—' a sudden spurt of anger flared, 'if the risk be overmuch for you or your master, then I must needs manage alone. Why should any man suffer because of me?'

'Never doubt the love of my master, nor my own goodwill to serve you; serving you in this we serve God. Nor do we consider any danger but your danger; your great danger. My master waits only for your final answer. I will come again in two days or three. . . .'

One day passed and then another and another. My preparations were made, those faithful few that should come with me, chosen. And still the days went by heavy with fear and waiting. It was nearing the end of April and the salt marshes aglitter in the sharp sunlight, and the sea beyond—my road to safety—lying pale beneath a pale sky when Van der Delft came to me again.

'Highness, with your plan my master will have naught to do. To depend upon one small boat is madness. You would be followed and taken. And if not, pirates that swarm in your creeks would fall upon you to take—need I say it?—treasure richer than gold. Now here is my master's plan. I am to be recalled. . . .'

I cried out at that and put out a hand as though to hold him back, this good, true man.

'Highness, be easy! It is the first step. I shall give it out that I am for Germany. Two ships, well-armed, will be sent for convoy; it is not unusual to protect ambassadors on the high seas—the times call for it. When we are clear of the Thames we alter course; we sail up the Black-water to Maldon. And there, Highness, God willing, you shall join us. The little boat belonging to your friend—' and he made a bow towards my Comptroller, 'shall bring Madam the Princess aboard my ship. And then—direct to Antwerp where you, Highness, shall find a most loving welcome.'

'May God bless my noble cousin; and you too, mynheer, servant worthy such a master. You will tell me, in good time, the hour and what company I shall take with me!'

'Highness, I will. There is much to do and so I take my leave!' He bent low over my hand; he was not a tall man yet I stood upon tiptoe to kiss him upon both cheeks.

The new ambassador Mynheer Schyeve had arrived; on the point of leaving Van der Delft came hurrying with news that bade fair to end all our hopes. A new law was about to be put into force—he had caught wind of it. Every road throughout the country was to be watched; every householder required to take his part.

'The Council has got wind of our plans?' And I wrung my hands.

'I think not, Highness. It is rather that the whole country is restless; discontent works like yeast. It is not only the hungry and the poor that complain; it is the rich merchants that lose their fair profits in ever-increasing taxes. Nor is it good Catholics alone because they fear the rope, it is all good men that will not willingly see God put down. It is all folk that know not when or where the hand will fall. Days are beginning to lengthen; and the Council fears the long hours of the summer nights; for then discontented men will always gather, ripe for mischief. So, Highness, you must leave at once, before the law comes into force. The ships are ready! . . .

'Madam my mistress, cannot go!' my Comptroller said, and it was as though the words came from a dying throat. And while we turned to stare at so strange a speech, he said, 'My friend cannot sail. His boat is damaged; laid up for repairs. He has this moment sent to tell me.'

'So much for one man's faith!' I cried out. 'Mynheer, you were right. Well, it does not matter! I will go on foot to Maldon; I and some half-dozen of my women—and all of us well-disguised. We shall go by twos and threes . . .'

'We dare not risk the roads now!' Van der Delft said. 'No! We must find another boat and a captain we can trust. For, Highness, if you are discovered and brought back, you are in worse case than before.'

I put a hand to my mouth to hold back the sickness that, these anxious days, forever threatened.

'I thought this might happen,' he said; 'and I have already planned for it. I have hired a boat at Ostend; a cornship. It shall put in at Maldon; cornships from the Lowlands are a common sight. My good friend Duboys shall be the merchant. A simple plan; it will work. . . .'

But now I was wild to go at once. *If not tonight . . . then never!* My heart knew it.

'I do not like this plan, it moves too far from England; it will take too long. I will risk anything, anything at all—save further delay. That I'll not risk. We leave tonight.'

'Highness, it is not possible. Go on foot and you will certainly be caught. Moreover, it is not yourself, alone, we must consider. Should my master's part in this be discovered, it must mean war; yourself a prisoner, my master discredited, and our two countries awash with blood!'

So in the end, with a heavy heart, I was forced to agree.

'It is but a few days,' he said. 'I will come for you, myself.'

'You swear it?'

'I swear it, God willing!'

But God was not willing. Within a fortnight he was dead; the plague had struck him down. He had died, wits wandering to me and my safety. But he had done his work first. Jehan Duboys was to bring his boat down to Maldon, while near Harwich three warships stood out to sea. I was to board Duboys' boat no later than the twenty-seventh of June. He would send full warning of the exact hour and day. All these things I heard; but of the death of that good man, Van der Delft, I was not told lest I take it as an omen.

The ships were late. Ships must wait upon wind and weather; but still the delay troubled me—I had waited so long.

The slow days went by. *If by the end of the month I do not hear, I will not go. It will be too late . . . too late.* June twenty-eighth, twenth-ninth . . . and then, last day of June the message; the longed-for message.

In the dark night Duboys already waited. In the early morning he would come into the town to sell his corn. That same night I must sail. I must not delay. The tide would be right, the river full, the night dark. The following night and every night thereafter until full moon the river would fall, the nights grow lighter. Moreover, tarrying we courted danger; he, himself, might be questioned, or the warships suspected. Rochester, my Comptroller, brought me the message. *If the packet is to sail, it is now or never!*

And now, as ever, when I must come to a decision, my mind pulled me this way and that. And Rochester whose true heart I could not doubt, Rochester that had once urged me to go, unsettled me further, urging me now to stay:

'Madam, have you considered what you shall lose by going? There's a wise woman foretells the King will die this year. And, God forbid—it could be so! And what then of the crown? Madam, does not heaven itself speak out? Why the accident to my friend's boat? Why the bad weather and the lateness of the Emperor's ships? Why the danger of the river falling? Are not these all warnings?'

When he was gone I walked about the room. Two selves within

me clamoured, tearing me, it would seem, apart. *Rochester talks good sense. Heaven itself speaks.* And then, *The ships are here, moon and tide are right. Does not God Himself say Yes? It is now or never . . . never, if not now!* And then, as so with me—the compromise. *I'll not stir until I see Duboys face-to-face, the manner of man he is!* And all the time I knew it was not omen of wind or weather, nor yet what sort of man Duboys might be. It was the sort of woman I was, I, myself, with my lack of courage, my doubts, my indecisions. I was not steadfast.

And now further trouble—as troublesome as unexpected; and none of my making. On the quay at Maldon there was quarrel, there was anger. Duboys had brought the corn for my household; a good opportunity, while bargaining, to make sure of every arrangement. He had contravened, it seemed, the town's laws. Now the mayor, very heated, was telling him that no corn should have been sold before it had been officially priced; and, having been so priced, should have been offered in the town first.

Duboys, quickwitted, managed to sweeten the man. 'I have spent the whole morning trying to get my corn priced,' he said, 'but there was no-one about. However, I have plenty more at home of this same quality. For you I will make a special journey and a special price.'

In the cool of the evening, his boat well-hidden, Duboys came all unwilling, making his way by devious paths lest he be seen.

'Madam, do not receive him!' Rochester whispered, 'I will take him a message that you cannot go. Remember the wise woman. . . .'

'You will repeat that once too often!' I said, sharp with my own doubts. 'To foresee the death of the King is treason—in me and in you; and in your wise woman that is maybe not wise enough to foresee her own death! See Duboys I must, whether I may trust him or no!'

Duboys came in and knelt before me. Rochester stood at my side; two of my women held the door.

I liked the look of Duboys; honest he seemed, keen of wit and brave.

'Majesty . . .' he began.

'I am not the King,' I told him.

'To us of the true faith you are the Majesty of England; you, your mother's daughter, not a heretic boy!'

'I am not the King!' I said again.

'If you are to go, Highness, it must be tonight.'

My heart that would once have lifted upon wings at those words dropped now like a stone. Suppose that wise woman had, indeed, been whispered of God? Should I fly now when any week, any day, even, might bring me the crown?

'Mynheer,' I told him, 'I must *think*. . . .'

He was plainly taken aback. 'Majesty, there is no time. . . .' And, kneeling still, stretched out both hands towards me.

And now all the miseries the homeless must endure swept over me . . . a stranger in a strange land, eating the bread of charity, my tongue learning to shape a foreign speech, Spanish and Dutch alike unknown. My welcome would be warm enough—at the first; but afterwards? What so cold, so bitter as the courtesies doled out to the unwanted guest?

The most important moment of my life had come—and I knew not how to take it. I rose and paced the room.

'Madam,' Rochester spoke in my ear, 'if you are not minded to go now, be sure the Emperor will send again. You are in no worse case than a month ago; and a month hence may be in a better!' And he was reminding me of the wise woman's prophecy.

I looked at Duboys that knelt still by my empty chair. I knew the pains he had taken for me, the dangers he had risked. I knew the Emperor's anger should I set all at naught; certainly he would never send again. And yet . . .

Duboys knew my answer before I spoke.

'Mynheer, I cannot come; not tonight. I have been ill and am not yet well. Give me, I beseech you, a little longer. Not tomorrow but the day after. Can you wait?'

Let me wait till Doomsday but you'll not come! His face answered me. Aloud he said, 'Madam, it will do. Not tomorrow but the next day; you must be aboard at four in the morning at the latest, lest we miss the tide. Every day the river falls and I dare wait no longer. Besides, there are more Dutch sailors than usual about the town; good men, but a little drink may loosen tongues. And there are the warships; already the mayor has asked some questions. So far I have satisfied him with tales of watching against pirates—he is not quick in the wits, that one! But any moment now those slow wits may come at the truth. . . .'

He was still talking when footsteps came hurrying. Rochester went to the door; he came back into the room.

'It is finished!' He spread empty hands. 'The mayor suspects everything—your cornships and your warships, you, Mynheer, and your sailors. If you do not leave at once he will take you all for question; your boat he will hold and yourselves put under lock and key. As for the warships he means to search them, but he must wait upon the tide. Mynheer, you must delay no longer. For my lady's sake as well as for your own, for the love of God, go now!'

352

Duboys stood upright. 'Madam, if it please you come at once. It can still be done!'

Rochester said, all rough with his fears, 'She cannot go. They have set a three-fold watch; men upon the road, men upon the church tower; men upon the quay. Take the field way—I'll show it you—and you can still reach your boat. Go at once; if you are taken it will be worse for my lady here.'

I said, 'Mynheer, God Himself has spoken. He will not have me go today!'

'Shall I come again?' He looked me full in the face and we knew each the other's mind. He would not come again nor I ever go.

He made a stiff little bow from the waist and went. Listening to his departing footsteps I felt empty, as though all the blood had been let out of me.

I had thrown away my last chance. I heard my voice come out sudden and high and thin, *What shall become of me?* I bit upon my tongue to keep back the words; but still that voice of despair cried out *What shall become of me? What shall become of me?*

Chapter Forty-Seven

So I was left, that out of fear had thrown away my chance. For I might have gone; with safety gone. No-one had challenged Duboys. The tale about the mayor, his suspicions and the three-fold watch was a lie. With the best intentions Rochester had lied. It had come to his ears that the Council knew something of my plans; they believed that the Scepperus—that is, the Dutch lord high admiral himself—had come in guise of a common sailor to take me away; that the Essex roads were full of soldiers and every likely port being watched. And so much was true; for after my brother's death, I saw in his journal, that strange revealing little book written in his own careful hand,

> I have sent into Essex to stop the going of the lady Mary because I was credibly informed that Scepperus would steal her away. . . .

Yet in that split second I could have escaped. The soldiers were still on their way; and though Harwich and every sizable port was certainly being watched, no-one, as yet, seems to have thought of little Maldon. But the fault was not in Rochester but in myself; myself that blew both hot and cold. So my moment passed. How often in the next three years did I pray my chance to come again! Yet I know—none better—that not chance but character is destiny.

The year of 1551 came in. All winter I had been a sick woman bewailing my lost hope, and half out of my mind with fear, not knowing when the blow would fall but knowing full well that fall it must; for the Council, driven thereto by Protector Warwick, would, no more than cat with mouse, let me free of their claws.

I had kept no Christmas festivities, deeming it wise to stay close and quiet; and having, besides, no heart for them. My brother did not send for me to share the festivities; nor did I expect it; I was clearly out of favour.

February came in with the first faint signs of spring—elm trees red against a pale sky and snowdrops. And because Beaulieu must undergo its cleansing after the long winter, I left it to its brushes and brooms and went to Hunsdon, my house in Hertfordshire. Since it is further from the sea I hoped to set my brother's mind at rest—for still he suspected I meant to run away; but alas, there had been no more talk of that, nor did I expect it.

I had scarce arrived when my brother commanded me again to court—and in no uncertain terms. Well, if to London I must go, it should be in fitting state.

It was mid-March when I took the road attended by a great train. Fifty ladies and gentlemen rode before and fourscore behind, and every one very fine in velvet and gold chains. And since I meant to plead my cause I myself all in black, and every one of us wearing a rosary of black beads. Maybe I had been wiser not to display these tokens; but I was never one to go roundabout in any matter and in this case I meant openly to declare my faith.

So along the country roads went the procession in clear sunshine and budding trees and the green look of the world in spring. And everywhere folk rich and poor came out with gifts and blessings; and some of the richer sort fell in beside me to bring us into London. Their love was comforting and, my spirits rising, I thought, *My brother loved me once; and will again.*

As we neared London, the people came out to meet me and bring me into the city; but not my lord mayor nor his aldermen—they must lick their finger and hold it in the wind to see which way favour blew. So long since I had seen this dear city—the familiar smells; and the river, my own royal Thames, and the people crowding the narrow streets to see me pass. For there was always love between the city and me, love which we showed each other unashamed; I with too-ready tears, the people with thrown caps, with cheers and salutations and blessings. It lent me some courage.

But as I neared Westminster my heart was down again; nor did it rise seeing no sign of welcome—neither trumpeter, nor standard, nor any member of the Council. It had not been out of place had my brother, himself, stood in the great doorway, but there was no-one save Mr. Comptroller Wingfield and he, though courteous, was cool. Such lack of greeting was meant to take my spirits down; and take them down it did. Nor did it help me that I must wait for audience. Very different his reception of my sister that had ridden in the day before.

When, at last, Wingfield came to conduct me into the Presence chamber he saw fit to remind me of the etiquette required. '. . . since, Madam, it is long since you were at court. Approaching the lord King you must kneel three times; and upon both knees; once at the door, once in the middle of the room and once at the foot of the throne. And there you must kneel, while the King speaks; nor must you rise until of himself he give you the nod.'

'Mr. Comptroller, I have known the ways of courts longer than yourself—' I began and stopped. For my father, in the midst of his family, had been wont to dispense with rigid etiquette—unless he were angered. Were Wingfield's words meant as a warning against the King's displeasure; or as an insult? Either way it was an ominous beginning.

In the great chair sat the King, that formidable child; the Council of twenty-five all about him, at his right hand Protector Warwick. I knelt at the door but he did not look up; nor when I knelt in the middle of the floor. When I knelt before his very feet, he bent upon me a cold look . . . and let me kneel. And all the time we spoke together, I knelt until the knees trembled beneath me.

'Madam and sister,' he said in his clear, young voice, courteous yet forbidding, 'too long we have suffered you to hear your masses and your prayers. We had hoped that, given time, you would, of your own will, reject heathen superstition unworthy of any Christian soul. But since that hope is gone we'll endure your heathen practices no longer. Our sister you are; but still a subject obedient to your King. That obedience I now demand!'

'Sir,' I told him, 'with a joyful heart I obey the King's grace in every command save that which separates me from God. My worship I will never change; nor shall I hide my purpose beneath crooked words.'

The pale boy went paler still, if paler could be; he stiffened—a boy in stone. It came to me then that he would be more formidable than my father, even, when he was grown—if he should grow. He said nothing but stared ahead as if I did not exist kneeling there; and I went stumbling on.

'Sir, two things only I possess for my own—my body and my soul. My soul I give to God; my body to you—for your service and your pleasure. Take my life but not my faith. With a good heart I will lay my head upon the block.'

At that, he half put out his hand. I was, after all, the sister he had once loved; and, for all his stiff composure, he was still a child.

'Sister, we intend nothing against you. Be comforted.' And a half-smile lay upon his pale face.

At that Warwick bent towards him and the smile was gone. 'But lean not too far upon our kindness,' he added.

He rose. I knelt until he was gone and all his Council with him. I dragged myself to my feet and could scarce stand for the strain of it.

For all his harsh words my brother entertained me to dinner—if *entertain* be the right word. For I sat upon a stool so far from the King that no shadow of the cloth of estate could fall upon me; my sister I caught sight of, seated also upon a stool, and though still beyond the canopy, nearer to the King than I. And all the time, behind the King's chair, Warwick stood, watchful.

Dinner being finished, the King rose and, all of us upon our knees, made his solemn exit, Warwick at his right hand, the Council following. From beginning to end he had not cast one look upon me; though more than once he had smiled upon my sister, sending her some especial delicacy from his own plate.

I had gained nothing beyond a solemn warning; how long before the King's strained patience broke? Not long—if I might judge by Warwick.

I had not been asked to stay nor had any room been assigned for my comfort; so I stood in the chill of the courtyard while they made the horses ready and there my sister found me. She wore a friendly look but her eyes were, as ever, wary.

'Will it please you, sister, to sit with me in my chamber till all is ready?' she asked. So we went together from the dust of the courtyard and the sharp March winds; and, as we went, I could not but contrast our looks—she but seventeen and I thirty-five. And I doubt not she did the same.

She was handsome—if you liked those sharp and shining looks. But that fine nose of hers would coarsen to a beak, and, with those black eyes, she had already a predatory look; and the skin that in childhood had been sallow but gleamed now like a cream rose, would darken again to sallow when she had lost the first spring of her pretty youth. Ah . . . but till then! From netted cap to narrow waist flamed the red-gold hair; she wore it free-flowing like any young maid, remembering, no doubt, the scandal and flaunting her virginity. She was slender rather than thin, small breasts sharp beneath the silk of her gown—white and green, our own colours. She wore no ornament—for still she played modest—save for the great square emerald upon the hand that held the gown; the exquisite hand of which she was so rightly proud. Very simple she looked in her virgin colours; not only the boy my brother, but a grown man however wise might well be taken in; a woman—never!

A flame of a girl; a shining blade of a girl. With those eyes, that nose, that skin, she had a foreign look—she that was pure English.

Strange! I am half Spanish; yet my skin pink-and-white, my nose short, my eyes grey, I looked perfect English. But the fine pink-and-white that had once made me the toast of Christendom was lined now with ill-health and sorrow. If she were slender in her pretty youth I was very thin; and though my physician assured me that marriage would put more flesh upon my bones, I could still see no chance of altering my state. My eyes, so they tell me, are true and kind. I was—and am—shortsighted; it gives me an attentive, friendly look. But, they tell me that, like my father's, my eyes can be terrible. Well, I am not sorry for that! I am not often angered, being more inclined to weep than to scold; but if I am able to strike terror at need, it is all to the good.

I had not lost all my looks and given good fortune might well regain some of my loss. But always she would be more than seventeen years younger than I; and now in her fresh green-and-white next to me in my black velvet, dusty from the roads, she made me feel old and dowdy as she always did—and as perhaps she meant.

'Madam,' she said when we were settled within her chamber, 'sister!' And her voice was clear and sharp as her person. 'It is long since we met.'

'Long and long indeed! But not by my goodwill. Could you not come to me? I go back to Hunsdon.'

It was clearly the last thing she had expected; or wanted. She said, 'I will come . . . one day; when I am free. Our brother commands me at present.'

So she was to stay on at the court; I all-but commanded to pursue my homeward way. She was in favour and I, out. No doubt of that!

Smarting still at being kept upon both knees the whole time the King was speaking, I could not forbear to mention it now.

'Our father did not use his family so. He would raise even me—save when his anger was at its worst. Is it to show how low I am fallen?'

'Why no!' she said at once. 'It is always so. Our brother *enjoys* it. The smaller the King, the greater the show of respect. Our father commanded full ceremony upon occasion; but this! He would have puked. Did you kneel but three times, sister! I have, believe it, kneeled as much as five, seeing I am further removed from the throne. Distance from the throne—that is the measuring-point.'

That last was not true and she knew it.

'At dinner you sat nearer the King than I!' I said, blunt.

The colour came up into her face, she burned brick-red; flushing does not become her, not with the colour of her skin.

'It was Warwick's doing,' she said at last. 'He rules all; and he is incalculable.'

Why did she blush speaking his name? And why had he seated her nearer the King than me?

'How is he incalculable?'

She was silent. I could see her assembling the words beneath that clever forehead; weighing, picking, choosing.

She said at last, 'Sister; if you should hear aught concerning my lord Warwick and me, you may put it out of your head!'

'What *should* I hear?'

She said, seeming-careless, 'This place is a hotbed of gossip. Lucky you are to be free of it!'

'*What* gossip?'

'They are saying Warwick means to put away his wife. . . .'

And still—so simple I was—I made no sense of her answer. Warwick had been long wedded and his children married or marriageable. How did he or his wife concern my sister?

I waited. She added, a little sulky, 'They say he means to marry . . . *me!*'

To put you on the throne, perhaps! Simple I might be; but the thought was simple, too. I said nothing; I waited.

'Put it from your mind, sister!' she said. 'It is talk; ta!k, merely. I'd not bed with him though I lose my life for it! Upstart Dudleys and royal Tudors!' And she tossed that head so that her hair flew like a flame in the wind.

'Then let us change so distasteful a subject. How long have you been at court?'

'Since yesterday.' And now, surely there was a gleam of triumph in that careful eye.

'And how received?' And why did I torment myself? But I must know; for my own safety I must know.

'Our brother came down to the Water-gate; and all the Council with him!'

She was silent, knowing I must compare her welcome with my own; and not unenjoying the knowledge. Then she said, and again triumph sparked her careful words, 'I might as well tell you; you are bound to hear it. Tomorrow I am to ride through London—in procession; King and Council and all. My brother commands it.' She shrugged, as though this was not her own dear wish.

'And Warwick?' Suddenly I lost my temper. I had endured over-much. 'Is this Warwick's doing too, Warwick whose name is coupled with yours? Does he show you off to the people—the Protestant hope and his bride-to-be? And young, *young*! Does he invite them to weigh you against me—me, old and sickly and bound hand-and-foot by heathen superstition? And where do you stand in this?'

I had begun hot enough but now my eyes were filled with tears so that I could no longer see this girl that knew no loyalties save to herself and those two or three she loved—among whose number I was not.

We looked at each other, she cool and thoughtful; I, furious and humiliated by my treacherous tears. In that moment she seemed older and wiser than I; certain of the way she was going and ruthless to take it. Upon the inimical silence came the trumpet sounding for departure.

'Farewell, sister,' I said; and could not for the life of me kiss her cheek. She curtseyed to the ground and kissed my hand. In spite of Warwick I might yet be Queen!

Chapter Forty-Eight

I rode home troubled; for, as I rode, my brother's words rang in my ears. *Presume not too much on our kindness.* Nor could I drive Warwick from my thoughts; Warwick whose name was linked with my sister's, Warwick that stood forever beside my brother to whisper in his ear. And I remembered how the boy looked to him as though to catch the man's every thought. The King was the instrument upon which Warwick played his own tune. Had I feared Wolsey? Cromwell? Somerset? Now I had cause and cause indeed to fear.

But had I not gained something, some understanding of this new enemy—Warwick, his eyes upon my sister and beyond my sister to the throne; the throne itself? Let Warwick beware! Dictators before him have walked the land . . . and the earth has opened to swallow them.

I reached home subdued and not a little fearful. Was it all to begin again—the persecution and the fear? But no further threat reached me, all appeared quiet; yet my heart was not quiet. Sometimes I would be certain that my brother had softened at the sight of my grief; other times, remembering Warwick and the way the boy's eyes were forever drawn to him, my heart would faint. I was restless. I could endure Hunsdon no longer. I left it, in its turn, to brooms and brushes, and rode for my house Copt Hall. But let me go or stay, there always walked with me fear in which hope and strength alike wasted. Sweet summer was passing; and now my hope was more than my fear.

And then Warwick moved.

My chief chaplain Mallett was arrested and sent to the Tower. A blameless man Mallett, gentle and true, liberal in his thinking and wise. I heard—as I was meant—that this good priest was chained hand and foot in the dark cell; that neither day nor night was he left in peace, that gaolers forever watched, keeping him from sleep, greedy for every word that might incriminate me.

For days on end I stayed within doors, curtains drawn. My women, fearing lest I injure my none-too-robust health in this self-imprisoning, sent Clarencieux, oldest and truest of friends, to reason with me; but I would not listen.

'Shall I walk in the gardens this August day, enjoy bright sun and sweet air—and he be shut within the dark cell? It is not only grief with me; it is guilt, it is *shame*! My word I never broke yet; now it has been broken for me. I promised my priests they should not suffer on my account. And such a promise I had the right to make, being myself promised I might hear the blessed Mass in my own chapel. And if I may hear, then some priests must say it. They have smeared my good name and I am ashamed!'

I wrote to the Council protesting this blot upon my honesty; again and again I wrote—but never an answer. And still my priest languished in the stinking cell; and once more sickness laid a wasting hand upon me.

From the Council no answer. But a faithful friend came to see me by stealth.

'Madam,' he said, 'do not push the Council too far. Many of us would give you the freedom you should have—some of us, indeed, desire it for ourselves. But Warwick rules all.'

'Tell me, in God's Name, did the Council promise the Emperor I should have freedom to worship, or no?'

'It was promised in the presence of the King; and the King himself understood it so. But he has been persuaded otherwise. To that some of us upon the Council could testify; but, Madam, do not ask it. We should be thrust from our office . . . and we are your friends!'

'Fine friends that fear to speak!'

'We fear for you, Madam, as well as for ourselves. We fear Warwick; and Warwick fears *you*.'

'Fears me; a sick and helpless woman?'

'You make trouble for him; you give courage to others.'

'If that be so I am content!'

'Madam,' he said, very earnest. 'I pray you trouble the Council no more, thus you keep yourself and your household safe. Sting the Council and it will turn and sting *you*!'

'Shall I sit quiet when my good priest is taken? And what safety for my household? Of myself I do not speak. . . .'

'Madam, *we* speak of you . . . your friends. . . .'

He stopped. I waited.

'Madam, there is much anger, much bitterness. Warwick is a hated man. The King is young; we cannot wait for him to grow. Everywhere the people are ready to rise; a national rising in your name. Madam, we look to *you*!'

Was he honest? Was this a trap? Whatever it was, I had but one answer.

'This is treason. And with treason I'll have naught to do so long as I live!'

'. . . which may not be long! Madam, if you will not allow your friends to rise in your name then you must keep silent. Continue as you do—and it will be, believe me, your death!'

'When I must speak, then speak I must!'

He looked at me with such pity that I knew him to be honest. 'Then, Madam,' he said, 'I fear for you; I *fear*!'

He left me in anguish of mind but in purpose firm. For we are as we are made and I could do no other.

He had spoken true, the Council would waste no more time on me. Submit I must; or come to my death. They preferred submission. It would make less scandal, arouse less anger. They wrote, not to me, knowing the request useless, but to Rochester, my Comptroller. He was commanded to send them the names of all my priests.

I forbade him. 'This is my affair—not yours nor the Council's. Disobey me and you leave my service.'

'Madam, I would die in your service.'

'It is God's service; and you may well die in it!'

So, there being no reply to their insolence, they sent for Rochester himself. He must appear before them together with two high officers of my household—Waldegrave and Engelfield. Go they must, lest they be dragged hence. I remained at home to tremble beneath a new burden of fear. Would they, also, be cast into the Tower?

But return they did. Before ever they spoke I knew the news was bad.

'Madam,' and I could see Rochester must force himself to meet my eyes. 'The Mass is forbidden. No priest may say it for you; not even in the privacy of your closet.'

'And who shall stop me if the priest be willing?'

There was no answer, one man looking to another.

'The burden is on us,' Engelfield said at last.

'And how shall you do that?'

'Madam . . . we are commanded. . . .' He could say no more.

'Force?' I supplied the word.

Dumb, he nodded.

By force; and in my own household! The sickness came up in my throat.

'And if I dismiss you, all three?'

'Madam . . . we must stay.'

363

'Treachery then; treachery in my own household?'

Rochester cried out at that. 'Treachery, never! Treachery comes from the heart; and our hearts are true. But, consider, Madam! If you send us from you, the Council will appoint others in our place; others whose hearts are not so loving.'

'Much good your loving hearts will do me!' I cried out, bitter. 'Now hearken, for I'll not speak twice! Dare to give any order but by my command and I leave this house at once. Here you shall stay as long as it may please your masters; but me you'll serve never again!'

There was silence, each man his eyes upon the ground. Something more then? At last my Comptroller spoke. 'Madam, we must return with your written promise.'

'That you shall never have!'

'A letter, Madam; something we must take!'

'A letter you shall have!'

They were to return to Westminster next day and down I sat at my desk; I wrote not to the Council but to my brother—and not with any promise. I wrote of my astonishment that any man should presume to command my servants or to direct my conscience. The meanest subject in this land, I said, would not endure it. And, at the very thought, anger took me so that the pen shook in my hand and I was forced to put it down. I must write gently; I forced down the anger in my blood.

> . . . I did trust that your Majesty would have suffered me, your poor humble sister to have used the accustomed Mass which the King, your father and mine, with all his predecessors ever used. And wherein I have been brought up from my youth; and wherein my conscience does not only bind me, but will by no means allow me to think one thing and say another. . . .

I reminded him of the promise made by the Council to the Emperor, though now they denied it. I reminded him of my last visit to Westminster when,

> . . . I desired your Highness rather than you should constrain me, to take away my life, whereunto your Highness made me a very gentle answer.

I said that, though the orders had been signed with his own hand I knew they were not truly his, but the work of his Council. And then, knowing his young pride, I added,

It is well known that though, our Lord be praised, your Majesty has far more knowledge and greater gifts than others of your years . . .

And this was not flattery; he was a child gifted above the ordinary.

. . . yet it is not possible that your Highness can, at these years, be a judge of religion. . . .

I stopped, considering these last words. Would they turn him yet further against me, extinguishing any last pale warmth that might yet remain? Yet I must speak plain truth; for my life I could do no other. I begged him, as once before, that he would bear with me until he should be of age to judge for himself. If not,

rather than offend God and my conscience, I offer my body to your will; and death shall be more welcome than life with a troubled conscience.

I prayed God's blessing upon him and signed myself his most obedient sister.

Rochester, Waldegrave and Engelfield had been cast into the Tower; it was all the answer I got. They had refused the Council's orders to disobey me and to spy upon me in my own house. God that has been fit to send me so many griefs has sent me this blessing, also—faithful, loving hearts for my service. It is a blessing that calls for answering love. It added not a little to my anguish that these dear friends should suffer for me.

Towards the end of August, Mr. Chancellor Rich—as sly a dog as ever bit the hand that fed him—together with the King's Comptroller, and Mr. Secretary Petre, came to Copt Hall. Rich handed me a letter from the King. I took it, kneeling, as though from the royal hand and kissed the seal. I'd give no man—Rich least of all—cause to say that, in any least thing, I scanted my reverence to the King.

A curt, cold note. It censured my obstinacy and commanded me to obedience. In every unkind word I heard the voice of Warwick. Short as the note was, Rich gave me scarce time to read it.

'Madam,' he said, 'the King's Grace bade me command you. You must hear the Mass no more; in private as in public it is forbidden. And, take note, Madam, also; any form of service that departs in any way from that laid down by law, is likewise forbidden. The King commands not you alone but your chaplains also.'

'I am the King's most humble servant; in all things but this, obedient to his will. But rather than obey in this, I will lay my head upon the block—if God judge me worthy to die in so good a quarrel.'

'That is your answer Madam?' Rich said, his voice heavy with omen.

'It is. Let me add this, also. The good, sweet King is wise beyond his years; but it is not possible for him to judge in matters of faith. For, sirs, consider—' and to my shame I heard my voice break as though I would weep, 'if ships are sent to sea, or any matter arise in the government or abroad, you would not think he had sufficient years to decide of himself what should be done. How then shall he judge on points of faith and the matter of a man's soul?'

And when they made no answer but stood, as it were, smiling as at some nonsense, my anger flared. 'If my chaplains are not allowed to say Mass, why then I'll hear none! But no other worship will I hear. It shall not be spoken in my house. Let the attempt be made and I leave at once. Then, seeing they would have begun again upon their commission, I cried out, 'Your Council says this and your Council says that! But what shall men say of a Council that breaks the sworn oath—not to me, alone, but to the Emperor, also? How shall any man believe you? You shame England this day!'

'There was no promise,' Rich said.

'You mistake; or lie. The promise was made. But even if not made, still you should show respect to the daughter of my father, my father that made you out of nothing—you, my lord Rich, and the best part of your precious Council.'

My lord Chancellor went an ugly red; he was, indeed, one my father had raised from nothing, nothing at all. He said, and it was clear the words gave him pleasure, 'Madam, since Rochester now lies in prison, the King sends you his own Comptroller, Mr. Anthony Wingfield, here!'

'Then you may take him back again! I'll not have him, nor any other, to spy upon me. I am of age to choose my own servants. Leave that man here and I go out of my gate at once. He and I cannot dwell together in one house!'

Mr. Secretary would have spoken but I cut him short.

'What use fair words to persecute me? I am sick, brought to death's door by your persecutions. If I should die—and it may well happen—my blood shall lie upon your heads!' And allowing them no further words I left them, each man upon his knees.

When I had a little cooled, I bethought me that my tongue might make yet more trouble for me, I that had sufficient already. I sent for Rich.

'My lord Chancellor,' I said, 'I give you a message for the King; and therefore I kneel as though I speak to the King's self.' And, kneeling, I put into his hands a rich ring. 'I beseech you, give this ring to the King. Tell him that in all things but one I render humble, obedient and instant service.'

I looked into his face and remembered that this man with his lies had helped to make an end of his good master Sir Thomas More in whose shoes he now stood. I knew that neither message nor ring would ever be given. It was too late now; I could not take back ring or message lest I make of him a yet more bitter enemy.

He made no answer. 'I have commanded your priests,' was all he said and, bowing, not too low, took his leave.

From my window I saw them about to depart—all three, including Wingfield that they would have thrust upon me. That little triumph was too much for me and I beckoned them to my window.

'I pray you,' and I was half-jesting, 'ask my lords of the Council to send back my Comptroller. Since he left, I, myself, must take account of expenses. I have learned how many loaves may be baked from a bushel of wheat; but I was never bred to bake and to brew— and I weary of the work. If they will send my Comptroller home they shall do me some kindness—a new thing to them!'

I had begun in jest; but, anger getting the better of me, I cried out, 'I pray God send you well in your souls; and in your bodies, also—for some of you have but weak bodies!' And I fixed the lean and sickly chancellor with my eye. Again the ugly red came up into his face and I regretted those last words before they were out. Again my quick tongue was like to make trouble for me. But we are as we are; and plain speaking relieves the heart as a leech the blood.

I sent my priests away; for their own sake I sent them. My chapel stood dark, empty; and there was no Mass heard for two years.

Golden summer passed into golden autumn. And still I lived in a torment of fear. I had but one hope—Warwick, overreaching himself, might, like the most part of dictators, fall to disgrace. My hope was vain. For he rode higher still: now he wore another, a greater, title. John Dudley, duke of Northumberland. Had he still, I wondered, an eye to my sister that he named himself thus magnificently? And, if now he offered her the throne along with himself, would she, for all her denying, refuse him?

Or did he play some other game? For that same October, Jane

Grey's father was elevated, also. He was now my lord duke of Suffolk. Why? Was there anything between those two new-made dukes? What could there be—the first shrewd, hard-headed; the second a fool? The shrewd man may use the fool to his own advantage; but the fool in his foolishness may fall, bringing the shrewd man down with him. I could make nothing of the matter; nor did I try overmuch. It was not, I thought, my concern. How much it was to be my concern I could not guess.

The new year of 1552 came in. That same month Somerset went to the block. He had allowed himself to be entangled in a plot to murder Northumberland and put himself, once more, in the Protector's place. A witless ploy; the King would never accept him again. But Somerset had his hopes; he counted upon the common folk, for, with them, the tide had turned. They longed to see him again in the seat of power; compared with Northumberland he was an angel of compassion. And certainly he could be generous and friendly, easy of his promises; so they forgave him Tom Seymour's death remembering only the man's many kindnesses and his debonair ways.

Again the King lifted no finger to save his *dearest uncle*; with no change of expression on his quiet face he signed the death-warrant. Let this word be said for Somerset. He knew how to die. When he stood upon the scaffold, debonair still and unafraid, one word to the crowds that had come to see him die—and they had surged forward to save him. But he made no sign. And when he laid his head upon the block, they wept; and that is another word in his favour.

At Copt Hall I prayed for his soul. He had been an enemy to my faith—but once he had tried to stand my friend. And I remembered Nann, his wife, and wondered how it had gone with her that bitter morning; and I prayed God comfort her stricken heart.

For us of the true faith that year of 'fifty-two was a bad one. Cranmer, that enemy of God, had remade his Englished prayer book. If I had not been able to accept the first, still less could I accept the second. For the first had at least kept many of our own prayers in true translation—so I am told, for I never read it. But, let it be never so true, in translation the spirit dies; for words hold thoughts as body holds spirit. In this second prayer book the words—and again this is hearsay —are too simple, too familiar to bear the weight of our entreaties and God's glory. And more; it denies all that by which I live. It denies the everlasting miracle of bread and wine made flesh and blood. It makes no mention, even, of intercession by saints; according to these new prayers we poor creatures must approach God in our own sinful selves. I would not, nor I could not, accept it.

Now was the time to break me.

The Council sent their archbishop of Canterbury to persuade me—Cranmer himself. They could have done no worse; as ever, at the sight of the man, my gorge rose. I could not look upon that self-righteous, well-preserved face but there rose beside it the worn sad face of my mother. This man that called himself a priest, this weathercock, had changed with every wind of my father's breath—providing him now with the new-desired wife, ridding him now of the wife unwanted; preparing each, as the case might be, for the marriage-bed, for the humiliation of divorce or for the axe. Cranmer blow-hot, blow-cold; that served the King and his own welfare before God.

I received him with courtesy; he was England's primate.

'Madam,' he said, bowing low, his prayer book in hand, 'all men love and esteem you; and rightly so. Knowing this, would you set yourself against the faith of the land to divide it in two?'

'My lord,' I told him, 'it is you that divide the faith; but God in His goodness will make it whole again!'

'When a nation is divided,' he went on as though he had not heard me, 'then the enemy will come to destroy it!'

'I do not put expediency before God, my lord; nor do I doubt His power to save.'

'Madam, you are too glib with the name of God. You should leave that to your priests—of whom I am the head.'

'Not of *my* priests—' I began; but he interrupted, holding out his hateful book.

'My lord archbishop. I'll neither take it in my hand nor allow it in my house. It is this unblessed book that divides the people one from the other—and some of them from God, also.'

'I beseech you, Madam, read it. The words are fair and fitting; they feed hungry souls as food hungry bellies.

'What sort of food? Fair-seeming fruit hangs from the deadly nightshade; such fruit is this book of yours. You have thrust it upon a starving people to poison their faith in God.'

'Madam, I use such words of prayer as simple folk may understand.'

'You rob them of God; for in such words the glory of God cannot be set forth!'

'Who led the way with such translation? Who set forth in English the work of Erasmus, that Papist who served his faith so ill? Who

369

translated his paraphrase of the gospel according to St. John—of which Protestants make full use?

Again, again, that unfortunate translation!

'It was an exercise meant for no eye but my own.'

'Yet you allowed it to be put out in print.'

'I was overborne; to my shame I admit it. But I never thrust it upon anyone. It is you, my lord, that use it for your own ends.' Without warning my anger flared. 'You renounced the lord Pope that speaks for God, you brought my mother grieving to her grave; you drove away the good monks, you desecrated God's churches and grow fat upon their lands. You . . .' I choked upon the words.

His face did not change nor his voice neither.

'Madam, if you will not read it, then take it and put it by. Do not refuse it; do not rush upon your fate. Let me tell the Council you have, at least, taken it into your hands.'

'My lord archbishop, would you so plaster the truth with lies?' And he still holding out the thing, I said, 'I hear that in Italy they know how to poison a book so that, turning the innocent-seeming leaves, a man draws forth poison to destroy himself. If such a book be deadly, how much more so the book that poisons the soul? Let come what will, with this book of yours I'll have no truck!'

So seeing I was not to be moved, he bowed himself out, leaving me to ask *What now?* and to pray the blessed mother of God intercede that I be given strength to take what punishment might come.

And now it was spring once more. I was thirty-six with the mark of my years and my tears upon me. I carried myself like a woman but in my heart I trembled like a child.

Within the Tower Waldegrave fell sick; he had committed no offence against the law and they were forced to set him free. And for that same reason they must release Rochester and Engelfield. Now, to my joy, I had all three back with me, dear and faithful friends. And it never entered my mind that the Council must be pretty sure of me; for when had innocence saved that man Northumberland judged better dead?

For still Northumberland ruled. Invulnerable, absolute. The King obeyed him as though the man were God. In the Council no voice lifted against him; Parliament was his instrument to play what tune he would. He did with the Church what he pleased. If a living fell empty he kept it so and put the moneys into his own pocket. He chose his own bishops, men obedient to him—and most obedient of all bishops was Cranmer, archbishop and tool.

King, Council, Parliament and Church—all in Northumberland's pocket.

Folk sickened of Northumberland—iron hand, iron heart. So many causes for anger, for misery! Some longed for the word of God as in childhood they had received it; some of the new faith, even, sickened at the sight, the stench of the gallows; nor could one, any way, avoid such sights; for the gutted, quartered human flesh was carried away to be set in public places, a dreadful warning, where all must see—and smell it, too. But some were too wretched to care one way or another, for ever-increasing taxes like rats gnawed at their very bones. It needed but a leader—a leader acceptable to all. Twice, at least, I had been asked to be that leader, and twice refused. Revolt against Northumberland was revolt against the King. I could not do it.

Chapter Forty-Nine

I kept myself close in the country; my chapel was empty, my priests dismissed. Yet I was not entirely without my soul's sustenance; now and again, a priest on the run for his life, would knock the secret knock upon my door in the dark night. Him we would keep close in some secret place till we could get a passage for France. I was fearful in that business; save in childhood I was never brave. But I had my reward; not only in good men saved but that I could hear the blessed Mass again; behind closed doors—alas! For to hear God's word was a crime.

In April my brother fell sick. First the measles, then the little pox ravaged his frail body and reduced him to a shadow of his pale self. I feared for him; he was but half-way in his fifteenth year—an age when Tudor sprigs have withered and died. At the thought that he might die, not grief, alone, but terror possessed me. If the crown came to me I must take it. I had never wanted it; now I wanted it less than ever. I did not feel myself able to stand against Northumberland and his Council—hard-headed, self-seekers all. I longed, God knows, to bring back His faith; but my body shrank from so heavy a task. I waited, hoping against hope, for good news of my brother; and when, at last, none came, I rode out of a June morning for Greenwich to see him for myself.

I did not like what I saw. He was very thin, very pale; not even upon his lips was there any trace of colour. He did not, I thought, seem pleased to see me. I was not surprised; he liked neither my faith nor me. But his displeasure seemed to extend to Elizabeth—and that did surprise me. She was no longer his *sweet sister*. She had been thrust into the background and our cousin Jane Grey more in evidence than I had ever seen that quiet creature.

I call Jane Grey *cousin* by courtesy. My true cousin was her mother —Frances, daughter to my father's favourite sister, the lovely Mary Tudor for whom I was named. Jane Grey was a true Tudor; she was, indeed, compound of my sister and me. In appearance she was, like me, small and slight, with an apple-blossom skin and red-gold Tudor hair. Her eyes, like mine, were grey but not shortsighted, so that her glance was prouder. She so resembled me that, coming upon her picture more than one have taken it for myself when young.

In understanding she was all my sister—quick, both in scholarship and the swift retort. Like my sister she was devious and like us both, obstinate. She carried herself meek and gentle. Oh she could play humble but she was proud beyond any—and proudest of all of her royal blood, Plantagenet and Tudor mixed. Yet, for all that, she will go down the ages, I make no doubt, as the gentle innocent—she that was neither!

She had taken my sister's place with my brother; and, since courtiers forever copy their master, was the darling of the whole court. I could see my sister nowhere; and, as before, not being invited to stay, was on the point of riding home when she, herself, came seeking me.

'Sister,' she said, 'Will you walk in the garden with me?'

So out we went into the summer garden, roses and picotees sweet upon the air, the river running green beneath full-leaved branches.

She looked peaked, a small frown between the brows. She came to the point at once. 'Our cousin Jane Grey is too much in favour!' she said.

'It is natural,' I told her. 'She and our brother are of one age. You are a grown woman now—going on for nineteen. To fourteen that seems old indeed!' I thought her jealous, and not unnaturally; she had been everything to him and I meant to spare her pride.

She made a small impatient gesture. 'It is not *that*! What troubles me is another friendship—where none ever was before. Northumberland and Jane Grey's father. Why this sudden friendship? Why the great new title?'

'I've asked myself that and can find no answer!'

'Why should Northumberland give so great a plum to that simpleton? Northumberland gives nothing for nothing! No! When he gives, he means to get more back in return. *What?*' She smote her two hands together. 'Our cousin's not an able man; he isn't even honest —except when it pays him to be. But he *is* Jane's father. *He's Jane's father!* I don't like this friendship. I don't *like* it!'

What—if anything—lay behind her suspicions? I remembered how, when we had last spoken together, her own name had been linked with Northumberland's. She had disliked him then; could that same dislike be blinding her now? Or was it that, sharper by far than I, she had allowed some monstrous suspicion to take possession of her?

I was about to question her when her hand gripped upon my arm so that I felt the pinch of it through the stuff of my sleeve.

'Look!' and there was a hiss to her voice. 'What do you make of *that*?'

Our cousin Jane Grey had appeared at the far end of the garden; she was walking with a tall youth, her face turned upwards towards him.

'Who's the lad?' My short sight could not place him at this distance.

'It's Dudley. Guildford Dudley.'

'Northumberland's boy? Betrothed it would seem by the look of them!'

'Not yet,' she said. 'Not *yet*. . . .'

'And a pretty pair they make!' And I meant it, never thinking what such a betrothal might mean to me. All I could see was a comely boy and girl in love.

'A pretty pair, indeed! There's mischief brewing. I don't like her. I don't trust her. Do you?'

'I hardly know her!'

'Oh she's quiet enough and sweet enough; but underneath she's *sly*. Why has her father brought her up from the country?'

'To find her a husband. And this explains the new friendship with Northumberland.'

'Exactly.' And her voice had a sour edge.

'Why not? The girl must marry.'

'Sister, you are too good to live!' And it was not meant for a compliment.

'Would that were true!'

'I'd not wish that for myself. I mean to *live*! *How* I shall live!' Her arms went out in a sort of ecstasy, her small breasts rose. It was as though she offered herself to life.

Her moment passed. She said, very urgent, 'Sister, ask her to visit you!'

I stared at her.

'Find what she's about!'

'What *should* she be about?'

She said very patient and, in that patience, showing her exasperation, 'I might guess; but my guess could be wrong and I'd not influence you in the matter. You are the honestest woman I know. Keep her under your eye; what you report of her I shall believe.'

'Your wits are sharper than mine; and you have her here, close to your hand!'

'Would to God I might have her *in* my hand!' She made a closed fist so that the knuckles shone white. 'Oh she pursues me with her shy offers of friendship—very humble. Humble—she? She's proud as

374

Lucifer. Whatever she thinks right—is right. She's a Protestant—and lets the whole world know it!'

'And you?' I asked, a little sharp.

'I am open to reason—always,' she said, careful. 'She—never! Sweet Christ! I weary of her and her friendship. Friendship! Speak with her and she buttons up that little mouth and says—nothing. She trusts me no more than I trust her!'

Two of a feather—but who the cleverer?

'Madam, sister; ask her, *ask* her!'

'I will think on it!'

My sister's words stuck in my mind—a thorn to prick. I reckoned over the things she had said . . . and the things she had not said.

I sent for Anne of Cleves; both her honesty and her wits I could trust.

'You know Northumberland's son and Jane Grey are betrothed?' I asked.

She nodded; and I caught a hint of disturbance in her eyes.

'My sister is troubled . . . and you, too, it seems.'

She nodded. 'This betrothal let us consider together! If the lord King should die . . .'

'Then Northumberland must make an end of me. He has been an enemy to my faith and to myself. So another must be found to wear the crown. . . .'

She said nothing; and I went stumbling on.

'Someone obedient to his will. He thought first of my sister—and then he thought again. Of all women in the world she's least likely to bend to his will. He must find someone more docile—someone that stands near the throne. And who but Jane Grey, so quiet, so humble; royal Tudor, royal Plantagenet . . .'

My mind took a leap.

'In his will my father left the succession—failing his own children—to my cousin Frances . . .'

'. . . mother to Jane Grey!' Anne finished that sentence for me.

'Or to her descendants!' I added slowly.

'Jane Grey,' Anne repeated the name.

'We never gave it another thought,' I said. 'We were not like to die, all three of us, before we could reach the throne. And if we did? The descendant of his elder sister that married the King of Scots comes first. The little Mary Stuart. For the crown comes in rightful succession; it cannot be willed away!'

'I think it can. Your Parliament did give your father leave. But—if not?' She shrugged. 'What the man Northumberland wants—he takes. No question of *cannot*.'

So forced to concede more than a little to my sister's suspicions and remembering her request, I sent for Jane Grey to visit me. I knew almost nothing of her; she had, of course, lived in Catherine Parr's household but she'd been such a child—my brother's age! I have always loved children but with her I could make no headway. A shy little mouse; so I had thought. Now I was not so sure. Lately—apart from my sister's suspicions and those I tried to put from me—the things I heard about her I did not like. Ardent in the reformed worship and in that ardour unbending, she was the last person I wanted in my house where we were once more quietly practising the true form of worship. But my sister had earnestly desired it; and she was one to do nothing without a reason. So I invited my cousin, hoping and believing she would not come.

But come she did. I was at Beaulieu and it was July when she arrived. In spite of everything, the moment I set eyes upon her pretty face my dislike melted—she was myself when young. Yet she seemed to me too quiet, too still, too watchful; my sister's word *sly* I would not, at first, admit. I think she was as unwilling a guest as I a host. She had been constrained to come, though I did not know it then, sent by her father or Northumberland, maybe, to spy out the land.

I tried to like her. God knows I did try. But for all her pretty deference, I sensed in her a will inflexible as my sister's. Northumberland would not find her easy to handle. Nor did she seem to me a girl in love. She never mentioned young Dudley's name, never blushed at the sound of it, nor seemed pleased to talk of him. Remembering what hung upon that betrothal of hers, I did try once or twice; but I am not one to force a confidence and I gave up trying. There was, indeed, little we could talk of together—I was old enough to be her mother. The one thing she would talk about was her faith—and then it was I that withdrew. I did not want my words carried back to Westminster.

In spite of her shy and pretty ways she could speak her mind like a rude child. Such speech we may look for in a child; but the child grows beyond it. In Jane, I believe it was not lack of tact but deliberate rudeness.

Her first piece of rudeness came early in her visit. She was, as I have said, a pretty thing, but always plain-dressed; she preferred it, she

376

said. Well that might be! But did she prefer the silk of her gowns rubbed and faded and cracked? I thought of my own girlhood, before my father's anger fell upon me, and the rich gowns I had loved; and I thought of myself after his anger had fallen and how the very look of my poor gowns had added to my misery, my humiliation. And I thought of my sister that went demure and elegant, every least of her gowns perfect. The Grey family had never been rich; and the new dukedom—no doubt well paid for—had strained their resources. I thought how charming Jane would look in a new gown and I sent her one. Cloth-of-gold it was, cut very plain, the only ornament fine parchment lace at neck and sleeves. A beautiful gown—rich and elegant and simple; well-suited to so young a girl.

My Comptroller that took it, told me how it had been received. 'She looked at it, Madam, and her brows went up!'

Fine arched brows in a blank face; I knew that look!

'She said, "I pray you take it back again. Such a gown is not for me. My humble thanks to your lady for her kind thought!"' And, as he stood without her door, the gown upon his arm, he heard her laugh; that pretty laugh of hers, her voice very clear, *It would be shame to follow the lady Mary against God's Word and leave my lady Elizabeth that follows it!* And he heard her laugh again. 'And, Madam, I think she meant me to hear them—words and laughter, both, and carry them back to you!'

Well, she was within her rights to refuse, though the refusal might have been more courteous. But why had she brought my sister into the matter? Was she resolving to set sister against sister? And had those been her orders?

She had hurt nothing but my pride. It was her second piece of rudeness that went deep. None could doubt her intention; by deliberate intent it happened in my own chapel.

It was Susan Clarencieux, that had charge of my young ladies, told me; she was much offended.

'As we left the chapel, little Jane Dormer curtseyed before the high altar. Jane Grey perfectly knows the reason; yet she must ask, all wide-eyed innocence, "Is the lady Mary here?"'

'Knowing full well I lay abed with a migraine!'

'When she received the answer she expected, she asks in that little-girl voice of hers, "Then why do you curtsey?"'

'"I curtsey to God that made me, Jane Dormer says."'

'"Did not the baker bake him?" Jane Grey asks all sweet wonder. She was laughing at us all, and at our blessed faith. I am not quick with

my hands but my fingers itched to slap that sweet innocent face. But—'
and she shrugged, 'we stood both of us in the house of God!'

'We must bear with her; to quarrel could make trouble for us all.
My sister says not to trust her.'

'Your sister is shrewd beyond her years!' Clarencieux said.

A guest in my house and she openly insulted my faith. I gave up
trying to like her, I matched her coldness with my own; but mine,
at least, was courteous. Old Clarencieux and young Elizabeth had
alike judged her—one that loved me and one that did not; shrewd
judges, both. And with their judgment I must agree. Jane Grey was
self-righteous, stiff-necked, impertinent and sly. I breathed more free
when she was gone.

That year of 'fifty-two was the last quiet year I was ever to know.

In the autumn came my lord bishop of London to persuade me to
the new prayer book. If any might persuade me it must have been
Nicholas Ridley; for he came not to browbeat nor to threaten, nor
yet to make dissension. He came in peace to save my soul.

Courtesy breeds courtesy. I was gentle; but I would not listen to
him. He looked at me and I could see his grief. His concern was not
only for his faith but for me, for me myself; and for the country whose
crown I might soon wear—for there was no happy news of my brother's
health. This was no chequer-board bishop to be moved about in a
political game; he went from me all-but broken-hearted. Yet a man
so strong in his own faith should have known his errand hopeless from
the start.

And now I waited for further messengers, further commands,
further bullying and threats. But the days went by with nothing to
break their peace. For, my brother continuing in poor health, the
Council deemed it wise not to anger one that might soon be in a
position to punish them.

The winter, too, was peaceful. We worshipped according to the
old, true rites and our congregation grew ever larger. In view of my
brother's illness I should have read significance in this; but I am a
simple woman; the significance passed me by. I thought, only, *The
word of God triumphs*.

Chapter Fifty

The new year came in. Fifteen hundred and fifty-three. That most fateful of years, cutting clean through my life as with a sword; or as a new channel forces a river in a quite different direction.

Yet it came in quiet enough. I was at Hunsdon; there had been no Christmas celebrations on account of my brother's sickness; but there had been extra alms, extra prayers. All too soon it was February—my birthday month. I tried to forget my years; but the years themselves reminded me. I was thirty-seven.

That same February, though winds were bitter, roads packed hard with frozen mud, and myself unwell, I rode—again unasked—for Westminster to see with my own eyes how it fared with my brother. In spite of the cruel weather, in town and village, folk stood to see me pass. The quality of their greeting had, I thought, changed. It was less the light-hearted love shown to a prince than the respect shown to a crowned King. I thought, maybe, I was mistaken, that my fears coloured my thoughts; but in London it was the same—a quiet and sorrowful show of respect. There were blessings and some cheering but all was subdued and solemn as though already the people wore black upon their arms.

If I had thought to have misinterpreted these greetings I was in no doubt as to their rightness as I took my way to Westminster. Very different my reception from my summer journey! For there came riding out to meet me a great train of ladies, and at their head—who but Northumberland's wife, Madam Duchess herself; and with her that other new duchess—mother to Jane Grey. Here was surprise, indeed! And behind them came riding the great ladies of England, marchionesses and countesses three-a-penny! And all hastening to show respect —to whom? Could it be to the rising star?

Not a doubt of it! For when leading the great procession I arrived at the palace itself, it was not a solitary Comptroller that stood there bareheaded. It was Northumberland, my lord Protector himself, and all his Council behind him; and all bonnets sweeping the ground.

Once I should have taken pleasure in this deference but now I had no stomach for it; I had still less when I set eyes upon my brother.

He sat in the great chair, padded doublet hanging loose upon his wasted frame, his legs thin and without strength as though the hose were stuffed with rags and not good flesh-and-blood. He sat limp as a puppet, upright only because fixed in his place by the number of cushions. But the head made his extreme weakness only too plain; it drooped to his neck, he could not hold it upright. Northumberland stood at his right hand; his physician—and I could not miss the significance of that—at his left. As I knelt at his feet I saw that he was iller, even, than I had thought. If he had been over-thin before, now he was emaciated; no flesh beneath the skin, and the skin itself stretched so tight you could see the skull beneath. The face, all pearled with sweat, was dead-white save for a spot of red that burned high on his cheekbones, and for the scabs that marred his comeliness—for he was not yet healed of the pox. The unhealed scabs a little comforted me—reminder that, since his illness, time was young. But the fire burning upon his cheeks mocked at this comfort, and so did his over-bright eyes. He was in a high fever and should have been in his bed.

But for all that his understanding was clear. He held out a hand to be kissed and I saw the fleshless bones white through the translucent skin. *Poor child! Poor child!* My heart beat out the words. To me he was no longer the King; he was a sick child, my godchild, the small brother that I loved.

He was, I fancied, pleased to see me. He greeted me with a faint smile; and then, as if at some wordless command, his eyes went slowly to Northumberland and the smile left his face. Eyes still upon Northumberland, his nod, barely perceptible, dismissed me.

Northumberland went with me to the door. 'The King should be abed,' I said at once.

He spread his hands. 'The lord King grows wilful with sickness!' he said, liar that he was! For in his last weakness my brother was utterly subservient to the man's will.

'Westminster is no place for him!' I said. 'Too much noise; too much coming and going. And the air from the river is sometimes foul, and the damp chokes in his lungs. He should be in the country.'

'Does Madam the Princess Mary think that will make him well again?' There was a mocking under-current both in the question and in the use of my title; he had never so named me before.

Within four-and-twenty hours my brother was removed from Westminster; but not into the country. They had carried him to

Whitehall where there was no more quiet than at Westminster, nor more freshness in the air nor less damp from the river.

'If he is not to be taken into the country they had done better to bring him here!' I told my sister, for we were lodging in St. James's—a quieter house, not so exposed to river-mists.

'Bring him where we two are staying? Give his sisters freedom to come to him?' Her smile was both bitter and sad. 'Northumberland will not let us near him!'

'Keep us from our brother . . . and he so sick?'

'Oh sister, sister!' She was half-pitying, half-impatient. 'It is because he *is* so sick! If you are to be Queen you must learn to catch the whisper in the mind before it find tongue in word or deed!'

I stared at her, so young, so wise. But, *if you are to be Queen . . .*!

'To be Queen; not yet, please God, not yet!'

She said nothing; but her eyes said all.

She was right. We were not let near our brother.

Day by day we waited. Northumberland forever sent his reassuring messages. *The lord King grows stronger. . . . The lord King walks in the garden. . . . The lord King is better . . . is better . . . is better. . . .*

To the messenger my sister said nothing; but when he was gone: 'Then why do we not see him?' she cried out, passionate. 'Why? Why? Why? I will tell you why! Because it is all a lie. He grows not better but worse!'

'We shall be kept no longer from him,' I said. 'I am minded to see for myself!'

I remember the day we rode over to Whitehall. At the great entrance the way was barred; not by crossed halberds but by the lord Protector himself bowing very low and requesting a moment of our company. So we went with him into his private room and very splendid it was; the place, I suppose, where he received ambassadors and the like. And there he faced us, Northumberland that ruled all England, including the King and the King's sisters; and, it seemed, life and death itself.

'Madam Princess,' and he bent the knee to me, 'the King's physicians are of opinion that you should wait a little longer. Soon you shall see him again. It will not be long now!'

Those last words had an ominous sound. I saw Elizabeth, that proud girl, hold out her hands to him, hands clasped in prayer; I had never seen her weep before; but now tears ran down her cheeks into her mouth. He looked through her as though she were glass; but she looked at him very steady, as though she saw and could not believe what she saw—the purpose in that smiling face of his. I saw her lift a finger to her wet eyes and bend to the table. I saw her write in her tears *For all my long waiting I go without that I came for.*

He did not so much as look at what she had written; written in her tears. She lifted her head and again fixed her eyes upon his. The silent passage between them was frightening.

He shall pay for this! I swore it to myself and did not know that already I had accepted my brother's death.

And now, as if to make clear to me that acceptance, there was a constant press of folk in St. James's, the whole court coming to kneel before me, to offer me royal homage. When I rode abroad, ladies and gentlemen rode with me, headed by Northumberland himself. But why Northumberland if he purposed me ill? Could it be that I had all this time misread him; and that my sister was wrong in her suspicions? No! We were right; we were right but she, not I, had plumbed the depths of his treachery. For there he was all smiles and reverence, his Council behind him, so that I rode in such state as was none of my seeking. And from the country the gentry rode in —those of the new faith as well as the old. I had known nothing like this since those far-off days when I was my father's only child and his undoubted heir.

Elizabeth, too, showed a new and startling reverence. Though never loving she had always paid the respect due to an older sister—neither more nor less. Now, like the others, she would have saluted me upon her knees; but I would, by no means, allow it. 'The lord King is not dead!' I cried out all sharp with my fears.

'No,' she said, 'not yet. . . .' She had a forlorn look these days, her young face sharpened by grief, those great eyes sunk in dark hollows. She was one to love seldom but greatly; when she set her passionate heart it could be forever.

And still we were not let to see our brother.

'Nor shall we ever,' my sister said. 'Never again.' And then she said, 'Northumberland that bars the way will bar it to the end.'

Yet still we heard tales of returning health . . . *The lord King waved to the crowd from his window and they cheered him with loving cries. . . . The King met Boisdolphin the French ambassador and they discussed affairs. . . .*

'Lies! Lies!' my sister cried out, bitter. 'Yes, our brother *was* at the window and the people *did* cheer. But Northumberland, may God damn him, took him from his bed sick as he was and held him against the window for the people to see . . . it might have been a dead boy for all the crowd knew! As for the French ambassador—he went into the presence chamber and no-one was there, no-one except Northumberland. To hoodwink the people—those two are in the plot together!'

'What plot?'

'I think to give Northumberland time. . . .'

'For what?'

'To complete a treaty with France before . . .'

No need for her to finish. My brother was sick to death . . . and I had never loved France.

'Boisdolphin is no man's fool. He doesn't trust Northumberland. He doesn't believe it's merely a question of making peace with France before you, sister, wear the crown. He's another that doesn't like this new friendship between Northumberland and Jane Grey's father. . . .'

And how did she know all this, the formidable girl?

She answered that question, unasked.

'His secretary told me so—the ambassador's private secretary himself! I can coax a secret out of any man!' And in that moment her eyes were her mother's eyes; Anne Bullen's eyes.

Two days later she sought me out. 'Sister, we do our brother no good staying; and ourselves much harm. I am for the country and my own house; and, for you, it would be wise, also. I smell danger to us both!'

'Go if you will,' I said. 'My duty is here.'

'Your duty,' she said, 'is to keep yourself alive. That is best done in your own house. In this place you must always be a step ahead of the enemy.'

'What enemy? If our brother die—which God forbid—there'll be no more Protector; there'll be a Queen.'

'*What* Queen?'

'There's but one Queen!' And in face of the behaviour of all, and Northumberland in particular—as though I were already Queen, the old suspicion made nonsense. 'My father's will; have you forgot it?'

'I remember it. And Northumberland remembers it.'

'Now, sister, you are indeed a step behind the times. Once he was my enemy; but not now. He recognises my right and shows it everywhere. Oh,' and I smiled, I actually smiled, 'he knows which side his bread is buttered!'

'He does, indeed!' Suddenly she cried out, 'Sister, sister, do you not *see*! He'll move heaven and earth to keep you from the crown. And once you knew it! But now—' she spread her empty hands, 'let a man wear a smiling face and you believe his heart goes with it. Madam, you are too honest for your own good. That man has sought your death and trampled upon your faith. He cannot afford to let you live, let alone come to the throne! He will choose his own Queen—believe it!' She caught at my hand; in that moment she was desperately truthful; truthful and true.

'Stay—and you'll lose the crown and your head with it! Our brother is going to die; for him I make one prayer only—that Northumberland let him die in peace. But it will not be allowed. He'll be kept adying until he give that man his way. Only then will he be let to die. But we shall not see him; not ever again.' Her voice shook. 'We shall not even know *when* he dies or where; we shall know nothing until it serve that man's purpose. Go away, sister—as I mean to go. And stay away! And if Northumberland send—even though it be in the King's name—stay away; as I shall stay away!'

She caught at my other hand and lifted them both to her breast so that I felt the beating of her wild heart. 'Sister, keep from the court. *If Northumberland send, do not go!*'

She kept her word—and no time lost. That afternoon she rode for Hatfield. She knew what she knew; she could coax a secret from a man's very breast. She could sense trouble before ever it cast its shadow—a Queen's gift; and one, alas, denied to me. She had been urgent with me and honest; hers was a warning I dared not ignore.

I rode home. At Hunsdon I waited; at Hatfield, Elizabeth waited. And still Northumberland sent his reassuring words. But for all that, he could not hide the fact that my brother was a very sick boy; too sick to ride the little distance to Parliament, or even to be carried thither. Parliament must come to him. That was a piece of news Northumberland could not hide.

In April they moved the King to Greenwich. *He is over the worst of his illness*—Northumberland spread it abroad; *quiet and country air will make him strong again.* And yet . . . so short a time ago he had not been able to stir from his bed. If he were truly on the mend why had I not been sent for to see him with my own eyes? Why had there been no message, if not by his own hand then by word of mouth? Was Northumberland lying? Did he mean the dying boy's obedience to the last; an obedience the boy's conscience would not permit? My sister had prayed that he might be allowed to die in peace; the only prayer she could make for him—and he but fifteen years old!

Northumberland, that implacable man, my enemy, sent me a gift, a strange gift—the blazon of my arms. Royal Princess of the house of

Tudor, no less; arms that I, proclaimed bastard since girlhood, had been forbidden to carry. Once I would have received them with utmost joy. But now? What need had I of this, I, that must, alas, so soon wear the crown itself? Why had he sent it? To win my friendship? A warning—very subtle—that the crown was not for me? I tried to put from me all thought of the crown; to think only of a young child dying; but in my mind, God and my faith and the crown and conscience were all knotted together—a knot there was no untangling.

'Why has he sent it?' I cried out to Clarencieux. 'Is it to win my favour? Or a warning, very subtle, the crown is not for me?'

'The lord King is not dead yet,' she said. 'And if we are to believe Northumberland...'

'We are not to believe him! My brother is dying; dying of what? Of poison, some say; poison at Northumberland's own hand! Well, that could be true. It could account for our being kept from him!'

She shook her head. 'A hard man, hard with ambition; and can be cruel with it. But not a monster. No! The measles and the little pox together have wasted the lord King's strength. There's some say he has a consumption also....'

'They say. They say!' And I did not add that some spread it abroad that he was hatefully dying of a rotting sickness inherited from my father's way of life. And that, God help him, could also be true! 'But we know nothing and shall know nothing until he is dead—and even then not until it please Northumberland. So my sister warned me; and, for all her few years, she has a way of being right!'

And now, to add to our distress, the air was full of rumours. My servants gathered them from the market, from wandering priests, from wandering musicians and beggars.... *The King is all-but sped. Let him breathe his last and Northumberland will seize the lady Mary and the lady Elizabeth, and make an end of them both.* And once it was, *The King is dead. Northumberland has seized the lady Elizabeth to wed to his son; the lady Mary he has taken to wed himself and make himself King....*

Who could pluck the truth out of such wild rumours? My brother, God help us all, might truly be dead; but I was safe in my own house. ... for the present. Yet they did point, these rumours, to a possibility —one that the people feared and my sister feared and that I myself feared. Nothing was impossible to this ruthless man. But from all the rumours, one thing stood out clear. Whatever he intended with regard to his own marriage, Northumberland meant to keep both hands on the crown.

In May, Whitsunday it was, Jane Grey married young Dudley.

Neither my sister nor I knew aught of the matter until some days later. And now Elizabeth's suspicions began to prick afresh; *He will choose his own Queen.* By my father's will Jane Grey stood very near the throne; and, should my brother die, stood nearer still. And if I should die, or Elizabeth—who would dispute our cousin's right to the crown? Scotland, France, on behalf of the little Mary Stuart? France was too busily engaged in war on her own account and Scotland too poor. And besides, it would all be done too quickly; Jane Grey accepted and crowned. For in England no-one would stand against Northumberland. He had made such marriages for his children that he had the most part of the Council in his pocket. Certainly it would be to his advantage and their own to make an end of my sister and me.

But my brother was not yet dead. *Christ that brought back the dead unto life, restore him!* I prayed for him unceasing. I longed, passionately, for him to live. I could not endure his young life to go down into the darkness—the darkness that is worse than death. Darkness of the lost soul.

Chapter Fifty-One

At long last Northumberland sent for me. It was the sixth day of July; and full afternoon when I received the message. *The King desires to see his sisters.* Nothing but that; yet it could mean one only thing. My brother was dying.

If Northumberland send do not go! My sister's warning rang clear, as though she stood by my side.

Was this message a trap then? If I rode to London, was I riding straight to my death?

If Northumberland send do not go! Had my sister received this same message? And what would she do? Would she go? Had she, indeed, already gone? Had she been honest with me? Had she meant to keep me from London, until she, herself, had married Northumberland and taken the crown? Was he already divorced and those two married? It was a matter they would keep secret until the right time. Was Jane Grey but a second string to his bow? My sister had not always been honest with me and she was cleverer by far than I. But I had seen her write in her tears, felt the beating of her wild heart, knew her implacable hatred for Northumberland. That time, at least, she had been true.

If Northumberland, liar and traitor, had laid his trap, I should find myself not at Greenwich but in the Tower. Yet I could not be sure. Dying and wanting me; how could I not go to this young brother, my dear son in God? Maybe even at this last I could save his soul. Let him repent but upon his dying breath, it would be enough.

I would go; but I would ride at nightfall when I should not be expected. I would go roundabout and take a boat on the Southwark side, a small, plain boat for hire. And I would ride not with a royal train but with two gentlewomen and four gentlemen, only—any lady upon a journey.

It was full dark when we rode out. The summer night was gentle and full of delicate scents, there came to me very strong the scent of dew-wet honeysuckle; and so riding amidst summer leaf and blossom I was troubled for myself, lest I rode into a trap.

And so we came into Hoddesdon which is some five miles or six from Hunsdon; we were scarce clear of the sleeping village when a horseman came spurring. He was covered with dust, he and his mare plastered with the sweat of hard-riding. I did not, at first, though the moon shone full upon him, recognise Montague, Lord Chief Justice. How should I? So old a man riding furiously alone in the dark night. He lifted a hand to wipe the dust from his face and then I knew him. He had, it seemed, brought me news; so we dismounted, he and I, and we went a little apart from the rest.

'God save the Queen!' And there, in that solitary place, he went upon both knees.

So my brother was dead! And I had not seen him. I should see him never again!

'God rest his soul!' I said; and in that first moment there was no thought in me of the crown; nothing but grief for the boy that had died in his short spring-time. He had died . . . and not one that loved him to hold his hand, to say a last word of love, of prayer, for him upon his lonely way. I wept there for the pale, proud boy that had never wept for himself. Had I known how he died, his fainting spirit bound to earth by Northumberland's cruel will, I had, I think, wept my very soul away.

'*When?*' I asked at last.

'Some few hours since.'

I stood there weeping, until Montague plucked me by the sleeve, 'I have ridden for my life; or rather for *your* life, Madam. This is no time for weeping!'

No time for weeping and my brother new-dead!

'Madam, this is, God help us, a time to move; to move before Northumberland lay hands upon you. He and his friends keep the King's death secret until it suit his purpose.'

So she had been right, my sister! We were not to know when our brother died, nor how, until Northumberland chose.

'Madam,' Montague said, 'you are in grief for your brother; you may soon be in even greater grief. It is a question of the crown; the crown itself!'

'What question? I am the Queen!'

'The King has willed away the crown.'

I put out a hand lest I fall and he caught at it, holding it within his own.

'He would not do it, nor he could not do it!' I cried out. 'The crown is mine; by right of inheritance, *mine*! My father himself acknowledged it, willed it!'

'Madam, he *has* done it. You have to thank Northumberland for this!'

'Northumberland must be mad to think the Council would allow it!'

'Madam, they *have* allowed it!'

I stared at him, not believing, 'Proof!' I told him. 'I must have proof!'

'With my own eyes I saw the thing done, with my own ears heard it. Northumberland commanded the Council into the King's bedchamber. The King was dying; not a doubt of it. He lay propped upon high pillows; he was flat and grey as a shadow and coughing his life away. The pillows were bright with his blood and the sweat poured from him.'

I listened, my bones melting with pity for this young child publicly dying . . . dying his hard death alone.

'A hard death, Madam.' He plucked the words from my thoughts. And Northumberland made it harder. He stood at the King's right hand and the physician at the other to keep the King from his release. The King was not let to die until Northumberland had his way.

'All about the room and in the ante-room we stood—the Council. Then Northumberland spoke to us. He said that you, Madam, and the lady Elizabeth were unfit to inherit. The crown must go to royal blood pure and unpolluted. The King's sisters, he told us—Madam, forgive me that I repeat so vile a thing—were bastards both!'

'And whose blood does he consider pure and unpolluted? Upon whose head would he set the crown?'

I knew my answer before ever it came.

Right again, my sister; in every judgment, every suspicion, right, right, right!

'My sister; does she know? Is she safe?'

'Madam, I sent to warn her. She'll not stir from Hatfield; it is a house well-guarded. Then, Madam. . . .' he went on with his tale, 'Northumberland cried out, "The King wills the crown to her that is most fit to receive it—the high and mighty puissant princess, the lady Jane Grey, in direct line from King Henry VII. You, my lords of the Council, are here to witness the King's will in this matter. You are to see him make his signature and thereafter to add your own.'

'I cried out then, *I am the Lord Chief Justice of England and I tell you*

it cannot be done! I knelt by the bedside to make the King understand;
but he neither saw nor heard. His dying eyes were fixed upon his
tormentor.

' "My lords," Northumberland shouted, forgetting the respect due
to any dying man, let alone a dying King, "you should think twice
before you take either of the King's bastards for your sovereign. They
will marry foreigners belike, and what shall become of us all? Shall
you welcome the foreign yoke or bare your buttocks to the whip?
From these things this good King would save us. He has chosen pure
royal blood, wife to an Englishman, one of ourselves. Only if you
sign now can you save us all from bloodshed, revolt and shame." So
then, Madam, we signed. . . .'

'*All* of you; even you, Montague?'

'All of us, Madam. Some of us were not willing; yet we thought that,
making a show of agreement, we might serve the Queen better!'

I searched his face. Could I believe him? He was of Northumberland's Council! *Is my brother truly dead? And is Montague sent to trick
me into treason, to hoodwink me into proclaiming myself while still the King
wears the crown? So many times I have been betrayed with lies. I know not
which way to turn!*

There he knelt in the dust, the old man shaking with the strain of
kneeling. I saw the slow tears gather in his eyes. One cannot weep to
order. I held out both hands to raise him.

'What must I do?' He was old, he was wise; and other counsel I had
none.

'Get you into some safe place. Thereafter proclaim yourself at once.
Every moment lost to us is gained to them. But, Madam, wherever
you may go—go not to London!'

Not to London, my own good city!

'Northumberland has made good use of his few hours! He holds
the city and the Tower. He holds the river and the Bridge—all strong-
fortified. He has the Mint and the crown jewels—and he means to have
your head, also!'

'Let him look to his own head, liar and traitor that he is! But—if
not to London—where?'

'We are on the Cambridge road. Keep from Cambridge also. In
the name of the Protestant faith he stirs the town against you!'

'Then where? *Where?* I have none to counsel me but you! I have no
men, no arms—Northumberland has them all. I have no money—'
and I held out my empty hands.

'Madam, you have three things Northumberland would give his

soul to possess. You have the right. You have the people's love. You have your faith in God. And you have one thing more. You have your own great heart. Councillors, men and money God will provide. He will not forsake you!

'Now, Madam, you must make for Sawston—the house of Master Huddleston, a true Catholic gentleman. It is a goodish way—some twenty miles by road. But you may save five miles or so if you ride cross-country.'

'The distance is no great odds—our mounts are fresh; but—cross-country? How shall we find our way in the dark night?'

'I have a man will take you, Madam. You should get there well before dawn. I have sent a man ahead to warn Huddleston of your coming. You may trust all three with your life. But, Madam, make no delay at Sawston. A safe place for a rest; but not a house for defence. And Northumberland's orders are to take you, alive or dead. Make for one of your own houses with all speed and every care; one of your Norfolk houses. Norfolk men know you well and Norfolk hearts are true. And, Madam, as soon as you are safe in your own house wait for nothing—proclaim yourself at once. Wait neither for men nor arms— you'll not, I warrant you, wait long! But to proclaim yourself at once—that, Madam, is a matter of life and death!'

'It is good advice. My lord, do you go with us?'

'No, Madam. I ride for London to rouse the Londoners. Northumberland may have city and Tower, Bridge and river—but not their hearts; he is a man much hated. It is you, Madam, that London loves. I go, also, to press the Imperial ambassadors to move the Emperor on your behalf!'

I looked at his jaded mare and he smiled.

'Fresh mounts await me along the road; it is all planned for!'

He gave a low whistle and from the darkness came a fellow leading his mount.

'My lord, I have nothing; not even words to express my soul's thanks. God willing, I shall, one day, do better!'

'I ask no better than to serve my Queen. And so God go with you and keep you safe.'

So back along the road I had come and on to the Royston road with my small company and then, in a little while, turned into open country; and all the while fearful of those that might lie in wait in the dark night to take me alive or dead. But the moon lit our way and the country was flat enough and our mounts fresh. And as I rode, I considered of my plans.

I would ride on the morrow for Kenninghall. There I would raise my standard and gather my friends; thence to Framlingham, my own house also. A very great house with strong walls and towers, the whole enclosed by a triple moat.

And so we came in the dark of the morning safe to Sawston. And while I sat my mount, wondering how with least disturbance we might make our arrival known, there came from the shadows the master himself and gave us warm welcome.

When we had supped I told him of my plans. 'Madam,' he said. 'If I may be so bold to counsel you! Kenninghall is too far for one day's journey and too dangerous. You have no company with you. You had best ride to Hengrave; it is on your way. . . .'

'And is like to be the end of my way! It is lord Bath's place; he's one of Northumberland's Council!'

'No longer! Madam, the messenger that brought news of your coming, brought other news, also. Bath has left the Council. He witnessed the King's will because he could not help himself. But he'll have no truck with traitors. Madam, I took upon myself the liberty of sending to Hengrave. My lord is at home and offers himself and his son to your service.'

'God raises up my friends!' I told him.

Night was at an end, dawn breaking. I had no mind for sleep; fatigue I did not, at that moment, feel. I must be up and on my way! So I heard Mass and broke my fast; and then came my host bringing with him a gown such as a lower servant might wear. 'Madam the Queen would do well to wear my poor livery. It shall, God willing, bring you to safety. And, Madam, if I might counsel you further. Send your own people to Kenninghall by a different road. Ride with one man only—the man I shall send with you. You may trust him; his heart is my own in the matter.'

'Sir, there is great wisdom in this. God does, indeed, send friends for my comfort!'

So I bade farewell to the rest of my company and off I went, alone with the serving-man. Riding my humble mare I looked anything but a Queen, being no better suited than the humble fellow that rode with me; and for the first time I thanked God that had made me small and in no way remarkable. Me you could hide in a poor gown; my sister, never!

We had ridden but a little when I turned to look at the kind house that had sheltered me. In the grey of the morning flames leaped and licked; black smoke cast streamers across the sky. I guessed that some unfaithful servant had carried news of my last night's coming; and that soldiers from Cambridge, arrived to carry me away, finding their bird flown, had taken revenge upon the house. I was sad for good Master Huddleston; and angry, too—for wanton destruction always angers me. I should, I resolved, build him as goodly a house, to console him a little for the house he had lost.

Now, as we crossed the border into Suffolk, there came a band of horsemen with intent to take me; and their captain—who but my old friend John Sulyard? My heart fainted within me; too often I had known the anguish of friends turned false.

We looked one at the other and his face gave no sign.

'Good fellow,' and he addressed himself to the servant, 'we seek the lady Mary; have you seen her upon the road?'

'Neither hoof nor hide, sir!' The answer came quick and with such disrespect as must allay the suspicions of those that rode with Sir John. 'We did hear, though, sir, that she took the road to Cambridge!'

So away went Sir John in the direction from which he had come and we set spurs to our horses and so came safe to Hengrave Hall. And there stood my lord Bath, John Bouchier himself!

'Thanks be to God that has brought you safe, Madam,' he said, and himself led my mare into the stable.

'Will it please the Queen's grace to rest here this night?' he asked. 'I have sent out my summons but some of my men come from a distance. They will be here by tomorrow and we shall all march with you.'

And to that I was glad to agree; not only because I was weary with hard riding—and no sleep the night before; but because it seemed to me a sound piece of wisdom. We talked together and he told me that, of all those who had signed to witness the King's will, the most part were unwilling—and especially the judges. Only those that were Northumberland's kin, or that hoped to better themselves thereby, had signed with a willing heart. As for my lord Bath, himself, he had left London with his son, they having no wish to see the usurper proclaimed.

Thereafter he led me to a fine chamber; but I could not rest, at first, for thinking of my dead brother and of Northumberland that had not let him die in peace. And I thought of my sister and wondered where she stood in this. . . . Very quiet, in her own house, I supposed, till she saw which way the battle went. And I remembered Jane Grey that carried herself so meek and was yet stubborn and most proud; and I remembered her rudeness to me that had sent her a pretty gown;

and her blasphemy towards the blessed Host. Afterwards when she lay in prison she blamed her parents; they had beaten her senseless, she said, so that for her very life she must consent to Northumberland's treason. But I knew her better than that! No pain of body could bend that spirit. She was self-willed beyond most and ambitious with it. Oh she made much of her unwillingness for the crown; and because she was young and went early to her death, there were many to believe her. Yes, certainly, she will go down in history—the gentle innocent.

Jane Grey to wear my crown; Jane Grey arch-heretic and traitor! Never while the heart beat in my body!

Next day we set out with an escort of knights and squires and simple serving-men. A small force; but enough to protect me at need. Now I rode openly and unafraid; and as we rode there came men to join us, and women to offer us meat and drink for the journey; simple and gentle alike, all loyal hearts.

It was late in the evening when we reached Kenninghall and at once I raised my standard; and, this being done, Sir Thomas Wharton, good steward, good friend, rode the countryside to advertise men of my cause.

Having thanked God for His goodness in bringing me thus far in safety, I sat down to write to the Council. A hard letter to write. I must, at one and the same time, demand their loyalty, remind them of their treason, yet assure them of pardon.

I said *we*—for the first time using the royal *we*—found it strange, indeed, that the King, our brother, had died and we had not been informed. I said we knew well their plotting to upset our father's will and our just claim to the crown. But, to avoid bloodshed, we were,

. . . right ready to fully pardon the same. Wherefore, my lords, we require and charge you, and every one of you that, of your allegiance which you owe to God and to us and to none other, you cause our right and title to the crown and governance of this realm to be proclaimed in our city of London and in other places, as in your wisdom it shall seem good. . . .

A long, long letter. I wrote steadily through the night, scratching out here and there and making additions until I was satisfied to make a fair copy. And so I came to the end.

Given under our signet at our manor of
Kenninghall. . . .

I raised my eyes and daylight was grey in the room. I had written the night through. And so I signed my name and the date,

this ninth day of July, 1553.

And that being done, I commanded masses for my brother's soul— prayers of that faith he had sought to destroy. God, I believed—as still I do—would show mercy to one driven always by the will of others; whose short life had been heavy and full of pain. I had forgiven him; should the God of Mercy show less kindness than I?

And now I must wait in fear and in hope for the reply; mostly I waited in fear.

Two days brought me my answer; and it was worse even than the worst of my fears.

. . . We have received your letter declaring your supposed title— which you judge yourself to have—to the imperial crown of this realm. For answer, thereof, this is to advertise you that our sovereign lady Queen Jane is, after the death of our sovereign lord Edward VI, invested and possessed with the just and right titles of the imperial crown of this realm, not only by the good order of the ancient laws of this realm but also by our late sovereign lord sealed with the great seal of England in the presence of the great part of the nobles, councillors and judges assenting and subscribing to the same. . . .

And that last was a plain lie. For my lord Chief Justice had protested and the judges been unwilling; and of the Council, some had been unwilling, also. It was Northumberland's mind I read in every hateful word; for the shameful letter went on to remind me of the divorce between my father and mother; and the reason whereof, whereby I was

justly made illegitimate and therefore uninheritable to the crown.

They announced their intention of true faith and allegiance to her they called Queen Jane; and—final insult,

If you will show yourself quiet and obedient as you ought, you shall find us ready to do you any service and will be glad of your quietness to preserve the common state of the realm wherein you may be otherwise grievous to us, to yourself and to the realm.

It was signed by every member of the Council and dated July 10th.
I am a mild woman with now and again a sharp tongue. But now I was, for the first time, possessed of a truly royal Tudor rage; the

spirit of my father fell upon me. Such anger I had never known in all my life . . . *the supposed title you judge yourself to have* . . . the usurper's *just and rightful title*; the old wretched tale of my parents' divorce and my bastardy. And finally the threat, for it was none other, that I must remain quiet beneath my injuries, roused in me the uttermost anger—a red-hot, boiling fury that must out, lest the body it housed burst itself into a thousand pieces.

Quiet! Remain quiet while they blackened my mother's honour, stained my birth and put that heretic in my place! Civil war there might well be—which God avert; but none of my making. I would fight; and the end should see me a dead woman or a crowned Queen.

Chapter Fifty-Two

This letter was but a harbinger of blacker news.

On July the ninth, that same day I had written to the Council, Jane Grey left her home in Chelsea for Syon House; that house whence my sister and I had been turned to make room for a young Queen to go hence to her death. Now Jane Grey had come to this house—her first step, also, towards death.

But now all was joy and triumph. The house was one of those that Northumberland had taken for his own use; leaving Greenwich Palace to the dead boy, he moved the court to Richmond—a stone's throw from Syon. Into this house, Northumberland, Arundel and Pembroke in attendance, the usurper came in royal state. There, in the presence of the Council assembled, Northumberland broke to her the news of the King's death—broke it officially; she must have known it already. How else had she been prepared for her proclamation? Northumberland would never have risked it; he was not a man to take chances.

I doubt not, also, she had been well rehearsed for her part. She wept at the news; and her tears may well have been genuine. Who would not weep at the death of the ill-starred boy? And, it is not unlikely that, for all her ambition, she feared the weight of the crown. I, myself, bred in childhood to know that I must accept my task, I, in direct accession and more than twice her age, trembled before the hallowed burden.

Then, she weeping still, the Council knelt before her praying her in the name of God, the late King and the people, to take the crown. And she, eyes still wet, yet smiling through her tears, stretched out her hand to be kissed, swearing she had no wish for the crown but must hold herself obedient to God's Will and the will of the people.

The next day, in royal robes, she went by water to the Tower, thence, like all new sovereigns, to ride through London and show herself to the people.

Hour by hour the messengers rode in; and always the news was black.

'Madam, the usurper came to London in royal state; she came in the royal barge itself. But there were few upon the water or on the banks to give her welcome. She landed at the King's stairs; traitor Northumberland knelt to welcome her, and the lady, her mother, carried the train. Into the Tower she went. . . .'

Into the Tower of her own will; there she shall stay for mine!

'Madam she is feasted and fêted. The lord Treasurer has put the crown jewels into her hand. And not only the jewels but the crown, the crown itself. She stood there, Madam, holding the crown in her hand. My lord Arundel urged her to put it upon her head, to see how it should fit and become her. She refused at the first; but soon, being persuaded, she bent her head and Northumberland put the crown thereon.'

Now she bends her head to the crown; soon she shall bend it to the block.

'Then, Madam, Northumberland told her that, by the will of the Council, there was to be a crown for her husband, also. She took fire at that! No! she cried out. A duke he may be but never a King! No crown for him; no crown! Northumberland was clearly taken aback and the Council looked from one to another—they did not think she had it in her. They say the lady, her husband's mother, is much incensed and that the young Dudley refuses her his bed. But she is constant to refuse!'

So much for the sweet and gentle girl! A husband is as God to a woman; wedding him she weds the church, and through the church, God. Selfish and presumptuous she showed herself in this, also. Northumberland, I thought, again, would get little good of her!

On that same day, the tenth of July, in the year of grace fifteen hundred and fifty-three, she went, the usurper, royally robed, riding through London—my London; and with her, the lord mayor come to hand her the keys of the city; behind him his aldermen and his high officers.

I cried out at that and the messenger said, 'Madam, they had no choice. Immediately the King's death was known, Northumberland sent for the lord mayor to Richmond and then and there forced him to swear allegiance in the name of the city to the usurping Queen.'

Certainly Northumberland had made use of his few hours! London's heart I might have but he held the whip!

'Madam, into every street the heralds went with trumpet to proclaim her title. . . .'

'And . . .?' *How did my London accept it?*

'She passed in silence. The archers and the heralds were left to cheer alone!'

Northumberland might hold the whip; but I held London's heart.

That same night, the usurper, and those that had made her so, feasting in the Tower, my letter was handed to Northumberland. He opened it and at once left the table. My lady Suffolk, her mother, and my lady of Northumberland her mother-in-law, catching sight of his face and knowing their own treachery, wept and could not stay their tears; but Jane, herself, sat composed though pale, until supper was ended. Then Northumberland sought her in her closet. He was much shaken; he had not expected my defiance, he had all the cards in his hand, I, nothing but my right and the people's love. And I am so small, so mild a person—he did not think I had it in me! But I am my father's daughter; that he forgot in his reckoning.

He had brought with him a proclamation to be signed by Jane Grey herself. It announced her 'true right' to the throne, it called upon the people to defend her 'just' title, to help her in her 'rightful possession' of the Kingdom and to

repel and resist the feigned and untrue claim of the lady Mary, bastard daughter to our great-uncle Henry the Eighth of famous memory.

I do not doubt her word that the letter had been written for her; and she may even have been reluctant to sign it. But sign it she did Jane Regina; as Queen she signed it.

This writing, the printer's ink still fresh upon it, was put into my hand later that same day of July the eleventh. The infamous document lies by me, as I write, and though it is five years since she that signed it came to her death, yet even now I shake at this insult to my most dear mother trumpeted throughout the land. For not London alone, but every town and village throughout the country, every market-place, church door and guildhall carried the lying slander.

Bastard and papist. At Paul's Cross, Ridley, that had once been so gentle, thundered against me; in Buckinghamshire the heretic John Knox prophesied *Woe, woe to England if she ally herself with the enemy of God and the true gospel.*

The usurper had been proclaimed and I, branded bastard. Northumberland's men were searching to bring me in alive or dead. The Protestant church declared me enemy to God. At this lowest point of fear and disaster, worse news could not be! And so it proved. For as soon as the country had time to draw breath, to understand Northumberland's treason, every hour increased the number of my friends.

Bastard and papist. The missiles fell short. Those that had known and loved my mother held me true-born; and papist? The reformed worship was still so new that many in their hearts longed for the old rites and the safety of obedience to Rome.

I had not yet proclaimed myself. I had hoped that the Council, having considered my letter, knowing their treason yet being offered free and full pardon, would come to their senses and themselves proclaim me. Now this hope being lost I dared wait no longer. I had myself proclaimed; and everywhere—save among the traitors—the proclamation was received with joy. Joy there was; but in some places, those that must look to the safety of the people—mayors and their officials—judged it right to keep silent. But for all that, men came steadily into my cause—from my own Norfolk they came, from Cheshire and from Buckinghamshire where sour Mr. Knox still sought to curdle loyalty. And from Shropshire that had known me as the young Princess of Wales, from Somerset and far Devon, men were on the march. They came in, gentle and simple alike, at their own cost, even to the poorest, casting aside their work and bringing with them what food they could lay hand upon and what weapons. I had nothing for them but my heart's thanks, for in my purse there was nothing.

Every hour saw the increase of my friends and soon I could choose experienced men to sit upon my Council so that I, being unskilled in policies, might lean upon their wisdom. From London came my lord Chief Justice bringing his news. Northumberland had commanded a great muster to meet at Tothill Fields, thence to march into Norfolk and make a quick end of me. 'But, Madam, the temper of the people is such they will, I think, refuse to carry out their orders.' But of one piece of news he was certain; the best of news. The Council, never at ease in the matter, were increasingly troubled in their minds.

Every hour saw more fighting-men beneath my standard. One of the first captains to come in was Sir Henry Jerningham, brave, resourceful, and a leader of men; he came bringing his followers behind him. Hard on his heels followed Sir Henry Bedingfield with a hundred and forty knights; and the promise of more.

It was but two days since I had written to the Council; yet so much had happened that time lost all its true proportions; hours seemed days, and days weeks. In these two days the usurper walked in royal state, men and women falling to their knees as she passed. I, myself, had been proclaimed and every hour brought loyal hearts to my service. And, most important of all, in so short a space of time, Northumberland's Council that had seemed to wear a united front was now seen to be full of doubts and dissensions.

I had much hope, some fear and no money. Were a purse given me or a handful of silver, I gave it to my captains for those that should need shoes or a coat or a weapon—a present from their Queen. It was little enough; yet all seemed content.

But Kenninghall was no safe place if Northumberland's great muster should come marching. I was all impatience for the safety of Framlingham; thence, my forces strengthened, to ride forth to deal with traitor Northumberland, to pull the usurper from my throne.

I had another reason, besides. I was expecting an answer from my cousin the Emperor and to Framlingham I had requested it to be sent. Of that answer I had no doubt. I had asked his help. He was leader of our Catholic faith throughout Christendom—the holy Roman Emperor; and he was my close kinsman. How should I doubt but that he would give it? But at Kenninghall I must stay until my captains gave the word. Patience comes hard to me—especially if there be danger; then I must come to grips with it lest my courage ooze. I have never been a patient woman, nor have the years taught me my lesson.

Northumberland, too, it seemed, must learn that same lesson.

'He has no longer to deal with a sick boy,' I told my Council, 'but with a determined and obstinate young woman intoxicated with her filched royalty!'

My lord Bath laughed aloud. 'In two days he's learned something of the girl's mettle! We all have, indeed! We could not believe our eyes when she stood there defying Northumberland and refusing a crown to her husband—even the consort's crown!'

'Northumberland knew from the first,' my lord Montague said, 'even in that moment of signing, that some of us were looking towards our true Queen.'

'And how swift was body to follow eyes!' I smiled upon Montague and Bath.

'Let Northumberland lift his own eyes from the rest of his Council and they'll follow suit,' my lord of Essex said. He had arrived in the early morning, the marks of hard riding upon him. Last night he had been constrained to approve the usurper's insulting letter; thereafter he had ridden the night through with every offer of a loyal heart.

His coming was great comfort to me, not only because he was a high nobleman and a late member of the rebel Council, but because he brought me further proof of dissension within that Council.

'Madam,' he assured me, 'the most part of the Council would have ridden with me but Northumberland keeps them close-watched within the Tower. They bid me say they will never take arms against their true Queen, but will join you, Madam, as soon as may be!'

It was in good heart, then, that next day we left for Framlingham which is some fifteen miles from the sea. It had belonged to old Norfolk; he had given it, a gift to sweeten my father but it had not saved him from the Tower. And glad I was to come within its strong walls; and to see how great its courtyards and offices to house all my forces and any more that should come in to me.

At Framlingham I found the Imperial ambassador. Simon Renard had been sent, ambassador extraordinary, to watch affairs, to consult with the resident ambassador and to advise me at need. I was disappointed at first in this quiet-spoken man, but soon enough I understood my disappointment was in the news and not at all in the bearer of it. Simon Renard was to become my wise counsellor and true friend.

But he came now with no good news; bringing me, indeed, nothing less than a warning. My cousin, it seemed, had little hope of my success and no inclination to help me in so useless an adventure.

Renard was gentle with his bad tidings. 'Madam, my master is well-pleased that you have moved nearer the sea.'

'I am pleased to be here. If he be minded to send me help I am well-placed to receive it.'

'Madam, he sends no help. He advises you to escape while you can! He says you were ill-advised to proclaim yourself—my master's words, Madam, not mine. He says the people may love you; but he bids me warn you that simple folk accept simple facts. The simple fact is that the lady Jane Grey is proclaimed and accepted. He bids me remind you, also, of one other thing. This country turns more and more towards the heretic faith; that you turn to Rome will not help you!'

Fine words from his most Catholic Majesty! I bit upon my disappointment.

'I had thought such faithfulness must assure me of my cousin's help. Well, if it is not to be I must make do without. But he knows little of me or of my friends; we have the courage to fight, we have right on our side and we have faith in God!'

'Then, Madam, God will help your cause!'

'He will—though my cousin will not! Sir—' and I led him to a window, 'you see my standard, the royal standard, floating free! The sight fills me with hope and strength and certainty of victory!'

'God grant it may forever float.'

'Mr. Ambassador, He will.'

But for all my brave words I was afraid; I was very much afraid. My cousin, the Emperor, that experienced man, had neither help nor hope for me; and Northumberland's Council, for all their goodwill, were still prevented; they could give me no help, neither, but must show a united loyalty to my enemies. But all my life, having had cause, I have learned to cover fear with a brave face. Cover much fear with a little courage—and fear grows less, courage more.

Courage in me now bred hope, and great hope. Things began to move fast in my favour.

Sir John Sulyard, the same that had let me go free upon the road, came in to my standard. In the pages of history his is no great name; but in the annals of Norfolk, a name of integrity and power. Young Howard came also; but seventeen, good Catholic, and afire with love of God and service to me. His grandfather old Norfolk, whose very house this had been, lay all these years in the Tower saved from death only by my father's own. Whatever he had done he had suffered enough; he was an old man now, and his faith was my faith. For the sake of his grandson I should, as soon as I might, set him free. That same day Sir William Drury came in together with Sir Thomas Cornwallis, and after them Sir John Shelton and Sir John Tyrell—and each one served me for love, for love alone.

And now God Himself showed signal mark of His favour.

I had come from early Mass when, booted and spurred, Jerningham came into my closet, scarce stopping to make his salute.

'Madam, there are ships of war in Yarmouth harbour; a round half-dozen—my spies have this moment ridden in. Northumberland has sent them to cut you off should you attempt to fly the country. They would have been watching Framlingham by now but the storm drove them into harbour.'

'Here or there, they lose their pains. Run I never will!'

'Madam, if they cannot take you on the sea, they'll attack by land, joining forces with Northumberland's army. They carry cannon, scaling-ladders and other engines of war. We have not one cannon. We have only what every man laid hands upon when he left home—a sword, a musket, a pike or a bow. Let the wind change and the traitors will be battering at our gates!'

'We are in God's Hands . . .'

'. . . and He helps those that help themselves!' He finished my favourite maxim.

Jerningham is small in body but great in heart. There is power in him to lead and his wits are as keen as his sword.

Within ten minues I heard the beat of hooves; and there he was with young Howard and one other agallop for Yarmouth.

Yarmouth is all of thirty miles from Framlingham. Let the wind change and all too soon I should see for myself the warships sailing; and thereafter the men disembarking, dragging their war-engines after them. But even if Jerningham found them still in harbour, what could three men do against six ships of war?

Restless upon the battlements, through the spy-glass I strained my shortsighted eyes.

It was growing dusk; the wind still held, the sea still blessedly empty. It was full dark when, having come within, I heard a clatter in the courtyard. It was more than three men returned; much, much more. They had taken Jermingham then! And now they were come to take me. There was a sound of footsteps without; in that moment I knew what it was to be a wild creature when the reapers close in.

Jerningham came in at the door, his two companions with him.

'Madam.' He bent the knee; white with his weariness he was but lit like a lamp. 'The ships are yours, all six of them, together with captains and men, engines and cannon. The men wait below in the courtyard. They are not here to batter at our gates but to batter the Queen's enemies. Madam, they march with us!'

And while I stood unable to speak before so great a wonder, young Howard said, 'We went full-tilt cross-country and all the time we watched the wind. Would it change? Would we be too late and the ships gone? We came into Yarmouth at last, and down to the harbour —and the ships were there; *they were there*, all six of them and every one flying the usurper's standard! Sir Henry here bade us wait; he took a boat and rowed himself out to the flagship. We could not believe our eyes; nor could the sailors, neither. They crowded on deck to see what was going forward. They made no attempt to hinder him; what could one man do? Maybe they thought he carried messages of surrender! Then and there, standing in the boat, he opened his business.

I turned to Jerningham.

'Madam, I told them the simple truth in simple words. *I come upon the Queen's cause; your lawful Queen Mary!* Then I told them what they did not know, what Northumberland had taken care they should not know. I told them how your father of glorious memory had willed the crown to you, his lawful heir. I told them how the young King, dying, had not been allowed to take his peace until he had signed traitor Northumberland's command. I told him how the most part of the Council had been unwilling but that Northumberland had constrained them. I told them how the most part of the country was with you in this—councillors and judges, nobles and simple folk; and how every hour brought more men to march beneath your standard. And then I cried out, *Who shall stand against such armies? Not you, though you had six hundred ships, for God aye favours the right! Have a care, therefore, how you run, each of you, to a traitor's death!*

'Madam there was a silence—long or short, I could not know. Time stopped. And then a fellow cried out, *If our captains be rebels we'll throw them into the sea!* And all the others shouted *Aye!* Thereupon captains and officers not fancying so wet a death cried out *Long live Queen Mary!* and surrendered. They wait below with the men; as for the ships and the cannon—the good, loyal folk of Yarmouth have them in trust for you!'

For such a man and such a deed there are no words. As, too often with me, tears must speak my thanks.

So now I had six ships of war together with their cannon and their sailors and the captains, all won to my defence; and the good port of Yarmouth to guard the sea!

And one man, unarmed, with his wits and courage and golden voice had brought this wonder about.

We had scarce made an end of speaking when in came my Comptroller. Sir Edward Hastings, that had been my brother's Master of the Horse, was without and desired to speak with me.

He came and knelt before me. 'Madam Queen; I was sent to raise four thousand men for the rebels together with arms and money. All this I have done; and now I bring them into the Queen's service.'

'Sir Edward, you have our thanks; we had expected no less from you. We pray you remain Master of our Horse.'

I asked him for his news. 'Nothing, Madam, but good. The people cry out for their true Queen, King Henry's daughter. Those that are left upon the Council look for their chance of escape to serve their Queen; they pray her gracious pardon for those things they have unwillingly done. Of all the Council two, only, remain true to Northumberland and they can do no other—Suffolk and Northampton, ringleaders both!'

'I give God thanks! Those that would have joined us shall have assurance of our friendship and free pardon.'

Early next morning came the mayors of Norwich, Harwich and Ipswich—port towns all—together with their officers and chief citizens to swear loyalty. Good news spreads fast. Hastings' four thousand had swollen to ten thousand. I had now above forty thousand men with their captains to march with me; in some towns I had my officers—mayor and sheriffs, judges and magistrates—to keep order; I had ships of war, I had cannon and other engines for my need.

That same day brought further good news. The militia of Middlesex, of Oxford and Buckinghamshire had mustered to march on Westminster to take the palace in my name. And still all these men served me for love since money I had none. It troubled me that I could pay nothing for their service; an army cannot march on love alone.

And now another gift from a smiling God. As though He, Himself, crowned my cause, there was brought to me a great chest of church treasure—gold and silver-gilt vessels and jewelled ornaments. I was not, at the first, willing to use it. This was not mine but God's, but my Council and my priests advised me otherwise. 'God has put into our hands the gold we sorely need. An army marches upon its feet and belly. Hungry and barefoot it cannot march however great its love. God lends you His own treasure into your hands; shall you throw it back into His Face?'

It made good sense; I would use the treasure. But first I had it counted and weighed that it might be returned to Him that lent it as soon as might be. And now—sign that God was not displeased—the Comptroller of Customs declared for me; all customs dues were to be paid direct to me. So, with money in my hands, I ordered my Comptroller to command fifty bakers from Norwich to bake good bread for my forces and the same number of brewers to brew good ale; I commanded him also to lay in stocks of meat and cheese for us all.

But we must also feed the soul. I ordered the blessed crucifix to be set up within the parish church where so long it had been cast down— a sign that now a man might, if he chose, worship in the old ways of his fathers.

Chapter Fifty-Three

Wild as the hounds constrained by the huntsmen when the scent of the quarry is in the air, so I to march; to ride high on the full tide of my fortune. But still my Council and my captains counselled patience. Who knew how soon the tide might turn again? Northumberland had not lost, nor we gained all. He still had the army and the navy, he had the Mint, the Tower and the Bridge. He held London. We must wait for firmer news, more reinforcements. But always the messengers riding in with their good news were spurs to my restless spirit. If a thing must be done—a God's name let us do it!

But yet it was forever, *Wait wait, wait!*

'Madam, we beseech you, in the name of God, wait!' Thus even Jerningham, my captain so swift at need. 'God, we believe, will give us victory without blood!'

I am never willing for the shedding of blood. If time should bring victory without blood, what better way for us all?

But it was hard to wait. It was hard.

On the fourteenth of July, Northumberland left London for New-market; he rode with an army to raise yet more men.

'He is a fool to leave London that hates him,' my lord of Bath said, 'and the Council that waits only to betray him!'

'He goes unwilling,' my lord of Essex said. 'He has no choice. The Council wills it and he can do no other. It is not he that commands now. He obeys!'

So out he rode with his four sons and a goodly force.

'Did he doubt in his pride that London hates him?' Sir John Sulyard said. 'He can doubt it no longer. The people stood sullen to see him pass; and one that stood near heard him say, *They gather to watch me go; and not one bids me Godspeed!*'

Next day Jerningham brought me the most unexpected, the most glorious news.

'Madam, the whole fleet has declared for you. There's not a captain nor seaman but has sworn loyalty to his Queen!'

Northumberland had, all unwitting, helped me beyond my wildest dreams. He had, it seemed, been bargaining with France. Our cities of Calais and Boulogne in return for men. And this, leaking out, had caused anger everywhere. The fleet had sworn to sweep the seas of French trash.

And now came news—to me a miracle. Pembroke sent his urgent message; he stood by me in allegiance. Pembroke so late-bound to Northumberland by marriage, Pembroke that next to Northumberland, himself, had been foremost in bringing Jane Grey into the Tower to ride forth—the Queen; the Tower where even now she sat beneath the cloth of estate, the royal escutcheon above her head, her friends about her. But the true greatness of the news lay in this—*Pembroke commanded the Tower*. He that commanded the Tower commanded the army, commanded the river and its shipping, commanded the Bridge; commanded London itself. Now the Tower was no longer a dog fierce to attack but a good dog to guard my house.

At Framlingham I ordered prayers to Him that in His infinite goodness had shown His manifold mercies.

And to His mercies there seemed no end. For there came my lord Treasurer together with the Master of the Mint and what gold they could lay hands upon. Now I should be able to pay my men some of their due; counselling patience, my Council had been wise. With God's blessing I might have no need of armies. Every hour, every minute, almost, brought me good news. Bedford came to join us, Bedford, shrewd man that knew which side his bread was buttered; and with him Shrewsbury and Winchester.

And now came ever greater news—and news, indeed!

The end of Northumberland's Council.

'Madam, what is left of the Council openly declares for you—every man! They come not here to Framlingham but forgather at Baynard's Castle to consider how they shall bring in all London to your cause!'

And even while I listened, came the crowning piece.

'Madam, while those lords at Baynard's were considering how best to serve your Grace, in came my lord mayor with all his officers and chief citizens. He came at the request of the whole city to offer loyalty, obedience and love.'

'Now God be thanked!' I said and up went my hand to hide the too-ready tears. Had London turned against me I think it had broken my heart; for between my capital and me there had always been a singular love.

But what of Northumberland? The news had not yet caught up with him. Newmarket had proved a disappointment. Few, if any, had come in to his forces; and those he had were melting away. He was marching for Cambridge to whip up public anger against me. In Cambridge his confidence strengthened; for the city was with him—university and church. The vice-chancellor preached against my faith to scholars and gentry; and the latter—remembering no doubt the fat lands stolen from the church and fearing lest they be required again—lent a ready ear. And to the simple folk went the protestant priests warning them against me—antichrist that would rule them all to their souls' destruction. Northumberland, himself, spoke in the market-place, whipping the mob into a frenzy against me—and in the frenzy felt himself secure. He should have remembered the fickleness of the mob.

On the eighteenth of July, those lords gathered at Baynard's proclaimed me Queen; and those same lords, Northumberland's chosen Council, put a price upon their late master's head. A great price. A thousand pounds to any noble that should bring him in dead or alive, five hundred to any gentleman; and to any yeoman a hundred.

And still Northumberland, forever busy, was unaware of his danger.

At five o'clock in the afternoon of the nineteenth day of July, in the year of grace fifteen hundred and fifty-three, I, Mary Tudor, that had been named bastard and papist—names of scorn—without so much as a letting of blood nor a blow was proclaimed Queen.

'A most glorious happening, Madam!' Master Huddleston, summoned to join my Council, told me. 'Glorious for England and for all true Christendom. And, Madam, the day matched it in glory. For the full afternoon sun fell upon houses and people—golden sun and golden folk. It fell upon lifted trumpets and quartered tabards and upon faces lit with joy. Madam, such joy was never seen. Men, women and children cast caps, cast ribands, cast flowers into the air; And some, rich and poor alike, cast abroad such coins as they had in their pockets and did not look to see their value. And everyone was crying out *God save Queen Mary!* over and over again; and all the time the bells ringing and ringing and the trumpets never ceasing. And the noise went up to the sky and filled the sky so that it was as if heaven itself rejoiced; and, Madam, I make no doubt it did!

'And then, Madam, came the most lovely thing. I would you had been there; it must have moved your heart beyond the cheers and the flowers and the flung gold. In the midst of the noise a priest lifted his cross, lifted it high; and, at the sight, the crowd fell silent. Then he lifted his voice in a *Te deum* . . . and the crowd joined him; first a voice here and a voice there, then full-throated. And, at the blessed words so long forbidden, many wept for joy. Madam, the old times, God's good times are come again!'

'God grant it!' And there fell upon me exultation, not so much that my people had proclaimed me with love, but that they had sung with joy the prayer of the true faith. And to Him I vowed myself again— true daughter of the true faith; and as He had shown mercy to me, so I should show mercy to others. A merciful Queen; my greatest glory to be known now and hereafter.

From Cambridge the messengers came galloping—the one hard upon the heels of the other.

Northumberland had heard the news at last; heard it, at first, with utter disbelief. He had ridden into the market-place still further to inflame bitterness against me; nor did he doubt of success. Yesterday the mob had been hot enough with their curses. But today . . . today! They crowded to hear the proclamation with joy; and with joy blessed me.

'Madam, he sat his horse as one amazed. Then he seemed to come to himself, for he shook himself as a dog shakes water from him. He dismounted and signed to a fellow to take away the mare. Then, Madam, slowly, he mounted the steps that he might be seen of all. With uplifted arm he silenced the trumpeters; and, in the silence, cried aloud *Long live Queen Mary!* And he waved his bonnet in the air. But the words died in his throat and the bonnet dropped from his hand and the crowds trampled it underfoot. And they cried *Long live Queen Mary!* with the full throat of joy; cried it again and again. No man could have stopped them; nor did any man try!

'Northumberland stood there and the tears rained down his face; and, Madam, they were not tears of joy.'

He was overthrown, so it seemed, by the collapse of all his ambitions. I think he did not, as yet, understand this was not the end of ambition, alone, but of life, itself. In the midst of the rejoicing that followed, the bonfires, the drinking and the dancing he might have escaped. No-one had a thought for him, the price upon his head being, as yet, not everywhere known.

He did nothing.

When Arundel and Paget that had been at one with him on the Council, old friends, came to take him, his jaw dropped, Arundel told me later, like that of a dead man.

For a while he made no sound; then, his face all working, his voice came out choking in his throat. 'I beseech you, speak for me both of you for the Queen's mercy.'

'You should have thought of mercy earlier!' Arundel said.

'I have done nothing but with the consent of the Council!' Northumberland told him.

'You constrained us. Our hearts were not with you!' Paget said; that and no more.

Surely of all his bitterness, bitterest of all was old friends turned false.

Northumberland was my prisoner. But how easily I might have been his! Yesterday he had been all-powerful; today taken through the country in shame. The shame I could not help; that was between him and the people. What I could do, I did. I commanded that all prisoners pass unharmed. And so, for the most part they did. The crowds were quiet enough until they saw Northumberland, the tyrant. Then they broke into hisses, into jeers and curses. In London it was worse. Londoners had an especial hatred for him; he had put Somerset that they loved to death. They flung whatever came to hand; stones and worse; had he not been well-guarded he had been torn in pieces. The mob is a savage beast.

The guards riding by his side took from him his fine scarlet cloak that he be not known. So he rode, doublet and hose all stained with filth, and blind as an image; and did not know that, behind him, his youngest son wept as though his heart would break.

'Madam, they have torn down the lady Jane's escutcheon from its place in the Presence chamber of the Tower; with his own hands her father tore it; and they have carried away the cloth of estate and every sign of Queenship. And there she sits alone save for the lady her mother that so proudly bore up the train and now sits weeping, and through her tears upbraids the most wretched of ladies.'

'And the lady herself?'

'Pale as death and cold as stone. She speaks no word nor sheds one tear.'

On the last day of July I rode out from Framlingham. With me rode my Council, my nobles and my priests; before and after, beneath their captains, marched my ever-growing forces. A procession worthy of a Queen.

It was on the point of departure that there came, craving pardon, Robert Dudley, own brother to Northumberland. Proclaimed, and in the midst of my loving people, I was riding to my capital. God had sent me a victory unstained by blood; should I, myself, stain it? God would not wish it. And, as we rode there came many another suing for mercy; and, all these, too, I pardoned—my Council looking sour and prophesying much evil from this. But evil, I thought, never comes from mercy. Ridley, that same bishop who had preached against me at Paul's Cross, pronouncing me *bastard* and *stiff-necked papist*, had come hurrying also; but at Ipswich he had been recognised and taken back to London. I was glad he had not found his way to me; for him, also, I must have pardoned—once he had been gentle with me. But the man was enemy to my faith and, these many years after her death, had slandered my mother. Pardon I must have found hard.

All this time I had no news of my sister. She had stayed, as she had promised herself, safe at Hatfield, ignoring Northumberland's summons to the bedside of a brother, for all she knew, already dead. During all the turmoil and the danger she had given no sign; she had not sent so much as a word of loyalty, neither to Kenninghall nor to Framlingham. Well, maybe she was wise! The great Emperor, my cousin, champion of my faith, had presaged disaster and sent no help. Not even these last days, when I had been proclaimed and Northumberland's own friends had come to kneel, praying for pardon and swearing loyalty, had she given a sign. Now, I was riding for London and my crowning, she sent word at last. She was setting out with a great train to ride with me into the city and swear loyalty to her Queen.

I was glad of even this late gesture; sisters should stand together. It added strength, were that needed, to my position. . . . But I must have liked her better had she sent one loving word when all was dark, and I, friendless.

My journey south is a thing to remember all my life. A triumph of loving welcome, a great and happy homecoming. From Framlingham to London, folk lined the roads—the women and children to fling their flowers so that more than once I must tremble for those little ones that, in their joy, ran right beneath the hooves of the horses. And the men, cheering, fell in beside my armies, to join in the triumphal march, to bring home the Queen.

At Beaulieu, where I had lived in fear and grief, I rested awhile. And there came my lord mayor of London with a great company to welcome, me, kneeling he, and every one of them, three times, as is custom. And, so kneeling, he presented me with a purse upon a cushion; and, within the purse, five hundred pounds in gold. A comfortable gift; for my own gold, laid out upon my armies, was spent, and I nigh penniless. There came, also, to Beaulieu those laggards of the Council that had not yet come into my allegiance, to swear loyalty and sue for pardon. And these, since I was sworn to mercy, did not ask in vain.

On the third day of August I reached my house at Wanstead, some few miles from London. And there came to me my lady Suffolk, mother to Jane Grey who—if we are to believe Jane herself, that with all her faults was no liar—had beaten her daughter into obedience to Northumberland's treason. She came most humbly, that had been so proud, beseeching audience. At first I would have none of her; she had been in the very heart of rebellion. She had slandered my birth with a cruel tongue . . . but she was my cousin.

She lay full length at my feet; she lifted a face all ravaged with grief. 'Majesty,' she said. 'Majesty . . .' and for a little space could say no more but lay face upon the ground. Then at last she spoke. 'Madam Queen and cousin; for my daughter I dare not plead—her offence against the Queen's grace is too great. But for my husband . . . for my husband . . . Madam, he is very sick. Shut within the Tower he must surely die. So wasted in mind as in body, he can do no man further hurt. Madam, I implore you, set him free!'

So they were going to abandon her, the young girl, the daughter they had driven—with her goodwill or without—towards a traitor's death!

'Three days in the Tower!' And the bitterness came up in my throat. 'Three days for a traitor that has spat upon my mother's name and upon my own name also! A traitor that has betrayed his Queen and sought to set up his daughter—*your* daughter, Madam—in the Queen's place! Three little days in prison! Is that just punishment?'

'Majesty, no punishment could be just; it could never be enough! But, believe it, Madam, no punishment can equal that of his own heart. For the love of Christ's mercy, Madam, set him free!'

I set him free. I could do no other. The word *mercy* had done its work.

My Council complained once again—and more bitterly. This *mercy*! An encouragement to all traitors! they said.

'Harshness is yet more encouragement,' I told them, 'for if their prayer for mercy fail, the rebels, for very fear, must continue in their treason!' To this first prayer for mercy made from within a prison cell I cannot shut my ears'. But they were right and I was wrong. False mercy is no mercy . . . I see that now.

To Wanstead came my sister with a thousand ladies and gentlemen all in holiday attire. She knelt at the door of my Presence chamber, and in the middle of the room, and again at my feet; so I had done to my father and to the child, my brother. She was all humility kneeling there. I looked at her and I thought, You should have come before! And then, so young she looked, I felt again the sudden rising of affection—she was the child I had loved; to whom from my own scanty purse I had once given a yellow satin gown. And I remembered that, if she had not always been loyal she had yet warned me against Northumberland; and, but for that warning, I had not been sitting here—her Queen. So I put away my suspicions; she was my sister. I raised her up and embraced her.

Chapter Fifty-Four

In the golden evening of that same day I rode into my loving and beloved city. My first entrance as Queen; I rode upon a high palfrey that I might well be seen; it was pure white and trapped to the ground in cloth-of-gold. And I, myself, dressed to honour the occasion. There had been much anxious thought between my women and myself upon the choice of a gown. I must use one brought from the Wardrobe; it must be fine enough for the occasion and small enough to fit my small stature—for I, being kept poor all these years, had nothing fitting.

We chose, at last, a gown of royal purple velvet opening upon a kirtle of pale violet sewn with raised roses of gold. I wore no jewel save my mother's Spanish collar of gold with the hanging cross—her cross. There it lay among the Queen's jewels that the Keeper brought me. So it had been my father that had kept it from me—my father and not Cromwell! There it had lain all these years among the great jewels forgotten, but dearer to me than all the rest put together. In vain my ladies besought me, holding up this ornament and that—a girdle all of jewels . . . *it sets off Madam the Queen's waist that is slender as a girl's*; a hair ornament of rubies . . . *the Queen's hair has not lost one thread of its red-gold, Tudor gold*; a collar of pearls . . . *the Queen can wear them— so clear and fine her skin and soft as silk*. All that was true enough; my waist as small, my hair bright as ever, my skin clear, fine pink-and-white and soft as silk . . . but like fine silk it bore the marks of wear . . . for I was thirty-seven.

Studying my face in the looking-glass—and not for vanity, God knows—I marked the lines about mouth and eyes. But the eyes surprised me. They had lost their soft, attentive look—look of the shortsighted; today they fairly blazed with authority—my father's eyes when young. I have always known how to carry myself so that, for all my smallness, I am seen to full advantage; today I could mark further my father's part in me. I carried myself—the Queen.

I was the Queen. The people's free-chosen Queen . . . but I was thirty-seven and my sister twenty.

She rode beside me now, all in green-and-white, our own colours and fresh as the spring. She was handsome, she was graceful, she was gracious . . . she was young. Dear God, how young!

I was the Queen . . . but I was thirty-seven to her twenty.

So we rode together through the summer countryside amidst the cheers, the blessings and the flung flowers . . . but how much of it all was for me; how much for joy in the splendid young woman riding by my side; the young, young woman?

I tried to put thought of her from me; to think, instead, of my mother that, at the very feet of God, must weep for joy this day. But with her came memories of that other; I looked at Anne Bullen's daughter riding high and handsome by my side—what trust could I put in her? But gradually the smiling countryside, the countryfolk all in holiday dress, the cheers and the blessings and the gay pealing of bells brought me back to the miracle of the occasion. I thrust dark thoughts away; I rode in my people's love.

And so I came in to London by the Aldgate; and there my lord mayor waited in the great robes of his office and his aldermen all about him. He held upright the ceremonial sword of my city and, kissing it in token of homage, delivered it into my hands. Exultation should uplift; it is the word's meaning. If that be so, there was no exultation in me then; nothing but humility and fear, lest I be found wanting. For that moment I held the sword in my hand was sacred as a hallowing. Then, he still kneeling, I gave back the sword and he held out, upon a crimson cushion corded all of gold, the keys of the city. And these, too, I took and then returned, in token that I gave back into the city's hands its own rights and freedoms.

Then, high upon my horse, I spoke to the crowds that packed between gutters and houses and looked forth from their windows, to thank them for their loyal, loving hearts. But I might as well not have spoken; for, in the pealing of bells, the salute of the Tower guns, the cheers risen to a roar, my voice was lost. And that was as well since the voice choked and trembled in my throat. Again I glanced beneath my lids at my sister—for my life I could not help it. Did they, for all their loyalty, wish her, and her fresh youth, in my place? And she; did she wish it, too? It would not be far from her way of thinking.

And suddenly my thoughts flew to one for whom the crowds had not cheered nor wished in my place; but stood silent as she went by. I was taken with unexpected pity for her—poor Queen of nine days. All my anger against her was gone.

I came from my thoughts by the halting of the procession; and there stood the charity children of the Spital scrubbed clean, and all in white and singing sweet as angels. I think it was that that gave me greatest joy that day; for children I love dearly and their joys, no less than their sorrows, move me to the heart.

And so through Leadenhall that all might see me; and then turning again towards the Minories where once the friars had their home— and God willing should have again—down to the river where masters, journeymen and prentices of every guild stood massed together all in their best livery and gay as a garden of flowers. And every hand held posies that were tossed to the air until the very sky rained flowers.

The Tower at last, whose grim walls had more than once threatened to close upon me; and there stood Sir Thomas Cheyney the constable, not to take in charge a prisoner but to kneel to his Queen and lead her into the citadel of her capital.

It was not Sir Thomas, alone, that kneeled. Behind him some half-dozen prisoners, grey with the long years of their suffering, lifted anguished eyes and hands clasped for mercy. Norfolk was there that had lain forgotten during all the years of my brother's reign. I scarce knew him at the first; he had gone into the Tower in sturdy middle-age; seven years had made an old man of him. He had been concerned in some plot against my father—so the charge. Well, it might be so; a good enough soldier but not a clever man. He was there, I believed, less for treason than because he'd had the misfortune to be uncle to Anne Bullen and Catherine Howard, both. The first he had been forgiven; the second time he paid for both. I had no cause to love this persecutor of my girlhood; yet once he had said a kind word to me. For that kind word he should go free; aye, and have his great house again!

There knelt also those two bishops Tunstal and Gardiner. The first had suffered because he had stood fast for my mother; the second had won a high place because he stood fast against her. But each had stood steadfast for his faith. They had refused the Englished prayer book and the Protestant service; they had been faithful to the old, beautiful rites and the immemorial prayers. And because of that I must alike honour them.

And now I saw my old friend Nann that had been wife to Somerset; and by her knelt a handsome boy I guessed to be Courtenay—son to guiltless Exeter come to his death for no reason save that he was of kin to my much-loved lady Salisbury; and for her dear sake my heart went out to the boy, his whole young life spent in this grim place, cut off from pursuits of his breeding and the companions of his blood and age. He should be Marquis of Exeter if he had his rights; those rights he should have.

There they knelt, old and young, hands lifted towards me—their last, their only hope. At the sight of these forgotten people long imprisoned for some light offence, or for none at all, the tears ran down my cheeks. From one to the other I went and with my own hands raised them; yes, even Gardiner that had brought ill to my mother and would have brought Catherine Parr to her death. For he had held to the truth, declaring it better to die for the word of God than to live denying it. I kissed them upon both cheeks and did not know whether the wetness came from their eyes or from mine; and I promised to restore them, each one to his rightful honours and possessions together with my friendship and favour as long as I should live. Then Gardiner that had been my enemy blessed me in the name of God, thanking Him that had sent this poor country a heart of mercy. And at that joy filled my heart and gratitude that God had given me power to forgive those that had done wrong and restore those that had done right.

That night, first night in the citadel of my capital, I could not rest but must pace the narrow confines of my sleeping-chamber, treading soft lest I disturb Clarencieux that slept without.

I was Queen. The poor, despised bastard, Queen. All my life lived beneath the shadow of the block, all my life walking in fear not for myself alone but for all good priests and for those that had openly declared their faith. All my life lived in grief for the insult to my birth and the dishonouring of my mother's name. Had I once thought I did not want the crown; that it must lie too heavy upon my woman's head? Now I knew the true meaning of exultation. I was filled with it, head-to-foot, because henceforth priests should be free to preach God's Word and folk be free to listen. And I exulted, also, because no-one could now question my birthright nor any more slander my mother's name.

Glorious days lay before me; but because they were glorious, hard; and hard, indeed! So much to be put right! First and foremost the country must be brought back to its true faith, the faith that was its heritage and its right; a country once more secure in God, both here and in the world to come. And, for this, the country itself was eager; of that I was certain; else why had it chosen me? I had made clear statement of my faith; in the teeth of disgrace and death I had, save for once long ago, held to it. Rejoicing, the people would come back to

God. Yet for some that had been born into the heretic faith it would not be easy. Those I must protect; they would come in God's good time; His voice, in the end, is always heard . . . and I was sick to the heart of the burnings.

And now, at once—the question. My brother's body lay in state as yet unburied. What must I do in the matter of his funeral? Bury him in the sterile rites of his new faith, lacking the true word? Or bury him according to the old true faith to save his soul at the last? I pondered the matter, weighing this against that, but could come to no decision. I must leave it to the Council.

But there were other things about which I needed no counsel. I must give back to the Church the lands and the treasure my father and my brother had carried away. I must restore the monasteries that the sick might be healed, body and soul, as heretofore. But all this must lighten a purse already too light for the calls upon it; yet I could not fill it at the expense of my people. Rather I must relieve them of the burden that had been laid upon them—the too-heavy taxes.

The Council would not be with me in this I knew full well; still less in restoring to the Church that which belonged to the Church. Then I must weed out from the Council those of Northumberland's men, that, trained to his way of thinking, could not rise beyond it. I should choose instead men of wisdom and worth to sit with those I had alread chosen—men like Montague wise in the law, like Huddleston strong in God, men that had come seeking my service in the dark and dangerous days; and by them I should be guided.

From Northumberland's Council my mind went to the man himself. He lay in his cell within this same Tower and his traitors with him. Here, too, was another problem; God had given me victory without blood and I had sworn to keep it so—if I might. But it would be hard, and hard, indeed! I must fight my Council aye and Parliament, too, on this matter. Northumberland's death I could not withstand. Him I dared not—had I wanted to—spare in face of their opposition; but I did not want to spare him. Heart and core of the treason; and, given a chance, would be again—a man that held his word of less value than a worn-out shoe. And not for that alone; but for the cruelty that would not let a dying boy die in peace. But the others? I would spare as many as I was let. I was Queen, but no ruler has power without limit.

And so my thoughts came again to that other prisoner—to Jane Grey, her royal escutcheon torn from the Presence Chamber in this same Tower, by the hands of her own father. For nine nights she had slept in this very chamber, in this my very bed. The thought was sudden, and sudden my anger. I could scarce breathe until reason came to lighten my wrath and give me back my breath again.

The father and mother that had coerced her, I had pardoned; the father I had set free, the mother kept by me at court. Guilty my cousin was; yet less guilty than they ... but it was she that had been proclaimed, before whom all had fallen upon their knees; she that, in her own name, had declared me a bastard, uninheritable to the crown!

What must I do with her? For the present, nothing. She was well enough. I had given orders that she be comfortably and privately lodged. She lay now in the house of Master Partridge chief warden; a comfortable house and she an honoured guest. But she could not remain there for ever.

What must I do with her?

Until I had settled the matter I could not hope to sleep. In the anteroom Clarencieux, upright on her chair, slept the light sleep of the old. She came awake at once and I bade her tell the guard send my lord Montague to me.

He came presently, old and wary and wide-awake; I think he, too, had not been in his bed for he was full-dressed even to his bonnet.

I went straight to my question.

'My lord Chief Justice, what must I do in the matter of the lady Jane Grey? Her father and mother I have pardoned. Must she not be pardoned, also?'

'Madam,' he said, 'it is a matter that troubles us all. How wise to spare my lord of Suffolk and his lady, it is too late now to discuss; but it has pleased your Council not at all. As for the lady Jane, herself— she cannot be pardoned. A little more time—and upon *her* head the sacred oil, the hallowed crown; upon hers, not yours!'

It was true; all true. And yet, did she, I wondered, sleep now? Did she pace restless as I? And what did she feel knowing me Queen, me she had named bastard and upstart, she that for nine long days had usurped the crown? Did she pray now those new prayers of hers all fearful for her life, shrinking even in thought from cold steel sharp upon her young neck?

I felt once more the sudden spring of compassion.

She had been an enemy to my faith and to me. But she was of my own blood. And if she were ambitious, was she not like my sister? And if she were obstinate and held fast to her own faith, was she not like me? Were not those things in our blood?

'My lord,' I said, 'she has writ to me. She says, at the beginning she knew nothing of the treason; when they broke the matter to her she swooned. And that I can believe; treason is a fearful thing. They beat and battered her, pinched and bruised, they kept her from sleep; and that, also, I can believe! She was in fear of her life and scarce knew what she did when, at last, she agreed *with an ill-will, with infinite grief and displeasure of the heart*. Read for yourself!' And I held out the letter.

'That may be—or it may not!' And he scarce glanced at the paper. 'She's ambitious and she's self-willed. See how she stood out, refusing her husband a crown!'

'Strong-willed she is; but Northumberland stronger! Suppose, my lord, she did truly stand against them all until even that strong will of hers could stand no longer? Suppose she did truly stand in fear of her life? She's but seventeen!'

And I remembered another girl of seventeen that had stood out against her father's will till, for very weariness, she could stand no longer. That girl had done worse. Jane had denied her earthly sovereign. That other girl had denied her faith and her mother's honour; she had denied her God. Could I, of all people, be surprised if in the end Jane had broken?

'Whatever the rights and the wrongs,' I said, 'she is too young to die!'

'Madam, the Council will not agree in this. They will fight you to the death!'

'Not to *her* death! I am the Queen! My lord, I thank you for your counsel; you have pointed the way. I pray your pardon that I disturb you at this late hour.'

'I have not slept. Like the Queen I am troubled. Like the Queen I do my addition; but I make a different answer.'

When he had taken his departure I stopped my pacing; my mind was clear and firm. As soon as I might I should set her free—and her young husband with her. It would not be easy. Already they had been judged guilty and attainted, both. My Council would be stiff-necked in the matter, setting out good reasons for her death; Gardiner would swoop vicious as an eagle. But I am stiff-necked, too; I would not give those two young creatures over to the axe.

The narrow chamber enclosing the hot summer night seemed to imprison me, myself. I must breathe the wider air. From the Queen's closet a few steps go up to the leads. I stood upon the turret of the keep and looked out upon sleeping London, my London bound to me in bonds of love.

The moon was hidden in a wrack of cloud; far below the Thames flowed dark and oily; ships' lanterns hung still with garlands, went up a forest, against the sky. To my right lay the Bridge, its houses huddled together like children for safety; I could hear the rush of water through its narrow arches. On left hand and on right, behind me and before me on the Southwark side, rose church spires. Had any city ever, so many? And all their bells, every one, had rung this day to welcome me home. And every one, please God, should ring out happy because the country had come home to God.

The happiness of this my city, the happiness of all my England, lay between my two hands. Was I able for it? I looked at my two hands pale and small in the darkness. They seemed weak enough; yet clasped in prayer they gathered strength. . . . *As God hears me I will try. I will work for this country that has chosen me. I will work unceasing, sparing myself nothing. And always I will show mercy. As God to me—so I to others. For mercy is the heart of God; it is the heart of a Queen; it is the heart of a government. Let Council and Parliament stand against me in this, still it shall be mercy, mercy, mercy.*

I sank to my knees; the flagstones struck cold through my bedgown. Once I had knelt upon cold stone for my father's mercy and it had not been given. Now I knelt to my Father in heaven. God send me a heart of mercy; and it would be given.

The moon shone out from a wrack of cloud; shone in splendour upon city and river; shone upon my folded hands. I took it for a sign. There would be cloud; there might well be danger; but always God would send His light to show me the way.

Some books consulted

BURNET, G. *A History of the Reformation of the Church of England 1679–1715* (1679).

CAUSTON, H. K. S. *The Howard Papers* (1862).

CLIFFORD, H. *The Life of Jane Dormer, Duchess of Feria* . . . transcribed from the ancient manuscript in the possession of the Lord Dormer by E. E. Estcourt and edited by J. Stevenson (Burns & Oates, 1886).

FRIEDMANN, P., *Ann Bolen*, 2 vols. (Macmillan, 1884).

FROUDE, J. A., *History of England*, ten vols. (1910–13).

MACKIE, J. D., *The Earlier Tudors* (Clarendon Press, 1952).

NEALE, J. E., *Queen Elizabeth* (Cape, 1934).

NICHOLS, J. G. (ed.), *The Chronicle of Queen Jane*, Camden Society, O.S., 48 (1850).

NICHOLS, J. G. (ed.), *Literary Remains of Edward VI*, 2 vols. (Roxburghe Club, 1857).

POLLARD, A. F., *Henry VIII* (Longmans Green, 1951).

PRESCOTT, H. F. M., *Mary Tudor* (Eyre & Spottiswoode, 1962).

State Papers during the Reign of Henry VIII, Vol. I (1830).

STONE, J. M., *The History of Mary I, Queen of England* (Sands & Co., 1901).

STRICKLAND, A., *Lives of the Queens of England*, 8 vols. (1851).

STRYPE, J., *Memorials of . . . Thomas Cranmer*, 2 vols. (1840).

UNDERHILL, E., 'Autobiographical Anecdotes' in *Narratives of the Days of the Reformation*, Camden Society, O.S. 77, pp. 132–76 (1859).

WARE, SIR J., *Rerum Hibernicarum Annales* (1664).

WHITE, B. M. I., *Mary Tudor* (Macmillan, 1935).

WRIOTHESLEY, C., *A Chronicle of England* by Charles Wriothesley, Windsor Herald, Vol, I, Camden Society, N.S.11 (1875).

The family group described on p. 297
is to be seen in Hampton Court.

The story of Mary Tudor is continued in two more books by Hilda Lewis:

MARY THE QUEEN

The second novel in this remarkable series shows us Mary as Queen. Seldom in all history can there have been such a reversal of fortune. From being despised and ill-treated, to ascend the throne of the Tudors amidst the acclamation of her people; and from being poor and unloved to find the treasure of England in her hands, and suitors crowding at her door.

BLOODY MARY

This book, though complete in itself, completes the triolgy with an account of the end of the reign and the burning of the heretics. Hilda Lewis portrays with supreme skill the conflict in the mind, heart and soul of a woman who felt herself threatened in her inmost being, and who was ravaged by an intolerable jealousy.

If you would like a complete list of Arrow books
please send a postcard to
P.O. Box 29, Douglas, Isle of Man, Great Britain.